MW00903810

Event Horizon

Book Two in The Perseid Collapse Series

a novel by

Steven Konkoly

First edition

© 2014. All rights reserved. Except as permitted under the U.S. Copyright Act of 1976, no part of this publication may be reproduced, distributed or transmitted in any form or by any means, or stored in a database or retrieval system, without the prior written permission of the author.

Event Horizon is a work of fiction. The names, characters, places, and incidents portrayed in the story are the product of the author's imagination or have been used fictitiously. Any resemblance to actual persons, living or dead, businesses, companies, events, or locales is entirely coincidental.

ISBN: 978-1495380433

Dedication

To Kosia—still my number one supporter.

To Matthew and Sophia—two awesome kids who put up with dad's long writing hours

Acknowledgments

To my wife, Kosia. I carry a notepad with me to capture her thoughts and recommendations—which can arrive, unannounced, at any time of the day. Sometimes I suspect she spends more time thinking about these novels than I do.

To the beta reader crew for another A-plus round of comments, observations and edits. Trent, Nancy, Jon, Bruce and the newest member of the team, Greg. Greg has been a long time reader and generous contributor to my veteran's donation campaigns. Welcome aboard!

To the production crew. Felicia A. Sullivan—editor extraordinaire. Thank you for the early delivery! Jeroen ten Berge—for producing another killer cover design and devouring the story as quickly as I could write it. Stef Mcdaid—for creating the final showcase product. He takes whatever I spit into the file and "nukes" it into shape. To Pauline Nolet for the exhaustively detailed proofing job. Once Pauline is done, I don't need to look at it again…and I don't.

Once again, a special thanks goes out to Randy Powers of Practical Tactical. He beta read *The Perseid Collapse* and *Event Horizon* with a prepper's eye and provided me with a copy of *Practical Tactical's Handbook*. Not only did his advice and guidebook help shape the final disposition of the Fletcher's wide array of survival gear and strategy, it currently serves as the "go to" guide for the Konkoly household. Look for a collaboration between us in the near future. Something along the lines of *The Fletcher's Guide to Surviving the Apocalypse*.

Finally, to the readers, friends and fellow writers who continue to support my transition to full-time writing. None of this would be possible without you. THANK YOU!

About the author

Steven Konkoly graduated from the United States Naval Academy and served as a naval officer for eight years in various roles within the Navy and Marine Corps. He lives near the coast in southern Maine, where he writes full time.

His first novel, *The Jakarta Pandemic*, reached readers in 2010, followed by four novels in the *Black Flagged* series: *Black Flagged* (2011), *Black Flagged Redux* (2012), *Black Flagged Apex* (2012) and *Black Flagged Vektor* (2013). *The Perseid Collapse* (2013) signaled his return to the post-apocalyptic genre. *Event Horizon* is the second book in *The Perseid Collapse Series*. Book three, *Point of Crisis*, will be released during the summer of 2014.

Please visit Steven's blog for updates and information regarding all his works:

StevenKonkoly.com

About The Perseid Collapse Series and Event Horizon

The Perseid Collapse Series takes place six years after the H16N1 virus ravaged the world in my first novel, *The Jakarta Pandemic*. Book One, *The Perseid Collapse*, unveils the "event" that catapults the United States into chaos and chronicles the first 48 hours "post-event," as the characters navigate an unfamiliar, hostile landscape to reach their destinations.

Event Horizon picks up where book one ends, spanning the second 48-hour period. That's all I'll say. *Point of Crisis* (Summer of 2014) will open the timeline and scope of the series, addressing some of the bigger picture questions posed by the previous books. As always, the Fletcher's will be in the middle of the action.

Time in *Event Horizon* is measured in plus (+) or minus (-) Hours:Minutes from the EVENT.

Happy Reading!

"Event Horizon"

*In relativity theory, an **event horizon** is a boundary in space/time, beyond which events cannot affect an outside observer.*

*In layman's terms, it is defined as **"the point of no return."***

Prologue

EVENT 00:00 Hours

Boston University
Boston, Massachusetts

Ryan Fletcher squinted at his alien surroundings. Unnaturally brilliant light penetrated the translucent curtains, exposing beige cinderblock walls and sparse furniture. The glaring view of his dorm room faded quickly, replaced by a soft flickering light. He raised his head a few inches off the pillow to view the digital alarm clock resting on his desk. A dark object stared back. He raised his left hand to his chest and stared at the illuminated dial until it made sense. 4:59.

Brutal.

His eyes eased shut, and he started to drift back to sleep, until the steel bedframe under his thin mattress rattled against the wooden dresser behind his head. Angry thoughts of the "T" waking him every morning of his freshmen year yanked him out of the murky depths, and he sat up, fully awake and pissed off at his room assignment. Nobody had mentioned the fact that the train made stops *inside his dorm room*. The vibration intensified, accompanied by a deafening roar.

"No way I'm dealing with this for an entire year," he mumbled.

The bed heaved upward, tossing him face down onto the carpeted floor. Distant car alarms sounded. He lay prone for a few seconds, stunned by the violent upheaval. Another massive jolt rocked the room. He needed to get out of here.

Ryan grabbed the bedframe and tried to stand, but the room pitched violently, dropping him to his hands and knees. He crawled in the darkness toward the door, tumbling sideways into the wooden dresser beyond his bed as the building swayed. Ryan scurried into the small vestibule next to the door moments before both of the room's heavy, wooden dressers crashed to the floor. He leaned his back into the cold cinderblock wall and pressed his bare feet against the opposite wall.

Adding and releasing pressure on his legs to stay in place, Ryan moved with the building, hoping the walls didn't collapse. Not that it mattered at that point. The building was nearly fifty years old, and if the interior walls failed, rescue teams would be lucky to find any of them alive. He dug his feet into the wall in front of him and closed his eyes. He was on autopilot, too disoriented and terrified to put any effort into anything beyond his immediate survival. He knew that he should be sitting under the doorframe, but he couldn't convince his body to give up the stable position he had established between the two walls.

Moments later, the shaking abated, and the thunderous rumble yielded to distant car alarms and screaming. Ryan stood on wobbly legs and braced himself against the walls with both hands, taking deep breaths to fight the nausea. A strong campfire smell drew his attention to the flimsy curtains flapping gently through the jagged remains of the window. A wave of dizziness struck, buckling his knees.

Bright yellow and orange light danced against the room's dark interior, arousing his curiosity. He had to see what had happened outside of the building. Testing his legs, he edged out of the vestibule and stopped in front of the fallen dressers. Glancing up at broken windows, a flash flood of rational, analytical thoughts overloaded him.

First things first.

He tilted the top dresser upward, letting all of the empty drawers fall to the floor as he heaved it against the opposite wall. His dresser was next, but he took care to keep the drawers pushed firmly shut. Ryan dug through the dresser and quickly replaced his athletic shorts with jeans. Thick wool socks covered his feet, followed by a pair of well-travelled, dark brown hiking boots. He saw no sense in cutting his feet on broken glass before he left his room. He stepped over to the window and brushed aside the flimsy curtains. Flames engulfed western Boston, extending as far as he could see from his sixth story window.

Ryan stared at the inferno, transfixed by the enormity of the blaze. Pyres undulated and crackled, draping the city in a dancing blanket of fire. He scanned for wreckage on Commonwealth Avenue, desperate for clues to explain the apocalyptic scene. He'd expected to see the tail section of a commercial airliner or a colossal crater, but the street looked untouched. Even the buildings across "Comm Ave" looked undamaged. Something was off, but he couldn't bring it into focus. He followed the fires lining Granby Street, tracing them toward the Charles River and beyond.

"Holy shit," he muttered.

The city's confusing grid of tree-lined streets had been brought to life by the flames, leaving the structures intact.

Could a solar flare do this?

Ryan had no idea. He started to pull away from the window, but stopped.

That can't be right.

He checked his watch again. 5:01. Sunrise was still an hour away, but the lights were out across the city. Despite the near daylight conditions created at street level, he couldn't identify a single light—anywhere.

Ryan fumbled for the desk lamp. *Click.* Nothing. He swiped his smartphone and wallet from the hutch and sprinted to the vestibule, trying the side-by-side switches. The room remained dark.

This has to be a solar flare. What else could knock out the electrical grid and set fire to the trees?

Another thought crossed his mind, but he dismissed it. They would have been hit by the shockwave already if it was a nuke. Either way, his only mission at this point was to reach Chloe and figure out what to do next. Stay in Boston or trek north? He lifted a blue, twenty-gallon plastic storage bin from the closet floor and dropped it on his bed.

The bin had been the last item to leave the car, hidden under a blanket by his dad. Ryan had nearly refused to take it up to his room. Of the 21,000 incoming freshmen, he didn't want to be the only one with a "paranoia pack" taking up precious space in his closet. Of course, that was the point of the bin. Boston University represented a small city of students, most of them completely dependent on the university's infrastructure for their basic survival needs. With his mom in tears over dropping him off at college, he decided to take it and spare her the worry. Based on what he had experienced over the last few minutes, Ryan was fairly certain that the university's infrastructure had ceased to exist. The emergency bin didn't sound so ridiculous anymore.

The container held an olive green backpack, two CamelBak water bladders and a sealed plastic bucket of dehydrated food pouches. The backpack had been outfitted with enough gear and food to support a two-day journey. Each of the bladders held three liters, which was the theoretical minimum he should drink per day if hiking. Realistically, he'd need more, which was why his dad had stuffed a Katadyn microfilter into the backpack. His first task upon leaving the dorm room was to fill both of the CamelBak bladders. Beyond that, everything he needed to walk back to Maine with Chloe was inside the backpack.

The pack contained a hat, old sunglasses, maps of Boston and New England, a compass, extra cash, parachute cord, a thirty-foot section of remnant sailing line, a small emergency radio, first aid kit, fire-starting kit, flashlight, three MREs, a Gore-Tex bivouac bag, N95 respirator and an emergency blanket. The only thing he didn't have was a knife. Any knife, no matter how small, was classified as a weapon by university police and strictly forbidden. Even a Swiss Army knife could get you expelled. He dug through one of the outer pouches and found the flashlight. He aimed the LED light at the window and tested it, relieved that it filled the entire room with a bluish-white light. He had no idea what kind of damage a solar flare could do to battery-powered equipment.

He considered unpacking the dehydrated food bucket, but there was no way he could stuff anything else into the backpack. The bucket would be awkward to carry, but it had a sturdy handle, and he wasn't going far enough for it to become a real problem. He'd cover the three miles to Chloe's apartment in thirty minutes. Forty tops. He heaved the backpack onto his shoulders and tightened the straps. With the bucket in his left hand, he leaned against the door and listened. The screaming had faded to sporadic yelling.

Ryan unlocked his door and stepped into the darkness. Without exterior windows, the hallways were pitch black. A beam of light blinded him.

"You all right, dude? Can you believe this?" said a male voice.

"Did you see what happened?" asked Ryan, locking the door to his room.

"The whole city blew up, brother. We got nuked or something."

A different voice spoke up. "It wasn't a nuke. There's a huge contrail in the sky, running from west to east. It disappears at about a forty-degree altitude over the southern horizon. We'll see more of it as sunrise approaches. I calculate that it struck somewhere off the coast, due east of here."

Ryan flashed his light at the two of them.

"Dude, watch it with the light. It's like a million times brighter than this," he said, directing his beam into Ryan's eyes.

"Thanks for the demonstration. What do you mean 'it struck'?" asked Ryan.

"I think we got hit by an asteroid or some kind of—"

The student with the flashlight interrupted. "That was probably an ICBM fired from China. West to east, it makes sense."

"I've seen the ground footage of the space shuttle reentering the atmosphere, and this is about twenty times thicker."

"It still doesn't explain why the lights are out. Nukes create an EMP," said the first student.

"Not if they hit the ground," said Ryan, pushing past the two of them.

"Where are you going?"

"Anywhere but here. If the power's out for good, you need to start filling up any kind of container that will hold water. Even a trashcan," said Ryan, pushing open the bathroom door.

"Wrong bathroom, dude," he heard as the door closed.

"Hello. Anyone in here?" he yelled, before flashing the light along the row of stalls.

"Definitely not the men's room," he whispered.

Directing the light in the opposite direction exposed several sinks set into a long Formica counter. The wall-length mirror anchored to the wall behind the sinks had shattered, filling the white basins and covering the tile floor with razor-sharp pieces of broken glass. Satisfied that he was alone, he dropped the backpack on the floor next to the nearest sink and pulled out both of the water bladders, filling them with cold water.

He hoped the others took his advice about the water. Without power to run the building's water pumps, pressure wouldn't last very long on the sixth floor—or any floor. He'd just tucked the second bladder into his backpack when a thunderous explosion rattled the bathroom, rebooting the hysterical screams he had heard earlier.

Maybe we did get hit with a nuke.

Ryan crouched against the wall next to the sink and waited several seconds in the dark, hearing nothing but continued screaming. Activating his flashlight, he opened the door, finding the hallway thick with dust.

Not good.

A female student bolted out of the cloud, knocking him out of the way. He grabbed her arm and held her in place.

"Hold on! The floor is covered in glass!"

Coughing and sobbing, she yanked her arm free and stood there in bare feet.

"What just happened out there?" asked Ryan.

She looked up at him with a vacant stare. Her jet-black, curly hair was coated in dust, and she had several small cuts across her face.

"Something exploded in Boston," she stated flatly and started crying again.

"Like a bomb?"

"I don't know. I was facing downtown when all of the fires started to go out. Then it hit us. It was like a shockwave or something. How is my face?"

"Small cuts. Nothing serious. Where's your room?" Ryan asked, shining the light on her.

"On the other side," she mumbled.

"You need to go back to your room and put on some shoes and long pants. Hiking boots if you have them. Then fill up any container you can find with water. Tell everyone to do this. It's extremely important," he said, stepping out of the doorway to let her by.

"Okay. Water—uh—all right," she said and disappeared.

Ryan directed his light forward along the left side of the hallway, looking for the door to the stairwell he had used last night. He pushed it open and heard the hollow echo of screams and feet clattering against the stairs. Air quality in the stairwell vestibule was markedly better than the hallway, and he could see across to the door leading to the other side of his floor. The far door opened, and a shirtless student wearing red soccer shorts and flip-flops entered the vestibule, shining a flashlight in his face. The student nodded and rushed past him, yelling unfamiliar names into the hallway Ryan had just left.

He joined the mass exodus in the dark stairwell and let it carry him to the ground floor, jostled and shoved until he spilled through a pair of double doors into the main thoroughfare connecting the three Warren

Towers dormitory buildings with the cafeteria and main lobby. The lighting situation remained the same on the ground level, utterly dependent on the few students who had thought to bring flashlights to college.

The emergency lighting system had failed to activate, which didn't come as a surprise to Ryan based on conversations with his dad. Hardwired into the building's electrical grid, the battery-powered lights were susceptible to a solar flare or EMP-generated electrical surge.

He spotted a gap in the oncoming flock of students and dashed to the other side of the hallway, his feet crushing gravel as he ran. He flashed his light at the ground, exposing small pieces of concrete and dust. Before he could aim the beam at the ceiling, someone yanked the light from his grip. The light moved quickly away, darting through the swarm of students headed toward Warren Towers' main lobby.

"Fucking asshole!" he screamed, pushing his way in the direction of the wavering light.

He considered chasing the thief, but quickly gave up the thought. The flashlight had already served its primary purpose, and the risks of pursuit far outweighed the return of an item he could replace at Chloe's apartment. If the crowd became agitated by his antics, he could lose his bucket of dehydrated food or, even worse, his backpack. Ryan turned his back on the stolen flashlight and moved along the wall, against the flow of students, searching for one of the lesser-known exit doors leading directly onto Commonwealth Avenue. He ran into the door handle a few seconds later and stepped into a pitch-black stairwell, closing the door behind him.

Ryan reached into the blackness and edged forward slowly, groping for the railing. He could pop one of the chemlights in the backpack to light the way down, but he wanted to save those for a real emergency. Walking down one flight of stairs while clinging to a railing didn't qualify. His hand found the smooth metallic railing, and he took the stairs carefully. Less than a minute later, he emerged from Warren Towers and stepped onto the glass-covered sidewalk. The fires in most of the trees and bushes had been extinguished by the blast, but a few continued to burn, casting a hazy glow over Commonwealth Avenue.

Burning ash, pulsing like orange fireflies, floated down the street—carried west by a warm breeze. A lone police siren wailed in the distance. Ryan walked into the eastbound lanes of Commonwealth, checking for traffic out of sheer habit, but he'd be surprised to see any cars. All signs indicated that the power outage had been caused by some kind of power surge, and he still couldn't find a single light on the horizon. He continued east on the deserted road until the southern sky appeared behind Warren Towers. Ryan stared at the sky in awe.

Definitely not an ICBM.

An ugly column of uneven gray and white smoke streaked diagonally across the sky above the four-story buildings set back from Commonwealth Avenue, terminating high above Boston. He detected a faint difference between the distant, shadowy buildings and the lowest points of the sky. He checked his watch. Only eighteen minutes had elapsed. The sun would be up in thirty-five minutes.

Staring at the trajectory of the contrail over southern Massachusetts, he roughly calculated that it must have landed in the Atlantic somewhere just beyond Boston. A chilling thought hit him. His family was on a sailboat off the Maine coast.

Shit.

Ryan took the smartphone out of his pocket and pressed the home button. The device activated, but couldn't locate a signal, further evidence that the grid had been taken down by some kind of electrical phenomenon. But did that make any sense? If this whole mess had been caused by a rogue asteroid or meteorite, there should be no EMP—maybe. He tried the phone one more time, hoping it just needed a few moments to locate a signal. "No Service." He really hoped his family was safe.

Warren Towers disgorged a steady flow of panicked and injured coeds onto Commonwealth Avenue, quickly blocking the eastbound side of the road and spreading laterally. The lone siren had faded. He glanced at his phone one more time, just in case the initial cell tower failure had been a temporary glitch. "No Service."

He assessed the dense crowd approaching from the center of the dormitory complex and decided to head in the opposite direction. He'd been one of very few students wearing a backpack during the exodus and the only student carrying a bucket of dehydrated food. The crowd was more confused than hostile, but it wouldn't take much to bridge the gap. If one enterprising and unscrupulous individual recognized the opportunity represented by Ryan's gear, the situation could be turned against him. His best strategy was to avoid crowds.

"Are you getting a signal?" yelled someone behind him.

Ryan turned to face two guys supporting a blonde female student. She wore a pair of running shorts and a loose fitting T-shirt. In the dim monochromatic light cast by a dying tree fire, her ankle looked severely swollen. A two-inch vertical cut above her right eyebrow bled down her face.

"We need to get an ambulance. She's really messed up."

"I can't get a signal," said Ryan, approaching them, "and I don't think help is coming. I heard one siren, and that's it."

"Shit. Her ankle is smashed, dude."

"Looks like it's broken," said Ryan, kneeling in front of her leg. "I assume you can't put any weight on this?"

She shook her head and grimaced.

"You need to get her to a hospital. I can patch up her head, put a compression wrap on her ankle—but that's about it," said Ryan.

"Where's the nearest hospital?" asked one of the students.

"On the other side of the turnpike," said Ryan, pointing south. "Brigham and Women's Hospital. They should be able to fix her up."

Ryan led them to a small park next to Warren Towers, where they could avoid the prying eyes of several hundred desperate students. He carried a limited medical kit with enough basic supplies to treat three people for relatively minor injuries. Attracting a crowd might end badly. Treating the girl carried enough risk, but it was the right thing to do for now.

"How far is the hospital?"

"Less than a mile. You need to go west to St. Mary's Street and take that south over the turnpike. You'll keep going south. I don't know the streets. What's her name?"

"Elsie. I think she's from Denmark. You don't think we can flag down a car or something to take her?"

"I haven't seen a single car. If we got hit by an EMP or solar flare, you might not see one all morning."

"This is un-fucking-real," said the student. "I need to get back into my room."

"You'll be better off at the hospital. Set Elsie down on this bench," he said, stealing a peek at the crowd.

The ground-level structure blocked most of his view of the crowd, which was good for now. He dropped his backpack while they set her down, and removed the kit. Basic was an understatement for a disaster scenario like this. He could easily go through most of the gauze pads just treating the cut on her head.

"Is this good?" one of them said, standing next to the bench.

"Perfect. Do me a favor and keep an eye on the crowd back there or any people approaching us. This isn't a big kit," said Ryan.

"Got it. Are you an off-duty EMT or something?"

"No. I showed up here with the rest of you."

"Where did you get all of this stuff?" said the other student.

"My parents are a little paranoid. Elsie? How are you feeling?" he asked.

"Dizzy and my leg hurts," she croaked in a faint Scandinavian accent.

"Swedish?"

"Ja."

"My parents took us on a tour of Scandinavia. Stockholm first, then we drove along the coast to Helsingborg, crossing over to Denmark. We stopped in Iceland on the way back. One of our best trips."

"I love Iceland. We travel there every other year," she said.

"Elsie, I'm going to give you some ibuprofen to help with the pain, but—"

"It's not going to help," she interrupted.

"Exactly. Better than nothing, though. I need to disinfect your wounds, which will hurt. I can't do much for your leg. Good to go?"

"Good to go," she said, extending a thumb.

A few minutes later, Ryan packed up the kit and donned the backpack. Elsie sat up on the bench with three butterfly bandages on her lower forehead and a clean face. He checked the compression wrap around her ankle one more time before replacing her sock and shoe.

"That should keep everything under control until you get her to Brigham," he said.

"I don't know if we should go. I have shit in my room, and—"

"Do you have any food in your room?" said Ryan.

The guys shrugged. "Some chips."

"Guess what? The cafeteria is closed. Permanently. The stores are closed. Permanently. This is a major deal. Relief efforts will naturally focus on the hospitals. You want to be at a hospital, not here. Warren Towers is an empty shell. Eventually, you'll have to leave. You safely deliver her to the hospital and find a way to help out. Get in at the ground level of volunteers.

You'll get a hot meal, water and a roof over your head, which is more than anyone around here will be able to say in two days."

They both nodded.

"You *cannot* abandon her. It's one mile. If you don't want to stay at the hospital, you can be back in your tomb up there within fifteen minutes. You guys good with this?" said Ryan.

"Do you really think this is an EMP? What about that?" one of them said, pointing at the sinister contrail south of Boston.

"I don't know what that is, but I guarantee this is not a regular power outage. We'd see some backup lights out there. I didn't see anything from my room. Get her situated at the hospital, and talk your way onto some kind of volunteer detail. It's the best you can do right now."

"Sounds like the best plan we've got. Thanks for helping out, man."

Ryan shook both of their hands and tightened his backpack.

"Where are you headed in such a hurry?" said Elsie.

"Boston College to find my girlfriend. Then north," said Ryan.

"How far north?" she said.

"Maine."

"Sounds like a long way."

"It's far enough to be trouble, but it's closer than Sweden."

"Thank you for helping," said Elsie, glancing nervously at her two caretakers.

Ryan nodded and walked toward the road that took him behind Warren Towers. He agonized over the decision to leave Elsie, doubtful that the two students would carry through with their promise. He muttered, pounding his fist against his thigh. A diversion to Brigham and Women's Hospital would cost him too much time. If he didn't show up at Chloe's apartment soon, she might come looking for him, which could put her in danger. Every scenario their parents had discussed led to the same conclusion. Ryan was the one to travel in the event of a disaster.

Ryan kept walking, fighting the urge to look back. He reached the street and stopped. *Damnit!* He couldn't shake the image of Elsie crawling along the sidewalk, trying to escape a wall of water. He returned to the park bench, noting that no progress had been made toward getting her ambulatory.

"I'll take her to the hospital. Go back to your bag of Fritos," said Ryan, grasping her hand and pulling her onto her one good leg.

The two students took off toward the dormitory without saying a word, validating Ryan's decision. They would have ditched her somewhere out of sight, where their cowardly act went unnoticed.

"Thank you. Those two would have left me for dead. They rushed to my room after the quake. You know—to help."

"Imagine that," said Ryan.

"Exactly. They've been attached to me like glue since I arrived, but they didn't look too enthusiastic to help when they saw my leg."

"A busted leg is a deal breaker, even if you're a hot Danish chick," said Ryan.

"Swedish."

"I remember," said Ryan, putting her arm around his shoulder.

"I really appreciate this. I know you're in a hurry," said Elsie.

"We'll have to move fast. As fast as we can manage," he said.

"I'm not sure how we're going to do this. I can't put any weight on the leg, and I don't think hopping a few kilometers will work."

Ryan looked down at her leg. She had it bent at a shallow angle to keep her foot from striking the ground. Judging by the pained expression she displayed when he pulled her to her feet, he knew she was right.

"How much do you weigh?" he said.

"Is that a polite question to ask?"

"It is if someone's going to carry you a mile," he said. "I don't see any other way."

"I'm sorry this became your burden. 48 kilograms—give or take."

"I'm sure our paths crossed for a reason. What is that, like 220 pounds?" he said, receiving a playful slap to the shoulder. "You ready? This is going to hurt you a lot more than me."

"I guess."

He kneeled and reached under her good leg.

"Now lean over my backpack and reach your right arm over my shoulder," he said.

She groaned as he lifted her off the ground into a fireman's carry. He hooked his right arm under her knee and grasped the hand she had draped over his chest, freeing his left hand to pick up the bucket. Ryan took a few uneasy steps forward, wondering how the hell he was going to do this.

PART I

"Freedom Trail"

Chapter 1

Boston University
Boston, Massachusetts

Alex Fletcher sat against one of the interior walls of the elevator lobby and dug through his front cargo pocket. He retrieved the magazine he had ejected after shooting up the truck and thumbed four rounds into the palm of his hand. He tucked the half-emptied magazine into a "dump" pouch attached to the left side of his tactical vest and ejected the magazine in his rifle, adding the four rounds. Marines consolidated ammunition whenever practical, and he had a few minutes to burn before stepping off for Brookline—without his new entourage. The magazine slammed home in the HK416, and he stood up to prepare for his impending departure.

"You can't just leave us here," said one of the students, standing in the semi-circle formed around Alex.

"You're not exactly equipped to survive on the streets."

"We don't have much of a choice. You said it yourself," said another student. "Nobody is coming for us. We're running low on food and water."

"It's not like I'm meeting my son at Denny's for a Grand Slam breakfast before heading north," said Alex, adjusting the straps on his backpack and checking for loose gear.

"What's a Denny's?" said a petite brunette sitting in front of him.

"You really don't know what Denny's is?"

She shrugged.

"How much water do you have?" said Alex.

"Each of us has a few water bottles, and we still have, like, how many trash cans filled?"

"Four. Some guy went around telling everyone to fill up containers right after the shockwave hit. It's the only reason we've been able to keep a low profile. We haven't left the floor," said Piper, the young woman in charge.

"Your son told me to do that. I saw him right before he left," said a dark-haired girl, stepping forward into the red glow of the chemlight. "He seemed to know what he was doing. Like you. You have to get us out of here."

"I can't take any of you out of this building. It's not safe. They're actively looking for me. The best I can do is let the marines know about your situation."

"Who's looking for you?" said the leader.

"I was hoping one of you could answer that question. A heavily armed, organized group appears to be in control of the streets. Any intel on who might be calling the shots out there?"

"It looked like gangs last night," said a pale kid to Alex's left.

"What do you know about gangs?" said the student with the bat.

"I'm West Coast. We have gangs all over the place."

"Not where you're from."

"I'm from LA, man. Ever heard of the Crips and the Bloods?"

"Dude, that's from fucking twenty years ag—"

"Bullshit! It's still the biggest gang in—"

"Shut the fuck up! All of you! You're at Boston University. The tuition is nearly sixty thousand a year. Nobody here has any street cred, all right? Just tell me what you saw," said Alex, cutting them all off.

"They were rough-looking dudes, mostly Caucasian. Armed with pistols and some hunting rifles," said the kid from LA.

"That changed today. There's been a ton of shooting. Men—and women— running around with rifles like yours, but without all of the fancy optics stuff. They looked more like regular people, you know? I saw a pickup truck go by with a couple of them in the bed. It looked like a citizen's militia," said a student holding a baseball bat.

"That might be a good thing. If it's a legitimate militia, you should be safe out there," said Alex.

"Why is it safe for us and not for you?" asked the leader.

"I'm pretty sure they think I'm one of the marines. I swam across the river from one of the marines' outposts on the other side."

"You swam across the Charles at night, with all of this gear?"

"I told you he was a mercenary," said someone.

"Believe whatever you want. I don't really give a shit. I'm leaving, and nobody is following. I'll leave a water filter behind for you. It's a hand-pumped type, good for five hundred gallons. You can catch rainwater in the trashcans or fetch water from the river. Whatever you do, don't let anyone see it, or you'll have a fight on your hands."

"So that's it?" said Piper.

He wished he could do more for them, but beyond the water filter, he had nothing to offer. The idea of leading them on some kind of predawn parade through the streets of war-torn Boston was absurd. The fact that none of the students seemed to understand this reality made it even more ludicrous. Most of them were still wearing shorts and T-shirts, in a building that could collapse or catch fire at any moment. They were clueless.

But they're kids—and you're a parent.

He felt responsible for their safety on some basic level, but rationally, he couldn't justify the risk. Ryan and Chloe were his sole responsibility right now. He had to let these kids look out for themselves.

"That's it. I'll do a radio check at the top of the hour. Then I'm gone."

Chapter 2

Harvard Yard
Cambridge, Massachusetts

Ed dropped his backpack on the wet grass and collapsed against a tree trunk, staring at Hollis Hall's shadowy facade. The steady hum of the battalion's generator pulled at his eyelids. He'd have to sleep soon. There was no way to avoid it. He just needed to hang on for another eight minutes to catch Alex's first broadcast on the stolen Motorola. He wished they could talk, but Alex explained why it had to be a one-way broadcast.

All transmissions sent from one of the battalion's handheld radios triggered an encryption protocol, even if Ed used one of several "uncovered" channels, and could be monitored by the communications platoon. If they discovered an unauthorized conversation emanating from one of the battalion Motorolas, they would block the radio and trace the source.

Alex assured Ed that he didn't want to be on the receiving end of that search. Ed would only transmit if the situation deteriorated enough to affect Alex's timeline. Alex agreed to keep his radio in "sleep mode," which scanned for channel activity on their preset frequency, alerting him if Ed transmitted for longer than three seconds.

Just thinking about Alex's transmission energized him. By now, Alex should have reached Ryan's dorm room. Everything depended on what he found there. Ryan was supposed to travel to Chloe's apartment in the event of an emergency, where they'd wait for their parents. He desperately needed to hear that Ryan wasn't in his room. It meant that Chloe was safe. He knew the discovery would be tough on Alex, but it represented the best chance that *both* of them were safe.

Ed unzipped the top of his pack and dug into one of the internal compartments for the hidden Motorola. He turned it on and inserted one of the earbuds, hearing the typical back and forth military chatter he'd been treated to every time he scanned the channels. He had no idea what they were saying most of the time; the marine lingo was as foreign to him as Chinese. SITREPS. POSREPS. SPOTREPS. None of it made sense. Line Alpha. Line Bravo. All nonsense. He wasn't sure why they bothered to use encrypted radios. Nobody could figure this shit out.

All he knew at this point was that "Shadow" referred to the Harvard Yard security detachment, "Striker" meant any of the units in the city, and "Raider" was the group along the river. He learned most of this by eavesdropping in the battalion headquarters tent. Sergeant Walker hadn't been totally useless. He leaned his head against the harsh tree bark and pressed the scan button, jumping to the next encrypted channel. The orange LED read "Shadow."

"Shadow Actual, this is Shadow 3. SPOTREP. I have four possible hostiles moving south across the Cambridge Street overpass, headed in our direction. Request permission to engage, over."

Cambridge Street? His head came off the tree.

"Shadow 3, can you confirm weapons?"

"Affirmative. Rifles. They're halfway across. We're gonna lose them behind Holworthy."

Holworthy Hall?

"Stand by, Shadow 3."

"This is Shadow 5! We have six—contact! I say again, contact! Taking automatic fire from the southern end of the old yard!"

Rapid, sustained gunfire erupted in the distance, followed by an overhead snap.

"What the…?" Ed muttered, rolling on his stomach.

A hiss passed to his right.

"Oh shit," he said and pressed his body flat against the ground.

"All Shadow stations. You are cleared to engage."

Flashes filled the darkness between Hollis and Stoughton Halls, followed by the staccato hammering of the M240G machine gun. Red tracers stitched outward, floating deep into the campus. The marines between Hollis and Harvard Halls fired their rifles at the same time, barely beating the 240 deployed between Stoughton and Phillips Brooks Hall. The

STEVEN KONKOLY

thunderous gunfire masked the frantic reports streaming through Ed's radio earpiece. The marine perimeter was under attack from all sides! The shooting slackened several seconds later, and he could hear the different perimeter stations reporting.

"Shadow 5 reports three, possibly four enemy kills. Hostiles have stopped firing."

"Shadow 5, this is Shadow Actual. Copy report. Continue to engage any hostiles in the open."

"Shadow 3 reports two enemy kills on the Cambridge Street overpass. One enemy wounded was carried out of sight behind Holworthy."

"Copy, Shadow 3. Scan the windows and watch the corners. All units cease fire and pass your SITREP. I say again. All units cease fire and pass your SITREP. Shadow Actual, out."

The firing died out just as suddenly as it had started, yielding to the occasional distant gunshot. Ed pulled the radio out of his backpack and shifted to the "broadcast" preset channel programmed by Alex. He pressed the transmit button, fairly confident that an all-out attack on Lieutenant Colonel Grady's command tent qualified as an event that bumped up the timeline. Alex had overestimated the time it might take for the city to implode. Ed couldn't imagine they had more than twelve hours until the marines had no choice but to withdraw.

"Durham Three-Zero, this is Durham Three-Two. Come in, over."

Chapter 3

Boston University
Boston, Massachusetts

Alex felt one of his chest pouches vibrate. Checking his watch, he muttered a few curses. Ed couldn't wait five minutes? He really hoped the marines were too busy to notice an unauthorized transmission go out over one of their encrypted Motorolas. It wouldn't take Lieutenant Colonel Grady more than a few seconds to figure out who had swiped the radio. He opened the pouch and removed the radio, switching it out of "sleep mode" and inserting the earbud. Maybe it wasn't Ed.

"Station sending on this channel, please identify," said Alex.

"Durham Three-Two!"

"This is Durham Three-Zero. First transmission scheduled for zero-five hundred (0500). Stand by for five minutes, please."

"I told you he was Special Forces," said one of the students. "Parent, my ass."

Alex dismissed the comment and turned up the volume. *"No. Negative. SPOTREP. Whatever the fuck you people say!"* said Ed.

Something was wrong.

"Take a deep breath, Durham Three-Two, and send your report."

"The headquarters was just attacked from all sides. I had bullets snapping right over my head," hissed Ed over the radio.

"Can you estimate the number of hostiles?" said Alex.

"Every gun on the perimeter started shooting at something. Multiple groups. One of the SPOTREPs mentioned a group of four with rifles. It's all quiet now."

21

"Understand. You're still in the safest place possible. Stick close to the marines and cease transmitting. I did not find either of the kids at Boston University. It looks like Ryan bugged out right after the shockwave hit. I'm moving to the second rendezvous location. Will report again at 0600 or upon arrival, whichever comes first. Switch to our backup broadcast channel. Durham Three-Zero, out."

He put the radio back into the pouch.

"Is something wrong?" said the student leader.

"Everything is wrong."

A powerful flashlight illuminated the walls of the hallway to the right of the lobby.

"Who's watching the stairwell door?" Alex asked quietly, shifting his stance to face the shaking light.

"Which one?" said Piper.

"The one I used," he whispered.

"I don't know," she whispered back.

"Shit. Move this way and don't make a sound," he hissed.

Alex snatched the red chemlight from the floor and pocketed it, corralling the group toward the hallway opposite the new light source.

"Get inside any room on this side, and lock the door. Let's go. Where's the other stairwell?" he whispered, aiming his rifle across the lobby.

"Down there. There's a door on the left side, past the lounge," said Piper, pointing down the long, murky passage.

"Does the lounge connect on both sides?"

"Yes. Same with the stairwell."

Students scrambled through the darkness, pouring into the rooms and shutting the doors. Alex made a mental map of the dormitory floor. Two long hallways ran parallel to each other, connected by the elevator lobby, lounge and second stairwell vestibule. Three points of access to this hallway and only one viable escape route.

"So, what's the plan?" she said, peeking around the corner with him.

"Get into a room, and don't open the door," he said, crouching. "I'm going for the second stairwell."

"You're ditching us?"

"If this is the same group that followed me from the river, you'll be glad I left," said Alex.

"What are we supposed to tell them?"

"Tell them I searched one of the rooms and took off, or tell them everything. It doesn't matter. Gotta go," he said and dashed across the hallway.

He reached the other side as a concentrated beam of light spanned the elevator lobby.

"Freeze! Step into the hallway with your hands above your head!"

Alex stopped long enough to see that the beams of light had settled on Piper, who covered her eyes with one hand and raised the other.

"Both hands!"

Alex flipped his night vision goggles down and sprinted away from the lobby, toward the opposite end of the hallway. He passed a door labeled "WOMEN," followed by an unmarked door, which he pushed inward. Several comfortable-looking chairs and a long couch faced a flat-screen television mounted to the wall. Two round tables with chairs sat beyond the couch. *Wrong door.* He started to back into the hallway when a light appeared under the stairwell door. Alex ducked inside the lounge and shut the door quickly and quietly. Crouched in the pitch darkness, he drew his suppressed pistol and remained absolutely still.

"You got anything!" someone yelled outside the door.

He couldn't hear the reply over the high-pitched screaming. His grip on the pistol tightened. The shrieking intensified, followed by crying.

"Open your doors and get into the hallway!" another voice boomed.

Alex crossed the room, careful not to bump any of the furniture, and listened at the far door. Hearing nothing, he cracked it open and stared directly ahead at the wall, interpreting the light. The green image of the cinderblock wall shimmered but didn't flare, giving him the confidence to open the door and verify that the hallway was empty. The hallway near the elevator lobby pulsed bright green, almost washed out by the powerful flashlights. He heard the men pounding on the students' doors and yelling threats.

He edged toward the lobby, knowing damn well he should leave. He couldn't skip out now, not after dropping a dangerous enemy right at their doorstep. He couldn't let the new world order play out on these kids tonight. They had a whole lifetime ahead of them to deal with the newest form of Darwinism that emerged from this disaster. Alex continued, walking heel to toe, constantly checking behind him. No plan materialized as he edged closer to the corner. The sharp sound of multiple slaps caused Alex to grit his teeth.

"I know he was here! I'm not blind!" said an angry male voice. "None of us saw him leave the building!"

"He was only here for a few minutes. He was looking for something in that room. I don't know if he found it," Piper whimpered.

"You better not be lying to me," he grunted. "Get those kids out of their rooms! Shoot the door open if you have to!"

Alex instinctively backed up and crouched, expecting one of them to run across the lobby, but no one came. The pounding intensified in the other hallway, followed by heated shouting. This was his last chance before the hallways filled with students. He holstered the pistol and gripped his rifle, disengaging the safety. Finishing one more scan of the dim hallway behind him, he flipped his NVGs out of the way. A quick peek around the corner gave him hope. Two men dressed in woodland camouflage and tactical vests stood in the lobby with Piper, one of them holding her against the wall by her long blonde hair. The second man shined a flashlight in her face with one hand and gripped her neck with the other.

"He didn't leave. My people came up both stairwells," spat the man holding her hair.

"He left over fifteen minutes ago!" she yelled.

Alex emerged and triggered the rifle flashlight. The 150-lumen beam blinded them, and they instinctively turned their faces away from the searing light. Alex fired one bullet at each of their heads, dropping both men to the floor. He deactivated the light and grabbed Piper, pulling her into the hallway before the rest of the militia group could investigate.

"Gerry? Ted? What's going—"

"They're dead!" screamed another voice.

"What the fuck are you talking—shit!"

Alex leaned out and aimed at the rightmost corner, hoping to catch the last voice in the open. He centered the red tritium dot on a partially obscured torso and fired twice, yielding an agonized screech.

"Get to the student lounge, quick," he whispered to Piper. "Don't open the door."

He followed her at half-speed, keeping his rifle trained at the corner they had just abandoned, until he bumped into her.

"We're at the lounge," she whispered.

Alex lowered his NVGs and gently pushed the door inward, checking the room for surprises.

"It's clear. I need you to follow the wall to your immediate left and keep going until you hit the corner. You'll stay there until I come back for you. Understood?"

"It's really dark in here," she said.

"You have a clear path to the corner if you hug the wall. How many of them did you see?" said Alex.

"Four."

"Minus three. See you in a few," he said.

With the door shut, he lifted the NVGs for a second. He couldn't risk using them in the hallway once he left this room. The NVGs gave him a considerable advantage in the darkness, but a beam of light directed at the device's sensitive lens would blind him. Switching to his pistol, he carefully opened the door. The hallway was pitch black. *Of course.* He lowered the NVGs and studied the green image. The hallway was empty. He closed the door and paused, thinking about his next move. If the guy had been smart enough to turn off the lights, Alex couldn't count on him to make a rookie mistake. He'd have to go out and look for him.

"Piper?" he whispered.

"Yeah?"

"He's not there."

"What?" she said too loudly for comfort.

"Sssshhhh! Keep it down," he grunted. "I have to search for him, but I'm going to need your help with something."

"I'm not going out there."

"You don't have to. Do you know how to shoot a pistol?"

"My father's a cop," she stated.

"Is that a yes or a no?"

"Yes. I can shoot a pistol, but I'm not a good shot."

"You don't have to be," he said and worked his way over to her.

"I just need you to cover my back. Sit in the doorframe, watching the second stairwell door and this door right here," he said, pointing to the door they had both used to enter.

"Are you pointing in the dark?" she said.

"No," he said, lowering his hand. "Can you do this for me?"

"I don't know. I can't see anything."

"It's dark out there, but not as dark as this room. There should be enough background light in the hallway to see either door open. I'm not asking you to get into a prolonged gun battle. Yell, pop off a few rounds and run for it. I'll take care of the rest. This would make your dad proud."

"You can spare me the proud parent speech."

"Sorry. Can you do this, or are you useless like the rest of your generation? Is that better?"

"Sort of," she said.

"The pistol has no safety. You pull the trigger, it goes boom. First trigger pull is a little tough—"

"Double action. Single action. I get it."

"Let's get you set up."

Less than a minute later, Piper stood in the doorway, propping the door open with her foot and facing the back hallway. Alex removed his boots and placed them inside the lounge.

"Just shoot and run in the opposite direction," whispered Alex.

"Uh-huh."

Alex lowered his NVGs and activated the IR laser. He had no idea what he was up against. He didn't know if the guy turned off the flashlights because they might give up a shadow, or if he had caught a glimpse of the NVGs on Alex's head. For all he knew, the guy just picked them up because they were expensive. It didn't matter. The rifle light would advertise his location, and it was too dark to effectively see without the NVGs. He could use the goggles to his advantage in this environment, unless his adversary was crafty. It was still too early to tell.

He took several silent steps on the cool tile, keeping the green laser centered on the empty passage ahead. The bulk of his attention was directed on the doors lining the hallway. As he passed each closed door, he checked the handle to verify it was locked. He felt comfortable enough to turn his back on a locked door. Not that he had a choice. Knocking on doors wasn't an option right now.

Approaching the elevator lobby corner, Alex tensed. A blood slick trailed into the elevator lobby, beyond his line of sight. His adversary had moved the wounded man, hopefully down the stairwell and out of the building. If that was the case, Alex needed to get out of here before reinforcements arrived. He studied the hallway beyond his son's door, convinced that the shooter couldn't have doubled back after dragging his comrade away. A significant pool of blood extended across the hallway where he'd shot one of them in the chest. The tile beyond held no footprints.

He crouched at the corner and executed a quick peek into the elevator lobby. Gunfire exploded, lighting the lobby and exploding the cinderblock wall in front of him. *Shit. Crafty.* Alex scrambled backward, desperate to escape the shower of fragments, as shards of cinderblock stung his face. Bullets pummeled the concrete on the opposite side of the hallway, sparking and ricocheting into the dark void behind him. The shooting stopped, and he heard the telltale sounds of a magazine swap. Alex sprinted to the corner and dropped to the floor, leaning to the left and placing the laser on the man's head.

The wounded man sat propped up against one of the elevator doors, desperately trying to change rifle magazines. He acknowledged Alex's presence by spitting.

"You'll never take this country from us."

"Stop loading your weapon. I'm not with the government," stated Alex.

Fighting to sit upright in a puddle of his own blood, the man's shaky hand inserted a magazine and reached back for the charging handle. A sharp bark from Alex's rifle ended the struggle.

Who the hell are these people?

He didn't have time to analyze the question. He felt certain that the remaining shooter had relocated to the other long hallway. The wounded militiaman effectively served the same purpose as Pip—*oh shit!*

"Piper!"

Gunshots echoed from the other side of the building, lighting the end of the hallway behind Alex. He scrambled to his bare feet and sprinted for the lounge, arriving to find the door closed, perforated by several bullets.

I killed her.

He kicked the door in and rushed inside, ready to engage any target without long hair. He caught a glimpse of a figure with a rifle crouched near the far wall, but his night vision flared before he could react. Gunshots erupted, and he dropped to the floor, firing blindly at the other side of the room.

"I got him!" screamed a female voice.

Alex raised the NVGs and stared upward at the voice. Piper stood over him, aiming a pistol and flashlight at the other side of the room. A bright red, clumpy stain covered the brightly illuminated wall.

"That's all of them. Turn off your light," he said, standing up.

He took the flashlight out of his pocket and guided her out of the lounge.

"You all right?" he asked, handing her the light.

"I hid inside the lounge when the shooting started. I'm sorry. The door opened, and he got halfway across the room before I fired. I couldn't move. We couldn't see each other. We just kept shooting," she said, crying.

"You did great, Piper. You're meant to lead this group, and that's not a bullshit, motivate the youngsters speech. Take a minute to get your shit together, and start working on a plan to secure the floor. You hear me?" he said, grasping both of her shoulders and forcing eye contact. "You have three points of access. Two on the stairwell back here and one by the elevators. You need to make it impossible for anyone to open one of those doors. Move the desks out of the rooms and pile them up. With four rifles and plenty of ammunition, you should be able to discourage any attempts to breach those barriers. Pick your shooters wisely. Anyone with prior shooting experience is preferred. *Call of Duty* does not count. Keep one rifle on each access point at all times. You carry the fourth to reinforce whichever door is under attack. Never leave a door unguarded. Ever. Good to go?"

"I think so."

"Search the bodies for a radio and listen. If you can talk to these people, do it. Let them know exactly what happened, and that I'm no longer here. Tell them that you'll defend the floor with your lives. Drag the bodies into the back stairwell vestibule and respectfully lay them side by side. They might leave you alone."

"What if they don't?"

"Then you know what to do," said Alex, picking up his boots and socks. "I guarantee your dad would be proud of you for this."

"You really think I'll see my parents again?" she asked.

"Not a doubt in my mind," Alex lied.

Ten minutes later, he sprinted across the Massachusetts Turnpike, seeking refuge in the maze of tightly packed west Boston neighborhoods he needed to traverse to reach Ryan and Chloe.

Chapter 4

Middlesex Fells Reservation
Stoneham, Massachusetts

Charlie Thornton put the key in the ignition and paused, his hands trembling. He'd somehow picked up a transmission from Ed on the primary broadcast frequency, after several hours of sheer radio silence. Ed's sudden, desperate report of an all-out attack had jarred him into action. Little of the report made any sense. Ed had used Alex's radio call sign, and they were clearly having a conversation, but Charlie could only hear Ed's side of the exchange.

Ed's report painted a horrible picture of the situation in Boston. From what Charlie could tell, Ed was in some kind of besieged perimeter with other survivors. How did that evolve? Why was he able to hear Ed? Did he turn back? Was he nearby? He'd lost contact with them in Medford, which was less than four miles away. Too many unanswered questions. He lacked the bigger picture, which was why he closed his eyes and took deep breaths until his hands stopped shaking. He pictured Linda and his girls, safe at the Fletcher compound, and the key came out of the ignition, his hand resting in his lap. He'd come perilously close to making a disastrous decision.

They'd barely navigated the tight roads and fallen trees in full daylight. Even if he somehow managed to miraculously get the jeep onto Route 28, then what? Drive south in the middle of the night until he made radio contact again? Alex reported that the exodus along the main roads leading north had intensified, with travelers looking to put as much distance between themselves and the city at night, while the temperatures were reasonable. How long would he have lasted driving through that desperate herd? He knew the answer.

Charlie opened the door and stepped onto the soft forest floor, taking his rifle and backpack with him. He took a few steps and lifted his rifle, using his night vision attachment to locate the IR chemlight that marked his makeshift camp. He'd taken Alex's advice and set up about twenty-five yards into the forest. Far enough away to avoid drawing immediate attention to the Jeep, but close enough to respond to one of his trip wires set across the forest road. He'd tied the ends of the two trip wires to thick sticks, which he kept under his armpits when he felt sleepy. For the most part, the night had been uneventful. Alex had been wise to bring the Jeep here.

Stuck between the Middle and South Reservoirs, a crumbly, raised road connected the island to the eastern and western sides of the reservation. He hadn't noticed any foot traffic on the road and guessed that most of the city's evacuees had no use for an east-west running trail. Everyone was headed due north. Charlie set his pack in front of the tree marked by the chemlight and lowered himself carefully to the forest floor, gingerly leaning against the soft pack.

He'd torqued his back carrying their packs to the Jeep. He knew better than to heave all of them at once, but he'd been in a hurry to finally sit his ass down and give his heart a break. One last chore, he'd told himself, and wham! He'd felt the telltale twitch, and his lower back muscles started to spasm. He popped a thousand milligrams of ibuprofen and laid flat on the ground for an hour. Surprisingly, the combination of drugs and rest kept his muscles from locking up and pulling his back completely out of place—for now. He was borderline useless when his back "went out." Linda could attest to that.

He chuckled at the thought of Linda chastising him for lifting three packs at once. She'd hover over him, pointing that finger, reading him the Linda Thornton Riot Act and setting a time limit on his recovery period. One day for a self-inflicted back pull. Two days if it wasn't his fault. He'd never received two days.

God, I miss her.

The thought of his family gave him the idea to check the satphone.

He powered the device and studied the screen. Eight satellites registered within line of sight; two more than earlier that evening. The government must have "asked" the major satellite communications companies to move a few of their more redundant satellites into geostationary orbit over the United States. Satellite bandwidth represented the only viable long-distance communication network available in the United States—for government use only. He autodialed the Fletchers' second satphone and pressed send. "Connection Unavailable" flashed on the muted orange display. He noticed a new message in the phone's inbox and sat up. Adrenaline flushed through his body. It could be a message from the wives! He navigated to the inbox and opened the message. Not the wives, *Uncle Sam*.

"Department of Homeland Security Bulletin DTG 210500Z AUG13—Effective Immediately: Citizens required to observe curfew from evening civil twilight (sunset) to morning civil twilight (sunrise). Citizens to remain indoors within personal dwellings or Military/FEMA designated shelter zones. Check with law enforcement, military or local government representatives for a list of approved zones if personal dwelling not available. Citizens in violation of the MANDATORY curfew may be detained and returned to their personal dwelling or held in a nearby detention facility until curfew hours have expired. Situation Update: Power outages persist nationwide. Authorities continue work to restore power to critical infrastructure and key population centers. Check with law enforcement, military or local government representatives for instructions regarding the distribution of emergency supplies."

"That's it?" he muttered, followed by a wide yawn.

How on God's green earth did the government expect to enforce a curfew when half of the population had taken to the road? Idiots. The latest government broadcast told him everything he needed to know about the state of affairs in Washington, D.C. There was a one hundred percent clusterfuck in progress. Only the most obtuse bureaucratic stooge would approve a nationwide sunset-to-sunrise curfew given what he'd seen on the approach to Boston. Didn't the government have any way to receive reports from the field? Was it possible they didn't know the cities had already started to empty? They had clearly hijacked all of the available satellite bandwidth—wait a minute! What if the government wasn't in control of the satellites?

His heart rate started to increase, followed by heavier breathing. None of this made sense. Either the government had purposely ignored incoming reports, or they hadn't received them. Either scenario carried chilling implications. Staring at the starry sky through the moonlit branches, Charlie couldn't shake the image of a sky blanketed with Chinese paratroopers. It beat the other image; a convoy of heavily armored DHS vehicles rolling into town.

Chapter 5

EVENT +47:45

Brookline, Massachusetts

Alex low-crawled along the hedge, fixated on reaching the corner of the narrow yard. Traversing over one hundred fifty feet of dew-covered grass along the apartment building's frontage had left him soaked. He arrived at the corner and lowered his head into the wet grass, thankful that the low hedge still held enough leaves to provide adequate concealment from the intersection. The cool, damp clothing felt refreshing against his skin. He'd spend a few minutes lying prone and taking in the ambient sounds at the intersection before poking his head over the bushes to confirm the road was clear.

The GPS receiver told him Stedman Road emptied into Harvard Road, but it couldn't know that the intersection rated a stoplight. He'd taken pains to detect and avoid traffic signals, having spotted militia patrols hidden at two major intersections in the past mile and a half. He'd started crawling toward the intersection of Stedman and Harvard long before detecting the stoplight. In all truth, he'd slipped up. He could have used his NVGs to scan from a distance, but he'd started to conserve the unit's batteries and had forgotten.

By the time he stopped to check, he'd already traversed half the distance and couldn't raise his head fully to scan the intersection. He decided to press onward and gamble that it was clear. If it were guarded, he'd have to crawl back. Not a big deal, but with morning twilight approaching in forty minutes, he wanted to put as much distance between himself and Warren Towers as possible.

Militia activity had been steady but not overwhelming in the areas south of the Massachusetts Turnpike, confined to obvious intersection outposts or easily detectable vehicle patrols. With little background noise beyond distant, sporadic gunfire, the sound of an approaching vehicle was impossible to miss. He'd effortlessly avoided several vehicle patrols within the first mile of his journey, decreasing markedly after Pleasant Street. With 1.4 miles left to reach 42 Orkney Road, he anticipated smooth sailing, as long as he didn't get sloppy.

He heard the repeated click of a disposable lighter and froze. A fit of hacking followed, drawing Alex's attention to the park across the road to his left. A small orange glow appeared through the hedge's foliage, quickly fading.

How did I miss that?

He couldn't determine the precise location, but based on the position of the glowing cigarette, someone had decided to sit his or her ass in the small park bordering the intersection. He'd caught a serious break.

Now what?

Crawling the same one hundred fifty feet didn't seem like a good idea anymore. The militia team had an unobstructed view of the hedge along most of its length. Rationally, he knew the result would be the same, but his mind had already closed off that route to further discussion. It didn't leave him with a ton of options.

The hedge turned at the corner and ran about fifteen feet along the sidewalk on Harvard Street, ending at the apartment building. If he could quietly squeeze through the bushes and crawl past the corner, he'd be out of their line of sight. Alex crawled the length of the bushes, reaching the building's rough sandstone foundation. The entire hedgerow appeared thick and well maintained. There was no way he could push his way through that without waking up the entire neighborhood. This left him with one guaranteed option. Eliminate the sentries.

While definitely the "tried and true" solution, killing militia this far from Warren Towers carried risks he'd prefer to avoid. Warren Towers to the corner of Harvard and Stedman in thirty minutes? A simple game of connect the dots on a city map would give militia leadership a fairly accurate prediction of Alex's intended travel route. Worse yet, a straight line drawn between the two locations terminated less than a quarter of a mile from Chloe's apartment at the Chestnut Hill Reservoir. They had no way to determine how far he travelled, but they could focus their search along this projected path, effectively trapping him in Chloe's apartment until nightfall. Based on Ed's report of the attack in Harvard Square, they couldn't afford to wait until sunset to cross the Charles River. Boston sat on the verge of a complete civil breakdown.

He pointed his body at the sentries and lowered the NVGs, peering through the bushes. Leaves broke the image, but he managed to form an actionable assessment. Two armed men sat on top of a picnic table, facing the intersection. The smoker was partially obscured by a tree stump, his head and legs visible beyond the lead edge of the table. He stared down the length of the hedge, wondering if he shouldn't try to crawl back. If they spotted movement and decided to investigate, he could take them down with little effort. If they skipped the investigation part, he'd be in trouble. The bushes would do little to protect him from a concentrated barrage of projectiles travelling at 3,200 feet per second.

He didn't have the time to dick around with crawling back and approaching another intersection, and the sun had no intention of waiting for him to figure this out. Alex crawled along the hedge and stopped, reevaluating his line of fire to the targets. Both men sat in full view.

Let's get this over with.

He started to rise, but stopped to reflect on his surprising indifference toward the prospect of preemptively killing them.

The sentries had been reduced to objects. Dehumanized for his emotional convenience. They fell into several convenient categories: Enemies. Targets. Obstacles. All true, but oversimplified—the way it had been done for millennia. Warfare relied on dehumanizing the enemy, no matter how "justified" the conflict. Raw human nature didn't embrace wholesale slaughter. It had to be manipulated, which wasn't an overly difficult task.

Alex had already convinced himself it was necessary and justified. He didn't stop to consider why these men sat here watching the intersection. Were they doing their part to protect family and friends? Did they believe they were connected to something bigger and more important? Defending their city from the government? Alex didn't care about the answers to any of these questions, because he was sure of one thing. If he stood up and tried to identify himself, his journey to reach Ryan and Chloe would come to an abrupt end—and that was the only piece of information that mattered.

With that in mind, he kneeled, keeping his profile below the top of the hedge. Rising slowly, he canted the rifle and braced it snugly into his shoulder. The IR laser broke the plane of the hedge and reached the man enjoying a cigarette. Alex moved the beam to the center of his head and slowed his breathing. One of the sentries' radios broke the silence, emitting a garbled transmission, causing him to delay the shot. The second man slapped the smoker on the shoulder and said, "Let's go," prompting them to jump down from the table and run across Harvard Street. They hopped into a two-door sedan parked on the street and drove urgently toward Beacon Street. Alex waited for the taillights lights to disappear behind the buildings before running in a low crouch to the hedge along Harvard Street. The red lights continued to recede into the distance, vanishing from sight. A quick scan in the opposite direction convinced Alex that he could cross the street unobserved.

The team's sudden recall from the area was a positive development. It signified a redeployment of assets away from his intended travel path, which might allow him to pick up the pace. Beyond Harvard Street, Alex faced a twisted path of obscure side streets leading to Chloe's apartment. At a brisk, alert walking pace, he could be there in less than thirty minutes.

Chapter 6

42 Orkney Rd
Brookline, Massachusetts

Alex squeezed between two tightly parked cars and sprinted across Ayr Road, burying himself in a stand of tall bushes next to a two-story duplex. Ed had advised him to turn on Ayr Road and look for the service street that ran between the apartments on the southern side of Orkney Road and Beacon Street. Access to Chloe's apartment from Orkney Road was limited to a single, street-level door, which should be locked. With the doorbell inoperable, he'd have no way to effectively signal Ryan and Chloe on the third floor without drawing considerable attention. He preferred to arrive at the apartment unnoticed. One radio call to the militia from a concerned citizen could jeopardize everything.

Resting against the building's brick façade, he measured his senses. The green image betrayed nothing behind the windows staring down at him. The buildings appeared uniformly green. No "hot spots" or movement. A few well-spaced crickets provided the neighborhood's only discernible background noise. The near absence of sound worried him. Ed's description of the ancient metal staircase attached to the three-story covered porch on the service street gave him pause. One way or the other, he was going to wake up some of the neighbors.

The service street connected to Ayr Road through a narrow paved drive surrounded on both sides by steep brick walls. Alex walked through the gap with his rifle raised, until it opened into a wide paved courtyard ringed with trash dumpsters and parked cars. He paused to scan the windows and was treated to a sea of uninteresting green. He counted porches, stopping at the fifth structure jutting out from an indistinguishable three-story wall of brick and windows. Ed had been adamant that 42 Orkney Road was the fifth porch—one of the few details he'd stood behind in his description of the apartment. The porches were supposedly marked with the street number, but in the sheer darkness of this alley, he wasn't sure the night vision could pick up the numbers.

Arriving at the porch, he was relieved to find the number "42" on a sturdy placard next to the stairs. He was almost there. He wanted nothing more than to rush up the stairs and pound on the back door, but he swallowed his excitement and took a cautious step forward onto the metal staircase bolted to the concrete next to the building. He hadn't made it this far to screw it up at the last possible moment. Halfway up the first flight of stairs, the metal groaned, causing Alex to stop and cringe. The sound echoed off the walls of the concrete enclave, repeatedly reaching his ears. His next step yielded the same result.

"Fuck this," he muttered and mounted the stairs at a normal pace.

By the time he stepped onto Chloe's covered back porch, Alex heard several windows slide open, followed by scattered mumbling. The night vision image flared bright green as at least one powerful flashlight swept the alley. Someone issued a halfhearted challenge, only to be immediately shushed. A whispered argument ensued, and a window slammed shut. They were afraid. Good. Maybe everyone decided this wasn't their problem.

Alex walked gingerly across the loose wooden planks, careful not to knock over the bicycles leaned against the railing next to the stairs. Four plastic chairs sat stacked next to a small plastic table in the far corner of the dingy platform. He raised the NVGs and let his eyes adjust, listening for any commotion below. His heart pounded, but not from the threat of discovery. He started to have doubts about finding Ryan and Chloe here. No effort had been made to discourage an intruder from walking onto the porch. At the very least, Ryan would have fashioned a crude early warning system by jamming the bicycles and other porch junk on the stairwell. If the kids had fled, he faced a tough decision, one with the potential to haunt him for the rest of his life.

He felt shaky approaching the door, suddenly overwhelmed by the gravity of the next few minutes. He shuffled forward and felt something rub the front of his thighs. A muted cascade of crashing aluminum cans exploded inside of the apartment, followed by footsteps. Alex reached along his leg and gripped a piece of slackened fishing wire.

They were here!

A light exploded in his face, followed by a gleeful shriek. The door swung open, and Chloe Walker rushed onto the porch, trailed by his son.

"Mr. Fletcher!"

"Dad!"

"Shhhhhh. Keep it down. Turn that light off. Let's get inside—quickly," he hissed, corralling them back inside.

"Is my dad here? Mom? Abby and Danny?" Chloe asked in a rush.

"Mom? Emmy?" added Ryan.

"Everyone is fine. Everyone. Chloe, your dad is on the other side of the Charles, sitting tight with a battalion of marines. I made him stay behind. It's so good to see the two of you," he said, tears flowing freely down his sweaty cheeks.

Alex hugged his son, squeezing him tightly. He wanted to say something profound, but settled for a comfortable, reassuring silence. No matter what happened from this point forward, it happened to both of them. The three of them. That was a promise he intended to give his life trying to keep. He reached out and pulled Chloe into the hug, and they stood there for several moments.

"I need to contact your father and let him know that you're all right," he said, breaking up the group embrace.

"Did you bring the satphone?" said Ryan, locking the door to the porch.

"No, I left it with Charlie outside of the city. It didn't work the last time we checked."

"You dragged Mr. Thornton into this mess?" asked Ryan.

"He volunteered. We wouldn't have made it without him. He's guarding Chloe's dad's Jeep about nine miles from here in the Middlesex Fells Reservation. We hid everything up there and walked in. Everyone else is in Limerick—at the pond."

"Let me grab some candles. You should sit down, Mr. Fletcher. Ryan, grab some water for your dad, or make a Gatorade," said Chloe.

"No candles, Chloe. We shouldn't draw any attention to the apartment. I ran into some trouble on the way over here."

"Street gangs or militia?" asked Ryan.

"I'd say militia, but I'm not sure. How did you guess?"

"We went out onto Beacon Street a few times during the first day, trying to get some information, but we stayed inside when the shooting started," said Ryan.

"Who was shooting who?"

"We didn't stick around long enough to find out, but people said the police were being targeted. That's all we needed to hear."

"The shooting intensified by nightfall and lasted all night," Chloe chimed in. "At about seven the next morning, we heard someone yelling through a bullhorn outside of the bedroom window. A pickup truck was cruising down Orkney Road announcing that the streets were safe," said Chloe.

"They called themselves the Liberty Boys. Camouflage uniforms, but not really matched. A hodgepodge of tactical gear, plenty of ARs. They were also looking for volunteers," added Ryan.

"Jesus," muttered Alex.

"What's wrong?" Chloe asked.

"The Liberty Boys. Holy shit," he said, dropping his rucksack to the carpeted floor. "It's linked to one of the oldest militia groups in American history. The Liberty Boys, aka 'Mechanics,' were an offshoot of the original Sons of Liberty run by Sam Adams. Paul Revere was one of the founding members. They gathered intelligence on British military activity in the Boston area and conducted limited sabotage missions during the lead-up to the Revolutionary War. The famous midnight ride by Revere on the eve of Lexington and Concord was one of their operations. I ran into one of them at your dorm. He said something about us 'never taking the country away from them.' It sounded like typical paranoid militia talk, but now I wonder. This group responded quickly, right? Within twelve hours?"

"I think, yes. They definitely took control of the streets within twenty-four hours," said Ryan.

"With rifles like mine?"

"That's what we saw."

"Only a well-established underground militia group could have pulled that off. The Liberty Boys never went away. They just went deeper underground and waited."

"What happened to the guy you saw?" asked Ryan.

Alex unclipped his rifle and walked toward the couch near the front of the apartment. He desperately needed to sit down.

"I killed him," said Alex, setting his rifle against the back of the couch.

He dropped his aching, deliriously tired body onto the soft couch and sighed. Ryan followed with a bottle of water, pushing it against Alex's hand. He sat in one of the chairs across from his father, his dark form barely outlined against the front window of the apartment. Chloe sat in the chair next to Ryan and posed the question that his son hesitated to ask.

"Why did you kill him?"

"Because he was trying to kill me. They all were."

"They all were?"

"Four of them followed me to the sixth floor of your dorm," said Alex.

"Four? What happened to the rest?"

"Same thing."

"Holy crap," muttered Ryan, "we're screwed."

"Why did they follow you?" said Chloe.

Alex lifted his legs onto the couch and leaned backward, wanting desperately to close his eyes.

"They were waiting for me when I got out of the river. I managed to shoot my way through their welcoming committee with the help of a talented marine sniper. They probably assumed I'm some kind of marine saboteur."

"That doesn't make...none of this makes sense. Right? What happened to the bridges?" asked Ryan, the shadow of his hand reaching over to Chloe. "Why do the Liberty Boys care if you're a marine?"

"Because they think this is all some kind of false flag conspiracy set in motion by the government to declare martial law. They see the marines, or any military unit on the streets, as the enemy. The bridges are still there. It's just that nobody's allowed across, in either direction."

"That's insane," said Chloe.

"I agree, but I don't see either side budging. Your dad radioed me about an hour and half ago with news that the marine headquarters had been attacked. The marines put an end to all northbound bridge traffic after they discovered a large weapons cache hidden among a group of refugees. They see the Liberty Boys as some kind of criminal insurgency. I need to call your dad," said Alex, opening one of the pouches on his vest. "He can't respond, but he'll be listening."

Alex detached the earpiece from the radio and increased the volume, filling the room with static.

41

"Durham Three-Two, this is Durham Three-Zero. Press the transmit button the preset number of times when you are ready to receive the broadcast."

The static clicked three times, and Alex nodded.

"Durham Three-Zero has arrived at the second rendezvous location. Both VIPs located. Stand by for separate transmission," he said, handing the radio to Chloe.

"Do I have to talk like that?"

"No. Just keep it short, and don't give away any information. Someone might be listening," said Alex.

"Daddy, it's me. We're both fine. I love you. We'll be together soon," she said and handed the radio back.

"VIPs are in good condition and capable of travel. Will advise when ready to move. Durham Three-Zero, out," he said and sat the radio on the coffee table.

"Thank you, Mr. Fletcher," Chloe said, breaking into a muted, controlled sob. "Thank you for coming to get us."

Ryan got up to comfort her.

"I'm just one part of the dream team. If you saw all of us at one time, you might consider taking your chances alone with the young master Fletcher," he said, feigning a British accent.

"Good lord," said Ryan, shaking his head. "When do you think we'll leave?"

"I don't know. I figure the Liberty Boys will make their big move on Cambridge tonight. We need to be across the river and out of Boston before the festivities begin. If we leave an hour before dusk, we should be able to reach either the Arsenal Street Bridge or North Beacon Street Bridge by nightfall. I have signal flares that will keep the marines from shooting us when we cross. We can swim if the militia has the entrances to the bridges locked down. I'm tempted to make a run for it right now, but..." said Alex, shaking his head.

"It'll be light soon," said Chloe.

"Too soon. And they're actively looking for me. We could consider leaving earlier, but it'll mean leaving most of my gear behind. We'd have to look and play the role of beleaguered travelers heading north. Make up some story about getting stranded during a camping trip somewhere in

Rhode Island. I don't know. I'm too tired to think about it," Alex said, barely aware that he had mumbled his last sentence with his eyes closed.

His last conscious thought of the morning revolved around Ed Walker. Chloe's dad was probably handcuffed to a dormitory bed somewhere in Harvard Yard. The pre-established code had been six clicks, not three.

PART II

"Homefront"

Chapter 7

Limerick, Maine

Kate refilled her coffee mug from the stainless-steel percolator on the stove and joined the adults at a rough-hewn farmer's table on the screened porch. The moist, early morning breeze felt chilly compared to the house, which had managed to retain much of the previous day's late afternoon heat long into the night. It still felt swampy, which wasn't a good sign for the rest of the day. Temperatures inland tended to run ten degrees hotter than the coastline, creating saunalike conditions remedied by a swim in the lake or air-conditioning—neither of which was an option today. They had too much work ahead of them.

She'd woken two hours earlier and strolled the perimeter of the 2.5-acre clearing with a thermos of coffee and her rifle. Stopping every fifty feet to listen for anything out of place, she walked the inner grounds until she spotted a light on the second floor of the main house an hour into her patrol. Returning to refresh her coffee supply, she found Linda Thornton filling a second thermos, rifle slung over her back. Having Linda at the compound made a big difference. They spent the next hour forming a basic strategy to protect the compound from the inevitable shit storm headed their way.

If the kid hadn't been lying about his association with local militia, they faced a serious threat. Alex's research into militia groups had been frightening, and she didn't share some of his more optimistic conclusions about their overall intentions. Heavily armed and highly organized, they were everywhere. If anyone in Limerick recognized her face or Emily's when they drove through town, the militia would find them. Being "from away" drew attention in rural Maine, and their land purchase from the Gelders hadn't exactly endeared them with the locals.

She placed her hands around the steaming cup and started the meeting.

"Linda and I came up with a rough plan to get the most important work done by the end of the day. We'll divide into three groups— security, IT and general prep. Samantha and Tim will head up the IT group, with Abby, Emily and Ethan to help. Your first task will be to figure out how to hook up the outer perimeter surveillance gear. Motion detectors, remote cameras, thermal detection stuff. Alex has a bunch of diagrams in a logbook down there. Once you figure out how to hook it up, the security group will install it, along with the trip flares. It's a massive perimeter, but Alex put a lot of thought into this."

"You think?" Linda laughed, eliciting a chuckle from Samantha.

"I know, but here we are. Once the IT group finishes making sense of the surveillance gear, the next task will be to restore power to the gate," said Kate.

"That's just a flip of a switch. Puts the camera, intercom, gate motor and the keypad back into business—on battery power," said Tim, raising an eyebrow.

"No worries," Kate said. "Getting the backup solar array up and running will be your third job. If we run minimal equipment, the backup array should replenish the batteries at a fast enough rate to keep us in business."

"I'll need some young athletes to climb into the barn loft to connect the solar panel coupling. There's a junction controller that looks like an electrical box and a plastic conduit tube running through the loft floor and down into the ground. I think you're supposed to run wire down the tube and attach it to the house. Nothing is connected. That's about the extent of my knowledge. Alex has a diagram."

"We'll put the kids to work figuring out the setup," said Samantha Walker. "You said he had spare inverters and stuff like that? It sounds like we have to recreate the control element. Shouldn't be too difficult if the system is like the one we have at home."

"The basic concept is the same," Kate said. "I hope."

"Alex stored everything in giant plastic bins and labeled them," said Tim.

"And everyone thinks Charlie is nuts?" Linda winked.

"Where the hell are they?" Samantha sighed.

"They're fine," said Amy Fletcher. "I can feel it."

"They should have been back by now."

"It's still early," Kate said confidently. "They didn't plan to enter the city until dark. If Chloe and Ryan are holed up near Boston College, they're looking at a fifteen-mile round trip on foot. That could take all night, especially if the city is hostile."

Samantha shook her head and exhaled. Kate looked around the table. Despite a full night of sleep, they looked even more exhausted today.

"Waterboro was hostile," muttered Samantha.

"Then it's going to take a while. Alex is cautious," Kate said. "Right now we need to get this place up and running. Once we get the solar panels feeding the batteries, we'll activate the perimeter security system."

"What about the other group?" asked Tim. "I suppose I'm in charge of that crew?"

"In title only," said his wife.

"Funny how we all have that same arrangement with our husbands," said Linda. "As long as they feel like they're in charge, they stay out of trouble."

Everyone but Tim laughed. The joke even managed to drag Kate momentarily out of her funk.

"Amy's group," said Kate, twisting her head toward Tim, "will do two things. First priority is camouflage. We have to make this place look like it's only housing Mom and Pops Fletcher, plus their grandchildren. The downstairs needs to be cleared of any evidence suggesting otherwise. The garage windows need to be covered from the inside. Nailed shut with ply board. The door to the backyard from the garage should be locked and somehow reinforced so it can't be kicked in. We can't have anyone snooping around and making a casual discovery. Can the big doors be jimmied open?"

"I tried last night," said Tim. "They feel solid, but I have no idea what might happen if someone really put some effort into lifting one of them."

"It should hold. Charlie was worried about the same thing at home," Linda said. "He nearly broke the damn door, but it held."

"Okay. This is going to sound weird, but are your daughters familiar enough with firearms to load magazines and match them up with Alex's weapons?"

"Alyssa and Sydney have been shooting and cleaning all of Charlie's firearms for longer than I care to admit. They can figure it out."

"Perfect. I know he has two more ARs in the basement. One is a .223, the other is a .308. There are a few pistols and shotguns. I think everyone should be armed. Alex has a Ruger 22, which might suit you or your son," said Kate, nodding at Samantha.

"Danny can handle the .22. I'll take one of the shotguns," said Samantha.

"Linda, can you tell your daughters to load the shotguns with—"

"Number one buck?" said Linda. "Way ahead of you."

Samantha shrugged.

"Number one is easier on your shoulders and still has the penetrating power that makes Alex happy. That's all I know," said Kate. "Once the firearm situation is sorted and the house is secure, the kids on the general prep team will join us on the perimeter, installing the surveillance gear. I'd like to have everything up and running by sunset."

"Sandbags?" suggested Linda.

"I think it's worth looking into, but only if we have spare bodies."

"Sandbags?" said Samantha doubtfully.

"Is that really necessary?" asked Amy Fletcher, looking to her husband for support.

"I thought Alex was kidding," admitted Tim.

Kate nodded. "I did too, but it doesn't sound so crazy now. Not if we have a price on our heads."

"How many sandbags are we talking?" asked Samantha.

"I'd have to look at the logbook tossed in with the empty bags, but I remember him saying something about a thousand, maybe more," said Kate.

Samantha frowned. "What is he planning to do, line the outside of the house with sandbags?"

"No. Unfortunately, he planned to drag all of that crap inside the house," said Amy. "I thought he was joking about the sandbags! We'll have dirt floors!"

"Inside?" asked Samantha. "This is extreme, even for me."

"Alex came up with a plan to create firing positions around the house, in front of enough windows to cover a full 360 degrees. Each 'position,'" Kate stated, using air quotes, "is three feet wide and two feet thick, with another foot coming back from the wall to give you some wraparound protection. You place a three-by-three piece of sheet metal against the wall under the window, then build the barrier."

"He has sheet metal in the basement?"

Kate nodded slowly. "He has sheet metal in the basement. Pre-cut."

"I thought those rifles could shoot through cars," said Samantha.

"According to Alex, a bullet from an AR will lose enough momentum passing through sheet metal to burrow harmlessly into the dirt. He planned to build two or three larger safe boxes within the house, with sandbag walls on four sides. If you can't get to one of the firing positions or hostiles break into the house, you throw yourself over the three-foot wall into the safe box and figure out your next move. With hostile militia in the picture, I don't think it's a bad idea to start filling sandbags once we finish the higher priority chores."

"I'm sold," said Samantha. "I think we should work on the safe boxes first, then key positions around the house. Once we get the surveillance system sorted out and the power running, I'll put the crew to work filling sandbags."

"What do you think about taking the screens out of the windows?" Linda asked. "For shooting and looking through binoculars."

"Maybe just the firing positions?" Samantha suggested.

"If we do one, we have to do them all," Tim countered, "otherwise they'll be able to map out our gun positions."

"We'll give that to Amy's group," stated Kate. "Prioritized ahead of the sandbags. Now the hard part…"

"The hard part?" said everyone in near unison.

"Waking seven exhausted teenagers at 6:30 in the morning and convincing them to work for the rest of the day."

"No convincing necessary. They work or they don't get fed. Right?" Linda said with a smirk.

"Sounds good to me," said Alex's mom. "I'll fix up pancakes and bacon. Fill them up with a good meal before we break the bad news. Slackers eat cold oatmeal moving forward."

"Hard core! I like it," said Samantha. "Need any help in the kitchen?"

"I'll take all the help I can get. The quicker we whip this up the better," said Amy.

"I can crisp bacon perfectly—on the grill. Meat handling is my specialty," said Linda.

Samantha spit her coffee onto the table, immediately swiping her napkin.

"That's not something you want to advertise too loudly," said Kate, stifling a laugh.

"Good heavens," mumbled Amy, blushing.

"This is why I pretend to be deaf around women," said Tim. "The bacon's in the basement freezer."

Chapter 8

Limerick, Maine

Eli Russell marched up the steps of the two-story red brick building and stopped at the entrance door held open by his deputy commander.

"The building is secure. We have one hundred and forty-three residents packed into the recreation hall. Standing room only," said Kevin McCulver.

"Secure the door and post a guard. Nobody gets in or out without my say-so. We have to be on our toes," said Eli, entering Limerick's "Brick Town Hall."

No longer housing Limerick's municipal offices, the historical Brick Town Hall building had been recently renovated to house the town's library and generate revenue by renting the large first-floor hall for private functions. The recreation hall served as the largest public meeting place within Limerick, aside from the elementary school a few miles to the east on the Newfield border. Eli had chosen the historical building for his debut public appearance because it was a familiar landmark located in the heart of town.

He strode into the room and grasped the podium, pushing aside the useless microphone.

"Citizens of Limerick. Please. I'll keep this brief," he bellowed.

The din of conversation diminished, but didn't stop.

"Please. I don't want to take up any more time than necessary! We all have enough going on at home," he said, smiling widely at the crowd, which finally fell silent. "I want to thank Selectman Keithman for arranging this meeting and getting the word out on short notice. My name is Eli Russell. Some of you know me pretty well—I'm a Waterboro native. Several years ago, I started the Maine Liberty Militia. Our ranks are filled with hardworking, patriotic folks just like yourselves from all over York County. Gary Flannery is one of our original members," he said, motioning for a thin man dressed in a MultiCam uniform to step forward from behind him.

"His family has lived in Limerick for nearly a century, and you've been eating his family's pizza for three decades, for better or worse," he said, slapping Gary playfully on the shoulder.

The tension in the room eased with the joke, setting the stage for Eli's main event.

"Obviously, I didn't come here to tell jokes. These are uncertain, frightening times for all of us, but one thing is certain: the hardest days lie ahead. Life as we've known it has come to an abrupt end and is unlikely to ever return to what most of you consider normal. This isn't an isolated incident. The entire nation has been plunged into darkness. This has been confirmed by ham radio broadcasts."

The crowd murmured in response to his statement.

"Trust me when I say that the situation out there will only get worse. The police and National Guard are overwhelmed at the border, which is leaking like a sieve right now, leaving us exposed to the same horrors that migrated into Maine during the 2013 pandemic. The sheriff's department personnel assigned to these parts are nowhere to be found and—"

"They've been murdered. Haven't you heard?" said an elderly white-haired man from the back of the room.

No kidding.

"We've been so busy helping the State Police at the borders, I haven't—this is horrible. What happened?" said Eli.

"Three of them were killed at home. Assassinated along with their families. The other is missing, along with his car. He lived in West Newfield. Residents in town heard gunshots soon after that airwave hit us."

The room launched into an uproar, which gave Eli the precious moments he needed to capitalize on the "news." He couldn't have planted a better link to what he needed to say next.

"This can't be happening," said Eli, feigning shock and indignation. "This has to be related to the massacre!"

"What massacre?" asked a woman near the front of the room.

"At the border," said Eli, counting on others to eavesdrop.

"Where?" asked a young man a little further back.

"Milton Mills. The whole border checkpoint was ambushed. All of my men were killed. Completely wiped out! We also found a possible mass grave behind the Methodist church on Foxes Ridge Road, just a few miles from the New Hampshire border. We'd brought supplies over to the church, since it was so close to the border. Figured it might be a good place to feed and shelter the folks trying to get home to points north. Mainers have been showing up on foot from all over New England. By the time they get to the border, they're spent and out of resources. We let at least fifty through in the first twenty-four hours, until I lost contact with the squad out in Milton Mills…" he said, trailing off for effect.

"What happened to them?" yelled a man from the back.

"What massacre?"

"Who was in the mass grave?"

One of the town selectman, standing along the wall near the door, shouted, "Everyone! Keep it down! This is important!"

"Once we realized that this was more than some freak power outage," Eli continued, "I drove Route 11 to the border to see if I could offer any assistance and—"

"Where did you find a car that worked?"

"We have a big organization," he lied, "and a few of our cars survived. We were lucky. Anyway, State Troopers at the border told me that they didn't have enough personnel to watch some of the smaller crossings until the National Guard fully mobilized, which may never happen, but that's a different story. They asked us to set up border checkpoints at some of the smaller crossings past Milton Pond, doing the same thing the police are doing—screening refugees for Maine residents. Nobody wants a repeat of 2013, right?"

The group nodded and muttered in agreement.

"I lost radio contact with the squad at Milton Mills the night before…" He faded off, shaking his head slowly.

The room fell silent, everyone holding their breath for Eli's next words.

"I drove out there myself yesterday afternoon and found them dead. Twelve well-trained, heavily armed militiamen killed in an ambush—by extremely accurate gunfire."

"Who killed them?" asked several citizens at once.

"The same unit that killed everyone at the Methodist church. We found fifty plus bodies in the forest. All shot in the head, execution style. I had a few guys helping out at the church. They put up one hell of a fight, but whoever did this…" another well-placed shake of the head, "I haven't seen anything like this since El Salvador."

At 58 years old, the closest Eli Russell had come to Central America in his lifetime was a one-time trip to an all-inclusive resort in Cancun, Mexico, with his ex-wife. He'd joined the army in 1981, completing the infantry basic training and airborne training in Fort Benning, Georgia. His airborne qualification earned him a duty assignment to the 101st Airborne at Fort Campbell, Kentucky, where he served in 1st Battalion, 327th Infantry Regiment as an M-60 machine gunner until 1986.

After an uneventful stint in the army, Sergeant Russell returned to Maine, immersing the local bars with nebulous tales of "classified" black-ops paramilitary operations in undisclosed countries. The Iran-Contra hearings in 1987 dovetailed perfectly with his newly created persona, and he quickly became an underground celebrity in York County. Sergeant Eli Russell, suspected military advisor to the Salvadoran counter-insurgency effort, was born.

"Death squads," stated Gary Flannery, intimately familiar with Russell's history as a military advisor.

"Worse. Special Forces death squads. It's the only logical explanation for how my men could have been taken out so quickly. I can't go into the details of what I saw in El Salvador. I probably shouldn't have mentioned it at all, but it fits the pattern and confirms my suspicions about this whole EMP thing. I think we're on the brink of a government takeover."

"Not this again," said a middle-aged man near the back wall.

"I'm sorry, did I say something to offend you?" Eli said. "I'm just passing along what I saw. I'm concerned for everyone's safety."

Eli knew he'd have to handle this carefully if he wanted to prevent a public relations backlash.

"Look, I'm just as displeased with Washington as anyone else, but I draw the line at this broad-reaching conspiracy nonsense," the man replied. "They blame the same bogeyman every time. That one Internet nutcase has thousands of people convinced that the 2013 pandemic was allowed to enter the U.S. by the CDC, with the help of—you guessed it—the biggest bogeyman in human history: Homeland Security. I suppose this is the latest in a long line of 'false flag' operations that never materialize in the militarization of America? Like the Jakarta Pandemic? The conspiracy lunatics were sorely disappointed when the thousands of armored cars allegedly purchased by the Department of Homeland Security didn't take to the streets with the billions of hollow-point bullets supposedly purchased right before the pandemic. This is more of the same."

"We lost a lot of good men out there! Mr. Russell's youngest brother, Jimmy, was among the dead," barked Gary Flannery, stepping toward the crowd.

Eli extended his right hand to hold Gary back. "It's all right, Gary."

"I'm sorry. I had, uh—no idea," said the man. "I didn't mean any disrespect. It just all seemed…I'm really sorry to hear about your brother."

"I didn't take it as disrespect, sir. Thank you," said Eli, pausing to let the crowd think he was struggling to get past the death of his brother. He continued when he saw a genuine look of compassion appear on the doubter's face, signifying that his last hurdle in this room had been cleared.

"I'll be the first to admit that all of this sounds outlandish, but only a Special Forces team is capable of doing that kind of damage so quickly. They even took one of my men for interrogation."

Eli let the implication of kidnapping and torture settle into the captivated gathering of sheep. He hoped the rest of the townships would be this easy. He'd triple the size of his personal army within a few days.

"These are textbook guerilla tactics for rural paramilitary operations. Trust me, folks. I've seen this before, in another life. It's a brutal, systematic process designed to strike fear into the local population and disintegrate your resolve. We can expect more of this until…"

"Until what?" said a woman clutching a young child.

"Until the new authority arrives to *save* and *protect* us from this terror. I'm telling you, this is by-the-book Spec Ops stuff. Psychological operations— PSYOPS. They want you afraid to leave your house. Afraid to close your eyes at night, lest you be snatched away," he said, snapping his fist shut and pulling it toward him. "Do you think it's a coincidence that our satellite phones don't work? I have a full signal on mine—tracking nine birds, but all I can do is receive government transmissions. They don't want us talking with anyone outside of our immediate communities. Keep us isolated until our saviors arrive."

"A false flag ploy?" asked the town selectman.

"The bigger event is the false flag. Whatever they did to turn off the lights, that created the crisis."

"The government announced that a space-borne object broke up over the U.S and hit the East Coast. It explains the shockwave," said someone deep in the crowd.

"But not the EMP. I've studied this stuff. Meteorites don't cause electromagnetic pulses. Only nukes and solar flares do that. Did you notice how they haven't given an explanation for why your cars don't work or why the lights are out? That's because it doesn't make sense. Instead, they say, 'widespread power outages have been reported.' No kidding, Sherlock. I couldn't microwave my breakfast burrito this morning. Tell me something I don't know."

The group broke into open laughter.

Man, I love this, Eli thought.

"I'm not buying the asteroid story, and neither should you. They're watching the skies 24/7, detecting and analyzing inbound space objects years away. Ain't no way they missed one as big as they claim. Judging by the blast wave we all experienced, I'd say they detonated a nuke over the water in the Gulf of Maine. Far enough away to minimize civilian casualties, but close enough to let us know that something big happened. I bet they did this up and down the East Coast where most of the people live.

"I know this sounds extreme. I've gone over it in my head time and time again, trying to come up with a different scenario. Until the Milton Mills massacre, that is. I recognized the military's handiwork immediately, I'm ashamed to say," he said, letting those words sink in.

"I've held you up long enough. If anyone is interested in learning more about the Maine Liberty Militia, we've set up a table in one of the smaller rooms down the hall. We're looking for volunteers. Prior military experience is preferred, but anyone with basic firearms experience or a willingness to learn is welcome. We'll provide the training and the firearms to keep the people of this town safe.

"I know what you're thinking; if the government hit team can take out fifteen of Eli's best-trained men, what chance do you stand? I'm not going to BS any of you; we're not training anyone to be a Navy SEAL. Militarily, we'll never be a match for the teams roaming these parts, but if we organize quickly, they'll back off. They're in this for the long game. If they can't keep us isolated and scared, they'll switch to less drastic tactics or disappear completely."

"Does that mean the government won't bother with us?" asked the selectman.

Eli shook his head and grimaced. "The government's still coming. They're too vested at this point. The only thing we can do is change their early tactics. Save some lives. Keep your eyes open for strangers and any suspicious activity. Once word gets out that we're not afraid, they'll start employing some hearts and mind shi…stuff. Pardon my language, ma'am," he said, directing his apology at the woman holding a toddler.

"He's heard worse, I'm afraid," she said, smiling nervously.

"One last thing everybody, before we all melt from the heat," he said, fanning himself with his hand. "Two of my men were shot dead in Waterboro yesterday afternoon. The suspects, who may be women, were last seen driving toward Limerick along Route 5. Witnesses say the suspects shot them in cold blood and took their vehicle, a Black SUV. This happened around one in the afternoon, so if they made it to Limerick, they might have cruised through town maybe fifteen or twenty minutes later. Was anyone in town yesterday afternoon?"

A few hands rose toward the ceiling.

"Do any of you remember seeing a Black SUV? I imagine a functional car would stick out, right?" said Eli.

A man with a grizzly beard and unkempt hair answered. "I remember it. We were out in front of Flannery's Variety," he said, nodding at Gary.

"I was rationing out the last of the ketchup," said Gary, stirring up a little laughter.

"The SUV went by pretty fast, so I didn't really see much. I don't think it's the one you're looking for. This one had out-of-state plates. The back passenger window was rolled down, and Ken got a good look. Said there was like six people shoved back there. Ken Haskell thought he recognized one of the kids in the back seat, but he wasn't sure. I just figured they were some lucky out of towners. Be a weird coincidence."

Eli had to proceed cautiously. Like his fictitious Special Forces hit-team, he was playing the long game. Nearly all of the vehicles acquired at the Milton Mills border crossing had out-of-state license plates, which would inevitably raise dubious questions about his fleet of functioning automobiles. He'd instructed his brother Jimmy to swap out the license plates at the church. Every vehicle they drove out of Milton Mills was supposed to have a Maine plate. Non-negotiable. Instead, Jimmy gave his son, Eli's nephew, the shiniest late-model luxury SUV on the lot, and trusted his shit-for-brains son to change the plates himself.

He wondered how many bong hits it took for his nephew to erase that data, knowing it was likely gone by the time the kid turned the key in the ignition. He was truly sorry to lose Jimmy, but in this newly arrived "dog eat dog" world, they were all better off without Nathan. Of course, that didn't mean he was going to shake hands and thank his nephew's killers. He still planned to personally skull fuck each and every person who left a mountain bike on the side of the road in Waterboro, before cutting their heads off and jamming them on a tall stake.

I'll blame it on the government, too!

"I'm not a big believer in coincidences," said Eli. "I assume Ken isn't here?"

"Out hunting. He's got a few hundred acres up Sawyer Mountain Road," said Grizzly.

"Mind pointing out his place for me? I should probably talk to him. It will save the sheriffs a trip, not that we're likely to see the cops again. Still, better safe than sorry. Right?"

"I'll show you the way, right after I sign your list. I've taken a few tactical carbine courses," said Grizzly.

"I'll take you up on both offers. How about we take a drive up together once this settles down?" Eli suggested, wondering where Grizzly might land in his organization.

Chapter 9

Sanford, Maine

Harrison Campbell heard the increasingly uncommon sound of a car engine echo through the barn. Car tires crackled along the dirt driveway a few seconds later, drawing his attention to the open door. One of his armed sentries stepped into the brightly contrasted opening.

"It's Glen. He's got a woman in the car. I don't recognize her."

Campbell placed the ham radio headphones on the communications desk and stood up, his back crackling as he extended fully upright. The past two days hadn't been kind to his aging frame. There was no doubt about that. He'd slept on a cot next to the radios, his Kenwood transceiver scanning preset AM frequencies used by militia groups regionally and nationwide.

Sleep didn't come easy, as reports of civil disorder, fires, and a near complete breakdown of the nation's essential services infrastructure travelled in high frequency radio waves to anyone who cared to listen. Information was spotty at best, but he'd gleaned invaluable information about the event from the airwaves. Cities beyond the Sierra Nevada Mountains in California and the Cascades in the Pacific Northwest seemed to have suffered less of an EMP disruption than the rest of the nation. None of the cities on the West Coast had power, which made sense given the interconnectivity of the nation's electrical grid, but vehicle and home electronics remained mostly unaffected. California was a long way from New England, but it gave Campbell a glimmer of hope. Not all of the country was down for the count.

News from the international community gave him mixed feelings. Amateur radio stations in Europe and other parts of the world confirmed that the event appeared to be confined to the United States. This was bad news, since it validated the growing theory that the United States had been targeted. It was also good news, however, since it left the international community intact to render aid.

The Council of the European Union had held an emergency session yesterday, to be followed later today by a full meeting of the European Parliament. The general consensus among radio reports seemed to indicate that the European Union would authorize a comprehensive recovery package, to be implemented immediately. Transmissions from U.S.-based radio stations questioned the intentions of these efforts, spurred by reports that the United Nations had reassembled in Geneva to discuss "options." To some, this was bad news. It didn't matter at this point. The United States was falling apart fast, and Campbell seriously doubted they could pull out of the deep dive without foreign intervention.

He rubbed his eyes and walked between the timber benches to the door, catching sight of Glen Cuskelly and his supposed mystery guest as they approached. He recognized her immediately.

"Carol, is everything all right? Is Brian okay?"

The grave look on Glen's face told him nothing was all right.

"Brian's fine, Harry. He's home watching the kids, but we have a big problem."

"Come on in," he said, gesturing for her to enter the barn, "unless you'd prefer to talk inside the house. Mary would be glad to fix you up a cup of tea. All I have here is some dreadful coffee."

"No, I think we better talk in here. Probably make sense to look at some maps while I'm talking."

"All righty then. Make yourself at home. Good to see you, Carol. Especially in light of what happened to Randy. You're all still more than welcome to stay on the farm here if you don't feel safe at your house."

"Feeling safe is a relative term nowadays," she said, "but we may take you up on your offer. They killed Randy's entire family."

"I'm really sorry. I know your families were close," said Campbell.

Carol's eyes watered, and he left the topic alone as they made their way to the "situation room" in the back right corner of the barn. He lit the two-burner propane camping stove under the tin pot.

"Hope you don't mind reheated coffee," he said, taking a seat across from her at the table, next to Glen.

"That's fine."

"So, what brings you to Sanford, Carol? It can't be the coffee," he said, eliciting a muffled laugh.

"My husband didn't feel comfortable leaving the property, given what happened to Randy's family, or he'd bring the report himself," she said.

"Perfectly understandable."

"We shut ourselves in after finding the Cushmans slaughtered—and they were truly slaughtered," she said, glancing at Glen.

"Never seen anything like it. Whoever did that is an animal," said Glen.

"His radio was stolen, along with the chapter's supplies. Paperwork too, as far as we could tell. We figured we were next, since Brian was his deputy commander. Maybe whoever did this just wanted the chapter's stockpile."

"Seemed a bit more personal than that," said Campbell's deputy.

Carol nodded and fought back tears.

"If Glen knows the rest, you don't have to tell it, Carol. I understand."

"No. It's our new reality. We have to get used to things like this, I guess," she muttered.

"Not if we can get to the bottom of it quickly enough," said Campbell.

"So, Bill Fournier stopped by on the way back from town. He had some interesting news. Eli Russell was at the Old Town Hall riling up the people about military assassination teams and an upcoming government invasion."

"That's Eli for you," said Campbell.

"Bill said he's recruiting. From what he could tell, Eli added about ten names to his roster after the meeting. I guess he really pitched his militia hard, saying it's the only thing that will stand between freedom and martial law. I guess there was some kind of Special Operations massacre at the border, or so he claims. Jimmy, his brother, was killed. Brian says good riddance. I didn't know the man, so I couldn't say."

"You're better off never having known him. Trust me on that. I figured it was Jimmy that killed the Cushmans. He's a hard-core ex-con. Spent most of his adult life in prison. I'd heard some rumors that he was putting together his own little spin-off crew. Sounds like they met with disaster out in Milton Mills. Good riddance indeed. With Jimmy gone, you guys shouldn't have anything to worry about, but the offer still stands. We have plenty of room out here, and Mary would love to have the company. Glen and the gang ain't cutting it for her," he said, patting his deputy on the shoulder.

"Here's the thing. Randy's truck was missing, right? Gray Chevy Avalanche?"

"Yeah," muttered Campbell.

"Bill remembers seeing a big gray four-door pickup truck behind the town hall. It grabbed his attention, because he thought Eli's meeting would be the last place on earth he'd find Randy. He couldn't get a close enough look to confirm it, thanks to the heavily armed goons keeping people's noses out of the parking lot."

"Carol, let's bring your family over to Sanford. Actually, we should bring everyone in the Limerick chapter here until we sort this out. If Eli is behind all of this, it's just a matter of time before he makes the rounds."

"How big of a group does he have?" asked Carol.

"He has pretty much everyone we kicked out over the past five years, plus anyone we won't take," said Campbell. "Best guess, Glen?'

"Sixty or seventy, depending on how many he can gather. Judging by the number of vehicles he has running, I'd say he gathered most of them."

"If he grabs ten volunteers every time he opens his mouth, York County is going to empty into his camp pretty quick. At that point, we'll welcome the government with open arms," stated Campbell.

Chapter 10

Limerick, Maine

Kate stood in the basement next to her father-in-law, listening to Abby Walker explain Alex's solar power diagram and the steps they took to hook up the bank of panels on the barn to the house's battery system. Tim had called Kate off the perimeter to verify their work before they flipped the transfer switch.

"Sounds like you followed his directions step by step, Abby. Not sure why Grandpa Fletcher and your mom called me in to check on your work, but I assume it has something to do with sharing the blame if the system self-destructs?" she said, raising an eyebrow at the adults.

"This is going to be a long apocalypse," grunted Tim.

"Wait until Alex gets back," said Kate, winking at Tim.

"It's working fine, Mrs. Fletcher," said Abby, waving a yellow handheld instrument. "The new controller is blocking the flow of electricity because it can't detect the battery bank charge. I tested the input beyond the controller with a voltmeter."

"Looks like you're having fun, Ms. Tesla. If everyone concurs this is set up right, throw the switch."

"We have Emily and Ethan watching the connection in the barn. You never know…Alex's log indicates that the bank of panels on the barn have never been tested with this gear. They have a fire extinguisher," said Samantha.

"Mom, it's fine. The electricity is already flowing from the panels through the barn. This won't change anything," said Abby, shaking her head. "Ready?"

"Go for it," said Kate.

Abby flipped the transfer switch, and nothing happened at the circuit breaker box. She pointed behind them at two side-by-side LED monitors wired to the battery bank, which consisted of 16 deep-cell, 12-Volt AGM batteries mounted on a thick wooden table in the center of the room. Red and black wires ran back and forth across the batteries, in a pattern that made little sense to Kate. She believed they were connected in parallel, whatever that meant. The monitors showed green numbers, which she assumed was a good sign.

"It's charging. The one on the left is set to measure the charging current and the one on the right is a multifunction monitor. It's showing 12.6 volts, which means the battery bank is about ninety percent charged. Based on the calculations in Mr. Fletcher's book, the system is rated to provide 2880 amp hours, which should be enough to run lights at night, the security equipment, the pump for the well, and other appliances if absolutely necessary. Long term, we'll have to closely monitor the charge and discharge rates. It's all in the book. We should probably take a close look," said Abby.

Everyone clapped and congratulated Abby, who looked slightly embarrassed, but continued.

"We replaced the controller, inverter and both monitors, but we don't have any more backups."

"Is the system still vulnerable to an EMP?" said Kate.

"We disconnected the grid-tie inverter, but according to Mr. Fletcher's book, the wires connecting the panels to the house will probably conduct enough of the EMP to fry everything. If we get hit again, we're out of luck."

"Well, I doubt that'll happen. How many times in one lifetime do you get EMP'd?" said Tim.

"Once is more than enough," Samantha remarked. "Great job, sweetie. Your dad would be really proud!"

"Thanks, Mom."

"I didn't understand half of what you said, but it sounds like we have a new power Czar at the compound. Congratulations on your promotion, Abby," said Kate.

"Sure, Mrs. Fletcher. Thank you. So, where are we going to set up the surveillance monitors?"

"We wanted to ask you about that, Kate," said Samantha. "Alex didn't leave any instructions about where to set up the station. Everything is wireless, so it can pretty much go anywhere. We just need to plug in the monitors and the receivers for the cameras and sensors. Abby said she'll have the wireless router set up in less than thirty minutes."

"Perfect. Bummer about the cameras. I was expecting more than eight," said Kate.

"The diagram shows eight mounting points, so I don't think we missed anything in the boxes. Three on the barn and five on the house. I took a look outside, and each point has a weatherproofed outlet under the mount. Camera specs say you can see in total darkness for sixty feet."

"That's fine. We can't be expected to watch fifty screens for activity. We'll have our hands full with the motion sensors. We have deer all over the place, along with the occasional moose," said Tim.

"I know. Linda and I have concentrated on the most likely avenues of approach through the property. Alex spent a ton of time walking the grounds and mapping that out."

"You know, there was a time when I thought Alex was a little touched in the head." Samantha chuckled. "But now? I'm pissed that he doesn't have more cameras!"

"Oh, he's still a little touched. Remember, this is all once in a lifetime odds stuff," said Kate, motioning to the storage shelves behind them.

"Twice in a lifetime," Tim corrected. "We should probably run an inventory or something later; see where we stand."

"It looks like we might get some substantial rain. We can sit down and hash it all out in the afternoon," Kate said. "I'm going to grab Ethan and Emily from the barn and drag them out to help. We might be able to get the sensors done by the time the rain hits. I should probably grab one of the cameras to put up at the gate, in case we have visitors. Linda said she could hardwire it to the gate's power source somehow."

"Sounds good," said Tim. "Let me know when she's going to do that, so I can shut the power off. I'm pretty good with wiring if she needs any help."

"I'll pass that along," said Kate.

"That's it, then," Tim said, ruffling Abby's hair. "Sam and I will install the house cameras and replace the motion-activated lights while the IT genius here sets up the surveillance headquarters in the dining room. We'll need the table for the monitors and the receivers. It's a good, central location. We can set up an air mattress or one of those cots for whoever pulls the midnight shift."

"Perfect. Amy's crew has secured the garage, and they're starting on the sandbags," Kate informed him. "They're going to fill as many as possible before the rain. I told them to dig east of the garage. They can walk the bags through the bulkhead door on the other side of the basement and stack them in the root cellar. We'll figure out how to build the safe boxes later. Hey, awesome job on this. Everything is coming together nicely."

Samantha nodded. "And we're ahead of schedule."

"Even better. Give us a holler on the radio when lunch is ready. Amy thought we'd eat around one," said Kate.

"Will do," replied Tim.

Kate smiled at Abby and walked across the basement, headed out of the "bunker." The basement was divided into two sides, like the basement in their home on Durham Road. The half beyond the reinforced door contained Tim and Amy Fletcher's basement storage, with room for seasonal yard furniture, bicycles and whatever else they decided to migrate out of the cold weather. Like Alex, they were particular about organization, which was Kate's way of politely rephrasing "anal retentive." The Fletchers' trademark 50-gallon plastic bins lined the walls, four high, apparently filled with everything that they had ever owned. She couldn't complain. Much of what they had brought with them when they moved with Ethan and Kevin from Colorado after the 2013 pandemic was too painful to display and sat untouched in the bins.

The bunker resembled an expanded version of Kate and Alex's Scarborough home. The far western wall, underneath the expanded great room, housed the furnace, hot water tank, oil tanks and electrical system. Sturdy metal shelves lined the rest of the cement foundation, containing enough food and essential supplies to support the Fletchers' core family for at least five years—well beyond the expiration dates on some of the canned goods rotated through the stockpile.

Supplementing the vast selection of canned, pickled and dry goods, a deep tower of pre-packed plastic buckets, each containing one hundred twenty individually sealed freeze-dried meals, occupied the entire wall next to the door. She knew that the buckets alone contained enough meals to sustain eight adults for an entire year, only requiring water to reconstitute.

With a shelf life of twenty-five years, the buckets represented their last option. She shuddered to think how they might feel after eating nothing but freeze-dried food for a year, but it easily beat the alternative.

Beyond food, the shelves housed routine and emergency supplies; extra prescription medications needed by Alex's parents, along with antibiotics and antivirals purchased online through Canadian pharmacies; vitamins, supplements and protein powders; paper products and toilet paper; hundreds of candles and a wide array of portable lights; rechargeable battery stations and thousands of dollars' worth of batteries, both rechargeable and disposable; communications equipment, including handheld scanners, walkie-talkies, headsets—much of this gear had already been moved upstairs by Tim.

The shelves' contents represented anything and everything Alex had discovered on the hundreds of prepper forums and blogs that he frequented and wrote about for a living since the 2013 pandemic. Kate never said a word about the pile-up of gear or the near daily UPS and FEDEX deliveries. As their accountant, she knew exactly how much money he spent annually on prepping, and his website consulting business income far exceeded the expenditures.

Over the past three years, they had turned a substantial profit, in addition to receiving the equivalent of her senior accountant salary in "test" items to review on Alex's site. Even without the additional income to cover the expenses, they had enough money invested to spend like drunken sailors for the rest of their lives and barely touch the capital.

Of course, the traditional concept of financial security in America and the rest of the world may have taken a long hiatus, unlikely to return in any recognizable form. Despite Washington's rhetoric, the nation's economy had barely reached the point of stumbling six years after the Jakarta Pandemic. Stocked shelves, off-the-grid house, vegetable garden and grain field, year-round water access—this was the new face of prosperity.

Chapter 11

Limerick, Maine

Eli Russell sat in the front seat of the York County Sherriff's Department cruiser with "Deputy Brown," looking for the entrance described by good folks on the other side of Gelder Pond. Standing in one of their backyards and surveying the eastern shoreline, he'd spotted a lone dock nearly halfway across. Three-quarters of the way down Gelder Pond Lane, he pounded the dashboard.

"Turn the car around, Jeff. We must have missed it. No mailbox. No nothing."

Jeffrey Brown, recently promoted to squad leader after the public execution of the previous one, had proven to be more than amenable to Eli's plan for him to impersonate a sheriff's deputy, never asking a single question about the three bullet holes in the left side of the cruiser or the missing rear driver's side window. He didn't even have a problem wearing the officer's blood-speckled duty belt over jeans and a tan short-sleeve, button-down shirt. In fact, he looked enthused and oddly proud when Eli wiped the blood off the slain deputy's badge and pinned it to his left pocket.

"There it is," said Brown, stopping the car.

Eli peered through Brown's window at the unbroken foliage, finally noticing the faint gravel path beyond a young spruce. He stepped out of the cruiser into the downpour and approached the tree. A four-foot-wide, one-foot-deep band of dirt and forest floor debris had been strewn across the gravel road leaving Gelder Pond Lane, blending one side of the driveway with the other. A common spruce tree, roughly eight feet tall, stood in the middle of the dirt, secured upright by green paracord, extending to stronger trees on each side of the entrance. He kicked at the base, expecting it to give way, but it remained firmly in place. A quick inspection showed that a two by four had been driven at least a foot into the driveway and screwed to the back of the tree base.

Clever. Clever.

He cut the paracord with his knife and pushed the tree toward the side of the driveway, letting the weight and leverage of the spruce snap the two by four. Soaked and fuming with anger, he kicked at the shard of wood sticking up from the faux forest floor until he was satisfied that the splinters couldn't possibly penetrate the cruiser's tire.

"Up to the house," he said, slamming the door shut and wiping his face.

Brown didn't say a word, which was one of several reasons Eli felt the young man had a promising future in the Maine Liberty Militia. His usual driver would have made some inane comment about the rain or whatever trivial detail suited his need to run his piehole in overdrive. Eli had extended that hole all the way through the back of his head when he kept bringing up the "coincidence" of two of Eli's men being killed in the same day. *"Ain't that an unbelievable coincidence?" "You'd swear this was Friday the 13th, if you didn't know it was Tuesday,"* and on and on, until he'd told the idiot to pull over so he could take a piss. One bullet later, he had his peace and quiet back. The car halted, shoving Eli forward in his seat.

"What is this place, Fort fucking Knox?" he said, staring at a sturdy metal gate. "Any way around that?"

"Doesn't look like it, sir. Are we sure this is the right place? This seems more like one of those setups on that *Armageddon Preppers* show," said Brown.

Even Brown's choice of words didn't piss him off. He used 'we,' instead of 'you' to avoid sounding like he was raining an accusation of incompetence down on Eli. He'd caught the innuendo, but it didn't bother him. And he had to admit, this didn't seem to fit the mold. Whoever lived here had a nice setup for waiting out "the big one."

"I agree, but our only witness swears that he recognized one of the kids in my nephew's silver BMW SUV. Seen them in town at the diner and pizza joint over the past couple summers. Every other house on the pond is a long-standing resident of Limerick. This has to be it. Son of a bitch, I don't want to walk it in. I can't even see the damn place."

Brown lowered his window and pressed a button on the keypad, illuminating the numbers.

"They even have power. Press the intercom button and smile. I'm willing to bet we're on camera," said Eli.

৶ৎ

An electronic chime echoed from the house. Kate dropped the grilled cheese sandwich on her plate and stood up. She pushed her chair back and rushed through the sliding glass door connecting the house to the covered porch, beating Samantha, who sat on the other side of the table.

They made it!

"Is that Dad?" said Emily, as Kate flashed by the teenagers huddled around the kitchen table.

"I think so," she whispered, creating a discordance of squealing chairs.

Everyone followed her to the digital intercom panel built into the kitchen wall, just outside of the hallway leading to the foyer and stairs. She reached her hand forward to press the green, blinking "Intercom" button. A surprisingly strong hand seized her wrist and yanked it back.

"What the f—"

"Alex knows the code," hissed her father-in-law, releasing her hand.

She seethed with anger for a moment before the full ramifications of answering the intercom without checking the camera sank in.

"Let's check the camera feed. Sorry to grab you," said Tim.

"No. That was my fault," Kate said, following him to the dining room.

Tim swiped his finger over the track pad on the laptop, conjuring a quad-screen digital feed. The top left image displayed the gate. The EMP had damaged the front gate security system, leaving them without a built-in camera feed or the ability to open the gate remotely. With the voice intercom still functional, they rigged one of the wireless cameras to the gate's power source and hid it in one of the trees beyond the keypad.

"It's the cops," announced one of Linda's daughters.

"Everyone upstairs. Right now!" said Linda. "Let's go!"

"Why do you always have to yell, Mom? Jesus," said Alyssa, her brown-haired, hazel-eyed daughter.

"Watch it, missy! Get moving."

"We could ignore it and see what they do. If they walk in, we can always say that the system got fried in the house," said Kate.

"I don't think that's a great idea," said Samantha. "We need to answer and see what's up. They might have news about our husbands."

"I hope not," said Amy Fletcher.

"Something's off with these guys. No uniforms and—"

"They have badges," Samantha cut in.

"Those could be from a gumball machine, for all I can tell," said Tim.

"A gumball machine? How old are you exactly?" said Kate.

"You know what I mean. I think they'd have uniforms no matter what the situation. Take a look at the passenger. That guy doesn't look like a sheriff's deputy. His hair is too long and—look right there! Guy has a tattoo on his neck. You can barely see it above the collar. No way we should buzz them through."

"It seems like we're asking for more trouble by not talking to them," said Samantha.

"Are those bullet holes?" said Kate.

Tim pointed at the image. "Looks like the back window was shot out. Why else would they have it down in the rain? The back seat is empty. I don't like what I'm seeing."

"Neither do I," Kate agreed. "The two crazies that stopped us kept saying they were the law. Who the hell knows what's going on out there? I say let them sweat it out. If they're real, and they want to talk to us badly enough, they can walk in."

"I agree," said Linda. "We should watch the eastern tree line and keep everyone upstairs for now."

Samantha nodded, but she didn't look convinced. "Will the motion sensors pick them up in the rain?"

"They should. It's a passive IR system. We created overlap zones by placing two sensors facing each other at about a hundred and twenty feet apart. Even if they pass through the middle, we should pick them up. Four of these zones cover the eastern approach from the road, placed in a line from one side of the property boundary to the other—maybe three hundred paces into the forest. That should give us enough of a buffer to react," said Linda.

"And the rest of the property?" asked Samantha.

Linda winced. "We only found thirty-two sensors. The north and south boundaries are roughly two thousand feet each according to Alex's diagram, four times the length of the eastern approach. The water frontage is..."

"Five hundred forty-two feet," said Tim.

"We installed five overlap zones on each side, about three hundred paces into the forest, focusing on the areas Alex highlighted. Mainly game trails and natural openings. It's pretty thick in there, with some ledge, so we'll get some natural channeling effect. We have two zones covering the center of the pond approach. The perimeter isn't airtight, but the odds are stacked in our favor. Anyone heading to the house should trigger one of the sensors. We didn't mess with the trip flares. They looked like World War One relics. I can't believe Alex stored those in the house."

"Neither can I," said Amy.

"I drew up a chart with all of the zones. The transceivers are labeled and arranged on the table in a rough representation of the perimeter for easy reference. Each transceiver simultaneously monitors four sensors. Two zones. You'll get a visual warning on the digital display and an audible warning, telling you which of the four sensors were triggered. It's pretty self-explanatory when you see the setup in the dining room."

"What do we do if one of the alarms goes off?" asked Samantha.

"We sit tight and stay out of sight. If they decide to pay us a visit, the only people they should see are Ma and Pa Fletcher," Linda explained. "Under no circumstances do we allow them into the house."

"What if they insist, as in open the door or we'll open it for you?" asked Tim.

"Then we'll know they didn't come here on official business and act accordingly," said Kate, patting her drop holster.

"If they produce a warrant, you better not produce a gun," said Samantha.

"If they produce a warrant, I'll serve as your personal butler for the remainder of the year," Kate quipped.

❧

"What are these people thinking? Flash the lights and hit the siren for a few seconds," said Eli.

He waited a long minute after the sound and light show.

"I guess they don't give a shit about the law. All right. Back it up and park us about fifty feet down the road. That way," he said, pointing north. "I want to take a little look before we call in the cavalry."

Brown pulled the car along the right side of Gelder Pond Lane and stopped.

"Should I bring the .308?"

"Negative. We'll map everything out and head back to base. This is strictly a reconnaissance mission."

"Roger that," said Brown, opening his car door.

"We have company!" yelled Linda. "Zone 2. Single sensor pick-up. If they head straight in, they'll appear due east of the garden."

"Shit!" Samantha yelled from the kitchen. "I told you it was the cops!"

"I don't give a shit who it is. They're trespassing," said Kate, slinging her rifle. "I'll head up to the master bedroom and keep an eye on the tree line."

"I'll join you," said Linda. "Sam, I need you to stay here and watch the sensors. Call us on the handheld if any of them are triggered."

"Got it. What are you going to do if they head toward the house?"

"That all depends on how they approach and what they're carrying," said Linda. "I'm sending the kids into the cellar with Amy until this is resolved. Tim, I want you to make sure all of the doors are locked, then keep Sam company."

"I'll check the front door on my way upstairs," said Kate, patting her father-in-law's shoulder.

He leaned his M-14 rifle against the wall and hurried after Kate, catching her before she turned down the foyer hallway.

"Don't do anything we'll all regret. If they're alone, we'll talk to them at the door. The last thing we need is the entire Sheriff's Department pitched in against us. We'll lose everything."

"What happened to the 'I smell a rat' speech?"

"Let's sniff them out a little closer. Trust me on this," said Tim.

Eli Russell crept to the edge of the tree line, pushing the underbrush out of the way, until he had reached the point where he couldn't go any further without breaking concealment. Brown eased into a position behind the thick tree to his left and nodded, staring straight ahead. Dense, unkempt bushes forced the use of a compass to stay on a due-west heading. The Fletcher compound remained obscured by heavy rain until they reached a point roughly fifty feet from the edge of the clearing, reinforcing his assessment that it would be nearly impossible for anyone in the house to detect their arrival. Unslinging a pair of powerful binoculars, he rose on both knees until he had a view of the house and the surrounding area.

Through the rain-splashed lens, he saw that they had arrived on the left side of the house, from the perspective of someone standing on the front porch and facing the front yard. They had agreed that all observations would be recorded relative to the viewpoint of this imaginary observer. Continuity of perspective was critical to recreating an accurate diagram of the compound.

Most of his view consisted of the eastern side of the house. A single window on the ground level facing them indicated that he was looking at the garage, which probably housed his deceased nephew's SUV. Further examination led him to suspect that they had boarded up the window from the inside. He could see wood through the rain-splattered window. That was all the evidence he needed to bring back a squad or two of soldiers.

"Well, looky here. A surveillance camera," said Eli.

"Got it," said Brown. "Along with that motion-activated light up on the second story. The camera looks stationary. Do you think any of that shit works, with the EMP and all?"

"Unless they replaced it all, I highly doubt it."

"Do you think they could see us if it worked?" Brown asked.

"I highly doubt it. Even if those are quality cameras, the image will be grainy. Throw in the rain, and we'll be washed out. Those windows up there are a different story. Someone with a pair of binoculars might be able to pick us out. Keep an eye on them for movement."

"Roger that, sir. Did you notice the screens have been removed from the windows?"

"Good eye, Mr. Brown. They're ready for action."

He panned right to a partial, long view of the back of the colonial-style house. A bulkhead door protruded from the foundation, next to a covered screen porch containing a table and some of that fancy outdoor furniture he saw in his ex-wife's Pottery Barn catalogue. He couldn't be certain, but the table looked like it had been abandoned in the middle of a meal—unless they were slobs. Five table settings and what looked to be like the remains of sandwiches. Definitely an open bag of chips. Five was one more than the neighbors reported to be living out here.

Set back from the house, a red, two-story barn with roof-mounted solar panels materialized between sheets of rain.

Damn. These people have it all!

"Looks like we just found our new headquarters. Did you see the solar panels?"

"Yeah. This looks like a completely self-sustaining operation. The vegetable garden behind the house nearly stretches to the trees. That's enough square footage to feed several families, and if you squint between rainsqualls, you'll see that they're growing a sizeable plot of something way in front of the house. Some kind of grain."

"Shit. I might have to keep a few of them alive to tend the crops and keep the boys happy," he said, finishing his sentence with a barely audible mutter and a grin. "Be a fitting life sentence for these bitches." He studied the layout for another minute. "What are you thinking in terms of tactics?"

"Definitely bring in the primary breaching team behind the barn," Brown said. "They'll probably have cameras back there and some motion-triggered lights, but at that point it won't matter. Once we have control of the barn, we can suppress them from the northern tree line," he said, pointing beyond the vegetable garden, "and move the team right up onto the screened porch and in. Probably keep another team right here. Be easy to suppress those two windows and move a group across once all of the shooting starts on the other side."

"Damn. You read my mind, son. Were you Delta Force or something?"

"3rd Ranger Battalion, sir."

"No shit? 101st Airborne. Screaming Eagles."

"Airborne!" they said, pumping fists in the air.

☙❧

"Are you seeing this shit?" said Kate, standing several feet away from the leftmost window, staring through binoculars.

"Cops, my ass," muttered Linda.

"I can't pick them out of the forest on either screen," said Samantha, over the handheld, "what are they doing?"

"Reconnaissance. If they were real cops, they'd ring the doorbell and state their business," responded Kate.

"Maybe they want to make sure it's safe to approach."

"They drove up to the gate and pressed the intercom button. I'm pretty sure they would have driven their cruiser right up the driveway. Not exactly the safest approach. Hold on—they're leaving," Kate announced. "No way this was legit."

"I'd probably be cautious too if no one answered," stated Samantha.

"But why leave once you checked the place out?"

"I guess it doesn't matter if they're leaving," the radio squawked.

"If they're leaving. Let's verify their departure. They should hit the sensors on the way out."

"Got it," said Samantha.

Kate let the binoculars hang and grabbed the rifle leaned up against the wall next to the windowsill. She sat on the edge of her in-laws' bed and wiped the sweat from her face. "So, what now?"

"How many sandbags did they get filled before lunch?" asked Linda.

"A little short of two hundred. Moving them into the house slowed down the process. We have enough to make five positions as described in Alex's diagram, or two of the safe boxes."

"I'd almost rather have the firing positions than the bunkers. We can give ourselves full coverage. Five positions, five adults. Keep the kids in the basement if all hell breaks loose," said Linda, still watching the tree line.

"Until the rain stops, and we can fill the bags with something other than mud, I think this is our best plan. If they're really leaving, we'll have time. Looks like we'll be working with the mosquitos tonight."

PART III

"A Bridge Too Far"

Chapter 12

42 Orkney Rd
Brookline, Massachusetts

The first sound of distant thunder drew Ryan to the open window facing the street. He leaned on the armrests and craned his head, examining the sky. The light gray cloud cover had thickened, replaced by darker clouds, but the real menace clung to the western horizon. A purple-tinged, charcoal gray band hugged the skyline, slowly creeping in their direction.

"How long is the rain supposed to last?" he asked.

Chloe stopped fanning herself long enough to answer. "Most of the afternoon, but that was the forecast Sunday night, from what I can remember."

"Take a look at this," he said, stepping back from the chair.

She didn't look thrilled to get up, and he didn't blame her. Without air-conditioning or any semblance of a breeze, the apartment sweltered from the unabated heat wave suffocating New England. Daytime temperatures had remained steady in the mid-nineties since his arrival at Boston University on Saturday. High humidity compounded the misery, especially once the power died.

The window air conditioners in Chloe's apartment had barely kept up with the demand, but it beat the hell out of his dormitory. He had somehow missed the part about no air-conditioning in Warren Towers and spent most of Saturday night awake, sweating through his mattress. He'd nearly cried walking back to the Chestnut Hill Avenue station Sunday night after respectfully declining Chloe's offer to let him sleep on the couch. At least the subway had air-conditioning. He'd contemplated taking the "B" train to Lechmere station and back.

She wiped her face with a damp towel and joined him at the window, giving the sky a quick look. "It's gonna pour. If it lasts long enough, it might drop the temperature."

"Do you think we should wake my dad?" he asked, nodding at the couch.

"Why?"

"I think we should take off during the storm," said Ryan.

Chloe wiped her face and stared down at Alex.

"Good luck waking him. I'll start filling our water bottles."

Ryan examined the filthy, disheveled man sprawled on the oversized couch and shook his head. He'd seen less realistic-looking zombies in *The Walking Dead*. Covered head to toe in a crusty, foul-smelling layer of muck, Alex Fletcher hadn't stirred since falling asleep in mid-sentence. While arranging him on the couch, they discovered numerous congealed cuts and scrapes on his face and hands. A tightly wrapped, rust-color-stained bandage peeked out of his left sleeve and completed the picture. He'd gone through hell to arrive at their doorstep. Ryan almost felt bad waking him.

"Dad. Dad!" he said, nudging his exposed shoulder.

Alex mumbled and turned away from the sound. Thunder boomed closer as Ryan tried to rouse his father from a near catatonic state.

"Try this," said Chloe, appearing behind the couch with a half glass of water.

He reluctantly took the plastic cup and held it over his dad's face. A loud clap of thunder reinforced the urgency of their situation, and he dumped the water. Alex came to life, flailing his arms and knocking Ryan to the floor. A thunderous boom shook the windows.

"What happened?" yelled Alex, sitting up and grabbing for the rifle Chloe had hung on one of the kitchen table chairs.

"Dad, everything's fine. I just dumped some water on your face. We're fine," said Ryan.

The room darkened, filled by another round of approaching thunder. His dad glanced around, still confused.

"There's a big storm coming, Dad. We could take advantage of the heavy rain to reach the bridge. At least get us into place for tonight," said Ryan.

"What time—how long was I out?"

"It's 2:15."

"You should have woken me earlier. I needed to check in with—never mind," he said, shaking his head and rubbing his eyes.

"Everything's been fine. You needed the rest."

"I know, but I can barely move right now," Alex said, straining to lift his right arm.

"What happened to your arm?" Ryan asked. "And your wrist?"

"I'm fine. Nothing a thousand milligrams of ibuprofen can't fix. Grab the medical kit out of my rucksack. It's near the top. How big is the storm?"

A powerful round of thunder answered his question before Chloe could respond.

"The news Sunday night showed a massive system moving across the Midwest, but you know how these things can go."

"Yeah. This could last fifteen minutes, leaving us high and dry—"

"Or it can last all afternoon," said Ryan. "We should be able to move faster in a heavy rain, right? Two miles? We could be there in thirty minutes if we bust our asses."

"It's tempting. Have you seen any militia activity on the street?"

"Nothing. It's been quiet."

"That's not always a good thing. How long until the two of you are ready to move?"

"We're waiting on you," said Ryan.

"Chloe, the smartass gene runs in our family, on the mother's side. Let's be ready to walk out of the front door as soon as the heavy rain hits," he said, extending a hand.

Ryan took his father's filthy hand and helped him off the couch. Alex grinned at him for a few moments.

"Look at you," said Alex.

"Dad, we've been apart for like three days…"

"Long three days."

A refreshing wind swept through the apartment, billowing the front curtains and sweeping a map off the kitchen table.

"Here comes the rain," said Alex.

Chapter 13

Harvard Yard
Cambridge, Massachusetts

Ed Walker sat on a folding chair in the battalion headquarters tent, dozing off. Heavy thunder jarred him awake, nearly toppling him from the chair. He glanced over at his unofficial "escort," a perpetually irritated marine corporal talking into a headset, before burying his head in his hands. The marine never acknowledged him. Nine hours on this chair, broken up by two escorted trips to the "head" in Hollis Hall and a single MRE—unceremoniously thrown at his feet. Every time he felt like screaming and running out of the tent, he reminded himself what Alex said: "Stay with the marines."

He'd been right. Despite the surprise attack on the headquarters and open hostility displayed by the marines, he felt safe here. Perimeter security had killed fourteen "hostiles" within the span of thirty seconds, repelling an attack that Lieutenant Colonel Grady assessed had taken "insurgents" over twenty-four hours to coordinate and launch. Grady felt confident they had sent a strong message back to insurgency leadership: Attacking marines was a bad idea.

He propped his head in his hands and stared vacantly through the mesh window at the red brick walls beyond the command tent. At least they hadn't stuffed him in a guarded dorm room. He could deal with the concept of house arrest, as long as he stayed in the command tent. A single raindrop streaked across his view, followed by another. Moments later, the pounding din of heavy rain masked the marine's chatter. Ed glanced from the mess of wires and power strips littering the sand-colored modular flooring to the battalion sergeant major sitting next to Lieutenant Colonel Grady, waiting for the command that would convert the headquarters tent into a sauna. The sergeant major stood, having no doubt made the same weather observation.

"Secure the tent flaps!"

Several enlisted marines left their stations, methodically lowering the windows.

"Colonel Grady! Durham Three-Zero just transmitted. I have the transcript," said the corporal.

Grady removed his headset and walked to his corner of the tent.

"How we doing, Sergeant Walker?"

"Could be worse, Colonel."

"Now you're catching on," said Grady, taking the corporal's notepad. "Looks like they're taking advantage of the weather. They just stepped off from your daughter's apartment."

"You don't look too enthusiastic," said Ed.

"METOC predicts periods of heavy rain and thunderstorms for the next three hours."

Ed thought about the bridge at Milton Mills. A heavy downpour had camouflaged their approach until it was too late for the militia. Alex knew what he was doing.

"That's a good thing, right?"

"Periods of heavy rain. Meaning this could stop five minutes from now and continue an hour later. Alex is taking a big risk. He should have waited until nightfall."

"He's not convinced you'll be here when he gets back, especially after last night."

"If that's the best the insurgency has to throw at us, we're not going anywhere anytime soon," said Grady.

"What if that wasn't their best? What if it was a probe?"

"Damn costly probe, Sergeant Walker. They didn't have to lose fourteen heavily armed insurgents to figure out we have this placed locked down tight. That's amateur hour by my book."

"You're not worried that they managed to assemble and coordinate an attack by more than twenty…insurgents?"

"I'm concerned by the high number, but not worried about their capabilities. They could have assembled one hundred of those idiots, with the same result—except we'd have a higher insurgent casualty count."

"I wish I shared your optimism."

"Stick around long enough, and it'll start to rub off. Do you think I can trust you not to swipe any more of the battalion's gear, especially the kind with embedded crypto? If one of my marines 'accidently' took one of these radios home, they'd face a protracted interrogation session sponsored by NCIS, followed by a general court-martial."

"I promise not to take or touch anything that doesn't belong to me."

"I can live with that. Corporal, Mr. Walker is no longer your responsibility. I still want you to monitor Durham Three-Zero's transmissions," said Grady.

"Understand, sir. Thanks for behaving, Mr. Walker," said the corporal, breaking into a grin.

Ed shook his head. "I didn't think you cared enough to notice."

"Corporal Maguire notices everything, and you have him to thank for your release. I take his word seriously," he said, showing Ed the notebook.

A short note scribbled at the end of Alex's transmission read "Recommend Sergeant Walker be released on his own recognizance."

"He's been a public defender in Lawrence for two years," added Grady. "Follow me."

"One surprise after another," mumbled Ed. "If you don't mind, I'd like to stay in the command tent. It's about the only place I feel safe."

"You're not going anywhere. I just need to give Maguire a break from your ugly mug. Bring your chair over to my table."

"Am I still under house arrest?"

"No. More like grounded."

"I can live with that," said Ed, folding his chair.

"Let's see if we can steer Alex in the right direction before the storm grounds my Ravens."

Chapter 14

Chestnut Hill Reservoir
Brookline, Massachusetts

Alex picked up the pace, transitioning from a fast walk to a light jog. He'd worked through the cramps seizing his legs, using an age-old method perfected by the marines. Keep going. Defying all scientific theories regarding muscle cramps, ranging from electrolyte depletion to dysfunctional reflex control, "pushing through it" never failed. He checked on the kids, who easily kept pace. Both of them ran cross-country and long-distance track events in high school, so he didn't anticipate any endurance problems. He wondered if they were thinking the same thing about him.

An unfamiliar buzzing sound penetrated the curtain of driving rain, causing him to stop. He scanned the deserted gravel path, expecting to see a motorbike tear down the trail. The gently curving stretch appeared empty, but he wasn't convinced they were alone. The driving rain had reduced effective visibility to a few hundred feet. The high-pitched buzz intensified, and he signaled for the kids to take cover in the bushes and trees to the right of the path. They scrambled through the thin foliage, pressing into the dirt behind the first stand of trees. Alex caught a fast motion in his peripheral vision and turned his head.

No shit.

A gray aerial drone streaked over the reservoir, bucking from the wind and passing within a hundred feet of the northern shore. He recognized the RQS-11D immediately. Slightly larger than its predecessors, the Solar Raven represented a breakthrough in the realm of organic unit reconnaissance capability. Fitted with integrated, high-efficiency solar panels, and day/night camera systems, a single Solar Raven provided unit commanders up to nine hours of continuous aerial surveillance coverage. Colonel Grady hadn't let him down. Alex stood and waved for the cameras. A sudden gust of wind dropped the remote control aircraft several feet below its flight path, and Alex knew it had a limited time on station (TOS).

"Wave to your dad. That's one of the marine UAVs."

Chloe stepped in front of the trees and waved enthusiastically. Alex hoped Ed was watching. It was unlikely that Ed had received Chloe's transmission last night, and this was the first time he could personally verify her safety. With Grady actively helping them, he felt far better about crossing during daylight hours. Even with the storm masking their approach, the chance of discovery en route was high. Crossing the river carried a near one hundred percent guarantee of being spotted. He'd transmitted news of their departure, pretending to speak with Ed, in the hopes of eliciting sympathy from an old friend. Now it was time to see how big he owed Grady. He extracted the handheld radio.

"Patriot Actual, this is Durham Three-Zero, over"

"Stand by, Durham Three-Zero."

The Raven banked left toward the center of the reservoir and was swallowed by the rainsquall. Visibility must be shit from above. Colonel Grady answered the radio a few seconds later.

"This is Patriot Actual. You don't look any worse for the wear Three-Zero. Sierra Whiskey sends his thanks."

Sierra Whiskey stood for Sergeant Walker.

"Your dad says hi," he said to Chloe, motioning for her to take cover. "Copy. Looking to reunite these two, sooner than later."

"That's what I suspected. Big picture is dim until weather clears. It's either retrieve or recover the birds. I'd rather recover. You know the drill."

"Roger. I'll take any intelligence you can pass," said Alex.

"Low-level passes indicate you are clear to cross Commonwealth due north of your position. Avoid closing within two hundred feet of any T-Station. High probability of contact. Low-level north-to-south flight in the direction of movement showed no signs of obvious or concentrated insurgent movement. All vehicle movement classified hostile. How copy?"

Insurgent movement? Both sides had this completely wrong.

"Copy all. Request that you notify all friendly units within vicinity of destination. Estimate travel speed to be twelve to fifteen kilometers per hour. Raider gave me flares for IFF. I will contact Patriot when ready to launch flares. Can you verify that Raider passed the right sequence to friendly pickets?"

"Roger. We'll ensure they have the correct details. Recommend that you demilitarize your look. Charlie Romeo to start."

"Understand. Old habits die hard," said Alex.

"Good luck, Three-Zero. Patriot out."

Alex pocketed the radio and dropped his backpack.

"Did you get all of that?"

"Most of it. Retrieve or recover?" said Ryan.

"He can't keep the Raven up in this weather. Five pounds is no match for heavy rain and gusting winds. He'd rather recover it in Cambridge than retrieve it from the river or a hostile street. Frankly, I'm surprised it's still flying. I'm going to strip down my tactical rig and stuff it in my backpack so I look a little friendlier on the streets. The two of you should be fine."

Ryan wore a gray T-shirt under a light blue, unbuttoned long-sleeve hiking shirt, a pair of khaki pants with cargo pockets and brown leather boots. With a medium-sized military-style rucksack and Alex's desert MARPAT bonnie hat, he might attract a second look, which was why Alex insisted that he stuff the HK P30, without suppressor, into his right cargo pocket. Tucking it into his front waistband was too obvious, and the rear waistband was obstructed by his pack. It was all about appearances and practicality, which brought him to Chloe.

Her backpack was a purple, off the shelf, day hiking rig, which didn't raise an eyebrow. Combined with a light blue Boston Red Sox hat, gray short-sleeved hiking shirt and dark brown convertible cargo pants, she looked like a lost, yuppie hiker. Her outfit wasn't the problem. Chloe's gender would automatically attract attention, and additional scrutiny could end in disaster. Wrong. *Any* scrutiny could be instantly lethal.

He had no idea what had happened to the students in Warren Towers after he left. If the Liberty Boys broke through the barricades, they'd show little mercy for Piper and her ragtag band of freshmen warriors. Most of the students could provide an adequate description of Alex if forced. They knew he came to rescue Ryan and that Ryan had a girlfriend at Boston College. It didn't take a Boston University level SAT score to put together the pieces. He'd even left photos behind for the Liberty Boys to pass around! *Stupid.* If the sixth floor of Warren Towers fell to militia guns, it wouldn't matter if Chloe grew a beard. Still, they had to do something.

Alex proposed outfitting her in Ryan's spare clothes and giving her a one-minute haircut, but Chloe pointed out the obvious problem that no last minute, gender-neutralizing efforts could camouflage. Even with her tightest jog bra cinched in place, she couldn't pass for "one of the guys." They'd have to do their best to stay out of sight.

"Rub some dirt on your face, Chloe."

"Do you really think that will make a difference?"

"I don't know; just do something. Help her out with that, all right?" he said, nodding at Ryan.

He unclipped the rifle and removed the sling, which had been layered over his tactical chest rig. A few minutes later, he jammed the waterlogged chest rig into the top of his assault pack and reattached the rifle. His external carry load represented the bare minimum he needed to cross the river. He'd spread the chest rig's eight rifle magazines into easily accessible pockets. Three in each cargo pocket and two protruding from the right back pants pocket. The dump pouch from the chest rig was now attached to the right front section of his Molle compatible rigger's belt. The water-resistant bag contained the radio, GPS unit and two 38mm aerial parachute flares. He'd fire those when they were ready to cross. Red followed by green.

The effort they had put into maintaining a neutral appearance seemed ridiculous with a military-grade rifle prominently displayed, but he couldn't justify burying it in his pack. Despite all of the restrictions placed on AR and military style rifles after the Jakarta Pandemic, it was still one of the most recognizable and commonly owned weapons in the United States. The appearance of a heavily armed parent travelling with two unarmed young adults might pass initial muster. It could prevent an undetected ambush, giving Alex a chance to react, or it might allow them to move far enough through an openly observed area to make a run for it. Either way, the rifle would prove decisive, and he had no intention of sidelining it.

"Ready to move? One point six miles to the bridge. Twenty minutes tops if we jog. Good?"

"If that's not too fast for you," said Ryan snidely.

"You're really enjoying this, aren't you?"

"We'll let you set the pace."

Chapter 15

EVENT+57:29

Middlesex Fells Reservation

The splashing and laughter continued longer than Charlie had hoped. He started timing them as soon as it became obvious that they weren't passing through. Fifteen minutes and thirty-two seconds.

Too damn long.

Two women and one man, in their twenties from what he could tell through the foliage, had appeared from the west, walking along the dirt road connecting Charlie's small island to the forest preserves on either side of the reservoir. They stopped almost directly in front of the trail leading to the Jeep and dropped their packs. At first, he thought they had spotted the Jeep, but it soon became apparent that they were more interested in skinny-dipping than forest exploration.

Charlie felt a little weird watching them through binoculars. Peeping Tom weird. Still, he had to keep a sharp lookout in case one of them caught a lucky glimpse of the Jeep. On the grand scale of threats, the three travelers didn't rank high in the dangerous spectrum, but looks could be deceiving, and a concealed, snub-nosed revolver in one of their back pockets could even the odds in a heartbeat.

He'd been lucky during his stay on the island. Only a handful of refugees had wandered across the island road, most of them at night when it was impossible to spot the Jeep. The majority of the traffic through his area had been confined to the eastern shore of the reservoir. He'd made a few trips to the edge of the island to observe the paths skirting the water. Families, lone wolf types, college-aged kids, mountain bikers with child carriages bouncing behind them. Now skinny-dippers. Few carried a pack larger than

91

one of the rucksacks sitting in the Jeep. All of them were headed north. Most would run out of supplies before they reached their destination. All the more reason for him to be cautious of everyone that set foot on the island.

He'd game-planned his reaction several times, still not decided on how to respond if one of them saw the Jeep and approached it. He was pretty sure he'd charge out and pull the "military special operations" card. Tell them to move along right away or—or what? He had no idea. Maybe claiming to be military was a bad idea. Then they might insist that he helped them. He was better off telling them that he'd kill them if they didn't leave immediately, and hope they didn't push the issue, or try to pull a weapon. People were desperate, and trying to predict the behavior of a desperate person was like trying to predict the weather.

Distant thunder reminded him that he'd be stuck in the rain without his Gore-Tex if the skinny dippers didn't pack up and leave soon. He couldn't risk trying to slip into the Jeep with them this close. What the hell was going on with Alex and Ed? He hadn't heard a word from them since Ed's panicked transmission this morning, over eleven hours ago. It sounded like Alex's end of the operation was moving along as planned, but he still didn't know what to make of Ed's predicament. The more he thought about the situation, the less he knew what to do. How long was he supposed to wait here? Hell, even if Alex called him and said they couldn't get out of the city, "good luck, you're on your own," Charlie had no way of moving the logs blocking the road by himself. More thunder threatened, and the trio in the water swam to shore.

That's more like it. Move along.

Rain started falling before they had dressed, causing them to seek shelter in the stripped trees. Charlie held his breath as they sat down to finish dressing. Lightning flashed, followed by an instant crack of deafening thunder, prompting them to stand up. He heard words, but couldn't tell what they said over the strengthening rainfall. Within seconds, they started to jog toward the eastern shore, sharing the same thought with Charlie.

It isn't safe out here.

When they disappeared from sight, he picked up his gear and piled everything, including himself, into the Jeep. His radio crackled a few seconds later.

"Patriot Actual, this is Durham Three-Zero, over."

"Stand by, Durham Three-Zero."

He pressed his palms together and smiled. Alex was still in the game—but who the hell was Patriot Actual?

Chapter 16

Harvard Yard
Cambridge, Massachusetts

Ed stared across the tent at the radio sitting next to Corporal Maguire. They should have reached the river by now. Something wasn't right. He scratched the sweaty stubble on his cheek and stole a glance at the battalion commander, who crouched next to a marine seated in front of a flat-screen monitor. Grady jabbed at the previously recorded aerial drone, and the screen froze. The marine enhanced the image, and Grady shook his head. He turned his head suddenly, catching Ed's stare, and for the first time since he stepped foot in the tent over twelve hours ago, Lieutenant Colonel Grady looked worried.

"Sergeant Major!"

With practiced efficiency, the battalion sergeant major silenced the tent with minimal words.

"Time to reinforce the concentration zone. Redeploy Bandit platoons in accordance with Charles River Op-order number two. Deploy QRF one to the Longfellow Bridge and QRF two to the BU bridge. I want Bandit platoons in place and briefed within thirty mikes," he said, turning to the sergeant major. "Make it happen, Marines!"

Grady rushed to his seat and pulled up the Raven imagery, sorting through the various feeds provided by the UAV team.

"What's going on, Colonel?"

"I'm collapsing the battalion's perimeter and reinforcing the bridge crossings," said Grady, peering intensely at the screen in front of him.

"I figured out that much. What's really going on?"

94

"The last Raven pass picked up some unusual activity near two of the bridges. Vehicles and personnel almost hidden out of sight. I don't think they were expecting us to keep the Raven up that long in the storm. Previous passes didn't show any signs of activity. I suspect they're up to something. I just hope Alex gets his ass across the river before it happens," said Grady.

"He should have contacted you by now. It's been twenty-one minutes," said Ed.

"I'm sure he's fine. Twenty minutes was a generous estimate, under the best of circumstances. I won't start worrying until we hit the forty-minute mark. Even then, he might have spotted an insurgent patrol and decided to hide out for twenty minutes. This isn't an exact science, Sergeant Walker. How long did it take you to get down here from Medford?"

"Way too long."

"Not long enough. If you had taken it slower, you might have detected and avoided Striker One's headquarters."

"I couldn't imagine going any slower than four miles in three hours."

"No wonder you got caught. Good thing Alex was in a hurry. If we hadn't crossed paths, your trip across the BU Bridge would have ended in disaster."

Ed considered his words and grimaced. Grady was right. Alex would have led him onto the darkened bridge, oblivious to the danger ahead. Dressed like Special Forces soldiers, they would have been gunned down as soon as practical by insurgents hidden in the buildings and trees along Storrow Drive, or run down by one of their cars. He'd started and stopped this pointless internal debate more than a dozen times since Alex left Harvard Square, fueled by a desperate sense of helplessness. His daughter's rescue was in the hands of Alex, and he wasn't convinced Alex made the best decisions.

Their entire journey had been marked by one close call after another, all precipitated by Alex's insistence on the most dangerous course of action.

With his daughter so close to safety, he needed to let it go. There was nothing left to do but trust in Alex—but he couldn't. Chloe's life was in the hands of a man with a lucky streak a mile long. What was that stupid quote? Luck is when preparation meets opportunity or something like that? He needed to stop dwelling on something he couldn't change. The outcome depended solely on Alex. He had no choice but to trust his friend to protect the kids at all costs.

Grady patted his shoulder. "My daughter is at UCLA. I could only dream of having someone like Alex Fletcher on a rescue mission like this. Your daughter is in capable hands. I still see a lot of the old Captain Fletcher in him."

"That's a good thing, right?" said Ed.

"A very good thing."

Chapter 17

Riverview Road
Boston, Massachusetts

Alex crouched in the thick bushes between two dilapidated houses and examined the rusty chain-link fence across the street. According to the GPS plotter, the Massachusetts Turnpike lay beyond the fence. Blackened treetops swayed with the wind beyond the stained crisscross barrier, indicating a drop beyond to the highway. This was where things would get interesting. The turnpike represented one hundred fifty feet of flat, "nowhere to hide" open space. Beyond that, they faced three to four hundred feet of unknown before reaching the riverbank. They'd have to make a quick assessment once they ran out of concealment. Swim the Charles or run for the bridge.

Fortunately, most of the ground cover in the area had been spared the blast's thermal radiation effects. With any luck they might be able to cut the distance to the river in half, which helped them address another challenge. The mud. Alex hadn't forgotten the thick layer of silt he'd trudged through on both sides of the river. Sprinting near the riverbank wasn't a viable option.

Despite these challenges, Alex was optimistic about the approach. Conditions favored a covert arrival. He didn't detect any high-rise structures in the vicinity of the North Beacon Street Bridge, which restricted militia observation to ground-level efforts. The Liberty Boys should have a presence at the bridge, but given the weather conditions, he suspected it would be confined to vehicles. Street visibility was limited to two hundred feet at best, even less through water-blurred car windows. By the time

Alex's group appeared, it would be too late to stop them, and if the Liberty Boys tried, they'd be cut to pieces with brutal precision by the marines. It was time to get moving.

Alex scuttled through the narrow space between houses and sprinted across the muddy backyard to a gray wooden shack nestled against a paint-chipped white picket fence lining the back of the property. The kids had sheltered on the leeward side of the utility shed, between an overgrown forsythia bush and the fence. He pushed his way through the branches, startling both of them.

"Jesus, Dad!" Ryan said, lowering the pistol.

Ryan and Chloe sat shoulder to shoulder on the ground, with their backs against the shed. A steady flow of water poured off the roof onto their legs.

"Time to go," said Alex, extending his hand to pull Ryan off the ground. "The street looks empty. There's a chain-link fence on the other side, then the turnpike. We'll cross at a dead sprint. Do not stop for any reason. If you spot another human being, call out the relative direction using the clock method. Add a rough distance and description. Keep moving. We can't get pinned down on the turnpike. There's no cover. Understand the clock method? Assume twelve o'clock is directly facing the river or across the highway. Check?"

"Check," said Ryan.

"Check?" said Chloe.

"I got her," said Ryan, pulling Chloe to her feet.

The screen door at the top of the back porch flew open, slamming against the warped siding. A man rushed down the uneven concrete steps connected to the house, pointing a double-barreled shotgun at them. Alex skidded to a halt, immediately reaching back with an open hand to signal the rest of them to stop. He locked eyes with Ryan and quickly shook his head, returning his gaze to the man holding the shotgun. He prayed that Ryan got the message. There was no way they could outdraw this guy. Someone died if either of them tried. He doubted the shotgun was loaded with anything less than #1 buckshot, which would obliterate anything in the gun's direct path. At a distance of twenty feet, the man could very easily kill two of them with one blast. He raised his hands and faced the gunman, relieved to see Ryan and Chloe do the same.

"On your knees!" the man yelled.

"We're just passing through. Headed north to Maine," said Alex, trying to stall.

Dropping to his knees represented a severe reduction in mobility and options. The man would order them to lay prone next, eliminating any chance of escape or reasonable discourse. They'd cease to be human beings on the ground.

"This is my son and his girlfriend. I came down here to bring them home. They were in college when this mess started," said Alex.

He studied the man's reaction. His deep scowl relaxed while he examined the kids and took a few hesitant steps forward.

"How do you explain the hardware?" he said, pointing the shotgun at Alex's gun.

"I had no idea what I'd be up against in the city. Better to be prepared, right? Do you have family?"

The man nodded imperceptibly, studying the kids again. The shotgun started to lower, but stopped. "I'm sorry. I can't take the risk. On your knees! Mary! Run down to the overpass and grab one of the guys with a rifle!"

A woman dressed in khaki shorts and a yellow tank top appeared in the open doorway. "Holy shit!"

"Don't gawk; just get down to the overpass! Tell them to get up here right away!" said the man, turning his head to address the woman.

The shotgun's point of aim naturally followed the man's head and drifted to Alex's left. He didn't want to kill this man, but time and circumstance presented no other option. Alex dropped to one knee, cradling the rifle in a single movement, but the gunman recovered swiftly, realizing his mistake. A sharp report beat the thunderous blast of the shotgun, which grazed Alex's left shoulder, knocking him to the mud. Screams erupted from the house.

He spun on the ground, bringing the rifle to bear on the man, but the fight was over. The guy lay curled up on his side, clutching his left elbow and groaning. Ryan stood next to Chloe, frozen in a modified Weaver stance, oblivious to the downpour. The pistol trembled in his hands.

"He's down. Grab the shotgun!" yelled Alex, testing his left arm for stability.

His upper shoulder stung intensely, but he couldn't afford to look at the wound. They didn't have time to stop and treat it, so there was no point.

Finding that the arm easily supported his weight, he stood and grabbed Chloe, who hadn't stopped staring at Ryan.

"He didn't have a choice, Chloe. Let's go," he said, pulling her toward the street.

Pushing through the dense bushes, he heard a door slam shut.

"Find Ryan and get over the fence."

"Where are you going?" she said, shaking her head and grabbing his left sleeve.

"I'll be right behind you. Go!" he said, pulling his arm away.

Alex scanned the street as soon as he emerged, cursing when he finally spotted the yellow tank top in the middle of the street.

She must be an Olympic sprinter.

The woman had a six car-length head start in the direction of the Brooks Street underpass, which may as well have been six miles. Even without the backpack, he had little chance of catching her. Brooks Street was six hundred feet away according to his GPS plotter, and she showed no signs of slowing.

Alex stepped into the road and considered his options. All of them sucked. He raised his rifle and stared at her magnified image through the ACOG sight. At one hundred feet, her entire body came into focus. Her arms pumped furiously as she tried to open the distance. He placed the tip of the illuminated red arrow on her upper back and applied pressure to the trigger.

What am I doing?

He lowered the rifle a few inches and squeezed his eyes shut in frustration.

Protecting family.

If she reached the underpass, they faced the possibility of a coordinated, concerted militia effort to kill them at the bridge. He hadn't asked for any of this shit. He should have been able to drive his car to pick up the kids without anyone stopping him or trying to kill him, but that hadn't been the case, and that wasn't his problem. Why should he be the one to pay the price for something that had nothing to do with him? They thought he was with the marines and decided to gun him down? Fuck them. The Liberty Boys decided to shake down the citizens and turn them into informants.

Not my problem.

He reacquired the target and started to squeeze the trigger.

"Damn it!" he screamed, unable to shoot.

The woman jumped out of the street, continuing her run on the sidewalk, mostly obscured from sight. Alex turned to find Ryan and Chloe standing in the middle of the street, staring blankly at the fleeing woman.

"Dump the backpacks! We go straight for the bridge!"

Chapter 18

Westbound Lanes, Massachusetts Turnpike
Boston, Massachusetts

The first Liberty Boys appeared exactly where he predicted. A raised concrete section interrupted the turnpike's featureless metal guardrail, marking the underpass. At an approximate distance of three hundred feet, he'd barely spotted the break using his 4X ACOG sight. The men materialized at the eastern edge of the anomalous concrete segment. He hoped the men that spilled onto the rain-swept highway carried the same type of unmagnified EOTech or Aimpoint sights he'd seen fitted on the militia ARs at Warren Towers.

"Run side by side and don't stop. Find a place to hide. Looks like plenty of concealment. Go!" said Alex, slapping Ryan on the back.

He sighted in on the group, trying to settle on the target with the best chance of detecting the kids. The strategy was pointless, since they all faced his direction, apparently aware that Alex's group planned to cross further down the turnpike. He could have delayed this if he had shot the woman. At that range, he could have put a bullet through one of her lower legs.

I will never hesitate again, he thought as he scanned for any signs that the Liberty Boys had seen them.

The kids crossed unnoticed, but by the time they traversed the highway, the militia group had covered enough ground that Alex could see their outlines without magnified optics. He should have followed his own orders and continued without stopping, but the figures appeared in his ACOG just as they reached the turnpike divider. He panicked and ordered the kids to take cover along the concrete barrier, overestimating the militia group's detection range. He knew he'd screwed up as soon as they stopped. Now he faced a higher probability of discovery. It was time to switch from passive to active avoidance measures.

He braced the rifle's vertical fore grip against the top of the cement barrier and centered the red arrow on the furthest target. The suppressed rifle kicked, dropping the figure to both knees as Alex snapped two hasty shots at the next man in line. While the men scrambled for the safety of the guardrail embankment, Alex hopped the divider and sprinted across the slick pavement. He reached the guardrail as his first target face-planted into the pavement.

Gunfire erupted to his left, but he didn't hear the telltale snap and hiss of incoming bullets. A discordant volley of gunshots immediately responded from the other side of the turnpike, followed by an intense, unremitting fusillade of semiautomatic and automatic gunfire. He expected the foliage and tree trunks around him to explode with deadly projectiles, but the wall of steel never materialized.

They're shooting each other! he realized.

Alex spotted the kids crouched behind a thick stand of trees at the edge of a chain-link fence. Ryan had his pistol drawn, peering around the trees at the dense brush to the east. A one-story red brick building peeked through the healthy shrubs along the fence. He slid down the ridge, scraping his backside on rocks or glass. Like his shoulder, he didn't care to check. They didn't have time for first aid. If it didn't involve running or shooting, it could wait until they were on the other side of the Charles River. A pungent, brackish stench hit his nose, reminding him of the muck ahead.

"What happened up there, Dad?"

"They're shooting at each other, but we need to keep moving. Must have been a shitload of them hiding out in the underpass. Follow the fence line right. Call out any targets. I'll cover the rear until we break out of this," huffed Alex.

He knew going right would bring them closer to the bridge, but it also put them on the wrong side of this building when the Liberty Boys figured out they had already crossed the turnpike. The volume of gunfire coming from each side suggested a squad-on-squad level engagement. They needed to avoid direct contact with elements of either group for as long as possible.

The shooting stopped by the time they reached the corner of the fence, which meant they were running out of time. He had to reach the bridge before the militia. Once on the bridge, the marines could provide heavy suppressive fire, enabling them to cross. The trick was getting his crew to the foot of the bridge. He'd estimated the distances using maps and GPS. They had to cover two to three hundred feet of open ground, slogging through thick mud, with a rifle and a pistol for defense. The only thing they had going for them at this point was the rain.

"Keep moving! When we get past the building, you make a straight line for the bridge. I'll peel left and give you a buffer," said Alex.

He took the lead and broke out of the tree line, running along the fence toward the parking lot next to the building. His boots sank well above the ankle, but emerged without the telltale sucking sounds that signaled painfully slow progress ahead. The rain hadn't penetrated far enough to make this a complete disaster. A quick look inside the fence told him that it had once been a municipal pool. Mangled lawn chairs and plastic tables lay in a heap along the far fence. The pool must have been covered with a tarp, because he couldn't tell where the pool started or stopped under the blanket of dark brown silt.

A red brick outbuilding stood between the embankment and parking lot, shielding them from view as they approached the street. Beyond the empty parking lot, Alex saw the outline of a wide traffic island containing several denuded, blackened trees. He led them through a gate into the parking lot and hugged the side of the building, approaching the street quickly but cautiously. There was no point making a run for the bridge if the Liberty Boys had set up a firing squad for them. He risked a peek around the corner and caught a glimpse of the street signals flanking the mouth of the bridge. A concrete Jersey barrier blocked the inbound bridge lane, but the barrier on the outbound lane was not in sight. He wondered if militia units had pushed the outbound barriers out of the way on all of the bridges last night. Something big was going down.

Tearing his eyes off their escape route, Alex scanned west along North Beacon Street for any signs of immediate trouble. He didn't see any vehicles, which made sense given the potential difficulty of the mud. The militia's quick reaction force for the North Beacon Street Bridge had most likely been positioned inside the underpass. He noted a concrete handicap ramp extending from the front of the municipal pool building to the sidewalk. A small staircase with thick metal railings sat in front of the ramp.

The brick structure directly faced the bridge, making it a logical place for one of the militia observation posts. He'd have to deal with that first.

"Straight to the bridge. Don't wait for me," he said, stepping onto the sidewalk.

Alex ran through the heavy mud toward the front entrance, glancing back to make sure Ryan and Chloe had started their run. He saw Ryan yank Chloe into the open by her arm, holding her in place as she clawed the air for the perceived safety of the brick corner. Returning his attention to the concrete steps, he squeezed against the wall and aimed down the canted iron sights as he approached. A quick look behind showed Chloe and Ryan making progress toward the bridge. They had reached the traffic island, gaining more ground than he expected and prematurely exposing themselves to possible observers in the pool building.

He heaved his aching body over the railings and landed on the top steps, firing his rifle before he had steadied. The first rounds out of the barrel struck the front of the thick wooden desk, startling the gunman seated behind it. The shooter recoiled and knocked a scope-equipped, bipod-fitted assault rifle off the desk into the tight space between the right edge of the desk and the wall. Alex adjusted his aim and fired two bullets center mass, knocking the man out of sight behind the desk. He let his HK416 dangle from the one-point sling and grabbed the scoped rifle from the muddy floor.

The weapon's heft indicated he had picked up a .308 caliber AR. When it emerged, the large, box-style magazine confirmed it. Shit. He'd probably picked up the one AR-style rifle within a mile that wasn't compatible with the ammunition he carried. He couldn't complain. Twenty rounds in the hands of a second shooter could make a big difference.

He leaped down the stairs, leveling the .308 rifle at the closed door at the top of the handicapped ramp. Nothing. He turned his back on the building, hoping the man had been alone, and slogged through the mud until his peripheral vision detected movement—in both directions. A pickup truck raced out of the Brooks Street underpass, followed by an SUV. The vague shape of vehicles emerged from the east, still mostly obscured by the rain. He'd forgotten about the other underpass. A bullet snapped past him, fired from an unknown location. He sprinted forward, not bothering to search for the hidden shooter. His first priority was to close the distance to the bridge. Another projectile cracked overhead, joined by the sound of revving engines, putting a hold on those plans.

Alex turned to face the pickup truck and kneeled in the mud, switching to his HK416. With the .308 propped upright against his chest, he steadied his firing platform and found the right side of the pickup's windshield through his rifle's scope. He fired three bullets, confirming that the windshield spider-webbed, before firing on the trailing SUV. A tight pattern of four rounds shattered the second vehicle's windshield in place.

Hurtling toward the intersection at forty miles per hour, the SUV slammed into the near stationary pickup, launching the SUV's front seat passengers through the opaque windshield into the bed of the truck. Bodies tumbled into the intersection, catapulted by the collision. Alex grasped the rifle and ran for the first Jersey barrier, bullets smacking into the mud behind him. A throng of Liberty Boys had emerged from the bushes beyond the wrecked vehicles, firing on the run. He needed to reach the reinforced concrete barrier before the shooting frenzy tapered and they transitioned to more deliberate and inherently accurate tactics.

❧

A thunderous metallic crunch forced Ryan to steal a glance at the intersection. A dark blue late-model SUV careened sideways, its hood bent upward from rear-ending an oversized four-door pickup truck. The SUV's front windshield was missing, along with the driver and front passenger, who he assumed had joined the tangle of bodies next to the pickup. Three tightly spaced holes and a bright red stain in the driver's side of the pickup's windshield explained why the pickup stopped in the middle of the intersection. Thirty feet away, his father lowered his suppressed rifle and ran toward the bridge, looking over his shoulder at several men running toward the intersection from the turnpike.

Ryan tugged Chloe's hand to force her along. Progress across the exposed intersection had been stop and go since the shooting started. She had dropped to the mud several times during their trek across the exposed intersection, the crack and hiss of near misses short-circuiting her legs. He just needed to get her behind the Jersey barrier and out of immediate danger. Ryan slid his right arm under her left arm and shoved her forward, pushing against her back. Bullets ricocheted off the barrier in front of them as they edged toward the temporary reprieve of the one-foot-thick, steel-reinforced concrete barricade.

She sank to the pavement behind the wall, placing her back against the concrete and burying her face in her knees. Her body twitched uncontrollably, and Ryan couldn't tell if she was hyperventilating or crying. He pressed his forehead against her pink ball cap and held her tightly, wishing he could soothe her. The maelstrom of incoming fire intensified, showering them with concrete fragments. Chloe flinched at every sound. There was nothing he could do for her right now, other than get her to the other side of the bridge.

He yanked the pistol from his waist and started to lift himself, but froze. This wasn't a day at the range with his father. The supersonic snaps filling the void above him represented lethal projectiles travelling over three thousand feet per second. Rising above the top of the barricade exposed him to a fickle domain ruled by chance and ever-slimming odds. Ryan had learned all about this world after he announced his intentions to follow in his father's footsteps and pursue a commission as a marine officer. A weekend camping trip materialized, during which his father unveiled the realities of combat and dispelled the myths. One of those realities pressed down hard, locking him in place. He grimaced, fighting against it.

"Combat is all about odds," Alex had told him. *"Ninety-nine point nine percent of ordnance fired on the battlefield never reaches its intended target. Long odds until you consider the sheer volume of projectiles fired in a battle."*

He tried to stand, but his legs refused. He had to break out of this paralysis. His dad would be devastated to find him cowering behind cover. The thought of his dad in the sights of every gun south of the bridge spurred him into action.

Ryan popped up and scanned right, finding a target aiming a rifle at the bridge from the riverbank. Three rapid trigger presses placed ordnance close enough to break the shooter's concentration, forcing him to seek concealment in the thick underbrush. His dad hit the pavement next to him, slamming his back against the concrete. Ryan dropped down, not seeing any point in pushing the "long odds." The intersection swarmed with heavily armed militia. Remembering another Captain Fletcherism, he slid past Chloe to take a new position along the barrier.

"Appearing in the same place twice during a gun fight is bad for your health."

❧◈❧

Shards of concrete stung Alex's hands as he vaulted the barrier and landed next to Ryan, who had just fired Alex's pistol at the riverbank. Ryan scooted past Chloe and rose to fire three aimed shots directly into the intersection. A sharp scream from the intersection penetrated the earsplitting chaos.

"They're all over us!" yelled Ryan.

Alex unclipped the HK416 from his sling and handed it past Chloe to Ryan. Chloe quivered against the obstacle, face buried in her knees and hands covering her ears.

"Spare mags in my cargo pockets! Lay down some fire while I launch our flares!"

Alex scrambled to open the dump bag containing the flares while Ryan rapidly fired two-round salvos at the militia. He felt Ryan's hands clawing at the rifle magazines in his left cargo pocket before he had unscrewed the top and bottom end caps of the first flare. His son burned through the rest of the magazine in seconds. Incoming gunfire struck the top of the barrier and the side of the bridge, spraying them with painful fragments. They needed to move to the next barrier, but he didn't dare risk running toward the marines without sending up the flares. He prepared the second flare and turned to face the opposite side of the bridge.

Ryan stopped firing and ducked behind the barrier to reload. "They're getting too close! I can barely stick my head out!"

"Just buy me a few more seconds!" said Alex, aiming the flare at a seventy-degree angle in the direction of the marines.

He withdrew the safety pin and depressed the trigger, launching the aerial rocket. The flare sailed skyward and disappeared in the rain. He heard a faint pop a few seconds later.

Fuck.

Alex had forgotten that the parachute flare travelled nearly a thousand feet before igniting and drifting back to the ground. He wasn't sure if it would drift down far enough to be seen through the gray curtain of clouds and precipitation before extinguishing. Firing another flare seemed pointless, but he aimed the next one skyward and fired it with the same grim result. Swallowed by the impenetrable squall.

"What happened to the flares!" yelled Ryan, changing magazines.

"Into the clouds! Stand by to leapfrog to the next barrier. I'll cover you and Chloe with the .308 from here. You lay down fire for me. Focus on the closest shooters. Three-round salvos. Go!"

Bullets snapped overhead as Alex and Ryan swapped positions at the end of the crumbling Jersey barrier. Ryan pulled on Chloe, but she didn't budge.

Wrong time for this!

Alex leaned around the corner and found a target crouched behind a thick tree in the traffic island. He centered the crosshairs on an exposed shoulder and pressed the trigger. The rifle bit into his shoulder. He scanned over the barrel for more targets, locating a shooter at the corner of the pool building. The 6X scope brought the man into focus; a .308 bullet dropped him into the mud. The volume of fire against Alex's edge of the barrier intensified, forcing him back.

"You have to get her moving!" he said, sliding in the mud to the other side of the barrier.

"It's only twenty-five feet, Chloe," Ryan said to her. "You can do it. My dad and I will protect you. We have to go, Chloe! You have to run!" pleaded Ryan, tugging furiously at both her arms.

Alex fired two shots from his new position, connecting with one of them before the Liberty Boys adjusted their aim and started to pulverize the corner. He pressed his back into the concrete and examined the rifle scope. Small miracle. The scope was attached to a quick-release mount. He flipped the levers and discarded the scope, raising the front and rear flip-up sights. That was better. He rose to his knees and braced the rifle's hand guard against the concrete, firing the rest of the magazine in two-round salvos at the militia squad that had taken cover behind the destroyed vehicles. The level of incoming fire dropped significantly for a few seconds.

Alex dropped below the barrier and processed the situation. He could suppress the militia and hand Ryan the rifle, giving his son a few seconds' head start. It might be enough to get him to a safer position. The Liberty Boys would focus their initial fire at the barricade, giving Ryan a few additional seconds to reach cover. No other scenario worked.

"Get to the next barrier and cover me! I'll carry her," said Alex.

"You can barely run! I'm not leaving her!"

"Get to the next barrier! That's an order! I'll unload the HK and give you the time you need to get in position to cover our withdrawal. It's the only way," said Alex, tossing the .308 into the mud.

Alex reloaded the HK416 with one of the magazines from his back pocket. He passed the three from his right cargo pocket to Ryan, who stuffed them in his pockets, shaking his head.

"Dad, I'll carry her. You shoot," said Ryan.

With Chloe on his back, Ryan would move at less than half of his potential speed. Alex was willing to fight and die behind the first barricade, but the high volume of fire required to momentarily quiet the militia guns would burn through the HK's thirty-round magazine in seconds. Ryan and Chloe would be caught in the open during the first magazine change. Only one scenario produced a guaranteed survivor if Chloe refused to run. Glancing at her shell-shocked, inert form, he didn't see a ten-meter dash anywhere in her near future.

"That won't work! You go first and get ready to cover us!" said Alex.

"You'll leave her here!"

"I won't leave her," muttered Alex, stunned by his son's accusation. "I don't get to walk off this bridge without both of you."

"Then let me carry her."

"Ryan—"

A red glimmer in the sky east of the bridge caught his eye. He craned his neck against the harsh concrete and watched a red parachute flare break through the murky ceiling, swinging wildly for a few seconds before extinguishing. The parachute landed on the northern riverbank, nearly three hundred feet away. A green flare appeared further downriver, visible for a brief moment. Red tracers streaked past on both sides of the bridge before he could turn to Ryan, followed by the thunderous pounding of heavy-caliber machine guns. Alex pulled Chloe and Ryan flat against the pavement as the air filled with the sharp, staccato crackle of automatic machine-gun fire. The deafening roar continued for a few seconds before Alex lifted his head far enough off the ground to see that the tracers raced north to south.

Hello 1st Battalion!

"Those are marine guns! Lift her up and haul ass. I'll be right behind you!" said Alex.

Alex crested the top of the concrete block and stared at the carnage for a moment. The municipal building's red brick façade crumbled into chunks of brick and mortar under a hail of tracers, each red streak representing four steel-jacketed bullets. Large and small projectiles punctured the thin metal on both sides of the pickup truck and SUV, hammering the men seeking cover from the onslaught. A geyser of blood erupted above the pickup truck's hood, followed by a headless body toppling into the mud. A group of panicked men scrambled away from the vehicles east of the traffic island as tracers ricocheted off the metal. The marine gunfire intensified, tearing into the men as they crossed open ground. He felt a solid tug on his shoulder.

"Ready to move," said Ryan, holding Chloe in a fireman's carry.

"Right behind you," said Alex, firing at the few targets of opportunity left by the marines.

He found it difficult to keep up with his son, who effortlessly carried Chloe to the next barrier. Ryan paused near the next barrier, waiting for instructions.

"All the way! All the way!" said Alex, pushing Ryan forward.

Two bullets struck the face of the barrier, stopping him from immediately following. He scanned the intersection through the ACOG scope, searching for a shooter the marines couldn't see from their firing positions or vehicles. The bridge rose a few feet higher than the north bank, possibly obstructing their view of low-profile targets directly in front of the first barrier. He focused on positions close to the ground, spotting movement under the front end of the pickup truck. With all of its tires flattened by machine-gun fire, the front fender sat several inches above the mud, providing a perfect firing position for anyone willing to burrow their way through the filth.

Alex centered the tip of the red arrow on the darkness beneath the bumper and fired twice, unsure if his bullets struck a target. Smoke erupted from the same spot, spitting several bullets back. Alex pressed the trigger once before the projectiles reached the barrier, shattering concrete and grazing his right cheek. He dropped to one knee, clutching his face with his left hand and firing indiscriminately with the other. More rounds hit the barrier, forcing him to crouch. Ryan cried out less than a second later. This wasn't working.

Chloe lay on the pavement next to Ryan, who struggled on one knee to pull her toward the next barricade. Bullets snapped overhead, but Alex ignored them. He had to get the kids out of the open. He waved at the nearest marine M-ATV for help, but the gunner kept firing the roof-mounted M240B in long bursts. A few seconds later, three marines in full battle gear appeared at the end of the bridge, running in their direction. Alex rushed across the exposed hardtop and helped Ryan drag Chloe behind the wall. His son had been hit in the leg, but he couldn't tell how badly. A primeval tunnel vision channeled all of his focus and physical energy into pulling Chloe out of harm's way. He instinctually knew it was the only way to get his son out of the kill zone. The marines slammed into the concrete before he could check Ryan, firing fully automatic bursts across the bridge.

"Ryan!" he yelled, scrambling around one of the marines to reach his son.

"40 mike mike! Send it!" yelled a short, stocky staff sergeant.

The marines grabbed the pistol grips beneath their rifle-mounted M320 Grenade Launcher Modules and filled the air with hollow thumping sounds. A pair of hands grabbed his collar and stopped him.

"We got this, sir!" said the staff sergeant. "Colonel will kick our asses if he finds out about this."

The marine lifted Ryan's right arm and draped it over his shoulder, pulling him upright. Blood dripped from the tip of his son's boot.

"Grady didn't send you?"

"Negative. My orders are to provide suppressing fire to aid in your withdrawal. I just happened to bump into you while repositioning."

Three successive explosions sprayed mud and invisible fragments across the distant intersection.

"Amazing how shit like that happens. I owe you one, Staff Sergeant—Williams," said Alex, studying the name patch sewed onto his Dragon Skin vest.

"Compliments of the house. We need to get your son to the BAS. He has a through and through to the outer right leg. You could use a little patching up yourself."

Alex touched his cheek and held his hand in the rain, watching the rain wash away the blood. A quick glance at his bloodstained left sleeve brought his shoulder injury into focus. He traced the arm and saw two deep red slashes across the deltoid area. A few inches to the right and he could have claimed a repeat. Six years earlier, a shotgun-wielding psychopath had shot him squarely in the same shoulder. He started to jog toward the marines lifting the kids when the sound of a fast-moving car on the other side of the bridge stopped him.

"Behind the barrier!" yelled Williams.

Alex took Ryan's other arm and helped the marine lower him to the asphalt.

Williams keyed his combat radio headset. "Raider One-Zero, hold fire on approaching vehicle. I say again. Hold fire on approaching vehicle."

The marines tracked the mini-SUV skidding through the intersection.

"Staff Sergeant?" said a corporal, fingering his grenade launcher's pistol grip.

"It could be some stupid-ass civilians trying to get across. Wrong place at the wrong time."

"Could be a suicide bomber," replied the corporal.

"Hold on. Raider Base, this is Raider One-Zero. I have an SUV approaching the south end of the bridge, moving fast. VIPs have been recovered. Request ROE instructions."

"Raider One-Zero, this is Raider Base. Apply ROE in effect. Signal vehicle using any and all means available. Do not let the vehicle across."

"Fire a grenade at the first barrier. Now!" said Williams.

The corporal's launcher thumped, sending a small, dark object in an arc toward the southern end of the bridge. The 40mm high-explosive grenade hit the Jersey barrier, blasting it in half and showering the oncoming car with cement fragments. The vehicle accelerated.

"Staff Sergeant!" yelled the other marine.

"Light it up!"

Alex canted his rifle to use the iron sights and fired alongside the marines, emptying the rest of his magazine at the speeding car. Heavier guns from marine positions along the riverbank joined the skirmish, sending lines of tracers at both sides of the SUV. The car disintegrated under the barrage of mixed-caliber steel, careening left and wedging itself between the second barricade and the bridge. Alex tried to stand, but William's hand held him firmly in place. The engine whined for a moment before the car exploded.

The force of the blast rippled across the bridge, shifting the four-thousand-pound Jersey barrier several inches. William's instinct had saved Alex's life, keeping his body shielded from the potentially lethal overpressure and fragmentation effects. Instead of flattened organs and punctured flesh, Alex was knocked onto his back. A cloud of cement dust and smoke settled over the bridge, obscuring his vision. Urgent, muted voices penetrated the haze.

"Sound off!"

"Leverone. Still in one piece!"

"Graham. Shoulder is trashed!"

"My VIPs?" said Williams.

"VIPs good to go!" answered Corporal Graham.

"Move them off the bridge! You all right, sir?" said Staff Sergeant Williams, extending a hand toward Alex.

"Did I spring any new leaks?"

"Just the old ones. Let's get your son into one of the Matvees, get you all back to HQ."

Alex helped Williams lift his son off the ground.

"You all right?" he said to Ryan.

"I can't hear you!" screamed his son, grabbing Alex with both arms and hugging him.

"It's going to be fine, buddy. We made it," he said into Ryan's ear.

"Where's Chloe?" Ryan said, craning his head over his shoulder.

"She's fine. You'll see her in a minute."

"What happened?"

"Car bomb," said Alex.

"Motherfucking game changer," added Williams.

Chapter 19

Harvard Yard
Cambridge, Massachusetts

Ed Walker bolted through the thick tent flap and skidded on the slippery, matted grass beyond the entrance. His legs swung out, dropping him straight on his ass in front of the command post sentry. The corporal shook his head slowly. Ed sat on the wet ground for a moment, glad to be out of the steamy battalion command tent. The lukewarm downpour washed the sweat from his face and soaked through his swampy clothing, revitalizing him. The distant sound of a humming diesel engine echoed off the buildings, drawing him to his feet. He dashed toward the opening between Harvard and Hollis Halls, slowing as he approached the two marines stationed behind HESCO barriers.

After last night's attack, Lieutenant Colonel Grady put all noncritical personnel to work filling the battalion's modular HESCO cages with dirt from campus. The work lasted most of the night, producing dozens of four-foot-wide by four-foot-high barriers for the defensive positions ringing Harvard Yard. Two HESCO cages formed most positions, placed in a "V" shape facing the expected threat direction.

The HESCO system put twelve inches of compacted dirt between the marines and incoming high-velocity rifle bullets. Ed had been a little disturbed to discover that they didn't have enough barriers to surround the command tent. Grady told him that if the command tent came under sustained fire, they were well past the point where a line of HESCO barriers would make a difference. He couldn't tell if Grady was serious or kidding.

"Sir?" said one of the marines, looking away from his riflescope.

"My daughter's coming in on one of the Matvees."

The marines glanced at each other with doubtful looks.

"Let him through, Marines!"

Both marines stiffened, standing at attention. Grady gave him a single nod and disappeared into the tent. Ed squeezed past the HESCO barrier's metal mesh exterior and searched for the vehicle transporting Chloe.

Holy Jesus!

Harvard University resembled a cross between a refugee camp and a third-world military outpost. The battalion's "hard" security perimeter now encompassed most of the Old Yard commons. Two ugly, obtrusive machine-gun positions cut the yard in half, facing south toward Gray's Hall. Three HESCO cages, arranged in a "U," protected each M240 machine-gun team. Muddy patches of ripped turf surrounded each nest, identifying the immediate source of filler for the cages.

The battalion's motor transport section sat directly behind the machine guns, taking up half of the remaining open space between Thayer Hall and the cluster of buildings sheltering the battalion command post. Eight behemoth MK25 MTVRs (Medium Tactical Vehicle Replacement) transport vehicles made up the bulk of the section, staggered far enough apart to maneuver independently out of the yard. Four M-ATVs ("Matvees") were parked haphazardly in front of the seven-ton MTVRs, facing Johnston Gate. All of the battalion's tactical vehicles mounted M240 machine guns, part of Homeland's Category Five load out. He'd learned a lot pretending not to listen to the marines in the command tent.

Ed spotted an empty Matvee near the front entrance to Stoughton Hall and jogged toward the vehicle. Part of the battalion's inner perimeter, Stoughton had been converted into the Battalion Aid Station. The aid station had started as a self-contained shelter unit, half the size of the command tent, in the northern part of the Old Yard. Citizens flocked to Harvard Yard as word spread through Cambridge, quickly overwhelming the medical section's capacity to house severely injured patients.

The worst cases were moved to the first floor of Stoughton Hall, where the battalion surgeon and four navy corpsmen scrambled to stabilize patients long enough to be transported to one of the overwhelmed hospitals near Cambridge. Options remained limited, since most of Boston's major hospitals were south of the Charles River. Few patients had been moved.

Patients with minor injuries packed the rest of the yard, hiding from the rain in a variety of commercial tents and makeshift shelters. Grady refused to allow them inside the outer perimeter building, citing security concerns for both the civilians and marines. Few people in the Harvard Yard shantytown complained about the restriction. They were inside the defensive perimeter, which to many felt like the only safe place in the world. They had no idea how quickly "Fort Harvard" could cease to exist if the situation north of the Charles deteriorated much further. He'd overheard Grady issue an order to activate "thirty minute" protocols. He assumed this meant "gone in thirty minutes."

His knees buckled as the rear cargo compartment came into focus. Bloodstains streaked across the composite benches on both sides of the vehicle. He slammed the rear hatch shut and charged the entrance to Stoughton Hall.

A marine stepped through the open doorway and put a hand on his chest, forcing him back.

"Sir, you need to be escorted into the building by one of the aid station's personnel. If you head over to the triage—"

"My daughter's in there!" he said, pushing back.

"Sir! You will step back and follow procedure!"

"He's good to go, Corporal! His daughter is part of our group," said a marine Ed didn't recognize.

"Daddy!" he heard from the dark hallway beyond the sentry.

"Sorry, sir! Orders."

Ed ignored the marine and pushed into the dormitory, searching for his daughter.

"Chloe!"

He heard footsteps rushing down the hallway and turned in time to grab his daughter. The fact that she could run toward him meant that she hadn't been hurt. He hugged her tightly.

"We got you. We got you," he struggled to say.

She buried her head in his shoulder and cried quietly, her bear hug constricting his ribs.

"You okay, sweetie?"

She nodded her head, and he held her, momentarily oblivious to the hard journey ahead of them. He remembered the blood in the back of the Matvee.

"What about Mr. Fletcher and Ryan?"

A familiar voice echoed in the dim vestibule.

"We're okay too."

"Alex?" he said, searching the hallway.

"We're in the student lounge!"

His daughter reluctantly released her grip and stepped back a few paces. She couldn't meet his eyes.

"Are you all right, Chloe?" he said, grasping her hand.

She sobbed and shook her head.

"She was caught in the middle of a nasty gunfight. Real nasty. You should have one of the corpsmen take a look at her," said one of the marines that had brought her in.

Ed crouched, scrutinizing her for signs of injury. She didn't appear to be bleeding. She was soaked like everyone else, but intact. In the hazy light cast through the entrance, he couldn't find a single tear in her clothing.

"Not that kind of injury, sir," said the marine.

He nodded toward the marine and hugged his daughter again. "You're safe now, sweetie. We're going home."

"Right now?"

"As soon as we can, Chloe."

"We need to go now," she said blankly.

"Why?"

She paused for several moments. "Because they're everywhere."

"Who's everywhere, sweetie?"

"The Liberty Boys."

"I won't let anything happen to you. Let's find Alex and figure out how to get out of here," said Ed. "Where's the student lounge?"

"That hallway. Second door on the left," said the marine, pointing him in the right direction.

"What happened out there?"

"They had a serious hard-on for your friend. Sorry, ma'am. Whatever he did last night, it really pissed them off. They blew up half the bridge trying to snuff him out. They're lucky we saw the flares. We thought it was an all-out attack on the bridge."

"Thanks for bringing back my daughter," said Ed, starting for the student lounge and holding his daughter.

"We were just batting cleanup. Your buddy and the kid did most of the work. Navy Cross material on the bridge. Sorry, ma'am. You don't see that very often with today's youth."

Ed stopped and stared at the corporal, who didn't look much older than his daughter. He didn't know how to respond, so he nodded and kept walking. All of this was beyond surreal. What the hell had happened on the other side of the river? Was this related to the Liberty Boys his daughter mentioned? Were they safe here? The sooner they left, the better. He planned to activate his own version of the "thirty minute" evacuation plan, rain or shine. When he walked into the doorway marked student lounge, his hopes of leaving drained faster than the blood in his face. Neither of the Fletchers looked ambulatory.

"Well, there he is. Sergeant Walker!" said Alex, lying on a cot next to his son.

The room's furniture had been stripped, replaced by cots and folding chairs. A table stacked with medical supplies sat against the wall next to the door. A smaller cart near Ryan and Alex displayed stainless-steel surgical tools. Ed's stomach pitched. Two of the medical station's personnel hovered around Ryan's bloody leg while another tended to Alex's shoulder.

"Same shoulder?"

"It's not bad. Barely grazed," said Alex.

"How's Ryan?"

Alex's son had his head turned to the wall.

"He got hit in the leg, but he should be fine. He'll be out of it for a while. Morphine."

Chloe pulled at his arm, keeping him from entering the room.

"What's wrong?" whispered Ed, turning to Alex and shrugging his shoulder.

"You should spend some time with your daughter. We had it rough getting back. She did good," said Alex.

"No, I didn't," she muttered. "I almost got all of us killed."

Alex shook his head and mouthed, "No."

Ed hovered in the doorway, feeling conflicted and guilty about leaving them alone in the makeshift surgery room. He owed Alex everything for this. He had so much to say, but his daughter clearly needed him more.

"I don't know what to—"

"We've been in this together from the start. This is just what we do. Go," said Alex, suppressing a grin.

"Still, I—"

"Ed, don't make me chase you out of here."

"All right," Ed mumbled, "but I owe you one."

"Negative. You keep forgetting the church."

"I haven't forgotten. Bringing Chloe back—I can't even." He shook his head, fighting back tears.

"I know the feeling," said Alex, reaching out to touch Ryan's arm.

Chapter 20

Harvard Yard
Cambridge, Massachusetts

Alex entered the command tent and immediately sensed that something was off. The staff sat tensed at their stations, silent. The battalion TOC (Tactical Operations Center) was never quiet. Ever. He took a few steps in and spotted Lieutenant Colonel Grady talking to the UAV section.

Not good.

UAV operations had been grounded for more than two hours, and the storm showed no signs of abating. He removed his boonie cap and twisted the water onto the floor. Grady saw him and patted the UAV pilot on the back before moving to greet him.

"This isn't a good time, Alex. Sorry," he said, pointing toward the hatch.

"You're putting a Raven up? In this?"

"It's just a precaution. I can't afford any more surprises like the car bomb. Sorry, but I can't have nonessential personnel in the TOC right now."

"This is the first chance I've had to get away from the aid station. My son's fine, by the way," said Alex.

"I'm glad they got him stitched up, Alex. He sounds like a fine young man. Staff Sergeant Williams told me about the bridge. Sorry I haven't been able to swing by, but things are a little tense right now. Insurgency chatter stopped three minutes ago. All channels," said Grady, with a severe look.

"I need to talk to you about the so-called insurgency. It might have some bearing."

"All right."

"You're not dealing with a rogue gang of criminals. This is something much bigger. My son says they refer to themselves as the Liberty Boys."

"He heard them say this?" said Grady, betraying a hint of recognition.

"From his apartment window." Alex nodded. "A group of heavily armed men and women drove a pickup truck down their street, assuring everyone that the streets are safe. From what Ryan described, criminal elements ran wild for about twelve hours. There was a ton of shooting the first night, and this Liberty Boys group appeared the next day. They were asking for volunteers to help them secure Boston."

"That could have been the same criminal group trying to draw out troublemakers," said Grady.

"You don't sound very convinced. What I saw was far too centralized for spur of the moment, post-disaster opportunists. They had an effective, grassroots communications network. We were ratted out by a family just south of the turnpike. I didn't give you a heads-up on the radio because we were running for our lives."

"You got lucky. Staff Sergeant Williams almost lit you guys up. Flares reach a height of three hundred thirty meters. Over a thousand feet, in case you were curious," said Grady.

"I remembered the forty second part. The name Liberty Boys has an interesting historical context."

Grady held a hand up to stop him from continuing. "Why don't we step outside for a second," he said. "Let me know as soon as the Raven is airborne!"

"Yes, sir," replied the UAV operator.

They walked far enough away from the sentry to avoid being overheard. The rain collapsed the brim of Alex's cap against his forehead before they stopped. Grady, however, appeared unfazed by the deluge against his ballistic helmet.

"I have a few hundred digital pages of information compiled by the Department of Homeland Security on the Liberty Boys—or the Mechanics. Top secret, limited distribution. Myself and the battalion intel officer. There's a reason for that."

"A reserve military unit drawing unit members from the greater Boston area? I can't imagine what the problem might be," said Alex.

"We left three marines at Fort Devens, including my XO. My first task was to privately open a sealed file stored in my secure Cat Five capsule. The file contained explicit orders for the immediate incarceration of three marines that had been in the unit for more than a decade. Homeland identified them as 'immediate, high-mission risks. Known affiliation to subversive anti-government militia groups.'"

"And you don't think Homeland found all of them," said Alex.

"That's why we're talking out here."

"Don't you find this a little disturbing? Homeland investigating your marines? Category Five Event Response with no information flowing from higher headquarters? Boston is falling apart because the two groups with half a chance to keep it together are working against each other. Maybe that's by design. By the way, I saw a few XM-9s out there," said Alex. "What exactly happened to the National Guard unit out of Brockton?"

"We don't know. They just stopped communicating with us," said Grady.

"I think they had a problem. An internal problem—and I think you know more about the situation than you're willing to admit."

"How many XM-9s did you see?" asked Grady.

"Does it matter?" Alex countered, studying Grady's poker face.

The XM-9 was a new combat carbine used exclusively by the United States Army and National Guard units. Civilian variants of the Heckler and Koch line of XM rifles had been specifically banned from importation into the U.S. by the 2016 Combat Weapons Reduction Bill.

"You need to reach out to militia leadership across the river before this situation spirals further out of control. I've studied groups like this in Maine and New Hampshire. Talked to their leadership. They're highly suspicious of the government, but they're reasonable. Most of them share the same mission as your battalion: to help the people in a crisis. I assume that's still the crux of your mission?"

"The Liberty Boys are making that mission extremely difficult," stated Grady.

"That's because you're working against each other. If the current organization has roots to the original Mechanics, you're talking about a league of New Englanders that has spent the better part of the past two hundred fifty years planning to fight a guerilla war against a possible government takeover. I'm surprised that I didn't come across this group in my research."

"They don't officially exist. You won't find a single modern reference to them on any website. They don't produce literature or host bean suppers like nearly every other militia group out there. They don't muster in the streets to fill sandbags when the rivers overflow or serve hot meals after a nor'easter. Instead, they donate sizable sums of money through untraceable proxies to support relief efforts. They have considerable resources at their disposal. We're talking generational wealth."

"You need to take steps to convince their leadership that your battalion isn't part of a master plan to subjugate the United States. That's the only way this won't end in a complete disaster."

Grady grinned and gripped Alex's good shoulder. "I need you to head this up."

"Excuse you—Colonel," said Alex.

"You have experience talking to militia leaders. You've studied their structures and drawn conclusions based on research. My education into this subject started two days ago with the arrest of my executive officer and two staff NCOs. I can give you a laptop and a private room in one of these buildings to sort through the digital file. Help me make sense of the Liberty Boys and form a strategy. I barely had time to read the executive summary."

"Sean, I was really hoping to head out as soon as possible. I need to get these kids home to their mothers. We've been gone for thirty-six hours with no contact," said Alex.

A marine appeared between Stoughton and Hollis Halls, walking the well-worn, muddy path toward the battalion TOC. They waited for him to salute Grady and pass before continuing their conversation. The marine sergeant glanced back at Grady as he approached the sentry stationed outside of the TOC.

"Your son really isn't in any condition to travel right now. Neither are you, for that matter."

"I was hoping you might spare one of those Matvees for thirty minutes. I have a Jeep stashed up in the Middlesex Fells Reservation."

"Not until I figure out why militia radio traffic went quiet. I should have UAV coverage in a few minutes. Could you give me a few hours of analysis?" said Grady.

Alex's attention strayed to the marine that had passed them a few seconds ago. The sentry was speaking into a Motorola. The sergeant leaned against the HESCO barrier and started to unclip his assault pack from his Modular Dragon Skin Vest (MDV).

"Who is that?" asked Alex.

"Sergeant Bruckman. Chief mechanic," answered Grady, craning his head to look at the marine.

"Why is he detaching his assault pack?" asked Alex, thumbing the snap on his drop holster.

The marine looked back at them, his eyes dropping to Alex's holster.

Shit!

Alex drew his pistol as Sergeant Bruckman dropped the assault pack and fired a quick rifle burst into the sentry's chest. He tried to turn the HK416 on the battalion commander, but Alex lined up the sergeant's silhouette with his front sight and fired first, joined a fraction of a second later by Grady's P30L service pistol. More than a dozen 9mm bullets struck Bruckman in rapid succession, driving him against the HESCO barrier and knocking the rifle out of his hands.

The marine's MDV stopped the bullets from entering his torso, preventing his instantaneous death. Colonel Grady closed the distance to the marine, firing his pistol at the mechanic's unprotected face with devastating effect. Bruckman's faceless corpse slid down the tan HESCO cage and toppled into the shiny grass. Grady had already disappeared over the barrier to check on the sentry, reappearing a second a later.

"Alex, get the battalion surgeon ready for a Class Two!"

Alex holstered his pistol and took off for Stoughton Hall, placing his hands on his head as marines scrambled out of the TOC. Tensions were high, and he didn't want to give any of the headquarters' staff an early excuse to fire their weapons. Given what just transpired, Alex felt confident that every marine in Grady's battalion would put their service rifle to work, sooner than later.

"Fletcher is friendly!" Grady shouted. "Sergeant Major, get Bruckman's assault pack out of here. Possible IED. Put it in one of the HESCO pits away from the TOC. Bruckman shot Kappleman at point-blank range. Help me get this marine to the BAS!"

Alex needed to get his crew out of Cambridge within the next ten minutes. Bruckman's aborted attack on the TOC was only the beginning. A cascade of destabilizing violence would ripple through the battalion positions in short order. He'd seen this before, and so had Grady. Alex reached the side entrance to Stoughton Hall and stopped. Beyond the fact that one of Grady's marines had just attempted to detonate a bomb in the battalion TOC, something nagged him about the rogue sergeant's actions.

Bruckman had removed the pack, which indicated that he either planned to throw it inside or leave it behind. Either method required remote detonation. Throwing it through the entrance hatch didn't make sense. With a bull's-eye painted on his forehead, Bruckman would have been forced to trigger the bomb well within the casualty radius. He probably planned to drop it next to the piles of personal gear stashed around the tent, setting off the IED from a distance. But how did he acquire the bomb? Did he bring it with him from Fort Devens? Each question led to answers he couldn't ignore. Not if his son was stuck in the battalion aid station.

"Notify the battalion surgeon that he has a Class Two casualty inbound," he said to the marines assigned to the sentry post between Stoughton Hall and Hollis Hall.

"Do it," said a corporal, dispatching a private to deliver the message. The corporal looked shaken, on the verge of tears.

"That wasn't your fault, son. Get that out of your head right now," said Alex.

"Why did Bruckman do that? I don't—"

"There's nothing to understand about it. Don't let *anyone* through, Corporal, without clearing it with the TOC first. Copy?"

"Yes, sir," said the marine, shifting his rifle toward the Old Yard.

"Colonel Grady!" yelled Alex, running back toward the TOC.

Alex passed two marines carrying the critically wounded sentry to Stoughton hall. He didn't see an obvious entry or exit wound, but the upper half of his body armor was stained dark red. Bright red blood streamed from his mouth and nose. He'd be dead within thirty minutes—if that. Grady leaned against the tree next to the TOC sentry station, his hands and uniform sleeves soaked in blood. He shook his head and grimaced.

"Fucking savages," he muttered.

"Sorry, Sean. Your marine…" said Alex.

"One of the rounds hit a centimeter above his Dragon Skin," said Grady, shaking his head. "You ready to give me a hand figuring out this insurgency?"

"Can you confirm that the IED is remote triggered?" said Alex, kneeling next to Bruckman's body.

"Hold on," he said, searching around. "Top? Can you take a look at Bruckman's pack and confirm the detonation mechanism?"

"Roger, sir," said a hulking Latino marine standing next to the battalion sergeant major. "Make a hole!"

The master sergeant ran toward the unlucky marine tasked to carry the backpack to one of the shallow pits dug into the Old Yard.

"Get the marines focused, Sergeant Major. We still have a shit storm brewing out there," added Grady.

"On it, sir! Back in the TOC! Let's go!"

Alex emptied the dead marine's pockets and vest pouches, trying to avoid staring at his lifeless, destroyed face and the brain matter seeping out of his combat helmet. He found a Motorola resembling one of the battalion's encrypted models and handed it to Grady.

"Can you confirm this is one of yours?" said Alex, continuing the search.

"What's your theory?"

"If it's remote triggered, either Bruckman or another marine has the detonator. I was hoping to find it on Bruckman."

"Doesn't make any sense. How did he know to bring a backpack IED to Devens? We were on a regularly scheduled AT," said Grady.

Alex finished his search, coming up empty. He stood up and shook his head.

"Maybe they bring bombs with them to every reserve drill—or maybe someone delivered it."

"Everyone camped out on the yard has been thoroughly searched…son of a bitch! Bruckman CASEVAC'd some of the civilians to Cambridge Hospital," said Grady, stepping toward the tent flap.

"Not by himself, I assume," said Alex.

"Correct. Another motor transport marine. Sergeant Major!"

The ground shook, followed by the sharp crack of a high-order detonation. Windows shattered above the HESCO barrier stationed between Harvard and Stoughton Halls, followed by a horizontal debris shower that instantly engulfed the marines shielded from the blast. Gunfire erupted outside of the perimeter as marines from the battalion supply point poured out of the back of Harvard Hall and rushed to the source of the explosion. Alex started to walk backward, toward the battalion aid station.

"Who am I looking for?" yelled Alex.

"Private First Class O'Neil. Caucasian. Short. Pale with freckles," said Grady.

The battalion sergeant major's acne-scarred face burst through the tent hatch. "Sir, we have movement south of the river. UAV picked up at least fifty personnel and multiple vehicles at the bridges."

"Which bridge?" asked Grady sharply.

"All of them, sir."

"Shit."

"I'll take care of your internal problem," said Alex, turning toward the Old Yard.

"Alex!" yelled Grady, bending over Bruckman's body. "You might need one of these."

Grady tossed Bruckman's HK416, which Alex snatched out of the air by the hand guard. The sergeant's Motorola followed. He started to open the dead sergeant's ammo pouches, but Alex stopped him.

"I still have a few of my own."

Chapter 21

EVENT +59:37

North Beacon Street Bridge
Boston, Massachusetts

Staff Sergeant Terrence Williams stood in the M-ATV's armored gun turret and squinted into his binoculars. The rain hampered his view of the intersection, but he didn't need a crystal-clear view to know that the situation at his bridge was about to reach critical mass. Raven imagery passed to his vehicle-mounted tablet showed at least fifty infrared signatures gathered in front of the Brooks Street underpass. That was two minutes ago. The Raven had started with the North Beacon Street Bridge and headed east, confirming similar IR signatures at every bridge over the Charles River. Combined with the report of a massive explosion at the battalion TOC, he wasn't looking forward to the next several minutes. Something big was going down.

He had a rapidly developing problem. The crowd approaching the bridge didn't appear to carry weapons. Not like the group that had thrown itself at the civilians over an hour ago. ROE was clear in that case, and the militia made it easy for all of them by displaying and firing weapons. Everyone south of Mr. Fletcher's group had been declared hostile and was targeted with extreme prejudice. He didn't like what he saw through his binoculars. They were going to have a serious problem when the growing mass of men, women and children reached the bridge.

"Raider Base, this is Raider One Zero. I have eyes on sixty-plus foot mobiles approaching south entrance to bridge. I see children. No vehicles present."

"Copy. Can you confirm weapons from that distance?"

"Nothing in plain sight. Request ROE update," he said.

"*Stand by.*"

His orders were explicit. Nothing gets across. And with the newly minted suicide bomber tactic in play, he faced a shitty decision point. If he couldn't confirm weapons, he would launch tear-gas grenades first, hoping to convince the mob to turn back. Failing that, Raider One Zero's only remaining option was to physically block the group and try to force them back, which put his marines at risk from hidden weapons or explosive vests. If they spotted weapons, his options didn't improve. He could use sharpshooters against the armed targets, followed by tear gas against the rest, or—he didn't want to think about his last option. There was no way he would give that order. Not with children in the group. He'd already lost the bridge. He just hoped the crowd marching through the intersection didn't realize it.

"*One Zero, this is Raider Actual. Hold the bridge. ROE version three still in effect.*"

Son of a bitch. Battalion wasn't going to cut him any slack.

"Graham, put our Matvee in a blocking position at the foot of the bridge."

"Ooh-rah, Staff Sergeant," said Corporal Graham.

He keyed the vehicle radio as the fifteen-ton armored vehicle lurched out of its hide site in bushes north of Greenbough Boulevard.

"Raider One Zero, unclassified foot mobiles, numbered thirty plus, are about to walk onto our bridge. All One Zero units will hold fire. I repeat. All One Zero units will hold fire. Observe and report. I need to know if you see weapons. I want Rottolico's Matvee forming a block with me on the north end. Load all grenade launchers with CS. Start ranging the second Jersey barricade from the far end."

The Matvee raced into position on the bridge and joined the second vehicle. Williams hopped out of the Matvee and directed Corporal Graham into a twenty-degree angled position blocking the southbound lane. He ensured that the front of the vehicle had adequate clearance from the side of the bridge, to allow a quick evacuation. The second tactical vehicle backed up toward Graham's, leaving a five-foot gap between the rear bumpers. Satisfied that both vehicles could simultaneously escape, he ordered the marines to take positions behind the Matvees. He walked the line, verifying that they had loaded tear-gas grenades, borrowing one from Private First Class Leverone for his own launcher.

After replacing the high-explosive grenade in his own M320 grenade launcher, Williams climbed into his Matvee's turret and raised his head far enough to rest his binoculars on top of the armored protection kit. He scanned the crowd channeling past the first barricade. The group funneled into the left lane, which had been cleared of concrete obstructions by a large bulldozer last night. At two hundred feet, with rainsqualls whipping across the bridge, the image was still fuzzy.

"Does anyone see any weapons?" he said into his radio headset.

Negative reports filled Raider One Zero's designated intersquad channel.

Williams stood up in the turret and leaned over the side.

"Fire one CS grenade each, at right side of the bridge, near the exploded car!"

With the crowd massed in the left lane, he hoped to avoid skimming a solid metal object the size of a Red Bull can into the crowd at two hundred fifty feet per second. Hollow thumps filled the air, and Williams watched several dark objects arc toward the south end of the bridge. Williams knew the tear gas had limitations in this weather, which was why he ordered a large barrage to be fired in front of the mob. He hoped to discourage the civilians by giving them a diluted taste of what lay ahead if they continued. Most civilians had no experience with the painful, debilitating effects of tear gas and retreated immediately when exposed to a light dusting.

Three of the seven 40mm projectiles overshot the smoking car. One hit a piece of debris and ricocheted wildly into the crowd, dropping an adult to the pavement and exploding. A cloud of white gas erupted and covered half of the group before quickly dispersing in the high winds and rain. The CS gas blinded everyone it enveloped, forcing his or her eyes shut with an excruciatingly painful chemical reaction. It then went to work on their lungs and mucus membranes, causing each breath to feel like inhaling fire.

The sudden, violent denial of sight and oxygen caused a tragedy he couldn't have predicted. With the sole intent of escaping the tear gas, the mob dispersed in every direction. Staff Sergeant Williams watched in horror as a woman holding a child disappeared through a destroyed section of the bridge's concrete side barrier, followed by several others.

Williams climbed out of the turret and scrambled down the side of the vehicle, hitting the pavement in a dead sprint for the side barrier. He leaned over and counted six people flailing in the water. The current dragged them slowly away from the bridge, into the middle of the Charles River.

Fuck. I killed those people.

He wanted to help them, but a rescue was out of the question. His team didn't carry any equipment that could possibly help.

"Staff Sergeant! They're still coming!" yelled the marine in the gun turret of the second Matvee.

Williams lifted the binoculars and saw at least forty civilians continuing the march toward the north end of the bridge. Still no weapons. The woman hit by the errant 40mm projectile lay motionless on the pavement behind the mob. Small clusters of people materialized in the traffic circle beyond the intersection, headed toward the bridge. If he could break up this advance, they might be able to hold the bridge. He kneeled and aimed his M320 grenade launcher at a point directly in front of the group. The grenade exploded exactly where he intended, obscuring the front rank in a toxic chemical cloud. He watched as the pack worked together to keep the momentum moving forward. He'd fired as close to the crowd as possible without striking it—to little effect.

"Raider Base, this is Raider One Zero. CS ineffective unless fired directly into crowd, causing hard casualties. No weapons visible. Estimate forty-plus civilians on bridge, with more approaching."

"Stand by," said the radio operator.

"Reload tear gas!" he said, running back to his vehicle.

He had just settled into the turret when Raider Base responded over the battalion tactical net.

"One Zero. Use 40 mike mike grenades to repel crowd."

"What the fuck?" Williams muttered, keying the microphone. "Raider Base, this is One Zero. Say again. I heard use 40 mike mike grenades. Do you mean tear-gas grenades?"

An explosion thundered in the distance. Several seconds passed with no response.

"Raider Base, this is One Zero. Did you copy my last?"

"Stand by, One Zero."

"Copy. One Zero standing by."

The explosion was bad news. With the same situation simultaneously unfolding at ten bridges, he knew Raider Base was too busy to hold everyone's hands. He'd give the tear gas one more chance, then order One Zero's withdrawal. He wasn't going to kill or maim more civilians.

"One Zero, standby to fire CS grenades. Leverone, Graham, Rottolico, Howard will fire directly in front of the group. The rest of you will fire to the right. Know your limitations and adjust. I do not want to put another round directly into the group. Five second stand by. Four. Three.

"All Raider units, this is Patriot Actual. Withdraw from your positions immediately and proceed to assigned secondary staging areas for further orders. I say again, withdraw from your positions immediately and report to secondary staging area. Acknowledge, over."

The battalion commander had just given up the Charles River.

Williams activated the intersquad communications net. "One Zero, mount up. We're headed to Medford."

He dropped into the vehicle and squirmed into the front passenger seat as Graham and Leverone jumped in. He waited for his turn to acknowledge the order over the battalion tactical net, the process apparently stalled with Raider One Seven. One Seven covered the Anderson Memorial Bridge two miles downriver. He hoped the explosion had nothing to do with the delay in One Seven's report. The thought of a bomb detonating on the Anderson Memorial Bridge triggered an instinct. He glanced across the cabin, through Graham's thick driver-side window. A man sprinted ahead of the crowd.

"Contact, left!" he screamed, kicking his door open.

Williams sprinted to the rear corner of the M-ATV and sighted in on a runner carrying an oversized olive green backpack in his right hand. A short burst of automatic fire stopped the man just as he passed the bridge's final Jersey barrier. Gunfire erupted from the second vehicle, directed at the advancing crowd.

"Cease fire! Cease fire!" he yelled into his headset, pounding on the second Matvee's rear hatch.

A deep, rhythmic thundering replaced the M240's rapid chatter.

No. No. No!

Tracers from the third vehicle's .50-caliber machine gun streamed out of its concealed position along Greenbough Boulevard and connected with the top of the bridge's side barrier. Chunks of gray concrete exploded, followed by body parts. Williams ran toward the third vehicle, frantically waving his arms and screaming the cease-fire order. The firing stopped.

"Raider One Zero, this is Raider Base. You're transmitting over battalion tactical. Did you copy Patriot's last transmission?"

Williams checked the transmit switch attached to his Dragon Skin vest. He had broadcast the cease-fire order over the wrong net. His marines never heard him. He switched back to the intersquad channel.

"Graham, pick me up by Howie's Matvee," he said.

The armored vehicles lurched off the bridge and roared onto Greenbough Boulevard, speeding in his direction. Movement in the river drew his attention to three figures struggling against the current to reach the far side. A hundred feet downriver, Williams spotted the rest of them. Four bodies drifted in a loose pack toward Arsenal Street Bridge. One of them was half the size of the others.

Anger and resentment overwhelmed him, directed at everyone. The idea of blocking these bridges had been an obvious zero-sum game, matched and raised in its absurdity by the lunatics running the show south of the Charles River. Now what? Rinse and repeat at the next set of bridges north of Boston?

"Raider One, this is Raider Base. Radio check."

"Raider One acknowledges the withdrawal order. Proceeding to secondary staging area," he said, opening the Matvee door. "I think we're done with this mission," said Williams.

Leverone and Graham nodded their approval. He'd assigned them to his Matvee for a reason. Like him, they all had young families in the Springfield area.

Chapter 22

Harvard Yard
Cambridge, Massachusetts

Ed piled out of the side door to Stoughton Hall, stopping in the middle of the red brick walkway connecting the dormitories. A bullet snapped against the building façade several feet beyond him, causing him to flinch.

"Ed!" Alex said, waving him back into the building.

Alex reached the corner of Hollis Hall and edged along the concrete foundation until he stood behind the corporal. Ed held the heavy glass door open, beckoning him to follow.

"I have to take care of something. Get everyone into one room, close the door, and don't let anyone in until I get back!" Alex yelled.

Ed grimaced. "What the hell is going on?"

"Cambridge is falling. We can expect to leave here shortly," said Alex.

"Ryan's leg won't support any weight!" said Ed.

"We'll have to make do, unless I can secure a ride with the marines."

Two bullets ricocheted off the red brick wall a few feet above and in front of the corporal. Alex grabbed the marine and moved him off the wall. Bullets striking a hard surface at an angle had a tendency to ricochet and continue travelling several inches along the surface.

"Get off the wall, Corporal. One-foot minimum."

"Ooh-rah, sir! Private, stay off the walls!"

"I should be back in five minutes, Ed. Hold down the fort!"

"Where are you going?" yelled Ed.

"Out there with the good corporal."

135

The marine turned his head as a few more rounds struck the side of Hollis Hall.

"Don't get shot again," said Ed.

"Funny."

"Where are we going, sir?"

"To stop Private First Class O'Neil. Colonel Grady's orders. Someone detonated Bruckman's bomb remotely after Top and another marine brought it out of the perimeter—"

"Top's dead?"

"Most likely. Whoever triggered the bomb had to be close enough to see them carrying the pack. Bruckman made the medevac runs with O'Neil. They could have picked up the bomb from someone along their return route."

"Sir, I need to confirm this with the battalion commander," said Corporal Blake.

"Do whatever you need to do. I'm headed over to the vehicles before he sabotages my only ride out of here," said Alex, taking off across the wet brick.

Alex entered the Old Yard and made a rapid assessment of the situation. Red tracers streamed across the empty half of the common, bouncing off the rain-obscured dormitory buildings and sailing hundreds of feet in every direction. Extended staccato bursts from the northern side of the yard engaged unseen targets beyond Cambridge Street. The HESCO position directly ahead of him, partially obscured by the battalion's MTVRs, stood silent, patiently waiting for targets to appear beyond University and Thayer Halls.

Screams rippled through the northern yard as bullets tore through the civilian tents and ruffled tarps tied between the trees. Militia gunfire directed at the marines raked the refugee camp, igniting a panicked stampede for the safety of the battalion's inner perimeter. The corporal intending to follow him was swallowed in the pandemonium, pushed back into the gap between Stoughton and Hollis Halls. Alex was on his own.

He dashed from the cover of a thick tree trunk to the front of the closest MTVR, briefly detecting figures beyond the quiet machine-gun nest. Bullets snapped past and pummeled the side of the truck during the quick trip, clearly focused on stopping him. Alex dropped to the muddy grass and leaned his head a few inches beyond the truck's oversized tire.

A partial silhouette appeared from the far corner of Thayer Hall, directly adjacent to the HESCO barrier. Craning his head another inch yielded the complete picture. The two-man machine-gun crew lay crumpled on the ground behind the barricade; the M240G leaned against the inside of the cage, pointing skyward. Bullets smacked into the ground near Alex's head, forcing him to take cover. The battle for Harvard Yard depended on holding this machine-gun position.

Alex rolled to his right and aimed the HK416 down the first row between vehicle columns. *Clear.* He stepped onto the MTVR's running boards and opened the door, climbing into the driver's seat.

He locked the cabin doors before climbing into the top-mounted, armored gun turret. He located the joystick for the Battery Powered Motorized Traversing Unit and slewed the independently powered turret to the right until the M240B machine gun pointed at the gap between Thayer and University Halls. He pulled back on the charging handle and slid it forward, chambering a round. With the synthetic stock dug firmly into his shoulder, he sighted in on the gap between buildings, hoping it wasn't too late.

Four men dressed in civilian clothes, carrying rifles, swarmed the HESCO barricade, firing point blank into the unresponsive marines. Alex depressed the trigger before the Liberty Boys added a M240G machine gun to their arsenal. The gun rattled the turret mount, ejecting shells downward into the cabin, but stayed lined up on the tightly packed group of insurgents. The first extended burst punched more than thirty 7.62mm bullets through the group, at a devastating range of fifty yards, detonating a dense cloud of red mist over the HESCO barrier. The second burst shredded the remaining upright bodies, splattering the pavement with bloody entrails, chunks of flesh and skull matter.

Bullets pinged off the front armor plates surrounding Alex's M240B, drawing his attention to a woman aiming a rifle from a covered position behind the corner of Thayer Hall. With her rifle jammed against the corner, she fired round after round at the weapon that had just cut her militia team to pieces. Alex fired the machine gun, not bothering to aim directly at her silhouette. The wall did most of his work. The first steel projectiles struck the brick wall at 2800 feet per second and ricocheted toward the woman before the rest obliterated the brick. When Alex's gun fell silent, the woman stumbled forward in a cloud of masonry dust and dropped to her knees. Most of her face was gone.

Automatic fire erupted from Alex's immediate right, cracking overhead and pounding the turret's side armor. He dropped into the cabin, catching a glimpse of a helmet through the thick, bullet-resistant driver's-side window. He drew his pistol and turned the door handle, kicking the hatch open. The reinforced door slammed into the traitor's rifle, knocking it from his grip and smashing his nose. The marine stumbled backward into another MTVR, and Alex fired the remaining 9mm rounds from his P30 at the marine's legs, dropping him to the grass in an agonized heap.

"Get back on the 240! That fucker took out one of the MG's covering the south perimeter. You have a clear field of fire! I'll get the east gun back into action!" yelled a familiar voice from the front of the truck.

Alex climbed into the turret and spotted a lone marine racing toward the gore-streaked HESCO cage next to Thayer Hall. The young corporal lifted the machine gun and placed its bipod legs on the barricade. Once he started firing across the eastern yard, Alex rotated the turret right until he had a commanding view of the south commons. The machine-gun position located on the western side of the Old Yard stood quiet, another victim of O'Neil's rifle.

Two figures snaked along Matthews Hall, using the uneven façade to mask their approach from the remaining gun. In the confusion, they had managed to advance within fifty feet of the southern perimeter line. Alex lined up the front sight with the partially obscured figures and centered the notch in the rear sight ring, depressing the trigger. Bricks exploded, and one of the targets tumbled to the ground a few feet into the grass. Alex fired a long burst between the body and the wall, guessing what might happen next. The bullets caught the second insurgent trying to grab his partner, splattering the concrete foundation behind them.

Two marines sprinted from the corner of Harvard Hall to the downed machine-gun position beyond his gun sights. Alex scanned for threats beyond Matthews Hall, keeping the sector secure until they arrived and put the M240G back into action. One of the marines left the protection of the HESCO barrier and ran toward the battalion aid station with one of the wounded machine gunners in a fireman's carry. Alex dropped into the cabin and opened the door, grabbing his rifle from the passenger seat. He jumped down on O'Neil's legs, causing him to scream, and tossed the traitor's rifle well out of crawling distance.

"I'll get this devil dog to the aid station," he said, intercepting the marine in front of the MTVR. "You go back and get the other. I'll meet you on my way back."

The staff sergeant shook his head and pointed at the marine on the ground between the two rows of trucks. "Ramirez is dead. You grab that one."

Alex stared at O'Neil, who clutched both legs, crying out in pain.

"He killed the marines. I need you to dump that piece of shit in the battalion TOC and tell the colonel it's a special delivery from Alex Fletcher."

The staff sergeant's right hand drifted toward his rifle.

"You have to deliver him alive. He might have information critical to surviving this nightmare."

The staff sergeant transferred the unresponsive marine into Alex's care and jogged toward O'Neil.

"Alive, Staff Sergeant!" said Alex, not encouraged by the marine's glare.

Alex carried the marine across the abandoned sea of trampled tents, backpacks and moaning bodies, noticing that the incoming militia fire had slackened. With the bomb plot thwarted, and all of the battalion's machine guns back in action, the attack had been reduced to a lethal, medium-range engagement. Lethal for the militia. By the time Alex reached the steps of Stoughton Hall, the yard was quiet except for the panicked yelling inside the building. He fought his way through the packed hallway, jamming the side of his HK416 against those unwilling to move.

"Make a hole! Let's go! Out of the way!"

"Take it easy! My wife's ankle was sprained in that mess out there," barked a man in front of Alex, holding a woman up by the arm.

"This marine was shot standing guard over you," said Alex, shoving past the man.

Alex pushed his way through the door to the triage center and helped one of the corpsmen lower the unresponsive marine onto the floor. All of the cots were occupied by marines or civilians with grisly wounds. The events of the past five minutes had quickly filled the station to capacity. The corpsman worked on the wounded marine for several seconds, conducting a trauma assessment.

"Class IV!" he announced, turning to Alex. "Sorry."

Class IV was a death sentence. The corporal's wounds required treatment beyond the aid station's capabilities, and they couldn't move him to one of the local hospitals. Grady didn't have the personnel to spare. Simple life-sustaining measures like emergency airway breathing and plasma replacement only delayed the inevitable, consuming resources that could be used to stabilize other casualties. If the marine revived on his own, they'd sedate him with narcotics. Combat triage was a bitch. Without the prospect of immediate medical evacuation to a Level Three medical treatment facility, triage was an angry, merciless bitch.

Alex dug through the marine's ammunition pouches, filling his cargo pockets with spare rifle magazines. He had a feeling they faced a protracted siege at Harvard Yard that required an "all hands" effort. He eyeballed the corporal's Dragon Skin tactical vest, wishing he could get his hands on a few of them. The level IV body armor could stop a .30-caliber armor-piercing bullet, along with high-explosive fragmentation. Unfortunately, it didn't protect you from traitors that understood the vest's coverage limitations.

Angry shouting erupted from the hallway, causing Alex to level his rifle at the open doorway. The battalion surgeon glanced from the door to Alex and went back to work on a squirming woman held down by a blood-splattered corpsman. A mud-encrusted marine stepped inside the room a few moments later.

"Colonel Grady just issued the thirty-minute withdrawal order, sir. No civilians."

"We're gonna need some help getting these marines to the vehicles," said one of the corpsmen.

"We have our hands full with the perimeter. You'll have to make do," said the staff sergeant.

"Transition to palliative care for the civilians," said the battalion surgeon, addressing the corpsman.

The navy petty officer beside him paused for a second before nodding slowly. "Yes, sir."

The lieutenant commander tossed a bloodstained surgical instrument onto the wooden table and turned to face the marine. Placidly composed, his face projected a stolid "don't fuck with me" expression. He spoke deliberately.

"Tell Grady we require an escort. When the crowd finds out that we're abandoning civilian casualties, it's unlikely that we'll be able to reach the vehicles without creating more casualties—and I have no intention of doing that."

"Sir, the battalion has its hands fu—"

"Take a look around you, Staff Sergeant. I have thirteen critical casualties. Four marine, nine civilian. I just issued an order that killed the civilians and violated my Hippocratic Oath. Their families are waiting outside that door. Guess who gets to face that music?" He paused. "Tell Grady to get his head out of Homeland's ass and figure it out, or he can find a new battalion surgeon."

"Goddamn it, Commander. I don't have the personnel to—fuck it; we'll clear the building. Be ready to move in ten minutes," said the marine.

"We'll be ready in five. What's our destination?" said the naval officer.

"Melrose Armory."

"What's the status on a Level Three MTF?"

"Not at Melrose. They're still working on the delivery of equipment and personnel to Concord or New Londonderry. I'll be back in ten, sir," said the marine.

"Lock the door on your way out," said the battalion surgeon, glaring at Alex. "Reclassify that marine as Class II and stabilize him for transport."

"Class II, sir," answered the corpsman.

"If you don't get moving, gentlemen, I'll put you to work," said the surgeon.

Alex left with the marine, pulling the door shut behind him and checking that it was locked. The civilians jammed against them, asking questions that Alex ignored. He broke through the crowd and jogged down the long, dim hallway to the stairs, passing open dormitory rooms filled with injured civilians. He wondered if these people might be better off without the marines at this point.

His legs protested halfway up the first flight of stairs, forcing him to stop on the landing and lean against the wall. A wave of exhaustion and ache washed over him, no longer confined to his left shoulder. The dirty bandages covering the shotgun wound showed signs of blood seepage. He fought the urge to take a seat in the stairwell, knowing he probably wouldn't get up. His mission was to get Ryan and the Walkers into one of the MTVRs for the battalion's withdrawal. Melrose was located a few miles due east of the Middlesex Fells Reservation, and he had every intention of hitching a ride as far north as possible.

He shuffled up the remaining stairs and entered the deserted second-floor hallway. Ed Walker poked his head out of the fourth door on the right.

"Ed! Battalion is pulling out in thirty minutes! We need to be moving!"

"Shit," said Ed, stepping into the hallway with Alex's original rifle. "Is it safe out there?"

"Safer than staying here. They're headed up to a National Guard Armory in Melrose, which isn't far from your jeep. Two miles tops. Charlie can drive the Jeep to meet us if Grady won't take us directly," he said, patting Ed on the shoulder. "We're almost out of here, man."

"I'll feel better when we're loaded up on one of their trucks," said Ed.

"Me too. How's Chloe?" whispered Alex.

"Better. She's able to talk to Ryan, but she still won't look at him."

"She didn't do anything wrong, Ed. I've seen marines freeze up way worse than that. Things got really nasty right before the bridge, and it got worse from there. She's going to need some time and distance, neither of which are in ready supply right now. She'll be the same young woman soon enough. Trust me."

"I don't think any of us will be the same."

"My guess is she'll be fine. Let's get our shit together and secure some seats on the last ride out of Boston."

The stairwell door behind him burst open, causing him to whirl and level his rifle. A marine first lieutenant stepped into the hallway and froze at the sight of the rifle.

"Captain Fletcher?"

"Mr. Fletcher works just fine," said Alex, lowering the rifle.

"Colonel Grady instructed us to call you captain. He needs you in the TOC."

"I'm a little busy right now."

"Give him five minutes, sir."

"I need to secure transport out of here before the civilians figure out that the battalion is abandoning Harvard Yard."

"You don't have to worry about that, sir. I've been ordered to facilitate your group's evacuation. As soon as they're ready to move, I'll escort them to Harvard Hall."

Alex looked at Ed, who shrugged with a 'why not?' look on his face. If Grady was offering them a ride out, who was he to turn it down? Especially if that ride came in the form of a small-arms-impregnable vehicle and only cost him a few hours of scouring through the Liberty Boys' file data. The Captain Fletcher thing was a little annoying, but he could understand Grady's need to give him some perceived authority in light of the chaotic circumstances.

"Fair enough. Tell Grady I'll be right down," he said, turning to Ed. "Stay close to this marine."

"What's that saying you like to use?" Ed said. "Glued to his ass?"

"That'll work. Lieutenant? I want them in Harvard Hall ASAP."

"Yes, sir. I'll escort them down as soon as we get their shit together." He extended his rifle toward Ed. "Trade you."

"They're the same," protested Ed.

"But that one's mine."

"I give up trying to figure out how marines think," said Ed, swapping rifles.

Chapter 23

Harvard Yard
Cambridge, Massachusetts

Alex weaved through the chaotic mess of refugees that had enveloped the battalion TOC. The wounded sentry had been replaced with four marines that barely held the crowd back. As he approached the inner ring of civilians, one of the marines pushed through the angry mob and pulled him through.

"You're good to go, sir," said the sergeant, pointing toward the entrance flap.

He stepped inside to find most of the battalion's gear packed into reinforced, gray travel cases marked "Cat Five." Lieutenant Colonel Grady stood near the operations station, taking reports from the battalion staff huddled in front of communications gear. Grady saw him and rushed over.

"Attention in the TOC!" said Grady, halting all activity. "Based on the authority vested in my command by the Joint Department of Defense and Homeland Security Directive Five Bravo, I hereby commission Alex P. Fletcher as a provisional officer in the United States Marine Corps reserve, at an O-3 pay grade, effective immediately. Congratulations, Captain Fletcher. As you were, Marines!"

A few celebratory "ooh-rahs" echoed through the shelter, and the marines quickly went back to work, scrambling to pack up for their impending evacuation. Alex remained at attention in front of Grady, coming to his senses a few seconds later.

"What just happened?" he said loud enough to draw a few hurried stares from nearby marines.

"I need your expertise, Alex, and your judgment. Corporal Meyers told me what you did out there. You prevented a serious perimeter breach."

"You don't have to make me a captain, Sean. I'll gladly help you sort through the militia file in exchange for a ride up to Medford."

"The Liberty Boys aren't my problem anymore. We're heading well north of the city. I need your help with something else."

"My top priority is getting everyone back to Maine," stated Alex.

"That's exactly where I'm sending you. One of my infantry companies is based out of Brunswick, Maine. Alpha Company. I've had no contact with them since the EMP."

"Now it's an EMP?" said Alex.

Grady raised an eyebrow. "What else could it be? Homeland hasn't confirmed it, but I don't expect them to. We have enough problems without rumors of a foreign attack or invasion."

"Yeah. Reports of a U.S. government sponsored invasion seem to be keeping everyone occupied at the moment," quipped Alex.

"I'd like you to lead a convoy of two Matvees back to Maine and establish contact with Alpha Company. First stop in Maine is at your discretion," said Grady.

"You don't need me to babysit your marines, Sean. What's the catch?"

"If this shakes out like I suspect, southern Maine is about to become a significant focal point in the federal government's recovery plan. I assume you're familiar with Sanford?"

Alex nodded, wondering exactly how much Grady knew about his compound in Limerick. Was he included in Homeland's file?

"Sanford has a 5,000-foot runway and sits strategically in the center of southern Maine. Rivers naturally define most of the state's southern border, which makes it easy to seal off from the bulk of expected refugee traffic. One of the joint FEMA/Homeland Recovery plans establishes Maine as a Primary Recovery Zone. When that happens—"

"*If* it happens," said Alex.

"Oh, it's going to happen. The tsunami, coupled with the EMP, likely caused critical damage to Seabrook and Pilgrim nuclear plants. Think full reactor meltdown."

Alex shook his head slowly.

"The refugee situation along the coast is already a mess. Wait until everyone within a thirty-mile radius of each plant hits the road. Southern

Maine is about to become one of the most valuable pieces of real estate in New England. Guess what's in this file?" said Grady, lifting a green envelope.

"Recipes for radioactive clam chowder?"

"Funny. Profiles of militia groups in Maine. *When* Maine is declared a PRZ, every reserve and National Guard military unit in northern New England will be sent to southern Maine to assist in recovery efforts. Homeland assessed that local militia, and Mainers in general, will not respond favorably to the sudden influx."

"How does this relate to me being conscripted into the Marine Corps?"

"1st Battalion, 25th Marine Regiment will provide security within the Southern District," he said, pausing. "And I don't want a repeat of Boston. The Liberty Boys may or may not have responded to battalion outreach efforts. We'll never know, and that's my bad. I want you to study these files and come up with a game plan to approach the groups in Maine. You know them better than anyone. Ideally, we'd want to incorporate them into the overall recovery structure. Get them vested in—"

"The success of the military's plan to speed the recovery and return control of civil functions to the local government?" said Alex.

"You know the drill. Think of this as a favor," said Grady.

"Who's doing who the favor? I kind of lost track."

Grady started laughing. "We're knee deep in favors. I'm giving you an armed escort back to Maine and a provisional commission in the Marine Corps Reserve, which gives you one of these."

He reached into the green file folder and withdrew a light blue card with a magnetic strip on one side.

"Military ID card?"

"Better. Provisional Security ID. If you accept my offer, I'll activate the card and upload your information to Homeland's database. I doubt any of the law enforcement agencies or Guard units have the capacity to swipe this card, but they can confirm your identity and classification via satellite phone. Instructions are on the back of the card. You'll be classified as security/intelligence, which will give you unrestricted travel and facilities access."

"Travel will be restricted?"

"Only if we run into trouble, which is why I'm putting you to work on this before we arrive. I'll provide you with a secure satellite communications kit and a ruggedized laptop. You'll communicate directly with me, or in some cases my S-2. Can I count on your help, Captain Fletcher?" said Grady, extending a hand.

Alex weighed the situation. Taking the "deal" solved most of their immediate problems. It provided a heavily armed, government-sponsored escort to Maine, which, given the acutely hostile environment, seemed well worth the price. Long term, the military rank and security ID gave them an additional layer of protection and privilege, regardless of whether Grady's predictions came true. Priority medical treatment for his son's leg or, at the very least, access to medical supplies. Transportation. He envisioned safely returning to Durham Road to collect his family's personal effects. Pictures, scrapbooks—everything they'd left behind.

Grasping Lieutenant Colonel Grady's hand, he knew the job involved far more than relaxing at the Fletcher compound, reviewing files and typing up reports. A deep instinct told him to walk away, but he brushed it aside and shook Grady's hand, standing at attention immediately after.

"As you were, Captain Fletcher. Welcome *back* to the Marine Corps," he said, handing Alex the thick file folder. "The papers contain executive summaries of the data found on the flash drive. You'll set your own password when you plug the drive into the laptop. I'll activate your ID card and meet you in Harvard Hall to release the electronics gear. S-4 will set you up with some battle rattle, and off you go."

Grady considered him for a moment and nodded slowly. "Alex, I really appreciate you doing this—on top of everything you've already done for the battalion. Our reunion here was providence. I'm sure of it."

"If not, it's one hell of a coincidence."

"Too big for that. I'll see you in a few," said Grady, walking toward the operations table.

"Colonel Grady?"

The battalion commander looked back.

"Does Homeland have a file on me?"

"Do you really want to know the answer to that?"

"Yes, sir."

"Let's just say that activating your ID will be a one-click evolution," said Grady.

"I didn't give you my information yet."

"Like I said," he smiled and knelt next to a monitor displaying a map overlay of Boston.

"Captain Fletcher," said a young marine from the left side of the tent. "You can sneak out the back door. Head right to supply in Harvard Hall. Your family will be there shortly."

Nausea hit him in a sudden, quickly passing wave. Homeland Security's omnipresent hand felt suddenly oppressive. The government's level of knowledge about everything and everyone was disturbing. Alex wondered what might have happened if he had refused Grady's offer. Would Homeland have changed his status and paid him a visit in Limerick? Did their banter about *favors* have more meaning than Alex realized? Maybe the choice had never truly been his to make.

Providence, my ass.

Chapter 24

Middlesex Fells Reservation
Medford, Massachusetts

Even the windshield wipers worked surprisingly well in the Matvee. He'd imagined the same shitted-up, blurry ride he'd experienced with the venerable Humvee, but everything about the Oshkosh Defense's M-ATV sang the words "major improvement." Visibility through the tiny bullet-resistant side windows sucked, but that shortcoming was more than compensated for by the small arms and IED impregnable armor design. He felt secure inside the tactical vehicle and wished he could convince himself to leave the Jeep behind. He pointed at the granite sign marking the entrance to the reservation's lower parking lot.

"Take a left at that sign."

The corporal driving hit the tactical vehicle's siren, which sounded like a police car, while the marine in the turret yelled at the thick stream of refugees blocking the entrance. They had stopped using the horn twenty minutes ago. The trip had been stop and go most of the way from Harvard Square, rarely exceeding fifteen miles per hour. News of the battalion's evacuation spread quickly, prompting a large percentage of the civilian holdouts in the areas surrounding Cambridge to take flight. Perceptions ruled the day. The past twenty-four hours had been marked by frightening exchanges of distant and nearby gunfire. With the marines gone and the bridges unguarded, Cambridge was now vulnerable to the threat south of the Charles River.

The convoy cleared the crowd and slowed in front of the concrete underpass.

"We gonna clear that, Barry?" yelled the driver.

"Good to go!" said the turret gunner, sticking a thumbs-up through the hatch into the cabin.

The corporal eased the Matvee under the train trestle and roared forward toward the main parking lot. A few seconds later, Alex stopped him.

"I think this is it. Chandler Road."

"Not much of a road, sir," he said, pulling the left side of the vehicle as close to the trail marker as possible. "Confirmed. Chandler Road. Is there room to maneuver in there?"

"It's not worth getting one of your vehicles stuck. The Jeep is a half mile away. I can walk it," said Alex.

"Your guy can't drive it out, sir?"

"We moved a few downed trees across the path. It'll take two of us to move them," he said, glancing back at Ed in the rear driver's-side seat.

Rain poured through the open turret hatch, soaking both the rear passenger seats. Ed raised an eyebrow and shook his head. Ryan and Chloe sat jammed in the rear troop compartment.

"Kids, I'm headed out to grab Uncle Charlie and our Jeep. I'll be back in less than fifteen minutes."

Ryan nodded, still wiped out by the painkillers.

Chloe smiled wearily, looking a little more like the joyful, carefree young woman he remembered. The further they drove from Boston, the more she emerged from the mental barrier she'd constructed at the North Beacon Street Bridge. Alex knew from experience that she would never fully step out from behind the wall, but given enough time and compassionate support, few would notice. He returned the smile before activating his handheld radio.

"Durham One-Seven, this is Durham Three-Zero, over."

"This is One-Seven. Solid copy."

"I'm coming in on foot. Tactical vehicles won't fit down the trail. Meet me at the first obstacle with the Jeep. How copy?"

"Oh, man. What are we talking about here? M-ATV? Fully armored troop carrier variant? It's an M-ATV, right?" squawked the radio.

Alex winked at Ed. "I brought two of them, my friend," he said to Charlie.

Prolonged static filled the cabin.

"One Seven, you still there?"

"You're gonna make me drive the Jeep back, aren't you?"

"How could I deprive you of this? You've earned it. The marines will stick you in one of the turrets, if you don't mind the rain—and promise to keep your hands behind your back."

"Holy shit! Are you serious? In the turret? What kind of firepower are we talking? Is there somewhere to sit, or do I have to stand the whole time?"

"One Zero, we'll work out the details when we get back. I'm starting my trek into the reservation. See you in a few minutes. Out," said Alex, turning off the radio. "You think the staff sergeant will let him in one of the turrets?" he asked the corporal.

Corporal Gibson shrugged his shoulders. "It's up to you, Captain. He sounds a bit excitable."

"I don't know if that's a good idea, Alex. He'll drive the staff sergeant crazy," said Ed.

"I wasn't going to put him in the rear vehicle," said Alex.

"What? No wonder you're so excited to drive the Jeep. Forget it. It's my Jeep. I get to drive it to—"

"With all due respect, sir, one of the marines in the rear vehicle will drive the Jeep," said Corporal Gibson. "Based on the current conversation, I'd feel more comfortable if both of you were present when Durham One-Zero steps into the turret."

"Apparently, Corporal Gibson is far more savvy than he appears," said Alex. "Let the staff sergeant know we'll need one of his marines to drive the Jeep back to Maine."

"My pleasure, sir. Truly my pleasure."

PART IV

"Remember the Alamo"

Chapter 25

Limerick, Maine

An unfamiliar digital tone resonated from the kitchen. Kate walked out of the steamy dining room and looked around, unable to identify the source of the sound. Her stomach knotted. More visitors? Maybe today's law enforcement visit had been legitimate. She hesitated, not wanting to leave Emily alone in the surveillance hub. The two "deputies" had triggered one of the sensors on their way back to the road, but they had agreed to monitor the room 24/7. Tim Fletcher bolted through the sitting room doorway next to the intercom station and saw where Kate was headed.

"That's the satellite phone," he blurted. "It's charging next to the coffee maker."

"Is that the satphone?" yelled Samantha from the great room to Kate's left.

"Yes!"

She snatched the phone off the granite and read the display: "GOVT."

"Shit. It says government. Are they calling us with messages now?"

"Who cares?" Samantha said impatiently. "Pick it up. Either way it's important."

Everyone crowded around her as she pressed the green button. "Hello?"

"Honey? It's Alex."

Kate found herself unable to answer for a moment. "Yes," she uttered finally. "It's me. Is everyone all right?"

"The kids are fine. Ed and Charlie are fine. I'm a little beat up, but I'm fine too. We did it, honey. The kids are with me right now, and we're headed home."

155

She started nodding, tears streaming down her cheeks. "Everyone's fine. They're on the way home," she said to the group gathered around her.

Everyone cheered, and Amy ran over to the dining room. "They got the kids. Everyone made it!"

"Honey, I'll talk to you in a couple of minutes. Pass the phone to Chloe so her mom can talk to her. She's worried sick," said Kate, holding the phone out to Samantha.

"Like you weren't worried," said Sam, eagerly taking the phone and walking onto the deck.

Kate hugged Emily and was quickly joined by Amy. They held each other while the phone was passed around. Tim peeked out of the dining room, smiling and nodding.

"How far out are they?" he asked.

Linda handed the phone to one of her daughters. "Charlie said they were still in Medford. They're moving slowly because the streets are jammed with people. They're thinking it might take four to five hours to get back. After dark for sure."

"I hate to have them drive into Gelder Pond with those nutballs out there. They could be waiting near the entrance for all we know, with more fake cops," said Tim.

"Charlie said they're with a convoy of marines," said Linda.

"What?" said Kate, making her way toward the screen porch.

"I love you too, Dad," said Alyssa Walker, handing the phone out to Kate.

She took it. "Charlie?"

"Kate? Great to hear your voice. You won't believe what we went through. *Apocalypse*-fucking-*Now* kind of shit. Your boy will heal up nicely and probably get a Silver Star! Alex too."

"What do you mean? Charlie, can I talk to my son?"

"Oh sure, sorry. Here's the hero right now!"

In the background on the phone, she heard Charlie say, "I think I screwed up, Alex."

"Mom, I'm fine," Ryan slurred on the other end of the phone. "Mr. Thornton was being a little overdramatic."

"You don't sound fine. What happened?"

"They had to give me morphine. I got hit in the leg."

Kate found herself unable to breathe. "Hit by what?' she said, sitting down on one of the chairs.

"A bullet. We had some serious trouble getting out of Boston, but I'm totally fine. Mom? You there, Mom?"

"I'm just a little…it's so good to hear your voice. We didn't know how bad it would get down there. I can't tell you how happy I am," she said, sobbing in between sentences.

"Me too, Mom. I thought about the sailing trip and—"

"I know. I know, sweetie. We barely made it back," she said, rubbing her eyes.

"How is Chloe doing?"

"She's doing great, Mom. I went to her apartment right after the shockwave hit. The city got pretty weird."

"You can tell me all about it in a few hours. I don't think I'll be able to sleep tonight. Let me talk to your father. I love you very, very much, Ryan."

"I love you too, Mom. I can't wait to get back."

"Me either."

"Here's Dad."

Kate waited for her husband's voice to fill the digital void.

"Kate, Ryan is fine. I didn't want to worry you. We ran into some trouble."

"You're bringing him back in one piece. That's all that matters. I love you," she said, her voice cracking.

"I love you more, honey. I would have done anything to get him back."

"I know you. That's why I was so scared. I wasn't sure I'd get to see both of you again," she said.

"You almost didn't see either of us. The situation down here is beyond comprehension. If we had waited another day…we might not be having this conversation. We can talk about it over an ice-cold dirty vodka martini down by the pond. How was your trip out? Sounds like everyone made it fine."

"I think happy hour will have to wait. We ran into a bit of a problem," she said.

"Everyone's okay, right?"

"Everyone is fine, but we were stopped by two drunken idiots in Waterboro claiming to be part of a militia group. It didn't end well for them. They wanted us to give up our weapons or pay a toll to use the road."

"How much did they want?"

"They didn't want money," Kate stated.

"What did they want?"

"I think they had something a little more personal in mind."

"Shit. Sorry, hon. One of us should have gone with you."

"I don't think it would have made a difference. Actually, it might have confused the situation. We did fine. Linda shoots an AR better than you do," she said.

"That's good to know," he said, pausing. "So what's preventing happy hour?"

"We ditched the bikes and took their SUV. I didn't want any of their buddies running us down on Route 5. I think someone in Limerick recognized us. The York County Sheriff's Department paid us a visit this afternoon."

"At the compound?"

"They buzzed the intercom from the gate, but we ignored it."

"Good. Trust me, Kate; the Sheriff's Department isn't making house calls, and they're certainly not launching murder investigations. They're tied up at the borders."

"That's what we thought. The guys had badges, but no uniforms."

"Definitely not legitimate. York County sheriff's deputies shower in their uniforms," he said, "How were you able to see them?"

"With the cameras at the gate," said Kate. *How else?*

"Wait. How were the cameras working?"

"We installed the replacement cameras at the gate," said Kate.

"Those are wireless."

"Abby Walker's a little IT wizard. She replaced the router and sorted out all of the surveillance equipment. Amazingly, she can read your hieroglyphics. Good thing she was here. Your dad was scratching his head."

"Motion sensors?"

"That's how we knew the bullshit deputies took a stroll through the woods to check out the house. Everything is up and running according to your nearly indecipherable logbooks, including the backup solar array."

"How-how close did they come to the house?" he uttered.

"They stayed in the eastern tree line, opposite the garage."

"Why the hell would anyone announce themselves at the gate, then trespass for a look at the house?"

"They were probably looking for the car," said Kate.

"Please tell me the car isn't in the garage."

"The car isn't in the garage," she said.

"It is, isn't it?"

"We covered it with a tarp and boarded up the windows. Dead-bolted the garage door. We couldn't leave it sitting on Old Middle Road—not that it took them very long to find us."

"Did the guys in Waterboro mention which militia group they were with?"

"No, and they weren't dressed in any type of uniform. They might have been full of shit. They were certainly full of beer."

"Maybe, but we ran across something *Deliverance*-like near the New Hampshire border. We're talking sick and twisted stuff, involving a militia group. The crew we ran into was disturbingly organized."

"This doesn't sound like the same thing," said Kate.

"Did they have out-of-state plates?"

"Yeah, how did you know?"

The line stayed silent for a few seconds.

"Alex, you still there?"

"Did you set up the sensors like I indicated?" said Alex.

"Yes, but we still have a lot of gaps in the perimeter."

"What about the sandbags?"

"We filled about two hundred sandbags before the rain started, and we'll start up again once it stops."

"You should have enough to build two safe boxes. I'd get started on that immediately. You'll have to run the table saw."

"Linda and I decided to focus on the firing positions. We can't repel an attack from the safe boxes," she said, expecting some pushback.

"Good point. You're right. Sorry to pepper you with questions. It sounds like you have things under control."

"If you want to call it that. We had enough sandbags to build five positions. One in the master bedroom covering the eastern approach; two in the great room, giving us full coverage of the barn and lake approaches; one in the sitting room facing south; and the last one upstairs in the small bedroom. You can see most of the backyard and some of the barn from that one. If something goes down, we'll herd the non-shooters into the basement with your mother."

"Make sure you stack some spare mags at each position. I'm sure Dad is still walking around with one mag for his Vietnam-era relic," said Alex.

Kate detected an ease that she didn't expect.

"Linda duct-taped a spare to the stock, with a quick release tab. She's like MacGyver."

"Night vision?"

"Both of the spotting scopes are sitting on the kitchen island."

"Sounds like you have the situation under control," he said.

"We'll all feel a hell of a lot better with you guys inside the perimeter."

"I'm not sure how much of a difference we'll make. Ryan needs crutches to get around, Charlie's a refrigerator trip away from taking nitroglycerin pills, and I could probably use a wheelchair at this point. Ed and Chloe are the only fish you won't throw back in the water."

"I'm sure I can find a few uses for you, if you know what I mean," she teased.

"I could use a visit or two from the naughty nurse," he whispered.

"We left that costume back at the house," she said.

"That's what you think. Did you check the bottom of your rucksack?"

Kate burst into laughter, drawing a few stares from the kitchen. Alex's mom hovered near the kitchen table, stealing glances at the phone.

"I'm getting dirty looks from everyone, so stop. Charlie said you were with the marines. What's up with that?"

"Crazy story. One of my old platoon commanders is in charge of the reserve marine battalion based out of Fort Devens. He kind of saved my ass down here. I'm doing some intel analysis on militia groups for him. Stuff I can do on the couch. Got us an official escort back, which is a good thing. The borders are pretty much closed."

"Well, I'm glad everyone is safe. Let me put your mother on before she blows a gasket. I love you. Call again when you're in Limerick."

"Will do. Love you too, honey."

"Here's your mother," Kate said, nodding for Amy, who abandoned all pretense of staring at the floor and ran for the phone.

Chapter 26

Parsonsfield, Maine

Tyler Hatfield's eyes shifted left and right through swollen eyelids when he lifted his bloodied chin to look Eli in the face. His breathing, made difficult by several broken ribs, appeared erratic and forced. The young man slowly cleared his throat and spat a mouthful of blood onto the dirt floor.

"You spit on me again, I'll cut out your tongue and force feed it to your fiancée, along with a few other select cuts of meat."

"Eli, I swear I was gonna come find you as soon as I could. I was on my way over right after—"

"After what? By my watch you're about thirty-five hours late, unless the EMP fried your watch and—"

Hatfield started to respond, but Eli cut him off.

"And opened a black hole that suspended time!" said Eli, rushing up and pressing the flat side of a serrated knife against Hatfield's cheek.

"Don't you dare lie to me, Hatfield! You deserted my brother's unit in the middle of battle. Got them all killed!"

"No. No," he whimpered. "It wasn't like that. Everyone was dead already. I had to get to the church to bring back reinforcements."

"They found a radio in your car, deserter," said Eli, twisting the blade and pushing it a few centimeters into his left cheek.

Hatfield screamed and twisted in his bindings against the thick wooden post holding up the dilapidated barn's loft, succeeding only in digging the knife deeper into his face.

Eli put his face next to the man's head and hissed, "You better come clean, boy, or I'm gonna gut your bride right in front of you. Tell me everything, and don't leave out a single detail."

"Okay. I'm sorry, Eli. Please don't hurt Mary."

"That all depends on you," said Eli, slipping the knife out of his cheek. "Gentlemen, I got this from here," he said to the two uniformed militiamen standing next to the closed barn door. "Why don't you head up to the house and grab a few cold ones. It's hotter than hell in here. Good work bringing this piece of shit in. Hatfield and I are about to have a heart-to-heart talk. Send Mr. McCulver down in about ten minutes."

Eli wasn't sure why he was congratulating these two idiots. It took them a day and a half to track down Hatfield's fiancée's home address and follow the trail to her sister's house in Buxton, where Tyler and his disgustingly plain bitch were hiding. God help them if he couldn't find better recruits. When the hatch next to the barn door slammed shut, exposing tendrils of dusty sunlight, he wiped his knife on Hatfield's pants.

"Start talking."

Several minutes later, Eli stood up from a scratched, unfinished wooden stool.

"You're a hundred and ten percent sure they weren't some kind of Special Forces unit? Just regular guys you say?"

"More than that. A hundred and twenty percent."

"You can't have more than a hundred and ten percent, Tyler. Everybody knows that."

Hatfield continued pleading for his life, oblivious to Eli's facetious comment.

"I don't know how they got the jump on Jimmy, but by the time we got there, the whole west side of the bridge was throwing lead at us. Bikers, women, everyone had a gun. You stuck your head up; you got shot."

"Is that so?" said Eli.

"I swear it."

"I believe you, Tyler. Don't go anywhere. I'll be right back."

Eli checked Hatfield's bindings, ensuring that his wrists, ankles and neck were secured to the post. Confident that his captive couldn't execute an embarrassing escape, he scurried to the left rear corner of the barn and pulled on a thick metal ring attached to the floor. A trapdoor inched open, revealing a rectangle in the hard-packed floor. Holding onto the ring, he leaned back, and the door swung on its hinges, stopping perpendicular to the ground.

He pulled a flashlight out of a pouch on his belt and descended the stairs. At the bottom, he activated the light and shined it in Hatfield's fiancée's face. Her head twisted away from the powerful beam. A muffled scream barely penetrated the thick layers of silver duct tape.

"Damn, it's nice and cool down here," he said, grabbing her thick brown hair and yanking her upright.

"You've been a good girl so far; don't fuck it up now," he said, breathing against her face.

He meant what he said. The underground chamber had been designed as a hide site and couldn't be locked from the outside, which presented a risk. Then again, the trapdoor weighed at least fifty pounds, which made it nearly impossible to open with hands zip-tied behind your back. Eli had kind of hoped to hear some faint knocking at some point in the afternoon. The thought of her ramming that ugly face pointlessly against the impenetrable slab made him smile. Some people have the good sense to know when they're beat. Maybe she wasn't as dumb as she looked.

"Up the stairs. You try to run and I'll kill your sister, her family, your brother, parents—everyone. You got me?"

She nodded repeatedly, and he pushed her up into the musty barn.

"Now, I'm gonna take this tape off your mouth, but you don't say a word, or your husband-to-be is going to lose something important for your wedding night."

She nodded again, and he went to work on the tape, which proved to be difficult to remove without taking a little skin along with it. She cried and whimpered, but kept quiet.

"Very good girl."

"Mary, is that you?" said Hatfield, straining his head to see around the square beam.

"Shhhh," said Eli, walking her right behind him, keeping her out of view.

He slipped a combat knife out of a leather sheath attached to his belt and spun her around, jamming the seven-inch marine KA-BAR blade to the hilt inside her stomach. His stabbing hand mechanically forced the razor-sharp knife in and out of her abdomen several more times while his left hand pulled her tightly against him. She dropped to the ground without making a sound. He nudged her onto her side with his foot, surprised to see her eyes wide open, staring lifelessly at his legs.

"You were supposed to scream like a stuck pig!"

"Mary? *Mary!*"

"Mary's gone," he said, stepping in front of the post.

Hatfield's bloated, black and blue eyes fixated on Eli's gore-covered knife and hand.

"You promised not to kill her!" he managed to choke out.

"No, I promised not to gut her in front of you," Eli said, reversing the grip on the sticky knife handle. "I politely did it out of sight."

"Why?"

"Because you told her the wrong version of what happened at the bridge," he said.

"No. No. I told her the same thing I told you!"

Eli buried the knife in the right side of Hatfield's throat, stepping left to avoid the bulk of his pulsing arterial spray. "Exactly."

The side door sprang open, revealing a wiry, red-haired man holding a short-barreled AR. Eli's second in command stepped through the opening.

"Clean up in aisle one," said Eli.

"Shit. Both of them?" he said, closing the door and latching it behind him.

"Unfortunately, it came to that," said Eli, wiping his blade clean on Hatfield's pants. "We've got a problem."

"We can get these two buried where nobody'll find 'em," said McCulver.

"I'm not worried about that. Hatfield confirmed what I more or less already knew. He said a black Jeep Wrangler with Maine plates approached the eastern bridge at Milton Mills right before all hell broke loose. Possibly fired point blank into the three men. It's the only way they could have killed them that quickly. Jimmy reported the Jeep over the handheld and heightened their security posture, but the fight on the eastern bridge was over before it started. The guys on the western bridge loaded up and raced over, but were caught in the ambush. This turd never got out of his vehicle. Turned tail and left his buddies behind."

"Is it possible that he was captured and released? Maybe to lead the hit team here? Finding them seemed a little too easy," said McCulver.

"No. Those two have the combined brainpower of a trash bag, plus I worked them over hard enough to get the truth out. That's why she had to go," he said, pointing his knife at the bloody heap behind Hatfield. "I had to be sure."

"Should I get some guys to clean this up?"

"I want to leave Hatfield up for everyone to see. This is what happens to traitors."

"The girl?" said McCulver.

"String her up behind Hatfield. I want the message to be clear. You die with your brothers, or you die with your loved ones. The men we have now will form the essential core of the Maine Liberty Militia. They have to serve as an example for the new recruits. We need committed, disciplined patriots for the fight ahead."

"There's a balance, Eli. I trust your judgment with my life, but remember that there's a line. If you go too far over, you run the risk of losing people."

Spoken by anyone but McCulver, the words would have resulted in an immediate, excruciating death.

"That's why I keep you close by. To reel me in when my temper gets the best of me," he said, patting him on the shoulder. "You and I go way back."

"I think we might want to bury the woman and limit Hatfield's viewing to current members."

Eli fought the urge to pummel McCulver with the base of his knife. "All right. Let's get her out of here. When we're done, we need to start looking for that Jeep. Maine plates? Either the Special Forces team is using local government sympathizers, or they've been here all along."

"Like a sleeper cell?" said McCulver.

"I caught something about it on the internet. Part of that Wikileaks thing. Domestic Indigenous Response Team. It was stripped off the web almost as soon as it went up, which tells you something," lied Eli.

"DIRT?"

"Yeah. They ain't very creative with their acronyms."

Chapter 27

Limerick, Maine

Alex scanned the road ahead through the AN/PVS-15 Generation IV night vision goggles (NVG) generously provided by 1st Battalion's supply chief. He held them like binoculars, instead of attaching them to the ballistic helmet at his feet. Battalion supply offered him a full set of "battle rattle," which he had graciously accepted, despite the unlikelihood of ever using any of the gear. You could never predict when a second set of Dragon Skin armor might be useful.

"The turn is coming up on the right," said Alex, lowering the NVGs.

"Striker escort turning right in five-zero meters," said the driver into his headset.

"Almost home," Alex said to the pitch-black cabin behind him, eliciting a few exhausted comments.

The marines drove without lights for most of the trip beyond the New Hampshire/Maine border. Human traffic disappeared after the state police checkpoint, making it safe to open up the convoy's speed. All standard operating procedure designed to minimize the risk of ambush. What seemed a little overcautious thirty minutes ago, felt reasonable now that they were close to Gelder Pond. The less attention they drew to the compound, the better.

Alex dialed the ruggedized MSAT as the tactical vehicle eased right onto an inky stretch of packed-gravel road.

"Where are you?" said Kate.

"Turning into Gelder Pond. We should be at the gate in a minute or two. What's for dinner?"

"Dinner? Didn't they give you a few MREs for the trip?"

"Road snacks didn't make the list."

"Your mother just volunteered soup and sandwiches," said Kate. "We're trying to unload the fridge."

"Good thing my mom's on the scene."

"We'll see how long that attitude lasts. Meet you in front of the garage," she said.

"Make that the barn. I want to keep the Jeep out of sight. Love you."

"Love you too."

The Matvee veered left onto the eastern side of the Gelder Pond loop, eventually straightening on a rutted dirt road. A sudden jolt reminded Alex that not everything had improved since the Humvee.

"Looks like someone forgot to pave this side, sir," said the driver.

"You should see it in the winter. Not too much further on the right."

The convoy crept down the road while Alex peered through his binoculars at the forest fifty feet ahead of the vehicle, looking for a break in the underbrush.

"You can hit the lights now," said Alex.

"Roger, that," replied the driver, raising his NVGs. "Lead vehicle, lights on."

Alex squinted as the road and surrounding trees appeared. Insects flashed in front of the tactical vehicle, streaking like meteorites until they cleared the beams. The Matvee slowed in front of the gravel driveway.

"Looks like a tight fit, sir," said the marine.

"It's designed to accommodate a small tow truck, but I think we can call it good right here, Corporal. We'll toss all of the gear into the Jeep and take it from here."

"Embarrassed of your new friends, sir?"

"Never, but I have a little explaining to do, and the fewer armored vehicles they see, the better."

"Embarrassed," said the turret gunner.

"Hey, I'm trying to let you guys down easy."

"We'll get your gear transferred and hit the road."

A few minutes later, the Jeep sank on its axles, burdened by five adults and twice the volume of gear they had originally packed in Scarborough. Alex opened the lead Matvee's front passenger door and extended a hand across the seat.

"Thanks for letting Captain Chaos take a turn in the turret. Sorry about the noise."

"Don't apologize to me, sir. That was the longest thirty minutes of PFC Jackson's life," he said, shaking Alex's hand.

"Sorry, Jackson."

"No sweat, Captain. He looked happier than my daughter at Disney World!" yelled the marine through the roof hatch.

An uncomfortable, palpable silence enveloped the cabin as Jackson's statement synched. Alex suddenly felt like a complete asshole. They'd spent nearly five hours in the Matvee, and he'd been too self-focused and tired to ask about the marines' families. They'd become an instrument, their sole purpose to deliver him safely home to his family amidst jokes and stories about their experiences in the marines.

"Sorry," said Alex.

"Nobody wants to talk about it, sir. Trust me. We all signed up for this," said the corporal.

"Still," he said, pausing. "Has anyone been in contact with their families?"

"Negative, but Jackson lives thirty minutes away in Fitchburg. His wife knows to head over to Devens."

"What about you?"

"Worcester. CO said they've started to evacuate military families to Fort Devens. I'm hoping they send a truck down. Four guys from the battalion live in the area. Good chance, right?"

"I think so," Alex said. "Either way they'll be fine. Corporal Lianez, see you on the other side."

"Not if I see you first, sir."

Alex left the door open for the convoy's senior marine, Staff Sergeant Evans, who stood behind the vehicle.

"Staff Sergeant, good luck with the rest of your mission."

"Same to you, sir. Give us a holler if you run into trouble. Colonel said they shifted our tactical SATCOM network one hundred miles north of Boston. Use the ROTAC to reach us. We're programmed into the system as Striker Five-One."

"Which one is the ROTAC?"

"Small, green handheld. Ever use ROTAC before?"

"Sorry, I'm a bit of a dinosaur. Sincgars was new tech in my day," said Alex.

"Shit. I'll have to break this down Barney style for you."

"Thanks," said Alex, sarcastically.

"Menu button brings you 'channel select.' Scroll to Striker Five-One and press 'Lock.' Push to talk after that. It works over EMSS, typically in a regional DTCS configuration," said the staff sergeant.

Alex shrugged his shoulders.

"Satellite stuff. Two hundred fifty mile range. PFM. You just press the button like a walkie-talkie, sir."

"Pure fucking magic is right. What's my station identifier?"

"I have no idea, Captain, but we don't screen our calls."

"I'll let you roll. You're welcome to swing by on your way south, grab a warm meal. Just saying."

"I'll keep that in mind. Welcome aboard, sir," Evans said, coming to attention and snapping a salute.

"Carry on, Staff Sergeant."

Alex jogged onto the gravel road, using the light from Ed's Jeep to guide his way to the gate. He turned to watch the last Matvee rumble past the driveway entrance, headed south on Gelder Pond Lane. The dark shape disappeared, swallowed by the trees and thick brush. He turned his attention to the gate's touchpad and pressed "Intercom."

"No solicitors," said a male voice through the speaker.

"Looks like I'll have to take your grandson elsewhere."

"We'll have none of that. Coffee's brewing! Welcome home, son!"

Alex inserted his key into the metal box and turned it clockwise to manually override the fried circuits in the touchpad. The gate sprang into action, squeaking on its track. He heard his mother above several voices yelling in the background.

Chapter 28

Parsonsfield, Maine

Eli leaned forward to examine a piece of stained poster board that featured a crudely drawn map of the Fletcher compound. The ancient velvet sofa creaked with his movement, causing one of the men standing in the background to break the silence.

"Damn, Eli. This is close quarters, and I'm not ready for a chemical attack."

A few of the men stifled laughs, but quickly straightened up when he fired a murderous stare at the disheveled, overweight bald fuck that made a joke at his expense. The room was pushing ninety degrees from the late day sun, compounded by insufferable humidity. The ten men jammed onto folding chairs in the cramped living room of Eli's mobile home had turned the place into a cesspool of body odor and shit breath. He'd have held the meeting outside if the mosquitos and no-see-ums hadn't pushed him to his limit earlier. He was looking for an excuse to reinstall some discipline in his organization, and Dennis whoever-the-fuck looked like a good candidate to serve as an example.

"Dennis, I need to have a word with you outside."

"I'm sorry, Eli. It was just a joke. I wasn't thinking, and it just flew out of my mouth. Won't happen again. I promise. Seriously."

"You done?"

Dennis nodded with a pained look of regret and fear.

"Outside."

"Eli, I really—"

The handheld standing on the kitchen counter next to the sofa squawked. *"Liberty Actual, this is Recon One, over."*

Now he had Jeffrey Brown dicking up his job, too? There was no feasible way for Brown's radio to transmit eight and a half miles. They had been lucky to get a mile and a half out of these pieces of shit. Either Brown had abandoned his assigned reconnaissance position early, or every hill and tree between here and Limerick had been obliterated. His bet was on the former. Eli reached out and grabbed the radio, never taking his burning eyes off Dennis.

"Why are you out of position, Recon One?"

"I saw something that needed to be reported, sir."

"Unless you saw my nephew's SUV, you better get your ass back into position."

"You need to hear this, Eli. I just witnessed a small convoy of military vehicles pull into Gelder Pond."

"Say that again?" said Eli, noticing most of the men in the overcrowded room shift uncomfortably.

"Three vehicles approached from the west on Old Middle Road and turned into Gelder Pond. Two Matvees and one Jeep Wrangler running with no lights. I say again. They were running dark, with no headlights. The two military vehicles reappeared seven minutes later and turned east on Old Middle, heading toward Limerick."

Kevin McCulver, his second in command, stood from his chair next to the couch and mouthed, "Jeep?"

"Are you positive that you saw a Jeep Wrangler?" said Eli.

"Affirmative. I watched them through night vision. Four-door model. Driver only," echoed Brown.

"Could you determine the color?"

"Negative. Too dark without the night vision scope. Definitely Maine plates, though. Do you want me to head back to the OP?"

A sudden combination of exhilaration and uncertainty forced Eli to pause. He needed a moment to process the implications and spin them in his favor. On one hand, he was thrilled by the sudden appearance of a Jeep matching the description of the one used to ambush his brother, especially in the vicinity of the Gelder Pond compound. Connecting the Jeep to the assassination of his nephew should remove any shadow of a doubt that the attack on the compound was legitimate, not that he had heard or detected any opposition to the proposed operation. His men seemed eager to put their training to use, however he suggested.

On the other hand, he couldn't readily explain the presence of a military convoy, unless the story he had concocted had been some kind of subconscious manifestation of his true suspicions. He'd blurred the lines between fact and fiction so many times in the past three days, he could barely keep it straight himself. Shit, maybe he'd been right all along. He hoped that wasn't the case. A government-sponsored, false-flag operation of this magnitude meant they were headed for trouble. Federal trouble. Once he mopped up the Fletchers, or whoever they claimed to be, he needed to accelerate the recruitment and training of his army, on the off chance he had to lead a real fight against a government occupation.

"How many men do you have at the OP?"

"Three, including myself. I left two behind to keep an eye on the road," said Brown.

"Roger. Here's what we're gonna do. Head back and tell your two men to stay in position and observe the entrance to Gelder Pond for the rest of the night. Then drive straight to HQ. We have some decisions to make. How copy?"

"Solid copy. Turning around now, sir."

"Good work out there. Make sure those two don't fall asleep. We need to know if those military vehicles return. Did you see any mounted weapons?" said Eli.

"Affirmative. M240s."

"Roger. See you shortly. Out." Eli placed the radio on the counter and resumed his position on the couch. "Dennis?"

"Yes, sir!" he said, standing at attention.

"You pull shit like that again and I'll hang you from a tree. Copy?"

"Copy, sir."

Dennis's ghost-white face betrayed no emotion. He stared at the middle distance like a good soldier. One more slip-up and he'd join Hatfield in the barn.

"Mr. Brown's sighting can't be a coincidence. Hatfield confirmed that a black, four-door Jeep Wrangler participated in the attack at Milton Mills yesterday. My brother reported it over his radio, right before the ambush.

"Here are the facts. Gunmen in Waterboro kill two of our own and steal their car. Witnesses have them approaching the two sentries on bicycle and shooting them in cold blood. Very accurate shooting, I might add. We

EVENT HORIZON

tracked this group to an isolated property on the eastern side of Gelder Pond, complete with security gates, cameras and solar panels. This place is not your ordinary lake house.

"Now the same Jeep involved in the bridge ambush arrives at the Gelder Pond location—under heavy military escort? This confirms it. We have a government-sponsored Special Forces unit operating in southwestern Maine, and I think we just found one of their safe houses, if not their primary safe house. We need to hit this location with everything we've got. Break these sons of bitches and send the government a message. They are not welcome in southern Maine."

The men stared at him, paralyzed by his suggestion for a moment.

"Tonight?" said one of the squad leaders.

"Against Special Forces?" said another.

"Early morning at the latest," said Eli, standing up to establish some dominance over these quivering bitches.

"Mr. Russell? I heard that the shooters were women."

"What's your point?"

"Well, I didn't mean to imply—"

"I didn't ask to hear you chatter away like a bitch. If you're gonna interrupt me, you better have a fucking point. What's your point?"

"I guess it's that a bunch of women with guns doesn't sound like a Spec Ops team," the man blurted.

The room catapulted into silence, everyone avoiding eye contact with Eli.

"Why is everyone so quiet all of a sudden? Bertelson had the first sensible question of the evening. Thank you, Mr. Bertelson. Look, I don't believe we'll find a Special Forces team here. I've read about this kind of thing on Wikileaks. We're looking at a government sleeper cell put into place after the 2013 pandemic. They go about their lives until the government initiates the next false-flag crisis. You should have seen the place by Gelder's Pond. Definitely a self-sustaining compound—with electricity.

"They probably got caught off guard by the EMP like the rest of us. No way the government would risk any kind of advanced warning, even for the sleeper cell. The bridge attack occurred around the same time. I bet the men took the Jeep and sent the women on bikes so they didn't miss the ambush deadline. Brown and his crew probably witnessed one of the sleeper agents returning from a face-to-face meeting with Homeland and military commanders in New Hampshire. Whoever they delivered must be pretty damn important to rate a heavily armed escort. I say we take them out before they have time to execute the next phase of their plan."

"How many men?" asked McCulver.

"Three squads. Twelve each. Two to breach the house, one to provide suppressing fire. We'll put the thirty-cal into action for this one," said Eli.

"No shit! That's what I'm talking about," shouted another squad leader.

"Count my squad in," said Paul Hillebrand. "I have two men trained to use the thirty-cal."

"The job's yours," said Eli. "Any more volunteers?"

Everyone stood at once, vying for Eli's attention.

That's more like it.

He settled on Bertelson's squad, against his better judgment, but looking around the room, the crew-cut wearing, beady-eyed ex-army specialist was the only squad leader beyond Hillebrand that didn't look like a crumpled bag of dog shit. He stepped outside to cleanse his nostrils of their stench. Nobody followed except for Kevin McCulver, who joined him for a cigarette on the muddy gravel driveway. They walked until they were far out of earshot of the mobile home.

"I'm a little concerned about the military escort," said McCulver, lighting Eli's cigarette.

"A little? I nearly shit my pants when Brown passed that over the radio. I thought he was fucking with us."

"What does it mean?"

"For what?" said Eli. He took a deep drag and blew the smoke at the mosquitos above his head.

"For the operation. What if you're right about this group being linked to the military?"

"What if I'm right?" he said, taking a step back from McCulver.

"Eli, it's me you're talking to. I knew this whole government angle was a ruse when you first suggested Special Forces kidnapped one of our guys. I played along, because I don't care. I'm in this for the long haul."

Eli stared at him, wondering if he should cut his throat and bury him or continue listening. McCulver had skills essential to the cause and had been a loyal friend for years. It bought him another minute of oxygen.

"You have a chance to make something big of this, and I'll do whatever it takes to help. I just think we need to evaluate the possibility that this operation may not be a walk in the park. They might have left some men behind, especially if the guy in the Jeep is a high-value local."

"Kevin, I feel like I've learned more about you in the last three days than the past twenty years. I made the right call bringing you on board after Campbell gave you the boot."

"Harry doesn't like explosives," said McCulver.

"But I do, and I think we'll need one of your special projects for tomorrow. Just in case we run into more than we bargained for," Eli said. "I'm thinking the fifty pounder ought to do the job."

"That'll definitely do the job."

Chapter 29

Limerick, Maine

Alex collapsed onto the couch next to Kate, fighting to keep his eyes open. A warm shower and change of clothes had sapped him of any remaining energy. The soft glow of candles combined with the warm evening air threatened to knock him unconscious. All he wanted to do was close his eyes for a few hours, but the day wasn't finished. His mother held up a coffee mug from the kitchen.

"Alex? Anyone?"

"No, thanks, Mom," he said, reaching a sore arm out to grab a glass of water. He stopped halfway, not wanting to put the effort into leaning forward.

"Still that bad?" asked Ed, holding Samantha on the love seat across from them.

"I think I pulled my back out at some point, and my body just figured it out," said Alex.

"You want to borrow my back brace?" Charlie offered.

"Thanks, but I popped a thousand milligrams of ibuprofen. I should be set through tomorrow," said Alex. "I might need a kidney transplant, but that's the least of my problems. Why don't we get this rolling so we can get a few hours of sleep."

"You guys can sleep in as late as you want. We can handle the security watch," said Linda.

"I'll pitch in for that," said Charlie. "All I did was sleep next to the Jeep while they were getting shot up in Boston."

176

"Don't listen to SEAL Team Six over there. We wouldn't have made it out of Maine without him," Ed remarked.

"Exactly, which is why I wanted to have a talk before we shut down for the night," Alex said. "We might have a more serious problem on our hands than any of us can imagine. I was only aware of one organized militia group based out of southern Maine, the York County Readiness Brigade. There's a group out of Augusta that has members throughout the state, but they're mostly focused in central Maine. We ran into something highly organized and heavily armed at Milton Mills. Called themselves the Maine Liberty Militia. I've never heard of it, and my contact at the York County group never mentioned it either."

"What were they doing at the bridge?" Alex's dad asked from his recliner.

"Blocking traffic, both ways, unless you were willing to pay a toll. Sound familiar?"

The women shook their heads slowly, looks of disgust flashing around the room.

"Not the same kind of toll, though I wouldn't be surprised if that was involved too. The group guarding the bridge let you across if you gave up your car. We found a church a few miles back from the border. The parking lot contained at least a dozen out-of-state vehicles, mostly SUVs and minivans, which is why I suspect they are connected to the two that stopped you in Waterboro. A luxury SUV with Massachusetts plates?"

"Who in their right mind would give up a working car?" said Samantha.

"It's nearly impossible to get into Maine unless you can prove that you're a resident. They promised these people a ride to Sanford, where they could hopefully continue their journey unhampered by law enforcement. Apparently, the prospect of getting into Maine appeals to a lot of people. Based on what we saw spreading north from Boston, I can't say I blame them."

"It doesn't sound like a fair trade, but it's their choice," Amy, Alex's mom said. "How is this a problem for us?"

His parents were the only two that hadn't received some kind of a debriefing from one of them. Most of their time after arriving had been spent hosting, gleaning a few details here and there from mostly private conversations.

"They didn't drive anyone to Sanford. They executed the people in the forest behind the church," said Charlie.

"That's what we think," Ed said.

Not this again.

"We found piles of gear in the church. Footwear, camping gear, jackets, electronics. They stripped the people clean and walked them into the forest. We found several child-sized backpacks in one of the piles."

"I'm just saying," Ed cut in, "until someone verifies the bodies, we don't have proof. They might have shaken the people down for the rest of their stuff and sent them walking. Still a shitty deal…"

"You know that's not what was going on."

"I agree with Alex," said Charlie.

Ed sighed. "All I'm trying to say is that we've all jumped to conclusions, some more than others, and it has the potential to put us all in danger."

"Why are you saying this now?" said Alex, finding himself wide awake.

"Because I can finally think! I'm out of the pressure cooker. At least I thought I was. Now I have angry militia stalking the forests around me. What if they weren't executing women and children in the forest? What if we killed the guys at the bridge for no reason, and now we're at the top of their shit list?"

"I didn't kill the guys at the bridge because they were executing civilians. I killed them because they chose to stand in the way of rescuing my son and your daughter," he said, glaring at Ed.

Ed looked away for several moments while the words hung in the room.

"It was the right thing to do," admitted Ed, running his hands through his hair. "I'm just exhausted. I didn't think I'd come back to living in the Alamo. Sorry to get riled up like that. What do we need to do?"

"We'll all feel a little less punchy after some sleep. Unfortunately, it's not going to be as much as we all probably expected. I think we need to have at least half of the house up by 4:30 AM. Firing positions manned to cover 360 degrees, minimal lighting, all guns ready. We'll need to stay like that until at least eight. If they attack, it'll most likely come between those hours. If they make a move against us, they'll probably use the early morning darkness to move into position, then spring the attack when the sun comes up."

"What about the rest of the day?" Ed asked.

Alex knew his words might not go over very well with Ed, but he didn't want to sugarcoat the truth. If Ed was going to have a problem living at the compound, he needed to know sooner than later, so they could adjust the plan. He hated to think like this, but the threat they faced was organized, lethal and depraved. A bad combination in Alex's experience. They couldn't afford to make any assumptions about the commitment level of anyone in the group. He'd never ask his friend to leave, but if Ed's heart wasn't in the fight, Alex would craft the plan around him. Nothing personal. Purely pragmatic.

"We'll have to be extremely cautious. If we want to work outside, we'll have to carry weapons and post pickets in the tree line, just in case they avoid the sensors. I say we stay close to the house, so we can get inside if the sensors pick up a threat or one of the pickets spots something. We have to work the garden. That's non-negotiable. We're in peak harvest time."

"Sounds like prison. How long will we have to live like this?"

"Until the threat no longer exists. We might be able to get the marines to help us with that, given my new role. If this group represents a threat to the region's stability, I could make a strong case for destroying it."

"What exactly *is* your new role, Alex?" said his father, eyeing him skeptically.

Alex decided to give them the short version, skipping the part about Homeland's extensive data files. The information was classified anyway, "eyes only" for three members of Grady's battalion at this point, so he didn't feel guilty about concealing it.

"The commanding officer of the reserve marine battalion down in Boston is an old friend. He served as one of my platoon commanders in Iraq. We were both injured by the same RPG outside of An-Nasiriyah. The situation in Boston required the battalion to withdraw and reform north. He thinks they'll eventually pull back to Maine. Apparently, Maine has been designated as a priority recovery zone, which explains why we saw an immediate deployment of National Guard units at the major border crossing chokepoints. I guess they're worried about militia groups starting trouble inside the recovery zone. He asked me to apply my knowledge of the Maine-based groups and provide a threat assessment."

Kate looked at him sharply. "Does he want you to go out and visit these groups?"

"No. I can sit right here and do the work. They gave me a laptop, satellite communications gear, everything I need. It's an easy gig."

"Until it isn't," she said, "and the Marine Corps sends you wherever they think you're needed."

"It's a provisional appointment. I'm more like a consultant. Colonel Grady did this as a favor," said Alex.

"Sounds like you're the one doing him the favor," said Samantha.

"He gave us an armed escort back to Maine, and this position comes with benefits. I'm designated as a security/intelligence officer, which is one of the highest tiers," he said, digging the provisional security card out of his pocket. "It gives me one of these, which I—we— can use to access significant resources. Unrestricted travel, hospital privileges, no more worrying about walking around with firearms. I can authorize any of our families to enter the recovery zone. Probably get them picked up and delivered. From what Grady said, Maine is about to become one of the most sought-after pieces of real estate in New England. This is kind of our golden ticket."

"Sounds good to me," said Charlie, followed by a swig of coffee.

"I don't know," said Kate. "Sorry to be a downer about this, but the sooner you get that work done and cut yourself off from the marines, the better off we'll all be, especially if Maine becomes a recovery zone, or whatever it's called."

"Grady did this as a favor. It got us a ride back and a little insurance policy if things get wild. I'll finish up the threat assessment, designate the Maine Liberty Militia as a critical threat to recovery zone stability, and we'll all be able to sit back and relax while the marines hunt them down. Threat neutralized."

"I hope you're right, Alex," said Kate.

"I'm only right when you say I'm right," he said, eliciting a few stifled laughs. "Who's on watch at 4 AM?"

"I'm on from two until six with Alyssa," said Linda.

"All right. Why don't you wake Kate, me, Ed and Charlie at 4:15. Have some coffee going and some snacks available."

"I'll get up and make sure everything is ready," said Amy.

"You don't have to do that," countered Linda.

"I won't be able to sleep anyway."

"Thanks, Mom."

"Well, if she's up, I'm up," said Tim Fletcher.

"Sounds like that's all we'll need. I like the idea of having all of our rifles available during those hours. It might make sense to modify the nighttime watch rotation to keep our rifles off the ten to two in the morning shift. Set it up so that one is in the two to six, and the rest get a reasonable night's sleep in preparation for the dawn watch."

Everyone signaled agreement by mumbling or nodding. The group was exhausted and needed to power down. Waking up tomorrow morning was assured to be miserable for the recently returned Boston group.

"Well, if Charlie's too tired to talk, we should probably break this up and catch some sleep," he said.

Everyone rose in unison, eager to put the day behind them.

"Prep your tactical gear and weapons before you lay down. Trust me. You don't want to be fumbling around with that stuff at zero dark thirty. You should sleep in your clothes too. That includes sturdy footwear. I know that sounds crazy, but you'll be thankful if something happens. Plus I'm pretty sure most of us could fall asleep on a bed of nails tonight. See you in the morning."

A few minutes later, Kate caught Alex washing his face in the downstairs bathroom and closed the door.

"You again?"

"At least you're cleaned up this time," said Kate. "How is your shoulder?" She reached out and gently touched his right arm.

"Which one?"

"The bad one. You're lucky you didn't get more than a grazing," she said, standing behind him and pressing her body into his.

"Ryan bailed me out of that one. He did an amazing job out there. Everyone did."

"What happened with Chloe? She doesn't seem herself. She barely looked at Ryan all night."

"It's not a big deal," Alex said, leaning backward into her. "She froze on the bridge. Complete lock down. Ryan was hit carrying her to the other side on his back. She's a little embarrassed. That's all."

"She always seemed really sturdy. Nothing else happened?"

"Not that I'm aware of. She needs a little time and distance. We'll need to make sure Ryan respects that."

"And doesn't feel like he did anything wrong," she added. "Ed sounded like he might go for round two of the blame game. If he's doing that right to your face, who knows what he's saying to his kids behind closed doors?"

"Ed has a bad habit of second-guessing everyone's decisions and input. It's his quirk, and I've learned to work around it while keeping an ear open. He comes up with some good ideas. Ed functions best when he's taking orders or making his own decisions. He saved my bacon again."

"How many times did you need saving?"

"More than I'd care to admit. We'd be dead if it wasn't for the marines. For Colonel Grady."

"I didn't mean to come down hard on you for that. I'm just nervous about the whole arrangement."

"I'm a little nervous about it too. Ed's hit the nail on the head," said Alex.

"About what?"

"Being out of the pressure cooker long enough to think straight. Accepting Grady's offer sounded pretty damn good with the city falling apart around us and a Boston militia unit chasing me down."

"You pissed off more than one militia group?"

"Look who's talking," he said, drying his face with a towel.

"I guess we need to steer clear of any militia groups from now on," said Kate, kissing his neck.

Alex turned around and put his hands on Kate's lower back, pulling her into him while kissing her passionately. They grasped each other tightly, lowering their hands until Kate pulled back.

"There's a line outside of the door," she whispered into his ear.

"What?" he hissed. "Are you serious? And here I was thinking this might be the one place we could get some privacy."

"We kissed privacy goodbye when we invited two families to join us."

"Maybe they could all stay in the barn. They'd have a wood-burning stove."

She squeezed his bottom. "Or we'll just have to make better use of our 22 acres."

"Not until those crazies are gone," he said and kissed her. "See you up in our communal bedroom."

"It's not that bad."

"I know."

Chapter 30

Limerick, Maine

Alex opened his eyes to pitch darkness. He lay on his back next to Kate, which was the extent of his situational awareness. A cool, pine-scented breeze poured over his face, providing the first clue. He gently worked his left hand from under Kate's head, careful not to wake her up, and checked his watch. 4:11. His alarm had been set for 4:15. It took him a few seconds to figure out why. *Shit.* He could use about eight more hours of sleep—and some real painkillers. The ibuprofen had clearly worn off overnight.

He pushed his torso up with his left hand, finding himself sore along the left side of his body, extending through his abdomen. He felt like he had done a few hundred atomic sit-ups right before retiring for the night. For a moment, he seriously doubted his ability to get out of bed without help. He lay there, considering his next move, when the back of his right thigh cramped, locking him in position on the bed. He extended his leg and fought the muscle spasm for a few minutes, until he was sure it had passed.

Not a good start to the day.

Kate hadn't moved throughout the ordeal, presenting Alex's next challenge. How in the hell was he supposed to wake his wife up at 4:00 in the morning? She was a notoriously deep sleeper, barely functional until two cups of dark roast coursed through her system. He'd wait as long as possible before attempting to stir her.

Alex grabbed his flashlight from the nightstand and illuminated the room. Nobody shifted—of course. They had all inherited their mother's morning gene. He walked around the bed, careful not to step on Emily, who lay in a sleeping bag between the full-size bed and the elevated air mattress supporting Ryan. The room had been reconfigured to accommodate a sandbag position facing the backyard. The bed, normally under the backyard window, had been pushed across the room against the opposite interior walls. They had done the same in all of the rooms, hastily rearranging couches, beds, end tables and chairs to free up space for sheet metal and sandbags. Ed was right. The house had been transformed into the Alamo.

The door cracked; Charlie Thornton poked his face through the opening.

"I couldn't sleep either," he said. "Brought some coffee for your wife. Linda said she'd need it."

Alex stepped into the hallway and closed the door behind him, taking the hot mug in his hands. After a long sip, he patted Charlie on the shoulder.

"Thank you, Charlie."

"It was Linda's idea," he said, reaching for the Walkers' door.

"No," he said, stopping Charlie. "Thank you for everything. I mean it."

"That's what friends do for each other, man."

"Friends collect your mail while you're away on vacation. You've redefined my concept of the word. It's not a word I'll use lightly again. Thank you."

"Dude, you're evoking man tears, which means—"

"No. We are not going to—"

"It's time for that hug," he said, embracing Alex.

Alex held the coffee mug away and let it happen. Charlie had been angling for this "man hug" since he arrived at the reservation with the battalion's armed escort, and Alex had deprived him long enough, artfully dodging his outstretched arms.

"When the two of you are done hugging, I'd appreciate it if you started waking people up," said Linda from the bottom of the stairs.

"He started it," said Charlie.

"Thanks for the coffee. See you in a few," said Alex.

Twenty minutes later, everyone was in position, scattered throughout the dark house with coffee. Alex found himself back in his bedroom, facing the forest behind their house. He'd moved Ryan onto the bed and given Emily the air mattress, sliding it against the bed to make room in front of the sandbags for a folding chair. Through the open window, he scanned the length of the tree line with his night vision goggles, catching the occasional flicker of a lightning bug. Linda had a similar view on one of the computer monitors in the dining room, but the surveillance cameras couldn't penetrate the forest like his generation IV gear. He could detect a smoldering cigarette or the glow of a night vision scope eyepiece deep in the trees.

Kate watched the open expanse of land in front of the house through one of Alex's old night vision spotting scopes, a Russian knock-off with 2X magnification and an infrared illuminator. With nearly one hundred fifty feet of clearing separating the southern tree line from the house, a diligent watch through the scope could pick up any unusual activity. Their concern with the southern approach extended to the buckwheat and oat fields, which could be used by intruders to close the distance undetected.

The eastern woods extending from the road to the house fell under Charlie's watch. The Generation III night vision scope attached to his rifle gave him better magnification than Alex's goggles, along with the best chance of catching headlights if their attackers were foolish enough to use them on Gelder Pond Lane. Tim Fletcher covered the pond and left side of the barn with the second spotting scope while Ed kept Alex's mother company in the kitchen, waiting to relieve anyone that needed a break. With Linda in the dining room, they had all of the "fighting" adults on station to respond.

Their defense had a few flaws, the most glaring being their inability to effectively shoot at targets in the dark. Only Alex and Charlie had integrated night vision systems, leaving the rest to scan with their devices and shoot in the general direction of movement. Hardly ideal. The motion-activated lights mounted to each side of the house and barn had been fried by the EMP. He'd kept two spare lights in the basement surveillance kit, which Tim chose to install on the unobserved sides of the barn to give them some advance warning if anyone got past the motion sensors.

Later today, Alex would rig trip flares in the yard, fifteen feet from the house, and run the trip wires back to the house. A solid tug on the wire by one of Alex's lookouts would detonate a 35,000 candle power M49A1 trip flare, illuminating the open ground for a minute and providing silhouetted targets for shooters in the house. With any luck, they could engage attackers in the open at relatively close range. Failing that, the flares served as a powerful deterrent against repeated attempts to reach the house.

Beyond the limitations imposed by a nighttime battle on his motley crew, Alex's second-biggest concern was the barn. Located less than fifty feet from the house, it blocked their view of a significant portion of the clearing's northeast corner and represented the closest point of approach to the house. The militia team that scouted the property yesterday afternoon would have seen the barn and recognized the opportunities it presented. If the militia managed to break through one of the unobserved outer walls, they could open the barn door and rush the house. Ideally, they should place a team in the barn to stop this, but nobody besides himself had the training required to pull it off, and he'd be needed inside the house to keep this motley crew from falling apart under fire—if that was even possible.

Like any static defense, their best strategy was to inflict as many casualties as possible within the first few minutes of the attack, forcing a withdrawal. He also planned to put as many guns as possible into the first few salvos to give his attackers the impression that they had a large number of defenders. Marine Corps and army infantry schools teach combat leaders that they need a minimum three to one attacker to defender ratio when assaulting a fortified position. If he could throw enough bullets out of several windows at once, regardless of the caliber used, he might be able to pound some battlefield sense into the rush and stop its momentum.

If not, and they persisted, he wasn't sure how long he could keep his civilian army in the fight under sustained gunfire. He hoped they were all wrong, and the men scoping out the house decided they had stumbled onto the wrong location. However, he knew that was wishful thinking.

A light flashed deep in the woods. Possibly a lightning bug, possibly not. Alex stared at the spot for a few minutes, not seeing a repeated flash. He considered "lasing" the area for Charlie's magnified scope, but dismissed the idea. If the militia guys had some form of night vision gear, his IR laser would draw too much attention. He settled in for a long morning.

Chapter 31

Limerick, Maine

Eli Russell waved the three oncoming SUVs onto the path leaving Old Middle Road and followed them past a thick stand of trees after checking the road for observers. He was going to skin these idiots alive. They were an hour late arriving at the rally point and had failed to respond to his radio calls. He'd considered abandoning the attack altogether, fearful that they had been intercepted by the returning convoy. Larry Bertelson jumped out of the SUV and sprinted to Russell, saluting as he arrived.

"Eli, I'm sorry about the delay. One of my guys wanted to grab a different scope from his brother. It was supposed to be on the way, but it turned out to be further than I had thought. Ended up in Limington; then we kind of got lost. Something's wrong with my radio, too," he said, keeping his salute raised and his eyes lowered.

Bertelson had definitely been the wrong choice of squad leaders for the attack. Unfortunately, Eli's pickings were slim beyond Hillebrand's and Brown's squads, and he didn't have time to call in reinforcements. Like one of the head honchos said during the Iraq War, "You go to war with the army you have, not the army you want." Of course, he'd have to switch things around a bit. There was no way he could trust this turd to co-lead the primary breach team.

"Sergeant Hillebrand! Front and center!"

A lanky man with unruly red hair broke free from a group of nearby men and snapped to attention in front of Eli.

"Hillebrand reporting, sir!"

Eli saw the barely concealed look of contempt on Bertelson's face and decided if the man survived the attack, he'd turn him into his personal piñata.

"I'm switching your squad with Bertelson's. You'll be my right-hand man for the breach. Bertelson's squad will provide suppressing fire from the northern tree line. Bertelson, you have a crew that can work the thirty-cal?"

"Yes, sir," said Bertelson, pausing. "I can bring the attack in with you."

"Negative. Showing up late for beers is one thing; putting me an hour behind schedule on an operation is another. We'll talk about this later. Brief your troops and transfer the thirty-cal. We step off in five minutes. End of discussion. Oh, Bertelson?"

"Yes, sir?"

"Make sure you get a working radio from one of the guys staying at the rally point, if yours is still broken," Eli said, frowning.

The two men dashed off to take care of the last minute adjustment, making room for Eli's executive officer, Kevin McCulver.

"Surprised you didn't beat him over the head with his rifle."

"I wanted to, Kevin. I really wanted to, but we need everyone we've got for this. Keep a close eye on the road. If the convoy returns, I need an immediate heads-up. You know what to do after that."

"Roger," McCulver said, nodding hesitantly. "I wish we had a chance to test it. This is my first ammonium nitrate bomb."

"And it won't be your last. Not with Homeland digging its heels into the area. Just make sure the guys jump out far enough away. A fifty pounder will screw you up a long ways out. They need to roll that thing into the military convoy."

"Copy. We'll follow them in and set off the explosive as they dismount."

"Hopefully, it won't come to that," said Eli.

McCulver nodded. "I'll send the rest of the vehicles in when you give me the signal."

"Primary extract will be at the gate. I'll march the men up the driveway when we're finished. Secondary extract is where the two roads split, right where we enter the woods."

"Roger. Once the pickup vehicles depart, I'll park the car bomb on the turnoff from Old Middle in case we have late arriving guests."

"Sorry to sideline you like this, but I need someone I can trust running rear security. If this goes south for any reason, you're the only one with the tactical awareness to unfuck the situation for me," said Eli, gripping McCulver's shoulder.

"I got your back, Eli. I suspect this won't be our last operation."

"Not if the federal government plans on imposing martial law on us. Not by a long shot. If you'd do the honor of mustering the troops, I'd like to kick this off before I melt. Gonna be a scorcher today."

Eli stepped into the shade and repeated the plan in his head. He'd accompany Hillebrand's squad, followed closely by Bertelson's, into the forest past Gelder Pond Lane. They'd head slightly southwest until they reached the lake, where they'd turn left and follow the water's edge until his rangefinder put the dock at about a hundred yards. At this point, he'd lead them away from the shoreline at a forty-five-degree angle until they could see the clearing.

He'd send a few scouts from there to scan for sentries before moving Hillebrand's group to a position hidden from the house by the barn. Bertelson's crew would take positions in the tree line behind the house, and they'd all wait for Brown's squad to settle in along the eastern woods in the same location they had used to survey the compound yesterday.

Once everyone was in place, Bertelson's squad was to pour rounds into the back of the house while Eli breached the door attached to the screen porch with Hillebrand's squad. Brown's team would establish fire superiority on the eastern flank and rush to the garage, looking for a second breach point along the front of the house. With two squads converging on the target, radio coordination played a critical role in avoiding fratricide, a point he needed to reinforce.

With the three squads formed up in the woods, he stepped forward to address the troops.

"I'll keep this simple. Today we strike the first blow against tyranny. I don't expect this will stop the government's plan to take over York County, but it'll sure as hell make them think twice about putting boots on the ground," he said, amazed that he could conjure this stuff up on a whim.

The men muttered in agreement. He might have heard a "hell yeah."

"We show no mercy here—like they showed no mercy at the bridge. Kill everyone in the house, no matter what you find. They're harboring the enemy, and we need the word to spread. Harboring the enemy is the same as taking up arms against the people."

More cheers.

Man, this is fun.

"Squad leaders, keep your radio earpieces in at all times—and listen up. I don't like repeating orders, and we have two squads breaching the house from opposite ends. There's potential for a blue on blue engagement if we're not careful. Got it?"

The squad leaders verbally confirmed his warning.

"Rifles on safe until I give the order to open fire. You do not want to accidently discharge your weapon and compromise the operation. If you do, just put the barrel in your mouth and pull the trigger. Save me the effort. Keep your eyes open and your mouths shut. Are we ready to take the fight to the enemy?"

A mixed garble of chants erupted, most of which seemed to indicate they were ready.

"XO, make a note. Task Force Liberty crossed the line of departure at zero seven forty-two hours. Let's move out!"

Chapter 32

Limerick, Maine

Kate checked her watch and rubbed her face. This wasn't how she wanted to start the day, let alone every day until the Maine Liberty Militia was—how did Alex put it? Neutralized? She wondered what it might take to make that happen. Did Alex really have the power to list them as a critical threat and summon a giant boot to crush them? She'd thought his statement sounded heavy handed and Gestapo-like, especially on the heels of waving his magic badge around, but now she'd gladly help him craft the words required to prevent a continuous string of 4 AM wake ups.

After breakfast, she'd suggest that he draft his first report, emphasizing the immediate need to hunt down and stamp out this group, if they even existed. Maybe the kids had been full of shit, running their mouths after four too many tallboys. Maybe Alex had crossed paths with a one-off gang of opportunistic weekend warriors. Unfortunately, it didn't matter, just the off chance of an organized attack meant she'd continue to experience the pleasure of studying a grainy, light green image while mosquitos found their way through the open window with the sole purpose of distracting her free hand from her coffee mug.

She sighed, knowing full well that she'd never complain about any of this in front of the others. Leaders didn't whine, and they certainly didn't put up with whiners.

"A few mosquito bites are a small price to pay for vigilance," she mumbled, imitating Alex.

"What was that?" said Alex, appearing in the doorway to the sitting room.

"Nothing. Just muttering to myself. I ran out of coffee, and I can't think straight," she said.

"I think we're out of the attack window for now. We'll resume these positions about a half hour before sunset and keep them manned until 10 PM. Militarily, these are the most likely periods of time for an attack. I'll put up a bunch of trip flares around the house later today, which should give us an advantage if they hit us in the dark."

"Good, because, uh, I couldn't see shit out there. I might have spotted them moving toward the house, but that's about all I could do about it," she said, standing up from the folding chair.

"I know. Tonight and tomorrow morning, you'll have two wires running through the window, each attached to a flare. If you see something through the scope, pull the wire and fire."

"You're a poet. What's for breakfast?"

"Chef's surprise. The fridge isn't working right, so my mom is clearing out the perishables, which somehow includes frozen bacon."

"She likes bacon. How much coffee do we have left?"

"There's a fresh pot brewing."

"No, I mean like, in the grand scheme of things. Stockpiled."

"The good stuff?"

"I don't really care at this point."

"You might once you taste the instant stuff."

"How close are we to tapping into it?" she said, suddenly looking concerned.

"Six pounds."

"That's not good. Time to switch to instant. Most of them won't know the difference. I saw Charlie watering his coffee down with tap water. What's wrong with that man?"

Alex raised an eyebrow.

"I heard that!" said Charlie from the kitchen. "Not my fault you're serving this fancy mud stuff."

Kate picked up her backpack, which was filled with spare rifle magazines, and slung her rifle.

"You can leave that stuff here. No sense clunking it around the kitchen," he said, stepping out of the sitting room.

Kate didn't argue. She hated carrying the rifle around, constantly adjusting the sling and checking the safety—worried that it might discharge accidently. Logically, she knew it was impossible, even with a chambered round, but the very act of carrying a deadly weapon felt awkward. Alex handled his rifle like a natural extension of his body. Barely an afterthought. He shifted it out of the way with no apparent effort while navigating tight spaces or working. To her husband, the rifle was a simple tool. To her, it was a killing instrument to be feared and distrusted. She wondered if she'd ever adjust.

Most of the kids were at the kitchen table, including Ryan. She didn't see Chloe on the screened porch or in the great room. Hopefully, she was still sleeping and not avoiding Ryan. He was crazy about her.

"How's my big man doing?" she said, approaching the table.

"Feeling better, Mom. My leg is still throbbing, but the battalion surgeon said I could expect that for a week or so."

She hugged and kissed him in front of everyone, noticing a rifle slung over the back of his chair.

"No more battalion surgeons for you. I can take this," she said, grabbing the rifle barrel.

"That's all right, Mom. I feel better having it close," he said.

Alex walked in from the screened porch. "I'm gonna check the barn. Make sure it's empty of guests."

Linda spoke up from the great room. "It's clear, Alex. The camera was on the door all night. I didn't see anything on the time-elapsed feed."

"Call me paranoid. Mom, why aren't you wearing the vest?"

"I'm not wearing that thing around the house. I can barely move in it. If the shooting starts, you're going to stuff me in the basement anyway. Give it to someone on the front lines."

"Dad?"

"I can't make her do it," said Tim.

"Then you can wear it," replied Alex.

"Put it on one of the kids that isn't going into the cellar."

"I'm not going down there, by the way," stated Ethan Fletcher.

"Yes, you are," snapped Alex. "You're in charge of guarding the bulkhead door."

"That's kind of bogus," returned their nephew.

"The house has five points of access, not counting the windows. The bulkhead is the only point we can't adequately cover from any of the windows. It's a bigger responsibility than you realize."

"I guess," said Ethan, not looking convinced.

"If I can't get the old folks to wear these," he said, patting the vest hanging over the five-foot-by-five-foot sandbag emplacement next to the kitchen island, "we'll keep one vest in each of the safe boxes. If you leave the safe box, you put the vest on. Fair enough?"

"Alex, I think you should wear the vest. You'll be moving around the house," said Ed from the table on the porch.

"I'd feel better if one of the kids wore it," said Alex.

Logically, Ed was right, and Kate hoped he took him up on the offer. They had talked about the vests last night and agreed that they could become a point of contention if not handled properly. Each parent wanted his or her children in one of those vests. According to Alex, the Dragon Skin's silicon carbide ceramic plates could stop a .30-caliber armor-piercing bullet. Alex's solution was to give them to his parents, but even that could be interpreted as favoritism. With Ed making the suggestion, it gave Alex the opportunity to wear the vest without raising eyebrows.

"Take the vest, Alex," said Linda. "You're prone to getting shot."

"Thanks," he shot back at Linda.

She locked eyes with Alex for a moment and nodded imperceptibly, giving him permission to take the suggestion.

"Fair enough," said Alex, unclipping his tactical chest rig.

Kate helped him adjust the straps to accommodate the bulk of the body armor, which was configured with MOLLE points to carry the same ammunition pouches attached to Alex's rig.

"Would it be easier to transfer magazine pouches?" she said.

"We can do that later. I'll be right back," he said. "Mom, don't mix the bacon with the tofu."

Alex was in rare form, which was good to see. He'd looked utterly sapped of energy and enthusiasm last night.

"You want some company?" said Kate.

"It's probably better to keep everyone inside until later in the day," he said.

Rare form and all business.

Chapter 33

Limerick, Maine

Eli Russell crawled beneath the fallen tree, cursing under his breath. The half-mile walk through the woods had turned into a slog through decades-old untamed forest, slowing their progress to the point of madness. Soaked with sweat and covered in mud and dried pine needles, he stopped twenty feet beyond the rotten trunk to catch his breath and scan ahead. They'd kept the pond at least forty feet to their right, avoiding the shoreline bog that had swallowed a few boots and painted most of them dark brown at the beginning of their journey.

He raised a pair of compact binoculars and peered through the dense woodland, following the reflective waterline. The gray dock peeked through the trees at the far edge of his view. Maybe another fifty feet and they could turn southeast for the barn. The men had started to gather around him, breathing heavily and wiping their red faces. He'd have to impose more rigorous physical standards for his men. He had no delusions about turning this crowd of thirty- to forty-something weekend warriors into a Ranger battalion, but anything had to be better than the sorry sacks that slithered under the rotten log and spilled into the forest. One of the men pulled a pack of cigarettes from his left breast pocket and fished around in his pants for a lighter.

"What the fuck are you doing?" Eli whispered.

"I thought we were taking a break," the man replied.

Paul Hillebrand stepped out of the foliage next to the man and slapped him on the back of the head.

"Stow that shit and form a hasty 180-degree security perimeter facing south. You know the drill!" he hissed. "Sorry about that, Eli."

The men scattered and took up positions in front of the log while Bertelson's squad struggled through. His crew looked worse than Hillebrand's. Watching them drag the thirty-cal through the dirt and dead leaves under the log made him want to cut off Bertelson's head and shit down his neck. Of course, Bertelson was nowhere to be found, because he led from behind. As the gun crew emerged, Eli sprang forward and ripped the vintage thirty-two-pound M1919A6 Browning medium machine gun from their grip.

"Do you cocksuckers realize you just dragged a vintage weapon through the dirt?" he said, shaking soil and leaves off the weapon. "You better pray to God this thing works, because we don't have time to field strip and clean it. Lucky for you, this son of a bitch is tougher than the two of you combined. Bertelson?"

"Yes, sir," he heard from the other side of the downed trunk.

"Get over here and square your men away."

Bertelson shimmied under the tree and stood up, staring at the machine gun in Eli's hands.

"I want you out in front of your men. We don't lead from behind in my army. You might have seen them trying to fill the barrel with dirt," he said, throwing the weapon at the squad leader.

Surprisingly, Bertelson caught it without stumbling backward into the tree, which had been Eli's intention. He'd hoped to crack his face open on the barrel.

"I like to keep an eye on the squad. I can't do that with my back to the men," he said meekly.

"It's easier to pull a string than it is to push it. Get out in front, or I'll find someone who better understands the concept."

"Roger that, sir," Bertelson said, walking over to his shamed gun crew.

Eli pressed the transmit button on his radio. "Liberty Three, this is Liberty Actual. We've reached the turn. Commence your approach and hold at the tree line, over."

"This is Liberty Three, commencing approach," squawked his earpiece.

He strode to the front of the group and held up his right hand without looking behind him. Forming a knife hand, he chopped the air in front of him, waiting a few seconds before stepping forward. A quick glance behind showed that nobody had moved.

"On your feet. We're moving out," he barked as low as possible.

Tactically, the regular arm of the Maine Liberty Militia was a mess, better suited for basic military maneuvers, checkpoint duty and static defense. If he had known how bad they'd look after trudging for thirty minutes, he might have considered a different set of tactics. Too late now.

Without the distractions of modern-day life, things would change at the training compound. He'd put the few remaining members of Jimmy's old unit to work squaring them away. One way or the other, he'd whip this crew into a reasonable fighting force, if they didn't kill each other this morning. He gave the hand signal to move out again, guiding the column forward on an old game trail.

Chapter 34

Limerick, Maine

Alex flipped the light switch, darkening the barn before stepping into the glaring sun. The impeccable blue sky held no clouds to shield the blistering orb peering above the eastern tree line. The house usually gave up the fight around noon, reaching intolerable levels of heat and humidity by two. The late afternoon was a complete loss, as the house absorbed everything the sun had to offer and radiated the misery inward. The pond served as their only possible refuge at that point. With the militia threat looming on the horizon, he didn't foresee frolicking in the water. He almost wished for rain.

"Alex, we have movement along the northern perimeter, near the pond," said Linda's voice from the radio.

Alex locked the door from the inside and closed it. "Right along the pond?" he said, testing the door.

"Close enough. Something triggered the sensor facing inland from the waterline."

"I'll take a look. Get everyone in their positions. Someone needs to keep an eye on the sensors, in case we have another group out there," said Alex, heading toward the front of the barn.

"Let's just hope it was a deer," she said.

Alex jogged along the red siding and reached the far front corner, taking a knee. He dug into one of his tactical vest pockets and removed the handheld radio's earpiece, plugging it into the radio. Hollow static echoed through the earpiece as he leaned a few inches beyond the corner and peered through the ACOG scope. Bright green from direct sunlight, the trees and bushes along the edge of the clearing formed a dense screen. He'd have to get into the woods.

"Linda, I'm heading into the forest to take a closer look. I can't see anything from here. I'll be right back," said Alex.

"Are you sure that's a good idea?" asked Tim over the line.

Alex had forgotten that everyone was on the primary tactical frequency.

"Just a quick peek to give us something to work with. I'll be back in less than two minutes. Out."

End of discussion.

Alex crouched and sprinted toward the northwest corner of the clearing, cursing the entire two hundred feet. He'd taken a questionable risk running across flat, exposed ground, gambling on the enemy force's concentration in one location. If others had slipped the sensor net and taken positions closer to the clearing, his darting figure would have attracted immediate, lethal attention. Maybe they were waiting until he stopped. He hit the ground next to a thick raspberry bush and crawled through a low opening in the thorny mess. Lush raspberry bushes ringed the edges of the clearing, where they thrived in the sun. They also formed a low-budget barbed-wire fence along the closest points of approach to the house. Anyone sprinting out of the forest was in for a nasty surprise.

Squirming onto the soft pine-covered forest floor, he pressed forward several feet and rested behind a thick spruce. Alex listened for a few moments, hearing a snap in the distance, followed immediately by another. Unless the clumsiest, bumble-footed buck in all of southern Maine had just wandered onto his property, they had uninvited guests. Alex eased his head around the tree, taking in the scene. At first glance, the forest looked like it always did—a shadowy, multihued canvas of greens and browns, dominated by tall vertical lines and random thickets. Organically alive, but typically motionless on a macro scale. A few more seconds of observation explained the sensor hit. Darkened figures moved in a line, spaced at least ten feet apart, due east.

He brought the rifle to his shoulder and examined the lead man in the column. MultiCam-patterned uniform, tactical vest—no body armor, same boonie cap worn by the militia at the bridge, AR rifle with unmagnified optics.

Definitely not Bambi.

Their trajectory through the forest puzzled him. They couldn't be more than two hundred feet from the clearing, which meant they'd have seen the barn through the trees. The best approach to the house was from behind the barn, pretty much taking the same path he had travelled to arrive in the forest. The barn put them less than fifty feet from the house. A charge from the tree line directly behind the house forced them to cross triple that distance, while navigating a fenced vegetable garden.

What am I missing?

A quick scan through the line of militia soldiers showed them all moving in the same direction. Parallel to the tree line. The last man in the line didn't appear to be moving. Alex peered through the 4X scope, centering the red arrow on the man's chest.

"Shit," he muttered, slowly retracting his head and rifle behind the knotted trunk.

It hadn't been the last guy. He'd found himself staring at the point man for a second squad moving in his direction. The militia deployment made more sense now. One squad could take advantage of the blind spot created by the barn, while the other provided suppressing fire from the trees beyond the backyard. He started to low-crawl back to the edge of the forest, but stopped. Did it make sense to punch a few holes in the squad headed toward him and make a run for the barn? The thought was tempting, but he preferred not to attract the combined effort of two dozen rifles to his return trip across the clearing. The suppressor might keep his position concealed long enough to make it through the raspberry bushes, but he'd be fair game after that.

He wiggled under the thorns and turned left, lying along the edge of the grass and surveying the land behind the house and barn. It was clear.

"*Alex,*" said Kate through his earpiece, "*we have a second group approaching from the east. Sensors picked them up about a hundred feet from the driveway, which puts them about even with the house.*"

"Roger. I have two separate squads inbound from the north. One looks like it will line up along the trees behind the house. The other will probably use the barn to get as close to the house as possible. I want everyone with optics scanning the northern tree line for their positions. We'll give them a full magazine welcome to make them think twice. Everyone who can shoot needs to be in on this. Once the initial salvo is finished, everyone goes back to their assigned positions. If they can safely aim and shoot a weapon, they need to be doing that. We'll only get one shot at making a strong impression. I'm heading back, so don't shoot me. Have someone open the front door."

"Got it," she said.

He gripped the rifle's hand guard and took off in a crouch, half-expecting to hear the supersonic snap of incoming bullets. Careening past the corner of the barn, he didn't ease up on his legs until he reached the front of the house, where he slowed to a jog and struggled for breath. No matter how many miles he put into running, sprinting three hundred feet remained a thoroughly unpleasant experience. Fighting waves of nausea, he took the stairs on the porch in a single leap, pulling himself up by the railing. The front door swung inward, and Kate, who looked all business, took his hand and pulled him inside.

"Are you sure you want the kids involved?" said Kate.

"Yes," he insisted.

"Then you need to provide some hands-on guidance."

"Is Ryan upstairs?" he said, running through the foyer hallway.

"Charlie and Linda took him up," said Kate.

Alex surveyed the kitchen and great room area, not pleased by what he saw.

"Samantha, just for now, get everyone behind the safe box, not in it. When I give the signal, Daniel and Chloe will move next to their father by the sliding door and you'll stand behind the sink. At some point, very soon after that, I'll order everyone to start firing. I want you to empty the shotgun at the far right corner of the garage. Try to hit it as many times as possible."

"You want me to shoot the barn?"

"Yes. Tear the corner to pieces. I want the kids to shoot six rounds each into the forest, wherever their father is shooting, followed by the rest of their magazines at the barn. Got it guys?" he said, staring down Chloe and Daniel until they nodded.

"Sam, when you and the kids have emptied your weapons, get inside the safe box and reload. You should be safe behind the sandbags before they fire back. The rest of you will rapidly shoot half of your rifle magazine at visible targets in the trees, the other half at the corner. Targets of opportunity after that," he said, running to his father in the great room.

"Dad, I want you to focus on both sides of the barn and anything to the left. Use both of the firing positions in the great room. I expect them to send a guy to the left corner to fire into the house. Concentrate on putting that target out of action, even if you have to slow down your rate of fire and take well-aimed shots. Yell out if you need backup."

His next stop was Ed, who kneeled behind a wide sandbag wall built five feet back from the open side of the deck slider.

"You good with the AR?" said Alex.

"I prefer the Ruger, but I think we'll need the extra punch for this one."

"If it jams, switch to the Ruger and yell for me. I'll put the AR back into action. Here's what I need you to do. After the first full magazine salvo, reload and cover the right corner of the barn, along with anything you can identify in the tree line behind the house. Take three quick shots at each target, reacquire or find a new target and repeat. If men push forward from the barn, yell out a warning and focus your fire on them until they are no longer moving toward the house. Their most likely breach point is this sliding door. If it gets too crazy behind your sandbag position, fall back to the safe box," he said, slapping Ed on the shoulder. "Easy enough?"

"Easy enough."

"Kate, you'll start out in the bathroom. After the first mag, you focus on the tree line. If the eastern group makes a dash for the garage, you relocate to the sitting room. You'll have a clean line of sight down the front of the garage, which is their fastest way into the house. Cover that approach until Linda and Charlie get downstairs. Check?"

"Check," she said and jogged toward the mudroom.

"I'll be back down in a few moments. Pass anything you see over the radio." He opened the door to the basement and came face to face with his mother holding a 20-gauge shotgun.

"Mom, I need—"

"The kids stay down here. You have too many moving parts up there as it is. A few shaky pistols isn't going to make or break the day," she said.

"I love you, Mom. Keep the door locked and watch the bulkhead. Tell Emily I love her," he said, heading upstairs.

At the top of the staircase, he turned left and walked into their bedroom. Ryan sat on a folding chair, pressing his rifle's vertical fore grip against the top row of sandbags, scanning the tree line through the 4X ACOG scope. The Enhanced Combat Helmet issued to Alex by the marines protected his head. Over his clothes, he wore a loose-fitting tactical vest jammed with rifle magazines. Several magazines lay flat on top of the sandbag wall, ready for immediate use. More sat stacked on the floor beside the chair. With twenty magazines at his disposal, Ryan would fire the Marine Corps issued HK416A5, providing their only source of automatic gunfire. The weapon was essentially the same as the M27 Infantry Assault Rifle used by the Marine Corp as a squad support weapon, without the bipod and higher capacity magazines.

"You all right?"

"Ready for action," Ryan said, knocking on the helmet.

Alex kneeled next to the chair, putting a hand on Ryan's shoulder.

"You're the closest thing we have to an infantry support rifleman. I want you to burn through mags as quickly and accurately as you can. Short, controlled bursts. Spread the love around. You'll draw a lot of attention doing this, so keep your head as low as possible. If you see men coming from the barn, you engage that group until they stop. We can't let them get into the house. I love you, buddy," he said, letting go of his son.

"Love you too, Dad."

"Call out anything you see on the radio," he said.

"Got it."

"If the volume of incoming fire makes it impossible to engage targets without getting hit, you're done. You call it in and stay out of sight."

"How will I know when it gets to that point?"

"You'll know, and so will your mother. No heroics," he said, patting Ryan on the shoulder.

Alex hovered at the door, afraid to leave. When the shooting started, his son would attract hundreds of bullets. They'd reinforced the position with leftover sandbags, extending the sides to protect against shallow-angled fire and adding an additional layer facing the front. An extra piece of sheet metal had been brought up early this morning and wedged against the right side of the fortification to slow down projectiles heading into the side extension. This had been the only modification to Kate and Linda's work that Alex had directed.

Alex had initially considered taking this position, since it offered the best view of the exterior situation, but the rest of the adults quickly talked him out of it. They needed him to remain mobile, constantly assessing their defenses. Much to Kate's dismay, Ryan was the next best candidate for the key position. He didn't like placing his son here either, but Ryan could fire accurately at a sustained rate, which was exactly what they needed overlooking both the barn and backyard. When explaining this to Kate, he left out the part about their son becoming the primary target on the battlefield. He took one more look at his son and sped down the hallway toward the master bedroom.

The second safe box sat about five feet beyond the door to the vast room, in the middle of a windowless sitting area extending from the entrance to the master bathroom to a bay window facing south. Both of the Thorntons' daughters poked their heads above the sandbags. Linda turned her head from a pair of binoculars to acknowledge his entry before returning to the critical business of spotting the group approaching from the road. He noticed that she wore the Dragon Skin body armor. A good decision, given her job of holding the eastern line. She'd draw a considerable amount of gunfire trying to keep an entire squad at bay.

"That you, Alex?" said Charlie from the window facing the backyard in the northeast corner of the room.

Charlie must have changed as soon as the alarm was sounded. Loaded down with tactical gear, he sported Vietnam-era tiger-striped camouflage and his famous raccoon cap. Everyone had their combat rituals, ranging from specialized uniforms to a simple mantra spoken before firing the first round.

"Looks like the Thorntons have this side of the house locked down," Alex commented.

"Damn straight," uttered Linda.

"Charlie, move to the other side of the bed. Any rounds fired from the north at your current position run the risk of catching Linda in a crossfire. Better to draw fire away from the corner. She doesn't have much protection on her left side."

He passed Charlie in front of the bed, stopping him for a moment.

"Stay low. No crazy shit. Fire three to five rounds at each target. Shift immediately to the next. Work your way down the line. If someone makes a break for the house from the trees, stopping them becomes your only focus. I suspect they'll use the northern tree line for suppressing fire in support of the breaching team, so your job will mostly consist of staying alive and reducing their numbers. Be ready to help Linda if the squad in the eastern woods makes a run for the house. I suspect they will."

"Got it, brother," said Charlie with a fearful look.

"It's gonna be hell, but we'll hold them off," said Alex, believing the first part more than the second. "Linda, your job is pretty straightforward. Keep them in the woods as long as possible. If they have any tactical sense, they'll feel you out for a minute before giving it a go. They'll send a few into the open under heavy suppressing fire. You bury your head in that rifle and keep it flush against the sandbags. Don't remove your shooting glasses for any reason, or you'll be put out of action by flying debris. It will not be a pleasant experience. Keep firing and call Charlie. Charlie?"

"Yo!"

"When Linda calls you over, take the window next to hers and concentrate on the men in the open. With a bit of luck and good shooting, you'll take three to four attackers out of the equation. Keep your heads low. If it gets too intense to fire accurately, rapidly empty a few magazines using the Jihadi method and assess the situation."

"Jihadi method?" asked Linda.

"Yeah. You just fire over the sand bags without looking," he said, demonstrating with his own rifle. "If you can't stop them from reaching the house, call it out over the radio. Charlie returns to his original position, and you head downstairs to watch the eastern breach points. Good to go?" he said, slapping Linda on the back.

"Don't you have somewhere to be?" said Linda, keeping focused on the trees.

He heard a branch snap in the distance.

"Good luck," he whispered.

On his way out of the bedroom, he racked his brain for anything he missed. *ROTAC.* The battle would be finished by the time the marine detachment sent to Brunswick could arrive, but it was worth a try.

Chapter 35

EVENT +75:20

Limerick, Maine

Eli stared at the barn through the trees, catching part of the gray colonial beyond the far left corner of the red siding. He needed to lead the squad to the right, on a due south heading, so they could enter the clearing safe from observation and direct gunfire. Of course, this theory assumed that the people in the house didn't have a man situated in the barn. A half-opened window high up on the roofline stared down at him, casting serious doubt on an uninterrupted, near football field length jog across the grass. Like every window on the house, the screen was missing. He'd have to position at least two men to cover the window, bringing them across if the journey proved uneventful. His radio squawked.

"Liberty Actual, this is Liberty Three, we have a problem."

"What is it, Liberty Three?"

"Last man in my column found a motion detector thirty feet from our ingress route. I can see another one, maybe one hundred feet away in the opposite direction. Looks like a wireless model. I think they know we're coming."

Shit.

He'd counted on cameras and motion-activated lights, but a perimeter of motion sensors was overkill for a bunch of summer folk. This might be a game changer.

"Can you tell if they're live? The EMP should have killed all of this gear."

"Most of our unplugged electronics gear survived. We have to assume this stuff works. They probably caught us watching the place yesterday. Might explain the late night

military convoy. What if they offloaded a surprise? This whole thing could be a trap," said Brown.

Double shit.

It was definitely possible. Eli glanced nervously around the forest, wondering if he'd already passed a hidden gun emplacement. Was his second squad lining up on the tree line to be hit from both sides? No. This was crazy thinking. A couple of stupid bitches got the drop on his drunken nephew and stole his SUV. Hatfield's description of the bridge battle didn't include a Green Beret A-Team. Jimmy's group was hit by three guys in a Jeep during a blinding rainstorm, helped by a bunch of Hell's Angels. Only one guy was in the Jeep spotted by Brown. None of it added up to a clever ambush by Special Forces. But how the hell did he explain a military convoy driving around at night without lights? Maybe the driver was some rich out-of-stater with connections. Who the fuck knew—or cared? They'd give it a try.

"Liberty Three, continue your approach. Hang back about thirty feet from the clearing to avoid visual detection and wait for second squad to engage the house. Give it about thirty seconds, then execute your mission."

After a lengthy pause, Brown responded. *"Roger. Liberty Three will advise when in position."*

"See you inside the house, Liberty Three. Actual, out."

"I say we send a few guys across to test the waters. Just in case," said Hillebrand, from a crouched position buried inside a familiar-looking plant.

"Don't touch your eyes, Paul," said Eli. "You're sitting in poison ivy."

"Son of a bitch," said Hillebrand, stepping out of the bush and kneeling next to Eli.

"You got a few volunteers to send across?" said Eli.

"We don't have volunteers in my squad. Ain't a democracy. We'll get set up on the edge and send two out. If we get hit by automatic fire from the barn, I'd say we might have a problem."

"I agree. If we can get the whole squad to the barn, it won't matter who they dropped off last night. Not with the thirty-cal firing seven hundred rounds per minute into the house."

"Liberty Two, this is Liberty Actual."

"Send it, Actual."

He hated Bertelson's radio protocol. The kid just didn't get it. You didn't tell your commanding officer to "send it." You answer with your call sign and wait for orders. Why the fuck couldn't he get this right? Now wasn't the time to let this kind of shit bother him, so Eli took a deep breath and pressed his lips together before transmitting.

"Keep your squad thirty feet back from the clearing until I give you the order to move up. I don't want them spotting you too early. The only exception will be the machine-gun team. I want them up near the edge of the tree line in a concealed position, prepping the thirty-cal for action. Bipod extended, round in the chamber. When I give the order, they will push that barrel through the foliage and sweep each floor of the house with sustained fire. After that, I want them focused on the right-side windows and the sliding door. Fire until the gun is out of ammo. How copy?"

"Solid copy, Actual. I'll be on the gun myself, so we don't have any screw ups."

How the hell was he supposed to direct his squad sitting behind a thirty-caliber machine gun? Bertelson was getting under his skin.

"Negative, Liberty Three. I need you in a command and control position, not behind a machine gun."

"Uhhh, I made the decision when we split off. I sent Raymond to lead the column across. He's on the far left flank."

Eli peered through the forest at the skirmish line formed by Bertelson's squad, barely able to see past the fifth man in line. He didn't need this kind of shit right before the attack. His gut instinct told him to relieve Bertelson before he made a decision that botched the entire plan. He could send Hillebrand to take over Liberty Two while Eli spearheaded the house breach. Tactically, it made more sense for him to leave Hillebrand in place and take over Bertelson's squad, but then he'd miss all of the fun. There was no way Eli was going to pass up an opportunity to put his pistol grip shotgun into action. He'd just as soon miss his own son's wedding, if he had one.

"Never mind. Just make sure nobody starts firing until I give the order."

"Roger. I'll let you know when we're in position."

Several minutes later, Brown had arranged his squad underneath the impenetrable raspberry bushes, with orders to cover the second-story barn window. Satisfied that they were ready, he gave Eli the signal to send the two men who lay in the deep grass on the other side of the thorny barrier. Twenty seconds later, Eli exhaled gently as the two men safely reached the closest corner of the barn. So far, so good.

208

He sent two more across, just in case they were dealing with a well-disciplined gunner. If Eli was positioned in that window, he'd let the obvious Guinea pigs cross, waiting for a juicier target, but he'd never let more than two attackers across. Four men represented a full fire team—almost half of a standard squad, which was more than enough to do some serious damage in close proximity. When the second pair lined up against the barn siding, he knew the barn was empty. There was nothing he could do about the camera mounted next to the window, though he suspected it was disabled. Plugged into the grid, it would have been fried by the EMP.

"Liberty Two, this is Liberty Actual. Bring the thirty-cal up to a well-concealed position and get it ready. Advise when the gun is ready to fire."

"Copy all. Out."

Chapter 36

Limerick, Maine

Alex watched the rest of the militia squad disappear underneath the camera view. Thirteen heavily armed men had streamed across the grass, utilizing procedures that indicated a high degree of tactical awareness. The good news was that Striker Five-One had just turned north on Route 5 in Waterboro, on their way back to cash in on Alex's offer of a hot lunch. He just hoped his group could hold out long enough to benefit from Five-One's arrival.

"Striker Five-One, I have twenty-five plus confirmed bad guys converging on the house. Suspect one additional squad east of the house, in the trees. I have to go."

"Copy. We're 16.9 kilometers from your position. ETA nine minutes, seventeen seconds."

"Roger. Patriot Two Alpha, out." He triggered the handheld on his way out of the dining room. "We have thirteen men behind the barn. Call out any locations in the trees. The marines are on their way. Ten minutes out," he said and turned toward the great room. "Dad, scope in on the left side of the barn. I saw one of them break off and head in that direction. If he's partially obscured by the corner, shoot the corner. Your .308 will punch right through."

Alex kept moving.

"Ed, got anything?"

"Nothing."

"Does anyone have anything?" he said into his headset, surprised they hadn't picked up any movement.

"Affirmative. Two in the trees," said Ryan.

"Alex, I have a small cluster of guys, maybe two, directly back from the house," said Charlie.

"This is Linda. I'm all clear."

"I have movement!" yelled Kate from the mudroom.

"Let's get all shooters in position for the first volley," he said into the headset, running past Samantha, who immediately stood up and moved around the sandbags.

Kate stood in front of the toilet in the bathroom, a few feet back from the open window. The sandbag position in front of her had been built taller to accommodate the bathroom's shoulder-level privacy window, a consideration he hadn't built into his theoretical calculations. To compensate for the additional rise, they stripped sandbags from the side of the barrier and jammed them against an additional piece of sheet metal higher up against the wall.

"When the shooting starts, stick the barrel out of the window and lean into the bags. What do you have?"

"I see the two Charlie is talking about dead ahead, and I have a few more moving to the right and left, a little further back in the trees," she said, staring through the EOTech STS magnifier.

"Sounds like this is it," he muttered, aiming his rifle into the bushes directly across from the window.

"How bad is this going to get?" Kate asked.

Alex had no intention of telling her the truth. Twenty-five rifles pounding away at the north face of the house would be cataclysmic, likely wounding or killing a third of them within the first minute. If they didn't significantly reduce the number of militia rifles, they stood little chance of surviving. He needed her focused on killing, not dying.

"The marines are eight minutes out. We'll get through this. I love you, honey."

"I love you more," she said, leaning her shoulder into him.

Her gentle bump shifted his scope's field of vision, exposing a thick gun barrel supported by a bipod near the ground. He centered the scope's red reticle on the barrel and sharply inhaled. The tapered, perforated barrel was unmistakable. Alex reached for his handheld radio, raising the reticle a few inches above the Browning thirty-caliber machine-gun barrel.

"Fire on all targets! Fire on all targets!" he said and pressed the trigger.

❧

Larry Bertelson pushed at the thicket with gloved hands, trying to give his gunner a better field of view. He didn't think Cole could see the second floor through the tangled mess. Not that it mattered. There was little chance of elevating the barrel high enough to reach it. The bipod wasn't tall enough.

"Fucking thorns!" he hissed. "Can you see the whole house?"

"Good enough for government work," said Randy Cole, spitting out tobacco on his shoulder and pushing the machine gun further into the opening.

"Not too far or I won't be able to reload," said Bertelson.

His radio squelched.

"Say again. I did not copy your last. This thing is a piece of shit," he said, adjusting the earpiece.

"Liberty Two, this is Liberty Actual. Commence firing on the house."

"Roger. This is Liberty Two. Firing on the house at my command," he said, patting Cole on the upper arm. "Just got the order to fire, bitch. Holy shit, this is going to rock."

"You want me to start firing?" said Cole.

"Fuck yeah!" he said.

"Does this thing have a safety?"

"I didn't see one," said Bertelson, examining the metal along the right side of the machine gun. "Didn't you train on this gun?"

Bertelson knew how to load the ammunition belt through the tray, remembering the trick with the extractor. You had to manually lock the extractor forward before closing the feed tray cover. Beyond that, he'd never fired it, which was why he swapped out with Randy. Rank had its privileges.

"I fired it once at a demo, but it was already loaded."

"Pull the bolt back and light these fuckers up already."

Randy Cole yanked the charging handle back and slammed it forward, sighting in for a few seconds. He pulled the trigger and nothing happened. "Are you sure this thing doesn't have a safety?"

"What's the hold up, Liberty Two?" he heard through his earpiece.

Cole examined the left side of the gun and the area under the trigger.

"Pull the charging handle back again," Bertelson said. "Maybe it didn't chamber right."

"Liberty Two, this is Actual. What the fuck is the hold up?"

Bertelson leaned on his side to access the radio attached to the front of his chest rig. A wet crack stopped him from pressing the transmit button.

What the hell?

The raspberry bush above the gun barrel snapped and fell on the metal cylinder, immediately followed by a sickening wet splash. He twisted on his back to face Cole.

"Pull the Goddamn—"

The gunner's head rested against the machine gun's stock, still facing down the weapon's sights. Eyes wide open, he looked fine except for the two small holes punched through his forehead. A bright crimson mist settled over Cole's gore-covered legs. Bertelson felt a deep, driving pain in his upper back, paralyzing him in place as gunfire erupted. He never felt the rounds that ended his life.

Chapter 37

Limerick, Maine

Eli Russell leaned against the barn and waited for Liberty Two to respond. By now, he'd expected to hear the comforting chatter of a thirty-caliber machine gun pouring seven hundred .30-06 rounds per minute into the house. Right now, he'd settle for a few rounds from the dozen AR-15s spread among the trees.

Anything but dead silence!

"Liberty Two, this is Actual. What the fuck is the hold up?" he said, squeezing the handheld radio to the point he felt the plastic start to give.

Two sharp sounds, spaced less than a second apart, reached his ears. Hillebrand backed away from the corner, nearly knocking him over. Before Eli could regain his footing, the morning stillness erupted in a vicious barrage of gunfire. The corner of the barn exploded, spraying Hillebrand and Eli with splinters. Bullets ripped past the barn, forming a virtual wall of steel that caused all of the men to drop to the ground. Screams from the trees rose above the sustained roar of what had to be dozens of guns raking Bertelson's men.

Short bursts of unexpected automatic fire added to the chaos, driving the men, including Eli, to hug the ground even tighter. Bullets penetrated the siding several feet back from the edge of the barn at waist height, showering them with sharp pieces of broken cedar. The gravity of their situation weighed heavy as Eli fought through the paralyzing fear that glued him to the ground. They couldn't advance against that much firepower. Not with the thirty-caliber out of action—and he had to assume it was out of action. The first two shots came from a suppressed weapon, likely a sniper

214

targeting the machine-gun crew. He didn't see much of a choice at this point. They'd have to retreat unless one of Bertelson's men put the machine gun into action. Judging by the cries of agony rising above the gunfire, he wasn't hopeful. He reached for his handheld to order a retreat when he noticed that the gunfire had slackened to a few scattered shots emanating from the forest.

"They're reloading! Fire! Fire!" he screamed, flipping his rifle's selector switch to automatic and lunging past Hillebrand.

Eli slammed into the ground at the corner, firing into the house without aiming.

❧

Alex sprinted into the kitchen, stopping in front of the safe box. He waited for Samantha to clear his line of sight and fired the rest of his magazine well over Ed's head at the barn, hoping to penetrate the walls and drop a few of the militia on the other side.

"Nice job, Walkers!" he yelled, nodding at Samantha as she climbed over the sandbags.

His hands automatically reloaded the rifle while he assessed the situation. He didn't detect any return fire, which confirmed his panicked suspicion that the thirty-caliber machine gun had been the centerpiece of the militia's attack. Panicked for a reason. If the thirty-caliber had come into play, most of them would be lying in their own blood on the floor. Designed to stop standard .223 projectiles, the sandbag barriers would prove little match for the .30-06 bullet fired by the Browning machine gun. He'd spent more than half of a thirty-round magazine putting the gun out of action, killing its crew and disabling the ammunition box. The gun was still serviceable, but he doubted anyone would heave the bodies out of the way and try to work the gun.

A bullet snapped through the pine cabinet to the right of the kitchen window, knocking the door open and spilling blue ceramic fragments onto the granite counter. Another bullet hit the top of Ed's protective barricade, spraying dirt over his clumsy attempt to reload the AR. It was taking everyone too long to reload. Ryan's HK416A5 answered the sporadic crackle of distant small arms with a sustained burst of automatic fire. Alex caught movement beyond Ed, near the corner of the barn.

"Get down!" he screamed, kneeling behind the safe box.

Bullets sliced through the kitchen, shattering the sliding glass door and splintering the kitchen table. He felt the safe box shudder as projectiles hammered through the sheet metal, their energy absorbed by the tightly packed dirt. He dashed across the open area in front of the basement door in an attempt to reach his father, who was firing rapidly at the left side of the barn. He slid into the great room on the hardwood floor, bullets puncturing the wood behind before he reached Tim Fletcher in the corner. A quick glance through one of the western windows showed a figure stumbling into the open, a victim of the .308 bullets that his dad had fired through the barn. A single aimed shot from Tim's Vietnam-era relic collapsed the man on his stomach.

"Focus on this side!" he yelled and sighted in on the men exposed beyond the right corner of the barn.

The sandbags and windowsill in front of Alex exploded, driving him beneath the top of the barrier. He spit dirt and pieces of wood onto his vest as the fusillade continued. An extended burst of automatic fire from Ryan's position slowed the rate of incoming fire long enough for him to put his rifle into action. Jamming the vertical fore grip against the sandbags, he canted the rifle and fired rapidly using the forty-five-degree angled iron sights. Under heavy fire, the men disappeared behind the barn; one pulled lifelessly out of sight by his legs.

Tim squeezed beside him, seeking some of the cover provided by the barricade. Bullets snapped and ricocheted through the great room, clanging off the wood-burning stove behind them. Alex glanced around the half wall separating the great room from the kitchen and watched their once beautiful kitchen methodically disintegrate as the rate of fire increased.

Most of the cabinets sat wide open, knocked off their hinges to expose broken plates and glasses. The stainless-steel refrigerator's door panel was dented in three places around small holes. Water spewed out of the shattered chrome faucet. A bullet burst through the half wall a few inches left of his head, splitting the distance between Alex and his father. Unfazed by the fresh coating of drywall dust, Tim Fletcher kept shooting his M14 at the trees.

The men hidden in the woods were finding their rhythm after the intense fusillade that sent over two hundred rounds of various calibers into the trees without warning. Even if Alex's crew managed to kill or disable half of the men, six ARs in semi-proficient hands were capable of returning the same number of bullets twice every minute. Alex wiped his yellow-tinted shooting glasses with his sleeve and leaned into his father's ear.

"Ryan, what's your status?'

A few nervous seconds passed.

"Busy. They're finding good cover behind the trees."

"Copy. Keep your fire rate high. Out."

Another round of bullets sliced through the drywall, stinging his face.

"Watch the left side, in case they send another guy. I'll be right back," he said to his dad and slid along the floor to Ed's position. "What are you seeing?" he asked Ed, firing three rounds at a head peeking around the barn.

"Not much of anything! I can't see shit anymore!"

Alex scanned the tree line through his riflescope and saw the problem. The bright light reflecting off the leaves and bushes contrasted with the dark forest behind them, making it nearly impossible to find a well-concealed, man-sized target in the short period of time allowed by the incoming bullets. The effect was similar to looking inside a dark house on a sunny day. The militia had the opposite situation. Even though they couldn't easily identify individual targets within the house, the windows and doors made obvious targets for their rifles. Dirt sprayed Alex's face, followed by several thumps against the sandbag barrier.

"It's holding together nicely," he said, patting the sandbags.

"Doesn't matter. It's getting harder to put my head over the top to fire," said Ed.

Alex checked his watch. "The marines arrive in seven minutes."

"That's too long," said Ed, rising to fire.

Somewhere in the distance, the sound of a second battle rose to a crescendo, competing with the gunfire from the northern tree line.

"What the hell is that?" said Ed, ducking as dirt sprayed and the sandbags thumped.

The Thorntons.

❧

Linda leaned into the sandbags and sighted in on the first man to emerge from the trees. Bullets tore chunks out of the drywall around her

STEVEN KONKOLY

and fractured the windowsill, stinging her face as she fired three steady shots into the man, dropping him in the tall grass. *Alex wasn't bullshitting about needing these glasses.*

"I need some help here!" she said, catching Charlie's arrival in the adjacent window through her peripheral vision.

A bullet or splinter grazed her hat, followed immediately by a metallic crack that almost knocked the rifle out of her grip. She jammed the rifle into her shoulder and stared through the EOTech, quickly determining that the sight had been destroyed. Linda flipped the sight's quick-release lever and yanked it off the tactical rail, tossing it aside. She triggered the rear flip-up sight and leaned into the gun, finding a staggered column of four men sprinting toward the house. One of them fell to his knees, a geyser of bright red arterial spray erupting above his left clavicle as he pitched forward. She aligned her rifle's sights with the next uniformed target and pressed the trigger rapidly, tumbling the man into the patchy field.

She shifted her aim and started to press the trigger when a bullet exploded through one of the sandbags in front of her, striking her in the chest below the rifle and spinning her forty-five degrees to the right. Unable to breathe from the hammer strike to her ribs, she attempted to turn and face the window. Still kneeling, a second bullet caught her in the left ankle.

☙❧

Charlie fired at the magnified target in the middle of the green holographic circle and shifted the rifle to find another. He aimed at the next man's stomach, knowing that the bullet would arrive a fraction of a second later, when the man's upper torso crossed the bullet's path. Leading a target moving toward or away from the shooter at this short distance required minimal adjustment. He eased the trigger as the man tumbled out of view, leaving a splash of red in his field of vision.

Linda's stealing my targets!

He glanced at her in time to see the second round explode her ankle, knocking her to the floor before she disappeared in a shower of dirt and drywall.

"Linda!" he yelled, diving between the spilled sandbags and his wife.

He slung his rifle and grabbed the drag handle at the top of the Dragon Skin body armor. A second fusillade of heavy-caliber bullets ripped through the second barrier, obliterating the barrier he had just left.

Sweet Jesus!

He had to get Linda behind the safe box before another burst of that tore into the house. Bullets punctured the sheet metal in front of them, hissing past Charlie as he dragged his moaning wife to the safe box. He saw blonde hair poke above the sandbags.

"Stay down! Stay down!" he screamed.

He lifted Linda over the top of the sandbag wall and dumped her in, eliciting a scream of pain and anger. Foul words chased him out of the room.

"Shit, sorry, honey!" he said.

"Dad!" his daughters screamed. "What do we do?"

"Use the first aid kit to stop the bleeding. I have to go!"

Charlie sprinted out of the bedroom, fumbling for his radio.

"All units. All units. The eastern flank has collapsed. I say again, the eastern flank has collapsed. They're using a heavy-caliber rifle. Went right through the sandbags!"

"Copy," said someone.

Bullets splintered the doorframe leading to Ryan's position as Charlie approached the stairs, answered by a long burst of automatic fire from the kid's rifle. He hit the stairs hard, smashing his right hip into the handrail before descending. A few steps below him, a bullet fragmented the stair riser, followed by a second projectile three steps higher, a few inches to the right of his left leg. The splinters of wood stung his leg, but he felt lucky enough to smirk. A third round passed through the stairs, entering his left calf and erasing his smile. Blood splatted the white balusters, one of the last details he'd remember after tumbling down the rest of the staircase.

�����

Kate ducked below the sandbag barrier, thankful for the momentary reprieve, despite the sinister implications of Charlie's report. Incoming fire from the backyard had reached the point where she barely aimed the rifle before firing a few rounds and dropping back down. Bullets snapped by her head each time or exploded dirt in her face. Struggling to activate her radio, she observed the bathroom behind her for the first time. The sink was shattered, most of it lying in large pieces on the tile floor. A few jagged chunks remained in place, attached to the drain and the faucet. The top half of the mirror clung stubbornly to the white frame, the bottom sprinkled in shards among the white porcelain on the floor. The toilet next to her remained intact, perforated in at least four places. Water flowed out of the tank, spreading across the tile. The bowl cracked in half and dropped to the floor, causing her to scream. She pressed the radio transmit button.

"Copy," she said, leaning her head down to speak into the radio attached to the top of her vest.

"Fuck it," she muttered, using the rifle to push off the sandbags.

She stayed low, running out of the bathroom and colliding with Alex, who gave her a once-over and hugged her.

"You okay?" he said, letting go quickly and pulling her toward the sitting room.

"I'm fine," she said, shaking loose of his grip. "I got it."

"It's just us on the eastern side," said Alex.

"What about Charlie and Linda?"

Alex pointed through the French doors leading to the foyer and slid behind sandbags. "We're on our own! Flip down your magnifier. This is close-up work," he said, pulling her in tightly behind him.

Kate stared through the oddly intact matrix of glass panes at a body slumped on the floor at the bottom of the stairs. Charlie's fur hat was visible through the lower left pane. Her gaze drifted up the stairs. The few intact balusters were sprayed bright red.

"What about Linda?" she said, releasing the lock holding the magnifier in place and flipping it out of the way of the EOTech sight.

"She's not answering her radio," he said, raising his head high enough to see out of the window. "Here they come!"

Alex lifted his rifle over the sandbags and fired rapidly, spurring Kate to react. She braced her weapon against the right side of the barricade and fired into the men advancing along the garage bay doors, not bothering to aim through the holographic sight. Crimson stains bathed the white garage bay doors as the men dropped in a maelstrom of .223 caliber projectiles. Kate kept firing long after they had plunged to the gravel driveway in twisted heaps, stupefied by the sudden, devastating violence they had unleashed.

"Get back," he said, grabbing her vest.

Dirt exploded through the center of the barricade, knocking Alex backward. Kate felt a hard tug and fell with him.

Chapter 38

Limerick, Maine

Eli peeked around the corner at ground level, only able to hold his head there for a few seconds before splinters burrowed into his face and neck. He'd seen enough. Three shooters, positioned to pour rounds into the barn—only one of them making a persistent effort. The guy with the automatic. He could take care of that for the breach team. Staying low and squirming back along the concrete foundation toward Paul Hillebrand, bullets tore through the siding above him.

"I got a plan!" he shouted. "We'll use our two automatics to suppress the gun position above the porch and the one inside the door. You'll lead your squad into the house, firing as you go. Send one more guy around the other side to draw fire from any other shooters. Make sure he has a radio."

"Are you sure, Eli?"

Eli's earpiece activated.

"Liberty Actual, this is Liberty Three, commencing assault."

"Copy, Liberty Three. Let me know when you've reached the house."

"Roger."

Staccato gunfire erupted in the distance, rising in tempo as Eli smiled.

"Brown's squad is tearing up their eastern flank. They'll have to pull people away to stop him. It's now or never, Paul!" he said, putting a hand on his shoulder. "I want you moving on the house in thirty seconds. Get everyone briefed and ready."

"All right. Let's do this," said Hillebrand, rising to a crouch.

While Hillebrand briefed his men and picked one to fire from the opposite corner of the barn, Eli jogged over to the guy with the automatic rifle.

"What's your name, son?"

"Bob Harper," said the stocky, goateed soldier, resisting Eli's attempts to physically lift him off the ground.

"Get up, Harper. If I'm standing, you're standing."

Harper got up slowly, kneeling and looking nervously past Eli at the splintered siding.

"You and I have a critical job. Your squad leader is taking the rest of the squad forward while we suppress the house. Reload your weapon and listen up."

Twenty seconds later, Eli and Harper lay behind the foundation at the corner of the barn, side by side with Eli closest to the barn. Two spare rifles sat propped against the side of the barn within reach of the edge. Paul Hillebrand crouched directly behind Harper's feet, holding a radio and his rifle.

"*Liberty Actual, this is Liberty Three. We're approaching breach positions,*" his earpiece announced.

"Get moving!" Eli yelled over his shoulder, waiting for Hillebrand's voice over the radio.

"Liberty One. Breach. Breach. Breach!"

Eli scrambled to his feet and kneeled next to the corner, feeling Harper pressed against his left arm. He leaned left and braced his rifle against the fragmented corner, quickly finding the bullet-riddled gray siding through his red dot sight. He caught the top of a Kevlar helmet as the gunner swung the smoking barrel in his direction. Eli's rifle bucked against the chewed wood, unleashing a steady burst of automatic fire. He released the trigger, adjusted his aim and fired again, repeating this until the firing bolt locked back. At some point during the fusillade, the rifle above the porch disappeared.

He let the rifle drop in its sling and grabbed one of the spares, putting it into action against the gun position inside the sliding door. Hillebrand's squad stumbled across the patio, knocking plastic furniture out of the way to reach the porch. After several trigger pulls, he noticed his hands and the rifle were coated red. Eli looked over his shoulder to see Harper twitching on the ground, a thick stream of blood pumping out of his neck onto the barn. A bullet snapped through the wood next to his head, forcing him back. He'd have to watch this one from a distance. The sight of a Kevlar helmet in the house didn't bode well for Hillebrand's men.

≈≈≈

The intensity of fire directed at his sandbag position had taken on a surreal, almost nonthreatening quality for Ryan. Pressing his automatic rifle down into a small gap between sandbags and burying his face into the ACOG scope, he presented little target area for the attackers to hit. Combined with his Enhanced Combat Helmet, eighteen inches of packed dirt and reinforced sheet metal continued to protect him from the barrage of projectiles.

He fired a long burst at a target he'd been dueling with since the start of the attack; his only goal at this point was to prevent the man from taking aimed shots into the house. Several tightly spaced .223 bullets had done the trick so far. He loaded a new magazine and searched for fresh targets. Movement in his left-side peripheral field drew his attention, along with his point of aim, to the barn. He didn't have time to analyze the scene. Dirt exploded in his face, and he pressed the trigger, focused on the two men leaning around the corner. Ryan started to shift his aim to the group of men that appeared behind the shooters, but never lined up a shot. Bullets hissed and popped around his head, one striking his helmet and knocking him off the chair.

Unable to stand, he grabbed the flimsy chair and tried to pull himself upright, but didn't gain any momentum. Hell-bent on putting the gun back into action, Ryan crawled against the sandbags and used the rifle to prop himself high enough to reach his hand over the top of the sandbags. He dug his hand into the splintered wood and pulled his body up. A bullet grazed his hand, burning like fire, but he held tight and heaved himself upright. The men headed toward the house were here for one purpose, and it was his job to stop them. Cresting the top of the windowsill, another bullet hit his helmet, snapping his head sideways. He braced the rifle against the top of the sandbags and pushed up on his good leg, giving him a view directly below.

Three men lay sprawled across the patio, one of them sliding face down off one of the white Adirondack chairs, leaving a thick, dark red streak. He caught the last man in the group rushing up the wraparound stairs leading into the covered porch. Without thinking, he fired the entire magazine into the shingles directly below him.

Chapter 39

Limerick, Maine

Alex rolled on the hardwood floor, clutching his stomach. Unable to breathe from the 2,800-foot-per-second punch to his gut, he lay there mustering the will to move. He had to move. He tried to call out for Kate, but couldn't expel enough air to form words. The sandbags had been shredded; most of the dark brown dirt poured onto the floor below the window or scattered across the room. Judging by the fact that he was still alive, he guessed a .308 or similar caliber had done the damage. Anything less would have been stopped by the barrier, anything more would have penetrated the Dragon Skin armor.

"Alex!" a panicked voice cried.

A pair of hands pulled him onto his back, and he stared up at Kate. A wild look crossed her dirt-covered face. Blood streamed down her right earlobe onto her cheek.

"You're fine," she said, peeling his hands off his stomach. "Thank God."

"They're coming!" yelled Ed.

Bullets punctured the wall connected to the kitchen, spraying them with chunks of drywall and passing overhead with the telltale snaps signifying a near miss. He managed to flip into the prone position, lying next to Kate, who had flattened herself in response to the automatic gunfire. Alex glanced at the window behind them. They had to get out of this room. Kate read his look and started to crawl toward the demolished sandbags. He grabbed her arm and mouthed "no," surprised to hear faint words. Alex pulled her close and strained to speak.

"You have to stop them from getting in the mudroom," he croaked. "Not from here. Go fast."

She dragged him through the doorway into the kitchen, leaving him behind the safe box before disappearing into the mudroom amidst exploding drywall. His first instinct was to check on his dad. He didn't see the familiar eight point woodland camouflage Marine Corps cap poking up behind the half wall separating the two rooms. He turned his attention to the backyard, just in time to see Ed push the kitchen table out of the way and throw himself behind the kitchen counter, the sandbags behind him finally collapsing from the concentrated stream of gunfire fired from the patio. Beyond Ed's darting figure, he saw the screen porch door crash inward.

Forcing himself to react, Alex raised his rifle and fired at the first figure to enter the porch, knocking him back. A concentrated burst of fire struck the corner of the safe box, one round hitting the rifle's side-mounted Surefire light and shattering it. Knocked off target, Alex pressed the rifle into the sandbags and pressed the trigger, firing two hasty rounds into the patio before expending his magazine.

A mass of camouflaged men barreled through the patio door firing, giving him a fraction of a second to make a decision that might decide their fate: Draw his pistol or reload the rifle. Habit brought his hand to one of his rifle magazine pouches, but survival instinct kept it moving to his drop holster. He didn't have time to reload before they filled the room. Sticking the pistol past the obliterated sandbag corner, he tracked the first man entering the house and fired repeatedly, acknowledging the fact that he couldn't win this gunfight. Two men breached the shattered sliding door before clouds of drywall dust and bullets rained down on the men still bottlenecked on the porch.

Ryan is still in the fight!

A distant, crunching explosion rattled the house, triggering a long-forgotten, frightening memory. A few more shots locked the pistol slide back, once again presenting Alex with a miserably lopsided decision. Not much of a decision, really. One way or the other, he was as good as dead.

❧❦

227

Eli peeked around the corner and watched the remains of Hillebrand's squad charge up the porch stairs, firing at the sandbag wall just inside the house. A figure darted across the kitchen, barely visible through the shower of dirt and debris, seeking refuge from the onslaught. Scanning the far right ground-floor windows over his rifle, he didn't see the shooter using the M14. He was glad to see that gun out of commission. One pop from a .308—end of story. He turned in time to see men pile through the screen door, screaming and shooting like marauders. That should do it. Movement above the porch caught his attention, and the men inside the screened porch vanished in an explosive storm of gray drywall powder.

Frozen by the sudden, unexplained annihilation of Hillebrand's squad, the sound of automatic gunfire pounded Eli's ears and jarred him into action. He lifted his rifle barrel and sighted in on the man leaning out of the window. A booming explosion shook the ground and knocked the red dot off target as he pressed the trigger, sending a short burst of automatic fire high and to the right of the window. He didn't bother readjusting his aim for another burst, instead opting to dive behind the barn and take cover behind the foundation. Bullets ripped through the barn, some passing inches over his back. When the incoming fire stopped, he crawled back to the corner of the barn and grabbed his radio. The not-so-distant explosion meant one thing—time to "get the fuck out of Dodge."

❧

Ed crawled around the kitchen island, ignoring the shards of glass and ceramics that dug into his hands. He prayed that the sandbags protecting his family hadn't disintegrated under the intense gunfire. The floor shook from a boom, which he could barely differentiate from the rifle fire inside the house. Rounding the island on his hands and knees, he emerged in time to see Alex charge into the open and throw his pistol. Ed poked his head above the granite and witnessed one of the most bizarre moments of his life. The pistol bounced off the furthest man's head, knocking him off balance as he climbed over the toppled sandbags and dropping him to the floor.

Alex collided with the second intruder, knocking him against the kitchen table. The two men grappled and slammed each other against the column at the edge of the hall wall, stumbling toward the safe box. Movement on the floor caught Ed's eye; the man on the other side of the table kicked one of the chairs out of the way and grabbed the table. Having left his rifle behind, and carrying no other weapons, Ed felt helpless—until he saw the barrel of Samantha's shotgun sticking up behind the sandbags. He sprinted forward and reached inside, trying not to expose his body to the gunfire still penetrating the walls.

"Sam, I need the shotgun!"

"It's ready to fire!" screamed Samantha.

The warm barrel pressed into the palm of his hand, and he pulled it over the side. Without hesitating, he shouldered the 12-gauge shotgun and fired around the sandbags, knocking the man down. Ed racked the slide and fired under the table, shredding the table legs and splattering the half wall with bright red gore. Three additional 12-guage blasts stopped all movement and groaning on the porch.

One more.

He shifted the smoking barrel toward the desperate hand-to-hand battle on the floor fifteen feet away, but saw no way to shoot the insane-looking redhead without hitting Alex. Screw it. He'd put the gun right up against the dude's head. Ed stood up and was immediately struck in the right hip by a bullet passing through the kitchen cabinets.

🙖🙔

Alex grabbed both of the redheaded attacker's wrists, trying to keep him from grabbing the pistol on his thigh or the loaded rifle hanging across his chest. One fact became obvious as soon as they tumbled to the floor in the kitchen. He couldn't beat this guy in a straight grapple. Red was either too strong, or Alex was too tired. Either way, the result would be the same. Afraid to release either wrist, he held tight and tried to roll on top of his growling assailant. No good. Bullets continued to splinter the wooden trim and shatter plates in the kitchen as they lay on their sides kicking at each other.

His grip on the man's right hand slipped, changing the melee's dynamic in an instant. Red struck his face with the bottom of a closed fist and rolled on top of him, pinning him to the floor. Unable to effectively block the torrent of punches directed at his face, Alex pushed upward with his right hand and twisted his hips. The desperate attempt to turn the tables failed miserably, and Alex lost his grip on the man's left hand. It was time to even the odds.

Alex jammed his right hand under the rifles pressed between their chests and dug between Red's legs. Squeezing and twisting what he could grab through the camouflage trousers, Alex shot his head forward and caught Red's nose with his forehead. Red screamed and pushed away, breaking Alex's death grip on his crotch. Blood pouring from his nose, Red rose to one knee and fumbled for his pistol. Alex kicked his raised knee from the ground, knocking him backward against the basement door and scrambling after him.

Alex slammed him into the door, pinning both hands against the bullet-riddled wood. He was back where he started, holding both wrists in a struggle he couldn't win. Except this time Red held a semiautomatic pistol in his right hand. A quick knee to Red's already obliterated groin yielded nothing but a snarl and a return knee, which Alex deflected by turning his hip. Red's strength surged, pulling him toward the foyer hallway. He couldn't go to the floor again, not with a pistol in Red's hand. A bullet penetrated the door a few inches from their heads, causing their eyes to dart to the hole.

That might work.

"Mom! Shoot the door! Shoot the door!" he screamed past Red's left ear.

They shifted a few more inches toward the foyer opening.

"Shoot the fucking door, Mom!" he yelled and buried his head under Red's chin.

Two rapid blasts scattered slivers of wood over their shoulders. A sharp sting bit into his right shin as Red's body shuddered and weakened. Alex let go of Red's left wrist and wrenched the pistol free with both hands, throwing himself behind the safe box as bullets continued to plow through the house. Red stumbled a few feet away from the ragged, bloodstained door and dropped to his knees, staring blankly at the mass of dead men in front of him. His right hand drifted slowly to his rifle while his gaze shifted to Alex's outstretched, pistol-bearing hand.

Click.

The pistol dry-fired. Red's fingers seized the rifle's grip as Alex frantically racked the slide and checked the safety. A single hole appeared in Red's chest, followed by the distinctive boom of a .308 caliber rifle. Tim

Fletcher's M14 rifle barrel protruded from the bullet-peppered half wall. Red stumbled into the foyer and crashed face first into the wall, leaving a thick red trail as he slid to the floor beyond Ed Walker. His neighbor lay flat on his back, bloody hands pressed into his right hip. Ed looked at Alex and winked. Seeing Ed reminded him of Charlie, whom he'd last glimpsed at the bottom of the stairs.

"You okay, Dad?"

"I've been better!" responded Tim, peeking out far enough for Alex to see the brim of his camouflage hat.

"Ryan! Send your status."

"*I can't talk now,*" Ryan responded, followed by a long burst of automatic fire.

"I want you out of sight. The backyard threat has been neutralized," said Alex.

"*Copy.*"

"Kate, anything?"

The mudroom exploded in gunfire before she responded.

છ∕જી

"*We're almost in,*" Eli heard through the earpiece and scowled at the radio, like it was defective.

"Liberty Three, I don't think you appreciate what I just said. McCulver reported two armored tactical vehicles headed your way. That's too much firepower. Pull your men out and head to the secondary extract point."

"*They can't get the vehicles into the compound, Eli, and it'll take them at least five minutes to work their way through the trees. I have seven guys ready to breach. If the initial breach fails, I'll pull them out. If it succeeds, we'll sweep through the house and be on our way to the secondary extract before they reach the eastern tree line. We won't get another chance like this,*" said Brown.

Eli hesitated. Any chance to properly avenge his brother and nephew was worth losing a few more men. Regardless of the final outcome, he'd spin this in his favor, explaining the drastic loss of life as irrefutable evidence that the government had planted secret agents and platoon-sized kill teams among their own citizens. Of course, his militia had emerged victorious, and anyone that wanted proof could take a trip over to Gelder Pond to see for themselves, and be graciously shuttled over by one of his own members. Word about this attack would travel far and wide. The further, the better. He just needed to make sure he survived to spread the good word.

"Liberty Three, this is Liberty Actual. Proceed with the attack. Watch the second floor. You have one shooter armed with an automatic rifle in the northwest corner, out."

Chapter 40

Limerick, Maine

Kate fidgeted, trying to find a comfortable position lying on the wet tile floor. Razor-sharp pieces of porcelain and glass dug into her knees and thighs, rendering the effort pointless. At least the fragments hadn't spilled the entire length of the mudroom. Her elbows rested in a thick puddle spreading from the entryway into the mudroom. She braced her rifle against the doorframe, using the wooden trim to shield her left shoulder and part of her face from the mudroom door. This was the best she could do to protect herself, and judging by the holes in the trim above her head, it wasn't much. Oh yes—sandbags protected her feet.

Wonderful.

All compounded by the fact that she had no idea what had happened in the kitchen. She heard a ton of shooting, then nothing. Her radio was somewhere in the sitting room, detached from the earpiece that still dangled from her ear.

It didn't matter at this point. She had a job to do. A shadow slightly darkened the mudroom. Bullets penetrated the door, concentrated on the door handle and deadbolt, and slammed into the wooden shoe storage rack attached to the wall. A few bullets ricocheted in random directions, but most of them plowed into the same one-foot-by-one-foot section of the shoe rack, giving her a solid idea where the shooter was standing. She aimed at the wall to the left of the mudroom door and fired several projectiles through the drywall and siding, hearing a muffled scream from the porch outside.

A fusillade of bullets tore through the mudroom, forcing her to press into the doorframe as glass, drywall and wood showered the tile floor. A figure rushed in front of the obliterated door, rapidly firing his rifle at shoulder height into the mudroom. She placed the holographic sight's reticle center mass and fired as he kicked the door loose of the locking mechanisms. A second man wasted no time following the door in, proficiently advancing and firing through the mudroom door and kitchen entryway. Kate's rifle killed him before he realized his mistake.

A cylindrical gray object glanced off the door and bounced on the tile, rolling in her direction. She had no idea what it was and had no intention of finding out. All she knew was that when people threw things during a gunfight, they usually exploded. She scrambled to her feet and sprinted through the kitchen doorway, colliding with Alex.

☙❧

Four bullet holes dimpled the right side of the refrigerator in a tight pattern facing the mudroom. Alex depressed the bolt release button, chambering a round from a fresh magazine, and switched hands in anticipation of firing onto the porch from a position on the right side of the kitchen doorway. Kate burst through the opening as he arrived, knocking him into the broken pantry door, which crashed to the floor.

"Grenade!" she yelled, yanking him toward the sandbags.

Alex stumbled for a few steps, gaining his balance in time to push Kate over the side of the safe box onto the Walkers. As soon as she disappeared, he dove behind the sandbags and waited for the explosion. A few seconds later, when the house didn't shake, Alex clambered to the corner of the safe box and aimed at the mudroom. Thick, red smoke poured into the house, followed by several .223 bullets fired from men positioned around the doorframe. He fired back, but his hastily delivered bullets failed to find targets. Focused semiautomatic fire forced Alex to stick his rifle around the sandbag corner and fire Jihadi style for the first time in his life. He emptied the magazine and scurried around the other side of the box, reloading as he approached the far end of the kitchen island.

The mudroom fusillade continued as Alex checked the kitchen island corner and confirmed that he was screened from the mudroom doorway by the refrigerator. He edged along the stainless-steel appliance, plotting his next move. He could stick his rifle past the refrigerator and blast away, hoping that the shock of the unexpected, close-up blasts sparked a panicked retreat, but then what? Charge into the mudroom? He had no idea how many men waited for him. As the scarlet smoke intensified, he decided to wait for the marines—if the enormous detonation he'd heard a few minutes ago hadn't taken them out of the picture. He just hoped Kate and the Walkers stayed in the safe box. A dark cylindrical object arced past the refrigerator, on a trajectory that flushed his decision down the proverbial toilet.

If the grenade landed in the safe box, Kate and Ed's family would panic, jumping right into the sights of several militia guns. Alex lurched past the refrigerator, pressing the trigger twice before slamming into the pantry shelves. Dropping to the floor, he aimed up at the right side of the doorway and fired at a dark red mass behind a protruding barrel. A foot stepped into the kitchen, and Alex shifted his rifle left, firing again into the opaque cloud. Confused voices and jumbled commands quickly turned into return fire. Alex felt a bullet connect with his upper right chest, knocking him flat on his back. Another grazed his left thigh. He brought the mangled HK416 over his chest and fired the rest of his magazine into the smoke.

Chapter 41

Limerick, Maine

Jeffrey Brown crouched at the tree line, ready to sprint to the house, when his radio crackled.

"Brown, we can't break through the mudroom. Request permission to withdraw," said a coughing voice over heavy gunfire.

Thick plumes of red smoke billowed out of the mudroom door, hitting the porch ceiling and dispersing over the roof into the stark blue sky. The idiots weren't supposed to pull the pin on the smoke grenade.

"I'm on my way. How many men do you have left that can fight?"

"Two, including myself."

"Copy. Pull back. Head north for the secondary extraction point," he said and pressed the alternate frequency button. "Liberty Actual, this is Liberty Three, the breach failed. Heading to secondary extract."

"Liberty Actual copies. Get as many out as you can. Pick up the thirty-cal on your way out. It's in the trees directly across from the leftmost, ground-floor window."

"Copy. I'm moving."

Two men stumbled down the porch stairs, coughing as they stopped to pick up their wounded squad mate. Brown stepped into the tall grass beyond the trees, but the sound of diesel engines stopped him. He dropped into the brush and crawled back to the trees as a dark blur crashed through the metallic gate fifty feet to his right. Two angular gray tactical vehicles burst into the clearing and raced toward the house. Brown crawled faster as the turret-mounted machine guns chattered in tandem, trading off deadly bursts that killed the last of his men.

Punching through the foliage, he risked a glance back at the house. Marines dismounted from both vehicles, firing single shots into the corpses lying on the gravel. One of the vehicles backed up and drove across the front of the house, heading toward the barn. He swung his scoped AR-10 toward the clearing, wanting desperately to take a shot, but there was no point. Killing one of them was a death sentence, even if he targeted the turret gunners.

The former ranger slowly eased his way deeper into the forest. He should be dead with his men, but his choice of rifles bizarrely kept him alive. With Daniel Boone and that crazy-looking bitch raining accurate fire down on his men, the .308 caliber AR-10 quickly became their golden ticket to cross open ground. He'd survived for a reason—which started to crystalize as he reached a safe distance from the clearing.

Chapter 42

Limerick, Maine

A low-pitched roar competed with the high, ringing tone in his ears, breaking the relative silence that had descended on the mudroom for several seconds. Alex flinched when long, tightly spaced bursts of automatic fire erupted in front of the house. He pulled a fresh magazine from one of the pouches on his vest and released the empty, which clattered on the hardwood floor. Hands trembling, he inserted the curved polymer magazine and released the bolt, ready for any militia that survived the Matvees M240s—however doubtful that might be. He lay on his back, pointing his rifle into the smoke, until he started to hear single rifle shots. It was over.

"Stay where you are! Let the marines clear the house. Ryan. Linda, acknowledge," he rasped, crawling toward them.

Just one asshole with a trigger pull left in him could steal a life. The marines were making sure they didn't, one bullet at a time.

"Copy. Marines clearing the house," said Ryan.

"I need to check on Ryan!" Kate called, and he saw her head emerge from the sandbags.

"He's fine! Stay where you are!"

Samantha Walker's face appeared next, quickly finding Ed.

"Ed!" she screamed, climbing over the side and scrambling into the foyer.

"Everyone needs to stay—"

Kate jumped out next, running toward the stairs.

"Damn it, Kate!"

"I'm checking on Ryan!"

"I'm fine, Mom!" Ryan yelled from upstairs.

Two heads emerged from the safe box at the sound of Ryan's voice.

"Heads down!" he barked at Chloe and Daniel Walker. "Where's the grenade?"

"I threw it on the porch when it landed in the box," said Samantha.

Alex leaned his head over the side of the sandbags. The Walker kids were shaking.

"Sorry about that, guys. I need you to stay in here until the house is cleared. Your dad's hurt, but he'll be fine. I promise."

"I need the first aid kit!" yelled Kate.

"Throw us the first aid kit, Chloe!" screamed Samantha.

"Keep it down," Alex hissed from the sandbag wall.

"Dad?" he whispered.

"Still ticking," said Tim Fletcher from a hidden position in the great room.

He slid over to the basement door and put his head near one of the large holes.

"Nice shooting, Mom. Everyone all right down there?"

"We're fine. How is my grandson?" Amy responded.

"He sounds fine. Stay put for now."

A brown tactical-style backpack hit the floor next to him, billowing drywall powder in his face.

"Thanks." He coughed, grabbing the pack and crawling next to Ed and Samantha.

"What are we looking at here?" he said, unzipping the bag and removing two flat, sealed packets.

"It doesn't look good," Samantha said, tears streaming down her cheeks.

"I'm fine, honey," insisted Ed, squeezing her hand. "It just hurts like a motherf—"

"He sounds fine and looks fine." Alex noticed a small pool of blood on the floor under Ed's buttocks.

"And he's not bleeding badly. That's a good thing. How does your ass feel, buddy?"

"Like I sat on a nail."

"We can definitely fix this," Alex said.

He heaved the pack behind Samantha's back toward Kate, who had turned Charlie onto his stomach and propped his left leg against the front door. She sat under the leg, pressing on his calf. The amount of blood on the floor in the foyer was unsettling, but not indicative of life-threatening arterial damage. Through sidelights next to the door, he saw one of the Matvees cruise past the house, headed west. The gray vehicle reappeared in the great room windows and stopped in the backyard between the barn and the house.

"Kate, use one of the QuikClot dressings and tape it up tight. The marines will take care of the rest. Ryan's good?"

"I haven't seen him, but he sounds good," said Kate, digging through the medical bag. "Emily is fine with your mother?"

Alex smiled at Kate and nodded. "Mom has them locked down tight."

"Let me see the wound here," he said, gently moving Ed's hand. "Definitely the entry, which means…"

He pushed Ed's right thigh up a few inches and stuck his head against the floor.

"Through and through. Lucky guy," said Alex, tearing open one of the packets and handing it to Samantha.

"I don't feel very lucky," grimaced Ed.

"Lucky it wasn't your head. Sam, could you slide that trauma pad under his head, I mean ass? I get the two confused," he said, winking at Ed.

"Was he like this in Boston?" asked Samantha.

"Worse," replied Ed, wincing as Alex lowered his buttock against the hemostatic pad.

Samantha held out the second pad for Alex.

"Press this firmly into his thigh," he said, moving out of the way. "It'll stop the bleeding. I need to check on Linda."

"What happened to her?"

"No idea. She stopped answering her radio," he said, walking toward the stairs.

"Stop! Hands on your head!" bellowed a voice through the sitting room.

Alex complied, glancing through the shattered French doors. A rifle pointed at him from the lower right corner of the sitting room windowsill, locked tightly into a woodland MARPAT battle helmet.

"Captain Fletcher?"

"Affirmative."

"Have all of your people stand fast while we clear the house. Hands visible and clear of any weapons until we positively identify all friendlies. Ooh rah?"

"Ooh rah," said Alex.

"Dad?" called Ryan from their bedroom.

"Place your rifle on the bed and wait for the marines," Alex said, leaning his head into the railing behind him. "Linda!"

"What?" she screamed.

Everyone made it.

Alex kept his hands in the air as the first marine appeared, aiming his rifle past the safe box toward the great room. He recognized Corporal Lianez immediately.

"Lianez, my dad's by the wood-burning stove."

Staff Sergeant Evans appeared on the other side of the kitchen island and aimed at the sandbags. "Hands up. Stand where I can see you."

Chloe and Daniel Walker rose slowly, with their hands on their heads. The marine activated his rifle light and swept it through the safe box.

"These two are clear. Lianez, check the room across from the kitchen table."

"On it," said Lianez, winking at them as he moved forward to check the dining room.

"Captain Fletcher, what is your dad wearing?" said Evans, aiming his rifle past Lianez.

"Should be old-school woodland camouflage marine cover."

"Check. Any tangos in that room with you, sir?"

"Negative," said Tim Fletcher. "I didn't let any by."

Evans turned his point of aim to the covered porch. "That's a no-shitter. Jesus."

A third marine glided through the sitting room, examining the damage to the sandbags and nodding at Alex.

"Clear in the front room, Staff Sergeant!"

"Same here," echoed Lianez.

"Clear on the first floor," said Evans, activating his tactical radio. "Lianez, get these two stabilized for transport."

"Copy that, Staff Sergeant," Lianez said, dropping his MARPAT assault pack on the floor next to Ed.

Staff Sergeant Evans glanced up the stairs.

"Sir, is there any chance one of them slipped by you and made it upstairs?"

Alex shook his head. "We stopped them here."

PART V

"Far from Over"

Chapter 43

Limerick, Maine

Eli Russell stumbled out of the forest with four of Bertelson's men, nearly collapsing on the dirt road.

Where the fuck is McCulver?

Flames leapt from the charred frame of a two-door sedan, superheating each breath of air he greedily sucked into his suffering lungs. He was at his breaking point and needed something to go right. Searching through the dense black smoke, he spotted the extraction vehicles crossing Old Middle Road. Finally. He took a knee and triggered his radio.

"Liberty Three, this is Actual. We are at the secondary extraction point. What is your location, over?"

A calm, composed voice responded, *"Switch to the emergency frequency. Over."*

Eli fumbled with the buttons, his fingers slipping from the sweat that poured from his hands. "Brown, I need you at the extraction point immediately. If the tactical vehicles catch up with us, we're done."

"You're good for now, Eli. No marines in pursuit. One of the Matvees is behind the house. The other is in front. Looks like they're loading up the casualties."

"Brown, why are you still there? You were supposed to head north and pick up the thirty-cal."

"Northern egress wasn't an option. I'm sticking. I want to know why I lost an entire squad to some guy wearing a Daniel Boone cap."

"What? Never mind. What's your E and E plan?"

"I'll head north in a few hours, tracing Route 5. Radio checks at the top of the hour on channel 18, code 93. How copy, over."

"Solid copy. Don't get caught. Actual, out."

Kevin McCulver's black, matte-finished Bronco sped past the burning wreckage and skidded to a halt in front of them. A mud-spackled red SUV followed, pulling up several feet to the left. He turned to the survivors and signaled for them to get in the SUV. McCulver leaned across the seat and pushed the door open for Eli, who heaved himself into the seat and slammed the door.

"What the fuck took you so long?"

"What about Brown?" said McCulver, eyeing the road to the compound.

"He'll be fine," said Eli.

"Did you see him on the way back?"

"What is it with the twenty goddamn questions? Back up and get us out of here!"

"All right," said McCulver.

"How about a yes, sir, once in a blue moon?" he said, pounding his right fist into the dashboard.

Without saying a word, his second in command navigated the truck onto Old Middle Road and sped west, with the rest of the convoy falling in behind.

"Are all of the drivers on your radio net?" asked Eli, lifting the handheld radio from the drink holder.

"Yes, sir," he muttered.

"Don't be a smart ass, Kevin."

"Liberty Mobile, this is Liberty Actual. It is imperative that the last vehicle in this convoy watches the road behind them. Report any and all vehicles spotted. I want the last car to respond, over."

"Liberty Actual, this is Jim Huxitt in the last car. I'm scanning the road with binoculars, over."

"Roger. Out," said Eli, leaning into his seat and closing his eyes.

McCulver looked over at Eli briefly. "Is this really all that made it out? Where's the thirty-cal?"

Eli breathed deeply and exhaled, feeling his heart pound at his chest. "Don't remind me. Brown's staying behind to gather intelligence. We'll pick him up tomorrow, when this settles."

"Is it going to settle that quickly?"

"What do you mean?" Eli barked.

"We just attacked a high-value military target. No doubt about that now. If any one of our guys were captured, the feds will be at the Parsonsfield site pretty quickly."

Eli buried his face in his filthy black hands. With a thirty-caliber machine gun and nearly forty heavily armed militiamen assaulting the house, he hadn't considered the possibility of failure, let alone that some of his men might be captured and tortured for information. Kevin was right.

"When we reach headquarters, have the men pack up everything and hit the road. I want the place evacuated in less than an hour. If those two tactical vehicles show up before we're gone, they'll put an end to this show before it starts. I'll head up 160 with Bertelson's men and find a suitable location in the Brownfield or Denmark area. Made some deliveries up that way in the past. There are some real isolated places near the New Hampshire border. I'll pick a spot north of Porter for a temporary rally point. School, campground, whatever. I'll come get everyone once the new site is secure."

"I should make a second trip to my house," said McCulver. "I have some bomb-making gear—old cell phones, wiring, detonators—some pipe bombs in the shed. It'll save us from scrounging around while we need to keep our heads low."

"As soon as I return to guide our boys to the new HQ, I'll cut you loose on that mission. You'll need to approach your house carefully, and you'll have to wait at the rally point for someone to contact you via radio, in case the feds follow you back."

"I don't think anyone back there knows where I live."

"Probably not, but they know your name, and I God-guaran-damn-tee Homeland Security has a functioning database that could spit out your last five known addresses in a heartbeat," said Eli.

"Maybe I should forget about it."

"No. They'll hit the Parsonsfield HQ first, then my house in Waterboro, working their way down the list. The biggest risk is running into them on the road. You can't take the Bronco."

"What about splitting off from you guys when we hit Cramm Road?"

"Negative. I need you organizing the pack up and withdrawal from Parsonsfield," said Eli.

"We have enough competent people to pull that off, Eli."

"I thought we had enough competent people to shoot a thirty-caliber machine gun, but apparently that wasn't the case! No. I need you personally in charge of this. I can't be there, and one of us has to be with the troops at all times until we get things back on track. They need leadership right now. Without leadership, they'll drift away to the four winds.

"I'll put the guys left over from Bertelson's squad directly under your charge, along with the guys that were part of Jimmy's crew. Spread them out and use them to keep the troops in line. I don't want one of the SUVs to slip out of the convoy with rations and ammunition. Reporting to the rally point isn't optional."

"Got it. I still think it's risky sending me south later in the day."

"The payoff is worth the risk. This'll be your last trip to the house for a long time. Make sure your wife knows that," said Eli.

"She knows. I'm more worried about the kids."

"You tell them this is like a regular military deployment and that their dad is gonna be a hero, with his name all over the county."

"You really believe that, don't you?"

"Now I do. After what I saw at that house, there's no doubt in my mind that York County is about to be invaded."

Chapter 44

Limerick, Maine

Alex helped the marines load the portable stretcher carrying Ed into the back of the Matvee. Samantha held his hand until she had to let go.

"I should go. I can leave the kids with—"

"I'll be fine, Sam," Ed groaned, partially smiling.

"You don't sound or look like you'll be fine. Why are you smiling?"

"Morphine," said one of the marines from the front seat.

"Why didn't *I* get any morphine?" Charlie griped from the passenger seat.

"Because one of us needs to stay coherent," grumbled Linda from the seat next to him.

Corporal Lianez raised his eyebrows and whispered, "You put two Thorntons in the same vehicle with me, sir?"

Samantha started laughing.

"The kids need you here," said Ed. "I need you to be with the kids. The corporal said I'd be fine."

"No offense to the corporal, but it's not like he put you through an MRI," Samantha snapped.

"None taken, ma'am," said Corporal Lianez. "Best I can tell, the bullet entered his hip high on the outside, skipped off his pelvic bone and exited through his buttocks. Bleeding is normal, so I don't think it took a deeper route through. I've seen enough bullet and frag wounds to tell. We'll keep the bleeding to a minimum until we get to the hospital."

"Sorry, I didn't mean—"

249

"Ma'am, there's no need to apologize. I wouldn't trust me either." The corporal winked. "You're welcome to come, but I'd want my wife to stay with the kids too. Captain, if you'll close the hatch when they're ready?"

"Thank you," Samantha said, hesitating to say any more.

"This is what we do—but you're welcome," said Lianez, climbing into the troop compartment.

"Tell the kids I love them and I'll be back soon," said Ed.

"I will. I love you."

"Love you too, honey."

"You ready?" asked Alex.

When Samantha nodded, Alex pulled Samantha to the side of the tactical vehicle. They hadn't swept the forest for hostiles, and he didn't want to expose her to the eastern tree line when the door swung shut.

"Be good, my friend. The marines will stay with you at the hospital and push for priority treatment. I can't imagine they have too many gunshot wounds, so it won't be a problem. If it is, I'll have the battalion commander press down on the hospital. Probably see you tomorrow."

"Watch over the kids for me," said Ed.

"Like a hawk," said Alex.

"Like your own."

Alex nodded. "I think you pulled off number three in there today."

"Number three?"

"Three times you've saved my ass."

"That didn't count," said Ed.

"No?"

"Everyone racked up at least ten ass-savings in there. We'll keep the tally at two."

"Fair enough. I still owe you. Keep those two from killing each other," he said and shut the rear hatch.

Alex opened the left passenger door, figuring he had to say something to the Thorntons. He knew he'd probably regret it.

"Why do I have to go to the hospital? I'm fine," Charlie insisted. "You need help here, and I can still get around."

Alex looked at Linda, who shook her head and mumbled, "Idiot."

"You have a bullet hole in your leg, Charlie," said Alex.

"So what?"

"Morphine kicked in, Linda?"

"Something kicked in. Feels like a bad ankle sprain," she said, wincing when she accidentally moved her foot.

"Better than before?"

"You have no idea."

"Lianez, you should probably figure out a way to suspend her leg."

"I can do that, sir."

"Don't bother. We're not that far away," Linda said.

"It's her call, Lianez," said Alex.

"It's always her call," grumbled Charlie.

Alex met the corporal's stare through the rear passenger seats. He didn't look happy.

"We'll watch over your flock. You did good in there," said Alex, closing the door before they could respond.

Alex pounded on the hood and gave the driver a thumbs-up before running into the house, keeping himself between the woods and Samantha. Once inside, they found the adults in the kitchen with two of the marines. His mother stood at the basement door with her shotgun.

"Where's Ryan?" he asked.

"He won't leave his post until the forest is cleared. Alyssa and Sydney are watching the east."

"The rest of the kids?"

"In the basement, under lock and key until the farm is safe," said Amy.

Alex nodded at his mom, who looked all business. "I guess we should take care of that sooner than later. Staff Sergeant?"

"You sure you don't want to sit this one out, sir? You look like you're about to fall over," said Evans.

Alex knew he should take a seat and close his eyes, probably for the next twelve hours, but he couldn't rest until he felt reasonably confident that their property was secure. Even then, they faced a full day of work just to put the house back into rough working order.

"I've looked and felt like that for the better part of seventy-two hours. I'll survive a few more," he said.

Tim Fletcher opened one of the pouches attached to his web belt, exposing two fully loaded magazines. "I'm ready when you are," he said.

"Tim, you've had enough. Let the marines handle this," said Amy.

Tim pulled the brim of his hat down, exposing the faded Eagle, Globe and Anchor symbol on its starched face.

"Never mind," Amy said.

"Keep a watch in every direction," said Alex.

"Be careful. Don't take any chances. Not after this," she said, glancing around at the mess.

"I'll be good," he said and kissed her dusty lips.

"We'll radio back with our locations. I want to test the motion detectors. Some of the transceivers were knocked onto the floor, but I didn't see any bullet holes. Wish I could say the same for the monitors."

"We'll check the transceivers and put them back in order," said Kate.

Alex nodded. "One last question. Did any of the toilets survive?"

"The one in the master bedroom," said Tim.

Alex looked toward the stairs. "I guess I'll take my chances out there."

Chapter 45

Porter, Maine

Eli adjusted the Bronco's passenger-side vents to direct the cool air in his face. Nearly two hours later, he was still running hot from the half-mile dash through the forest in Limerick. He looked up from his GPS receiver and watched for the turnoff to Camp Hiawatha.

"Turn up here at the camp," said Eli, pointing to a rustic sign on the right side of the road.

His driver eased the SUV off Route 160 and drove them through a worn flagstone entrance. The dirt road gently wove through the dense forest, until they arrived at a two-story post-and-beam structure, which he guessed to be the main activities lodge. The road looped in front of the lodge, designed as a drop-off area for campers. A pickup truck and a small bumper-sticker-covered sedan sat in the back of a shaded dirt parking lot situated across the road from the lodge. Beyond the presence of these two vehicles, the camp appeared deserted, which suited him fine.

"No kids, huh?" he asked.

The driver started to open his mouth, but thought better of it. An even more uncomfortable silence hung in the truck's cabin. He'd made it clear to Bertelson's men that if they didn't have anything useful to say, they shouldn't say anything at all. They were on probation simply by association with their fuck-up of a dead squad leader. The slightest infraction of discipline or demonstration of incompetence would put them in front of a firing squad. Throughout the trip north, the four men had remained silent, dutifully watching their surroundings. It was amazing what a little leadership and a healthy dose of fear could do for the troops.

253

"Let me clarify something. If I ask a question, I expect an answer. As long as it's an answer and not some excuse to run your suck. Now, does anyone know why this place is empty?"

The driver, a serious-looking soldier type wearing thick-rimmed, corrective glasses, glanced at him and nodded. "I think most of these camps break up after the second week of August. The cars might belong to the camp director or something," he said, slowing the vehicle as they entered the loop.

"I want to see the whole place. That path looks wide enough," Eli said, pointing to a gravel path flanked by brush and a "no vehicles past this point" sign.

Several seconds on the camp's central pedestrian thoroughfare yielded tennis courts and a cluster of six cabins nestled into the woods. Shimmering water peeked between the trees behind the bungalows. A few minutes later, they returned to the loop in front of the lodge. He liked what he saw. More than enough structures to house the militia—with room to grow with each batch of recruits. Fresh water on both sides of the camp. The place was located between two sizeable "ponds," forming a land bridge between them. The idea of a ready-made barracks appealed to him the most, along with the lodge, which gave them a central meeting place. His biggest problem with Camp Hiawatha was its location.

First, it wasn't set far enough back from Route 160. The area wasn't exactly a high-population zone, but at the end of the road, near the lake, he could see several houses on the water. Located less than two miles from Porter, Maine, the high volume of vehicle traffic and activity generated by his militia would undoubtedly attract attention. The camp was an obvious choice for investigation if the government caught wind of them. He needed something more remote. Eli really wanted this place to work, but there was no point in forcing a round peg into a square hole, or whatever the stupid saying was.

"Take us back onto 160. North. I have a better idea," he said.

Less than a minute later, he ordered the driver to turn left on Porterfield Road. GPS indicated that the road forked about a mile and a half away, Porterfield Road continuing north and Norton Hill Road heading east. He liked the idea of heading east toward the New Hampshire border. Eli also knew from experience that the areas east of 160 were mostly empty. He'd be shocked to find more than four or five homesteads on this road. Easy pickings out here, unless they stumbled onto another government safe house. Just the fleeting thought of his failed attack enraged him. The driver's eyes darted nervously to his balled-up fists.

Eli counted the turnoffs along the hard-packed dirt road, jotting notes into a sweat-stained pocket notebook with a stubby, dull pencil. Five so far, mostly mobile homes or dilapidated saltboxes set close to the road. One dirt driveway extended out of sight, but it was too close to Route 160. They passed a patchy field on the left, which gave Eli hope, but he didn't see a driveway or a structure. It looked like someone had cleared the land and given up. A few minutes later, they approached a possible intersection.

"Stop at that intersection. Windows down," he said.

The word "intersection" was a generous description for the accidental convergence of two rural dirt roads in the middle of nowhere. The path heading south looked more like a well-worn ATV trail, which could prove useful for winter movement. No way anyone was getting around southern Maine once the snow started falling. He had a feeling that plowing the roads to facilitate insurgent movement wouldn't be high on Homeland's priority list. The road north held promise. Penetrating a thick stand of trees along the road, he caught glimpses of open fields in the distance. Best of all, it wasn't shown on GPS.

"Let's recon this road," he said, pointing north.

A rectangular field flanked the road once they broke through the trees. Measuring roughly two football fields long and one field wide, the grasses had been recently cut. Another tree break separated the field from a vast, open farm, easily stretching three times the length of the first field. Lush fields of late August produce bloomed on each side of the road, planted in organized rows that suggested the use of industrialized farm equipment. A house and barn stood amidst a clump of trees at the top of the road. Rows of corn baked under the sun in fields barely visible beyond the house.

"Jackpot," he said and removed the York County Sheriff's badge from a pouch on his tactical vest.

"Go slow when we get to the end of the road. No sense in scaring anyone."

The road emptied into the farm compound, which gave Eli goose bumps. This was more than a jackpot. It was the grand prize. Easily measuring fifty feet on all sides, a thriving vegetable garden greeted them on the left. The barn dwarfed the generous farmhouse, serving as a backdrop for three neatly parked green tractors. A few other well-maintained structures stood in the shadow of the barn. Chicken coop? The smell of livestock and hay washed through the Bronco's windows, reminding him of the York County Fair. This was the place.

"Why don't you stop up here," said Eli, pinning the badge to the left side of his vest while the car slowed to a stop.

"Keep your weapons out of sight, and do not get out of this vehicle unless I tell you to—or if I'm shot dead. Understand?"

A cacophony of "yes, sirs" reassured him that they got the message. He opened the door and stepped onto the dusty driveway, his sweat glands immediately responding to the direct sunlight. He pulled a black ball cap from the cargo pocket of his mud-crusted pants and pulled it tightly over his head, exposing the words "York County Sheriff." Unsnapping his hip holster behind the car door, he glanced at the driver.

"If you see something that ain't right, honk the horn," he said, shutting the door and walking toward the house.

He got halfway to the covered porch when a man wearing jeans and a dirty white T-shirt appeared on the right side of the house. He cradled a pump action shotgun across his chest, the wood fore-end nestled into the crook of his left elbow, finger in the trigger well. The brim of a faded green John Deere hat shaded his eyes, which never left Eli. Tufts of gray hair poked out of the hat.

"Can I help you, Deputy?"

"Sorry to startle you like this. Deputy Russell. York County Sheriff's tactical response team," he said, pointing at his hat.

"A little out of your jurisdiction, aren't you?" said the man, glancing from Eli to the SUV.

"We had two families murdered in Cornish yesterday and a report of three men staying at Hiawatha. Oxford County couldn't spare the manpower. We didn't find anything at the camp. We're doing a quick sweep before we call it quits. Getting crazy out there," said Eli, keeping his hands open at chest height.

"We haven't seen or heard anything unusual since the morning of the 19th."

"Well, sorry to trouble you. Stay safe," he said.

"Same to you, Deputy," he said, relaxing his grip and taking his finger out of the trigger well.

Eli's pistol cleared the holster before the farmer could grip the shotgun in both hands. Not taking any chances, Eli started walking left, firing his .45 Colt Commander with both hands as the farmer tried to bring the shotgun around. The first bullet grazed the man's left shoulder, slowing his efforts to turn the shotgun on him. The next three bullets missed entirely, forcing Eli to stop and kneel as the barrel swung precariously in his direction. Any further and the buckshot spread might have a chance of hitting him. Quickly forming the sight picture between his match-grade sights, he pressed the trigger, snapping the farmer's head back. Another trigger press blew out the back of the man's neck. Eli reloaded as he sprinted to the side of the house.

The temperature dropped several degrees in the shade next to the house, clearing his head a little. He grabbed the shotgun and pointed it at the door located toward the back of the house. A screen door swung open, and Eli discharged the shotgun, punching several holes through the loose screen and knocking a gray-haired woman into the backyard. Eli signaled for the rest of the men to join him, hearing doors open and slam shut as he slowly approached the side door. A revolver lay in the grass a few feet past the door, directly underneath a shiny patch of blood-splattered siding. The air wafting out of the door reminded him of a bakery.

Home sweet home.

Chapter 46

Limerick, Maine

Alex stormed out of the side door to the barn holding a bloodstained map in one hand and his rifle in the other. Staff Sergeant Evans and his two marines sat on the porch steps, drinking out of their CamelBak hoses and eating MREs. They had just finished hauling the last of the militia bodies into the trees behind the barn.

"Staff Sergeant! Have your team mount up. We have a mission."

"A mission, sir?" said Evans, stepping down from the porch.

The marines behind him started packing up their food.

"Two of the terrorists confirmed the location of the Maine Liberty Militia's headquarters in Parsonsfield—less than nine miles from here. We'll roll up with the Matvee and tear the place apart. I want M320s attached to all rifles. Full grenade load-out."

"The men in the barn, sir?" he asked, raising an eyebrow.

"What's going on?" demanded Kate from just inside the screen porch.

"They aren't going anywhere," whispered Alex, eyes on Kate as she strode across the porch.

"Sir?" he said, locking eyes with Alex.

"One of them expired from natural causes. The others are a little worse for the wear, but they'll be fine. I want to be on the road in under a minute."

"Shit," muttered Evans, "this isn't good."

"I plan to file a full report detailing the entire interrogation—after we get back."

"Where are you going?" said Kate, standing with her hands on her hips in front of the Matvee.

"I know where their headquarters is located," he said, waving the folded map. "We have to hit them now and put an end to this."

"You and three marines? You're out of your fucking mind," she said. "No offense, Staff Sergeant."

"None taken," Evans said, slowly backing away.

"We're bringing the Matvee. With the 240 and grenade launchers, we'll blow the place to pieces. You're not changing my mind, Kate," he said, knowing that he was unlikely to get off that easy.

"I'm not doubting that you could level the place, if they let you get close enough."

"What is that supposed to mean?"

"It means that this militia group detonated a car bomb at the entrance to our neighborhood. What makes you think they won't have something bigger ready for you at their secret hideout?"

"Headquarters," said Alex.

"Whatever. One, they won't be there, unless we're dealing with the stupidest militia group ever. Two, they probably left a nice little surprise behind for you. You're not thinking this through right now, and the staff sergeant knows it," she said, shooting Evans a nasty look. "You're running on empty, Alex. No. Actually, you're running on those stupid STIM things. Look at your hands."

Alex didn't have any intention of producing his hands for general examination. He'd fought to keep the trembling hidden since he arrived last night.

"How many P-STIMs have you taken, Captain?"

"See?" Kate said. "He knows."

"Four in the past thirty-six hours."

"Jesus," muttered the staff sergeant.

"It's the only way I've been able to function like this."

"Is that a lot?" asked Kate.

"They're recommended for one-time dosage, at night, during extended combat operations. Yes, he has a shit-ton of amphetamine in his system. Frankly, I'd feel more comfortable if the captain had a seat inside and let this filter out of his system."

"I'll take a break once this Eli Russell character is dead," said Alex.

"Who's Eli Russell?" asked Kate.

"Our prisoners identified him as the leader of this group. I haven't walked them around to look at the bodies, but I think he escaped. This was only half of their group."

"You're not going anywhere. Your family needs you in one piece. You have the vast resources of the Marine Corps and Homeland Security at your disposal; why don't you let them handle this?"

"Are you being sarcastic?"

"Not really. Call Grady. Maybe he can send a helicopter or a drone to blow the place up. Designate the location as a critical threat."

"Sounds like a better plan, sir, for now," said Evans.

"I'll contact Grady."

"Thank you," Kate said, hugging him tightly.

"I'll go check on the prisoners," said Evans, slipping away.

"Staff Sergeant?" said Kate, standing next to Alex.

"Yes, ma'am?"

"Thank you for moving the bodies. It would have been too much for us right now. We'll get your men some real food tonight."

"Not a problem, ma'am, and we're fine with MREs if it's too much trouble."

"It's no trouble. I'll throw some beers in the freezer a little later—if Captain Fletcher doesn't have a problem with that."

"As long as I get one, there's no problem," said Alex.

"Thanks, ma'am," Evans said and jogged to the barn.

"Sorry, hon. I just thought I could put an end to this right now. What if they come after us again?"

"I can't imagine they'll return with the marines here. Let Grady worry about this. Designate this guy, Eli Russell, as the top threat in southern Maine. It's not like you'll be out of the loop on what happens."

"You're right," he said. "Let me call Grady and see if he can scare something up while Russell's trail is hot."

Kate nodded. "I want you inside taking a break when you're done. Mopping and sweeping doesn't take a lot of energy. We have most of the bigger pieces cleaned up downstairs."

"What happened to resting?"

"Yeah, that's not happening. We'll be at this most of the day just to get the house in basic shape. All hands on deck."

"I'll be right back," he said and kissed her on the forehead.

Alex walked toward the garden, looking for a little shade behind the house. He still felt exposed outside of the house, despite walking nearly every square foot of the forest to the north and east of the clearing. The prisoners told him far more than he had conveyed to Kate, and he had no reason to doubt their words. Not after what he did to the scumbag who kept insisting Eli would return to "rape every bitch in that house." Dying of natural causes involved a long, painful process in front of his scared-shitless comrades. They nearly talked over each other to give Alex information.

The ROTAC indicated a full signal from his resting spot on the slanted metal bulkhead door. He scrolled through the preprogrammed directory and selected "Patriot." It was the only call sign listed without a follow-on number or letter. Had to be Grady. He pressed "Lock," which initiated an encrypted protocol connecting his radio to Grady's. "Connected" flashed on the digital display a few seconds later. He remembered it was "push to talk" technology just as Grady's voice broke the silence.

"Alex, Evans called as soon as Lianez hit the road. Sounds like you gave it to them good. I've arranged for priority treatment of your wounded at Goodall Hospital in Sanford. Is everyone else okay?"

"We have some minor injuries that can be treated here. Thank you. I have a situation that requires immediate attention. Can you spare a full squad right now?"

"Right now?"

"Affirmative. I need additional marines to conduct a raid against the militia headquarters. I interrogated a few of the surviving militia and confirmed the location. It's less than nine miles from here."

"Alex, I can't spare any marines right now. A quarter of the marines I had in Boston are missing or en route. We're getting ready to evacuate north to the Londonderry Reserve Center."

"What happened to the rest of the battalion? Where are you now?"

"National Guard Armory in Melrose. As for the missing units, I think we've had some desertions. Striker units found an abandoned Matvee in Watertown. At least they zeroed out the crypto in the vehicle radios. Homeland's Cat Five plan estimated a forty-three percent no-show rate for my battalion in the event of an EMP-related scenario, so we're actually in good shape, according to the plan."

"I'll take one vehicle with half of a squad. The group that hit my house is the same group I ran into on the way out of Maine," said Alex.

"The group executing civilians at Milton Mills?"

"Affirmative. Somehow they figured out where I live, and it doesn't sound like they're going away. This was only half of their group. Trust me when I say they will be big trouble for the Recovery Zone. They planned for the possibility of your marines returning and set off a sizable IED next to one of the Matvees."

"Evans briefed me about it. High-order detonation car bomb. No damage to the Matvees."

"They have a bomb maker in the group. He won't make the same mistake twice."

"I can't send anything your way, Alex," said Grady.

"Can you pull some strings and detach some National Guard folks in Maine? They're standing around in droves at the border crossings."

"I'll give it a shot, but I'm not optimistic. FEMA hasn't officially designated the Regional Recovery Zone yet, so technically, I don't have any jurisdiction in Maine. I do, however, have a mission, which is why Staff Sergeant Evans was on his way to see you."

"Hold on, Colonel, let me put my wife on. This sounds like something you might need to clear with her," said Alex.

"Funny," uttered Grady. "I do have your signature accepting an emergency commission in the Marine Corps for an indefinite period of time."

"Sounded like a good idea at the time. What are we talking about?"

"Babysitting duty. The remnants of Bravo Company are headed to the Sanford Regional Airport. ETA two to five days, depending on what I can scare up for transportation. Bravo Company is in bad shape. Thirty-two marines have reported for duty as of this morning, and the company gunny isn't holding his breath for any more. They're scattered all over the state. A good number are likely dead from the tsunami."

"Sounds like they're in good hands," said Alex.

"Gunny Deschane is squared away, but without an officer, he'll have problems cutting through the red tape that's bound to clog up that airport. With your provisional identification and rank, he should have smooth sailing."

"None of the officers showed up?"

"Two are confirmed casualties, and the rest live too far north. They may show up eventually, but until then, you're Bravo Company commander."

Kate was going to love this. Alex went from sitting on his ass typing reports about militia units—about a day's worth of work—to leading a marine rifle company, which in his previous experience took up about twenty-five of the twenty-four hours in a standard day, plus time on the weekends. At least it was only thirty-three marines. A typical rifle company could field nearly one hundred forty.

"Sounds easy enough for now, Colonel. Any other good news?"

"Bravo Company has no equipment. The reserve center at the former air station was wiped out by the tsunami. Nothing was salvageable, including weapons and ammunition. I have arranged the delivery of replacement gear for two platoons. Vehicles, comms gear, weapons, everything."

"Delivery date?"

"TBD, but I anticipate it will leave Hanscomb Air Force Base within three days. I need you to secure hangar space at Sanford Airport. Preferably, enough space for the entire battalion. I need this done ASAP. An Air Force Combat Controller Team is onsite, preparing the field for sustained 24-hour flight operations. Combat engineers from Maine's 133rd Engineer Battalion will arrive tomorrow to reinforce the location. It's about to get busy in your neck of the woods."

"I can't leave my family here unprotected. Not until the Maine Liberty Militia has been destroyed. I'll run back and forth to Sanford. All other business will be conducted over the ROTAC."

"Why don't you relocate everyone to the airport? In a few days' time, it'll be the safest location in Maine."

"I'm not moving my family into a hangar to eat MREs, drink funky-tasting water and sleep on cots indefinitely. I plan to call on one of the top militia guys in the county tomorrow morning. I'll secure hangar space immediately after that."

"Anything stopping you from doing it this afternoon?"

"Yes. Her name is Kate Fletcher. I believe the two of you have met?"

"Fair enough. Contact me when you've secured space at the airport. And Alex? I'm glad to hear everyone pulled through the attack. I'd hate to think what might have happened if you hadn't returned before this morning."

"Me too. I owe you for the ride back to Maine."

"It all worked out for a reason. Talk to you tomorrow, Captain Fletcher."

Alex turned off the phone and lay there for a moment, staring at the deep blue sky. Even with the amphetamines coursing through his body, he could fall asleep in a second if he closed his eyes. Glancing at the gauze holding a 4x4 dressing against his left thigh, he realized he should probably spend some time tending to his injuries. His efforts up until now had mainly consisted of applying some kind of hemostatic dressing or powder to stop the bleeding. He really needed to properly clean and possibly stitch the thigh.

Staff Sergeant Evans emerged from the barn and walked toward Alex. He sat up and planted his brown hiking boots into the grass, preparing for the painful ordeal of standing.

"Natural causes, sir?"

"Metal poisoning." Alex nodded.

"Lot of that going around," said Evans.

Chapter 47

Limerick, Maine.

Kate sat down for the first time since the motion sensors had been triggered. Soaked through every layer of her clothing, streams of sweat poured down her cheeks, dropping from her chin onto the table. Alex stepped through the empty slider and set two red plastic cups in front of her. He took the cushioned seat next to her on the porch and squeezed her hand. He looked utterly exhausted, his red face covered by rivulets of perspiration. She closed her eyes.

"I'm willing this into an ice cold beer," she said.

"Well water. Compliments of the house."

She drank the cold water in a single gulp and stared through the bullet-riddled porch screen next to her.

"Round one of the cleanup is done. There's only a one in twenty chance of getting a splinter stuck in your ass—or a piece of glass," he said, digging into the cushion under him.

He placed a sliver of glass on the table in front of her.

"We'll get there. Stroke of genius pulling all of the window screens yesterday. Linda's idea," she said.

Neither of them spoke for several moments. She felt terrible for her friend. The same .308 that had almost killed Alex and her in the sitting room had effectively destroyed Linda's ankle. Alex wasn't too optimistic about her prognosis. Unless she got extremely lucky and the bullet passed cleanly through, the damage likely caused by the steel-jacketed round would require serious orthopedic surgery. Repeated surgeries if she wanted to walk normally on her left leg again.

"They took a beating up there from that .308. We never did find it."

"Find what?" Kate asked.

"The .308. It wasn't on any of the guys in front of the garage or in the mudroom. Someone slipped away."

Kate looked over her shoulder at the eastern tree line. "You don't think—"

"We scoured the eastern woods," he said, shaking his head. "No sign of the shooter."

"They're gone, honey. They lost twenty-nine men. You don't come back after that."

Instead of agreeing with her, he reached out and plucked the porch screen.

"We won't be able to sit out here at night. Mosquitos will eat us alive."

She sensed he was holding back. Alex usually played the role of cheerleader.

"We have rolls of screen in the basement. We can pop this stuff out and replace it. Same with the slider. We'll have to board up one side, but it'll work," she said.

"Then there's the rain. Almost every window in the house is broken, and of course, these are custom windows."

"We'll be fine. We can cut enough plywood to cover the windows. We prepared for this possibility. It's not ideal, but it'll have to work for now."

"One rainstorm and all of the insulation will get soaked. We'll be living in a mold experiment by the end of September. This house was so perfect," he hissed, crumpling his cup.

Kate had never seen Alex like this and wondered if it had something to do with the amphetamine tablets. His hands looked steadier, but they still shook while he held onto the cup of water. This was something bigger. Something he didn't want to tell her.

"It's still perfect," she said. "The kids are fine. Your parents are fine. We have everything we need to thrive here. It'll take time, but we'll eventually patch up every single hole in this house."

Alex sipped his water and stared at the lake beyond the trees.

"What's going on?" she said, grasping his hand on the table.

"I don't think we can stay here," he said, slowly shifting his gaze to her.

His eyes looked distant, almost vacant, which terrified her.

"Honey, you're starting to scare me."

"I just scraped chunks of internal organs off the walls inside our house. The bloodstains will never come out, as far as I can tell. I've tried scrubbing with bleach. We'll have to sand the spots and repaint them," he said softly.

"Then we'll sand them tomorrow," she said, searching for something in his eyes.

They softened for a moment, watering.

"Ryan's helmet had two rips in the fabric covering, one right above his left eye. Without the helmet...I couldn't clean that up."

"What aren't you telling me?" she said.

His eyes sharpened. "There's a reason I wanted to take the marines to Parsonsfield this morning," Alex said carefully. "I don't think this Eli Russell character will ever leave us alone."

"We already agreed on a strategy to handle him."

"I didn't want to tell you this earlier, because I didn't want to start a panic, and I didn't want to leave you alone here with the kids. The attack this morning is connected to Milton Mills. I killed Eli Russell's brother on that bridge."

"This Russell guy is in charge of the Maine Liberty Militia?"

He nodded. "I killed his brother, and apparently, you killed his nephew in Waterboro. He's never going to stop, and worse yet, he's somehow convinced his whole gang of shitheads that we're some kind of Homeland Security-sponsored, covert operations team. Part of the government's false-flag operation. He's using this story to recruit people for his militia."

Alex's revelation changed everything. No wonder he had been reluctant to let the kids out of the basement. It had nothing to do with the blood on the walls or the stifling heat. He didn't think they were safe here.

"So, what do we do? Pack up as much as we can and go back to Durham Road until the military deals with Russell?"

"If we leave the area, I don't think this place will be here when we get back. We have one option as I see it. We could move everyone to Sanford Airport—temporarily. I'm supposed to secure hangar space for the rest of the battalion tomorrow, and Grady said we could grab extra space."

Kate stared at him in complete disbelief. Now he was driving around the state for Grady?

"What are you doing in Sanford?"

"Maine is about to be designated as a Regional Recovery Zone and—"

"Yeah, I get all of that. I thought you were putting together reports for Grady. Now you're making trips to Sanford? When were you planning on telling me?"

"This is the first chance we've had to sit down and talk since this morning. I think we can make this work," he said.

"I can't see how. The idea of living in a hangar doesn't sound appealing. Better than dead, but there has to be another solution."

"Just until Russell is put out of business. The airport will have tight security, and we'll have a battalion of marines around us. I can billet a squad here to keep an eye on the place, so it's here when we come back. Part of a forward operating base or something like that."

"Why don't you just make this a forward operating base now, and we stay?"

Alex smiled. "I might be able to sell that to Grady. Russell won't move his militia's base of operations south. It's too risky. He'll head north, but not too far away. Keeping a full squad or platoon of marines here as a quick-reaction force makes sense. If Grady doesn't agree, we're back to square one."

"Then we reinforce the defenses we already have with Staff Sergeant Evans and his men," said Kate.

"Our fallback plan can't include the marines. Grady could yank them out of here tomorrow depending on his needs."

"I don't think he'd do that to you."

"He's running a marine infantry battalion, not a babysitting service. Judging by the scope of operations planned for southern Maine, Grady's going to need every marine in the inventory to do his job. We can't count on any organic support at the house. If he doesn't buy the forward base idea and pulls the marines out of here, the best we can hope for is a thirty-minute response time for reinforcement—if available."

"That's too long," she said.

"I agree. We need to make a decision on this within the next day or so. Space to house civilians at the airport will vanish quickly once the recovery zone is officially designated."

"Can we defend this place without the marines?" Kate asked.

She didn't think so, not with three out of their seven riflemen limited to static positions by their injuries and one out of commission. Charlie, Linda and Ryan could take up their same positions on the second floor, but they'd require assistance to switch windows. Ed's injuries put him in a different category. They could lay him in the basement to watch over the kids, but that might be the extent of his usefulness in a battle. Putting a rifle in Samantha's hands didn't help their overall defensive posture. Asking her for more than a few shotgun blasts in the general direction of the enemy was pushing it.

"With a working thirty-caliber machine gun and seven hundred fifty rounds? It depends on what they throw at us. Same as this morning, I'd say no problem, even with half of our crew injured. If they add a few more .308 rifles to the mix and stick to the trees?" he said, shaking his head. "I'm not so optimistic."

"The machine gun works?"

"As far as I can tell. Evans plans to test fire it a little later. We also need to fix the gates, or at least harden them to SUV-sized vehicles. If they drive up on us too fast, in large enough numbers, who knows?"

"We'd have some warning, at least," she said.

"Not until we unscrew the sensor situation. The two damaged transceivers correspond to the eastern approach, which means we have a huge gap in our coverage along Gelder Pond Lane and the gate. We should probably do that before dark."

"If we have the marines here tonight, we can worry about that tomorrow," Kate said.

Alex looked relieved by her suggestion, but still hesitant to agree. He nodded slowly and forced a smile, which beat the distant and defeated look he had brought to the table several minutes ago.

"At some point, we'll have to lay this out for the whole group. Let them weigh into the decision. If I were Charlie and Samantha, I'd be thinking real hard about relocating to their house up near Waterville. If they left, the Walkers wouldn't be too far behind them," said Alex.

"Then we better have that meeting sooner than later. If the rest of the group decides to leave, we can't stay, and I don't want to miss out on Grady's airport offer. Not with that psychopath running around."

"I'll talk to Grady tomorrow and see what he thinks about establishing a forward base in Limerick. If he goes for it, we don't have to impose a rushed decision on anyone."

Kate leaned back in her seat, glancing inside the house. "I'd still like to know where everyone stands."

Chapter 48

Porter, Maine

Eli Russell sat in a wobbly rocking chair on the wide front porch, admiring the vast vegetable garden past the dirt driveway. He didn't know the first thing about growing vegetables, but he could worry about that next year. Right now, all he had to do was figure out how to harvest everything and store it for the winter. Too bad the farmer hadn't been friendlier. Maybe they could have worked something out, where he let them live in exchange for running the farm. No big deal. He'd find another farmer or two to take the deal, no matter how far and wide he had to travel. There was no way he could let this bounty go to waste. They'd need every scrap of it to survive the winter, unless they could put a stop to the Homeland invasion within the next few months.

He still wasn't sure what to make of the Gelder Pond situation. The tactical vehicles arrived after he ordered a general retreat, so technically, the hostile team inside the house stopped the attack without help. He saw at least two sandbag emplacements on the first floor and had to assume they had created reinforced firing positions at the windows. The gray siding around each window had been riddled with .223-caliber bullet holes. Anyone shooting from one of those windows should have been killed immediately. Instead, he lost twenty-nine men, not including the men lost two days earlier in Milton Mills.

No. There was a whole lot more to these Fletchers than met the eye—and he planned to kill every single one of them. Nobody fucked with Eli Russell like this and got away with it. He'd find a way. One of them liked to drive around in a Jeep and cavort with government forces? Sounded like a perfect target for his initial string of attacks.

"Liberty Actual, this is the Liberty Gate. I have two vehicles requesting permission to enter the compound. One containing McCulver and Brown. The other with the escort team. The road looks clear in both directions."

He grabbed the handheld radio perched on the wide railing in front of him.

"Did you say Brown? Jeff Brown?"

"Affirmative."

"Did the escort team search the passengers and vehicles thoroughly at the school?"

"Affirmative. No obvious tracking devices. McCulver's back seat is packed with electronics, which might be worth a second look."

"It doesn't matter at this point. Send them on up."

"Copy. Sending two vehicles your way."

Eli thought about it for a second. How the hell could Brown have turned up this quickly? Brown would have put some distance between himself and Gelder Pond, staying hidden until things settled. He couldn't imagine Brown having moved more than a mile or two from the site of the attack, in either direction—and McCulver had no reason to swing that close to Limerick. After leaving the Ossipee Valley Fairgrounds in Porter, McCulver headed east to Route 25, where he'd logically take Route 117 south and work his way around Limerick to reach his home in Hollis. If their stories didn't make sense, he was pulling the plug on both of them, along with the farm. He hoped it didn't come to that. He needed both of them.

A gray Suburban, followed closely by a red, four-door sedan, emerged from the distant tree break and raced toward the house, casting long shadows over the green field. A low dust cloud followed the convoy, illuminated by the deep amber rays of sunlight peeking over the western trees.

"Viper One. I want you visible when these cars stop. Don't crowd us, but make your presence known."

"Roger. We'll keep our distance."

Eli stepped onto the hard ground with his rifle and signaled for the vehicles to continue on the jeep trail that disappeared behind the house. A minute later, he met them in the grassy, makeshift parking lot next to the jeep trail. Viper One, the four men from Bertelson's squad, appeared between the house and the barn, staying in the shadow cast by the barn. McCulver stepped onto the jeep trail with Brown, who looked unperturbed by the day's events. The escort team, consisting of two heavily armed men, walked discreetly toward the barn.

He eyed Brown for signs of distress. The man remained impassive, as always. McCulver looked edgy, but that wasn't unusual either. Upon first impression, nothing looked out of place. Brown's AR-10 was slung over his shoulder, and McCulver appeared unarmed. Maybe he was being paranoid.

"Look what the cat dragged in!" he said, extending a hand to Brown. "Glad to see your face, though I'm a little surprised to see it so soon."

Brown shook his hand firmly. "Lucky day, I suppose."

"Can't wait to hear your report," he said, turning to McCulver. "Did Jeff show up at your doorstep? You sure as shit better not have driven back to Limerick."

"I finished up at my house around 3:45. Figured I might swing close enough to try the handheld. Brown answered on the first call. Picked him up near the Chesterton Farm just outside of town."

"So you drove through Limerick."

"The roads were empty," said McCulver.

"Damn lucky nobody stopped you."

He was glad McCulver hadn't run into any trouble. His explosives expertise was irreplaceable. If they couldn't hit the government head on, as the Gelder Pond encounter had painfully demonstrated, they'd have to rely on the same kind of tactics proven effective against U.S. forces in Iraq and Afghanistan. Improvised Explosive Devices (IED) and isolated ambushes. Still, he was pissed off that he had taken the risk. Driving that close to Limerick didn't show good judgment, not to mention the fact that they'd been out joyriding.

"So, where the hell have you two been for three hours?" asked Eli.

"Since I had Brown, I thought we'd visit Southern Maine Drilling and Blasting in Windham."

"You did *not* drive into Windham."

"Eli, there's nobody on the roads, and SMDB is south of town—for a good reason. Most of that reason is sitting in the back of the Suburban. You're gonna be really happy about my little side trip," said McCulver, motioning toward the SUV.

Standing behind the Suburban, Eli had one more moment of doubt as McCulver grabbed the handle to open the hatch. What if they had somehow smuggled commandos onto the ground in the back of the truck? Maybe the men guarding the entrance along Norton Hill Road had made their transmission under gunpoint? His eyes darted to the security team near the house.

"Jesus, Eli. Really?" said McCulver, opening the truck's gate.

Wood crates filled the spacious cargo compartment, stenciled with chemical names that looked sinister, but meant nothing to Eli.

"I couldn't believe they left this stuff unguarded. Slurry explosives, perfect for setting off bigger bombs or making concealable explosives. I found other stuff too, like dynamite, blasting caps, det cord, detonators, even a little C4. All just sitting there for the taking."

Eli grinned, no longer mad at McCulver. He'd been wrong. His second in command had shown excellent initiative.

"This is exactly the kind of stuff we'll need for the upcoming fight. This may sound like sacrilege, but now I know how the insurgents must have felt in Iraq. They couldn't beat our troops in a face-to-face battle, so they resorted to IEDs, isolated ambushes and targeted sniper operations. The Taliban did the same thing. We have to come up with a list of materials essential to fighting a guerrilla war and start assembling a stockpile—before Uncle Sam gets smart and shuts down our access. I'd say we have a week, probably less. Same goes for our recruitment efforts. Let's hit Fryeburg, Bridgton and Naples tomorrow. We only look north of here."

"We're more or less strangers in those parts," said McCulver.

"We'll just have to get acquainted with the good folks of Oxford and Cumberland counties. If we run into trouble rounding up volunteers, we'll start grabbing folks. Desperate times call for desperate measures. I don't mind dipping south for that. We can start spreading rumors that the government is kidnapping people."

"I'm not sure kidnapping is a good idea. I'd be concerned about loyalty," said McCulver.

"They'll come around once they see what we're trying to accomplish. If not, they can work on the farm. We'll need a ton of help getting this harvested."

"Was it abandoned?"

"I served a few eviction notices," said Eli, patting his holster.

"I'll need some help getting this stuff offloaded," McCulver said. "Best place to store it will be in a basement. Everything but the dynamite is highly stable."

"There's a gigantic root cellar attached to the barn. North side. Cool as a cucumber in there," he said, waving his security detail over.

"Perfect. Hate to blow up the house," McCulver said with his back turned.

Kevin's statement bothered him. Blowing Eli to pieces in his sleep solved most of the government's problems. Without his leadership, the men would throw down their weapons at the first sight of a tactical vehicle. He stared at the back of Kevin's head as his deputy commander started to offload some of the smaller containers. The man had been alone today for the better part of six hours. He'd have to keep an eye on his old friend.

"I don't think you have anything to worry about," said Brown, glancing at McCulver's back.

"Probably not," said Eli. "Gutsy move staying back. I thought you had lost your fucking mind, frankly. How many did we kill?"

"Zero."

"Bullshit. We tore that place apart. You said they were loading up one of the Matvees?"

"Two men and a woman were evacuated. I recognized two of them from the windows above the garage. I hit them hard with my .308 at one point."

"We need more .308s in our arsenal. That goes on the list. You sure we didn't kill *any* of them?"

"Unless they buried some folks on the other side of the house, where I couldn't see. I watched them drag our KIAs into the woods through my scope. All MultiCam uniforms. Nothing else. It took them over an hour."

Eli's eye twitched. Twenty-nine killed for three wounded? He couldn't accept that. A dangerous thought flashed across his synapses and hid in the dark recesses of his mind, waiting to be retrieved. He knew he should turn away from it. Nothing good could come from dragging it into light.

Twenty-nine dead in Limerick, twenty-five dead in Milton Mills. Jimmy. Nathan. These assholes had to pay.

"How many do you think are in the house? How many marines?"

"I counted five different civilians and three marines. One tactical vehicle stationed in the backyard. The other vehicle hadn't returned by the time I left. Probably stayed with the wounded."

"How did the marines get past the gates?"

"Busted right through. Those things are built like tanks," said Brown.

"Tell me about it," said McCulver, facing the crates in the truck. "We'll have to build shaped charges to do any damage."

"So the gates are broken?" said Eli.

Brown nodded, and McCulver turned around with a wary look.

"Eight total?"

"There could have been a few more in the house," added Brown.

"How are the marines set up?"

"One guy on the 240. The other two helping out around the house."

"Only one marine in the vehicle?"

"That's what I saw when I left."

Eli ran the scenario in his head and started to tremble. He might not have to wait as long as he thought to get his revenge.

THE END...To be continued in June 2014.

Please consider leaving a review for *Event Horizon* at Amazon. You don't have to write a novel. Even a quick word about your experience can be helpful to prospective readers.

To sign up for Steven's New Release Updates, send an email to:

stevekonkoly@gmail.com

Please visit Steven's blog for the latest news of future projects:

StevenKonkoly.com

37209984R00170

Made in the USA
Middletown, DE
22 November 2016